A Broken Kind *of* Beautiful

BOOKS BY KATIE GANSHERT

Wishing on Willows
Wildflowers from Winter

A Broken Kind of Beautiful

A Novel

Katie Ganshert

Author of *Wishing on Willows*

WaterBrook
Press

A Broken Kind of Beautiful
Published by WaterBrook Press
12265 Oracle Boulevard, Suite 200
Colorado Springs, Colorado 80921

Trade Paperback ISBN 978-1-60142-590-4
eBook ISBN 978-1-60142-591-1

Cover design by Kelly Howard

Published in the United States by WaterBrook Multnomah, an imprint of the Crown Publishing Group, a division of Random House LLC, New York, a Penguin Random House Company.

Library of Congress Cataloging-in-Publication Data
Ganshert, Katie.
A broken kind of beautiful : a novel / Katie Ganshert.
pages cm
ISBN 978-1-60142-590-4 (pbk.) — ISBN 978-1-60142-591-1 1. Single women—Fiction. I. Title.
PS3607.A56B86 2014
813'.6—dc23
2013046053

Printed in the United States of America
2014—First Edition

10 9 8 7 6 5 4 3 2 1

For the broken ones.

Fear not, for I have redeemed you;
I have called you by name, you are mine.

—ISAIAH 43:1

1

The girl with the haunted eyes reentered his life on the other side of a lowering casket, humidity and the shrill song of cicadas tangling together in the South Carolina heat. Aunt Marilyn pressed trembling fingers against her lips and swayed as if the wet ground had risen up and pitched her forward. Davis Knight tightened his grip beneath his aunt's elbow and looked away from her pain. That's when he saw her—standing like a statue, her waif-like form shrouded in grief.

Ivy Clark. All grown up.

A distant rumble of thunder rolled across the blackened sky, leftover remnants from a tropical storm. A raindrop brushed his ear; another grazed the tip of his nose. Pastor Voss bowed his head. So did everyone else, including Ivy. A slight breeze ruffled wisps of hair around her downturned face and fluttered the butterfly sleeves of her dress. The last time he'd seen her in the flesh, he had just returned to Greenbrier for a short summer stint after completing his freshman year at NYU. Ivy had been twelve going on fifty. Tall and gangly with eyes too large for her face—twin souls the color of honey, staring and deep as if she saw and understood every sadness in the world.

Then she had disappeared, and so did he, in a way. A few years later he began following her career because it was in his interest to follow it, but even with all professional motives stripped bare, he would have followed it anyway.

Pinpricks of sweat beaded along Davis's temples. His sister, Sara, wrapped her arm around his and squeezed. Pastor Voss's prayer ended in time for Ivy Clark to look up and catch him staring. Familiar territory to her, no doubt, given her career. Not so familiar to him.

He would have looked away, but her awareness of his attention triggered an intriguing metamorphosis. It seemed her eyes had learned some tricks over the years. Like how to bat in just the right way. How to dance in invitation. How to swallow the grief that had wrapped around her shoulders moments ago, when she thought nobody watched. She smiled a smile Davis knew well, one he'd seen hundreds of times on a hundred beautiful faces—the type of smile that had lost its allure two years ago.

He glanced down at the grass—thick green blades framing his black loafers—and patted his sister's hand, his own personal reminder of why a woman like Ivy Clark could not be a part of his life. Ivy belonged to a world that took and took and took so subtly and connivingly that a person didn't notice until there was nothing left to give. It was a world he never wanted to be a part of again.

Still, he looked one more time. Ivy stared back, a smirk on her face.

"Now's not the time to talk about this, Ivy." Bruce strode through the long grass toward a line of cars parked along the brick path, texting a message into his phone.

The drops of rain turned into a mist that settled over Ivy's arms, cooling her skin. If only the drizzle could quench her fear. Who was he texting? She lengthened her stride, trailing him like a long evening shadow. "You're the one doing business."

"How do you know it's business?" He dug into his pocket, pulled out his keys, and clicked the button on the remote to unlock the car doors. Two short beeps interrupted a chorus of chirping birds hiding somewhere in the Spanish moss that dripped from gnarled tree limbs overhead.

Ivy rolled her eyes. Only Bruce would lock his car inside a cemetery in Greenbrier, South Carolina. "This isn't New York City." The two places existed on opposite poles. "I don't think any burglars are prowling around waiting to break into your car."

He stopped in front of the black Lexus with rental plates.

She stopped too. "I need to know, Bruce. It's my future we're talking about here."

"If you were so concerned, you should have kept your mouth shut."

"I made one lousy suggestion. You're telling me O'Banion's getting bent out of shape because of one small—"

"It's not your job to make suggestions, especially not to a photographer like Miles O'Banion."

Ivy's stomach knotted. What would happen if that one slip cost her two years of security? Her twenty-fifth birthday crept closer each day. As hard as she tried, she wasn't getting any younger and people were starting to notice. If she wanted to continue modeling, she needed that contract.

Bruce ran his hand down his face. "It's your job to keep your mouth closed and work for the camera. That's what you get paid for. Nobody cares about your opinions."

"So I've been told."

"Then why didn't you listen?"

A small group of women dressed in black stopped conversing. Bruce painted on a smile and gave them a polite wave. He leaned close to Ivy and spoke from the corner of his mouth, his smile unwavering. "We're not talking about this here. Let's show a little respect."

Her muscles coiled. Respect? James didn't deserve her respect. She didn't care how touching the eulogy, how beautiful the flowers, or how crowded the funeral. Why should she care about losing a man who never wanted her in the first place? Why should his unspoken *I love you* echo in her mind? She refused to pretend her father's death had any bearing on her life. Because it didn't. She wouldn't let it. She gathered her mounting anger and stuffed it in the empty place inside her chest.

Bruce opened the passenger-side door. "Get in the car."

She folded her arms. "If you know something, as my agent, you have no right to keep it from me."

"I don't know anything. And when I find out, we can discuss it back in New York."

"Why did Annalise tell me I lost the contract?"

"Because Annalise feeds off gossip, or haven't you figured that out yet?"

Despite the stagnant heat, a chill crept across Ivy's skin. As her friend, Annalise wouldn't have pulled this out of thin air. It had to have some substance. She gripped her elbows, as if the harder her fingers dug into flesh, the less any of this would matter. "Gossip always starts with a seed of truth."

"Look, either get in the car or I'm leaving you here. Your choice."

Ivy looked over her shoulder at the rows of polished tombstones. Her throat tightened. She hugged her arms and stepped closer to the car. "I want to go to the airport."

"We're going to the luncheon."

"Why?"

"He was my brother and your father. We're not leaving now."

"He was hardly my father." The emptiness expanded, carving her out like a pumpkin-turned-jack-o-lantern. She was nothing but a shell. A beautiful, empty shell.

An SUV pulled out from behind them. An engine rumbled in front. Except for a few stragglers in the distance lingering over her father's grave, the cemetery cleared.

Bruce drummed his fingers on the top of the car.

"I'm not going to sit in that house, eat cucumber sandwiches, and pretend to care that he's gone."

"You don't have a choice." Bruce opened the door wider.

Her shoulders sagged. Ivy slid into the passenger side, pulled the seat belt across her body, snapped it into place, and stared straight ahead. Why had she said anything to O'Banion? So what if he wanted to keep her in the same overdone pose? She shouldn't have said a word. If there was one mistake to avoid in her world, it was wounding the pride of a notoriously prideful photographer.

Bruce's door opened. He got inside and set his phone in the cup holder. As soon as he started the ignition, the phone vibrated, rattling loose change in the console. He swept up the device and held it against his ear. "Bruce Olsen."

Nothing but the unintelligible chatter of a female voice from the other end.

A muscle pulsed in Bruce's jaw. He scratched his chin and looked out the window, hiding his expression. "I'll be back tomorrow. Could we meet then and talk this over?" He clicked his seat belt into place and nodded. Another long pause. More unintelligible chatter. A sigh from her uncle. "I understand. Thanks for getting back to me."

He hit the End button and started the car.

Ivy pressed her fingers against her sweat-dampened palms.

Bruce pulled out onto the brick street and steered toward the iron gate. "It seems Ms. Reynolds wants a fresh face for her cosmetic line." He flipped on the radio. Bon Jovi's "You Give Love a Bad Name" blasted Ivy's ears. "Sorry, kid. They're not renewing your contract."

2

The sound of chattering guests and clinking plates swirled around Davis as he leaned against a door frame, unable to erase the sorrowful image of Ivy Clark standing over her father's grave. The first time she entered his life, he had been the one who had just buried his father—the one who had stared in disbelief as the ground swallowed up the man who gave him life—right before moving with his mom and sister across the country to Greenbrier, South Carolina. Away from his friends in Telluride and everything he knew at the impressionable age of sixteen. And what had gripped him about this mysterious wisp of a girl moving silently about his aunt's house were her haunted eyes.

She, too, had been taken from all that was familiar and plunked into a world where she didn't belong. Her prison, however, would only last a month each summer. His, it had seemed, would last forever.

But now, as he scanned the crowd, Davis knew that Greenbrier was not the prison he had made it out to be. In fact, it had become just the opposite—a sanctuary. Sure, it had some thorns, but they were tolerable. If only he had realized this as a teenager, perhaps he wouldn't have been so eager to escape.

Across the entry in the great room, Grandma Eleanor leaned against Grandfather's arm and cooled herself with a handheld, rose-patterned fan. She chatted with Mom and her husband, Mike—a high school math teacher with a paunch and an expanding bald patch on the crown of his head. Much to his grandparents' chagrin, Davis's mother met Mike on an Internet dating site, married him two years ago, and moved to his house in West Virginia, escaping the reach of Grandfather's indomitable thumb.

Grandfather met Davis's stare. He wasn't sure what Grandfather hated more—Davis's first career as a fashion photographer or his current one as a church maintenance man. Not in the mood to discuss his professional future at a funeral, he looked away, shifting his attention from the chandelier hanging over the dining room table to the art decorating the foyer walls before catching sight of his sister. She stood on the landing of the wide staircase with one arm extended in front of her, fingertips grazing the frame of a water-colored fresco Marilyn purchased several years ago, her posture etched with such longing Davis could feel her ache.

He frowned and moved toward her when Aunt Marilyn descended the stairs. With a ghost of a smile and red-rimmed eyes, she took Sara's elbow, whispered something in her ear, and guided her down the rest of the steps.

Davis walked to the north-facing wall instead, covered in arched windows that opened to a manicured front lawn spotted with azaleas and shaded by a large oak. A line of cars wound down the long drive and spilled onto the cul-de-sac. He closed his eyes and leaned his forehead against the cool glass.

"She sure is a beauty."

His attention perked.

"Someone said she was on the cover of *Vanity Fair.*" This voice belonged to somebody different, slightly younger, and not quite so southern.

"And *InStyle,*" the first voice whispered, loud enough for Davis to hear.

"Is she really James's daughter?"

"Can't you see the resemblance? Those eyes. Her hair. She's the spitting image."

"But James and Marilyn celebrated their thirtieth wedding anniversary last spring. That girl doesn't look a day over twenty." A pregnant pause followed the statement, saturated with so much subtext Davis could practically hear their churning thoughts. "You mean Marilyn stayed married to him after such a scandal?

"Bless her heart, the poor thing must have loved him."

"Well, he couldn't have been all bad. I heard he donated a lot of money to the county hospital."

"I don't care how much money he donated. If my George unzipped his pants for another woman, he'd be out of the house quicker than that." Fingers snapped.

His own dug into the frame of the window.

"She could never have kids of her own, you know. Such a shame. And then to find out about this girl. News like that would have sent me straight to the grave. I wouldn't have been able to forgive him."

Enough gossip for one funeral luncheon.

Davis stepped out of the shadow cast by the heavy velvet curtains and cleared his throat. Trudy Piper, daughter of Pastor Voss and wife to Cal—the owner of a local bar and grill—stood face to face with someone Davis didn't recognize. Likely an out-of-town guest. The two women blanched, then strained their eyes and tightened their lips into appropriate funeral expressions.

"Davis." Trudy clasped her hands. "I'm so sorry for your family's loss. It's a shame for James to have passed so young."

"The cancer took him fast," the other woman added.

Trudy gave him a hug, the floral scent of her perfume overpowering, and the pair melted into the crowd in the dining area. He watched them go, his jaw clenched. Pastor Voss had two grown daughters. Trudy was the younger of the two and, much to the pastor's chagrin, the town gossipmonger. Aunt Marilyn didn't need a woman like that gossiping behind her back. She had enough to deal with. He turned around and set his palm against the window frame, then straightened to his full height.

Ivy Clark was in Marilyn's front yard, sitting on a white bench with one sinewy leg crossed over the other. Shaded beneath the oak, her toffee-colored hair fell in long waves past her shoulders as she stared off toward the street. He noted the elegance of her neck, the angle of her body. Except for her bouncing foot, she invoked an almost ethereal stillness, one that had him leaning closer to the window. There was a story there—hidden beneath her frame and her posture—and it begged to be captured.

Davis stepped away from the window and wove through the crowd. He plated a sandwich from the dining table and walked out into the humidity. If Ivy noticed him coming, she didn't look up. Not even when he sat beside her on the bench, holding up the sandwich as an offering. "Hungry?"

She traced lazy circles around her kneecap. "Not much of an appetite at the moment, thanks."

He set the plate down on the grass.

She leaned back on her palms. "Do you stare at women at funerals as a rule or should I be flattered?"

It took him a while, but he found it. In her irises. A barely there pulse of the girl he remembered from way back when, before the world had its way with them both. It kept him on the bench when everything else begged him to leave. "You don't remember me, do you?"

She shifted away and looked him in the eyes.

He decided to help her out. "Marilyn's nephew?"

"Davis Knight, you don't say." She tipped her chin. "So what does that make us—cousins?"

"Stepcousins, I guess." If there was such a thing.

"And here I thought I was running out of family." She looked him full in the face, her expression bored or maybe challenging. Like she dared him to entertain her.

"You're a lot different than I remember."

She raised her eyebrows. "And just how much do you remember, Dave?"

"You were sad a lot."

"Well, there wasn't much to be happy about back then. And I'm not a little girl anymore." One corner of her mouth quirked into a private grin. "But I think you noticed that all on your own."

Of course he'd noticed. Any man would. "I've followed your career."

"Oh yeah?" She leaned so close her shoulder brushed against his. "Are you a fan? You want me to sign something?"

The woman in front of him bore no resemblance to the one he'd watched out the window. That woman had looked lonely. This one wielded seduction like a weapon. So which was the real Ivy Clark? "It's hot out. You should come inside."

"I'll pass."

"So you're just going to sit out here the whole time?"

She slipped her phone from her purse and checked the display.

"Are you waiting for someone?"

"A cab."

"In Greenbrier? I didn't know they existed." The island town might boast twenty thousand, but something about its slow-moving pace made it feel half that size.

"Apparently they only have one. It's taking a long time."

"Where are you going?"

"The airport."

"Already?"

"Why the twenty questions, Dave?"

Why indeed? He nudged the plate with his shoe. A red ant scuttled toward the bread as silence settled between them every bit as pronounced as the humid air. A swallow filled the void with song.

Ivy sighed. "I never hear the word 'escape' without a quicker blood…"

He cocked his head. "Emily Dickinson?"

"You know it?"

The surprise in her question matched his own. She was as unlikely a candidate as he to quote poetry. "I had an English lit professor who was in love with Ms. Dickinson. That's what he called her too—*Mzz Dickinson.* I think her postmortem status truly depressed him."

A genuine smile tugged at her lips, but before it could take full form, she looked down and fiddled with the charm bracelet around her wrist. "If you really must know, Dave, I'm running away. Do you know what that's like?"

"Unfortunately."

She raised an eyebrow, like she didn't believe for a minute somebody like him would have anything to run away from.

"It's something I did for a long time," he admitted, wondering, even as he did, why he was opening up to her.

"Oh yeah? And how did it work out for you?"

Sadness spread its fingers and lay a heavy hand over his chest. "Not well."

A cab grumbled down the cul-de-sac and stopped behind the line of parked cars crowding the driveway. Ivy stood. He joined her. In her high heels, she came almost level with his six-foot-two frame. He wasn't used to looking a woman in the eye, especially not on his feet. "Good luck," he said.

"With what?"

"Stopping. We all have to sooner or later."

Something broken flickered in her eyes but disappeared before the lethargic shutter in his mind could capture it. She leaned forward and brushed her lips against his cheek, her breath minty and warm. "Happy mourning."

She pulled her purse over her shoulder and sauntered to the cab.

Taking a temporary respite from the condolences, Marilyn Olsen clasped the cross on her necklace, sliding it back and forth along the silver chain, watching as Ivy slid into the backseat of the yellow taxi.

Marilyn's house was full of people—if not mourning, at least acknowledging James's end—yet from the moment she caught sight of Ivy at the funeral, her thoughts ceased being about her late husband. Some might think that callous, but in truth, Marilyn did not dread widowhood as many women might. Her good-bye to James was not one of holding on and clinging tighter; it was more akin to slowly stopping after a long, grueling race. The flood of emotion she felt now was all about the girl riding away in the backseat of a cab.

Lord, my heart…

Sometimes obedience could feel like trudging through the mud, each acquiescent footstep weighted with resistance. That's how it was with James. Marilyn didn't want to forgive him, but who was she to ignore the words God continued to place in the palms of her outstretched hands whenever she prayed? *Absolve. Pardon. Exonerate.* Their crisp, sharpened edges left no room for misinterpretation.

Other times, though, obedience was unavoidable.

During her dark years, when James started drifting away and infertility defined her days, Marilyn took on the morbid habit of reading labor and delivery books. One author described the act of pushing like a train barreling forward at full speed. The doctor says push and the woman in labor doesn't have to think twice. Her body takes over her will, bearing down with a fierceness that is nearly impossible to thwart.

As a woman who had never experienced such a phenomenon, Marilyn couldn't fathom what that might feel like. Until she saw her—an eight-year-old girl with a Cinderella backpack who kept looking at James with a mixture of timidity and admiration. Only he never looked back. He didn't acknowledge her at all. And as Marilyn beheld this girl standing in their foyer for the first time, taking in all the ways Ivy resembled James but not her, she could hear the whisper…

Love this one.

It was as if God had shouted in a holy voice, "Push!"

She couldn't have stopped it if she tried.

"Marilyn." The greeting sounded so much like James that for one illogical second she thought it actually belonged to him.

Pressing the silver cross into the hollow of her clavicle, she turned around. "Bruce." His name escaped on an exhale. What James and his younger brother lacked in closeness, they more than made up for in resemblance. Looking up at him now brought on an eerie sense of déjà vu.

He reached out and squeezed her elbow—as close to affection as the two had ever come. "I'm sorry for your loss."

"And yours," she said.

"Yes, well." He slid his hands into the pockets of his trousers, his attention not quite meeting hers. "I didn't know the cancer would take him so quickly. If I'd known..."

Marilyn let the unfinished sentiment fade into the chatter around them. She might have offered something comforting. *Nobody imagined he would go so fast.* Or *James knew you loved him.* But in truth, she didn't have the energy to offer Bruce placations. Her concentration returned to the white bench where Ivy had been. Davis sat there now, elbows on his knees, playing with a sandwich he'd picked up from the plate between his feet. "How's Ivy doing?"

"Hanging in there, I think."

"I see her on those makeup commercials from time to time."

"Unfortunately, she won't be on them anymore."

Marilyn looked at her brother-in-law. "What do you mean?"

"Reynolds has decided not to renew Ivy's contract. They want a younger face."

"What will she do?"

Bruce puffed up his cheeks and released a long breath. "I'm sure she'll figure something out. Ivy always does. I know you had your doubts, but the kid's had quite a run. A lot better than most."

The words smarted. How could Bruce be so shrewd in business, yet so obtuse in other areas of life? Yes, Marilyn had had her doubts, but they were never in Ivy.

"Speaking of our girl, have you seen her?"

"She left in a cab just now." Marilyn spoke the words to the glass.

Bruce stepped closer, following her line of vision. "She left?"

The disapproval in his tone raised her hackles. Of all the things he could care about, it was this? Never mind the fact that Ivy was barely fourteen when Bruce invited her into a world built on empty promises. Never mind the fact that he saw nothing wrong with exploiting a hurting girl's God-given beauty.

"I'm really sorry, Marilyn. I didn't think she'd call a cab."

"She's not a prisoner, Bruce."

Isn't she?

The question might as well have been another one of God's holy shouts. Just because the bars weren't visible didn't mean Ivy wasn't a prisoner. They'd only grown stronger, more resilient in the ten years since she had last walked out of Marilyn's life. Still, the whispered words that wrecked her all those years ago echoed in the deepest part of her heart. The place where mothers were made.

3

Ivy tore through her closet, pulling tops off hangers and discarding them onto the floor. A trail of black, turquoise, and plum, Versace, Chanel, and Vuitton made its way onto the tile of her bathroom. She removed a black sequined top from a plastic hanger, held it up to her chest, then flung it out the door.

"Whoa!"

Ivy poked her head out from the walk-in closet. "Annalise!"

Her friend was dressed in a black miniskirt, silver Louboutin heels, and her signature red beret. She dangled the sequined top off the ends of her fingers. "Clothing crisis?" Crisis came out sounding more like *cry-sees.* Even after ten years in America, Annalise still spoke in a thick French accent.

"I can't find the top I'm looking for." Ivy gave up her futile search and stood in front of the large bathroom mirror. "How was Miami?"

"Very hot." Annalise dropped the shirt alongside the others and sat her lithe body on the edge of the Jacuzzi. "You know, Ivy, you really should not leave your front door unlocked. I could have been a crazy stalker. Haven't I taught you anything?"

Apparently, Ivy was a slow learner. Otherwise she'd have kept her mouth shut and would still have a contract with Reynolds Cosmetics. A full week after Bruce delivered the news, and weariness still dragged at her soul—a cloying, oppressive heaviness that refused to leave. Ivy leaned over the counter, close to the mirror, and scrutinized her hair. She fished out a bobby pin from the top drawer of the vanity and wedged it between her teeth.

"I put your mail on the counter. It was sitting in front of the door. Along with a vase of flowers." Annalise wagged her black eyebrows at Ivy's reflection. "A dozen red roses and a box of gourmet chocolates. Who is the guy?"

Ivy pulled back a lock of hair and removed the pin from between her incisors. "Probably the one who took me out on Friday."

"*Si romantique.* The sparks flew, no?"

Ivy lifted her shoulder.

Annalise chuckled. "One of these days, you are going to mess with the wrong man. Tread carefully, my friend. You do not want to get hurt."

Ivy's insides twisted at the irony. The only man who ever had the power to hurt her lay six feet underground. And even there, he managed to reach up from the grave and clench an iron fist around her heart. She stuck the pin in her hair, freezing the pouf in place. James only had as much power as she allowed him, and she'd allowed him too much already. "I'm pretty sure my heart's safe."

"I was not talking about your heart. We all know that is untouchable."

Ivy studied her reflection. She needed to look perfect tonight. Clara Vans—the new fashion editor for *Friction*—would be at the launch party. Maybe Clara would want Ivy for an editorial shoot. How long had it been since she'd last done one? Nine months? They paid hardly anything, but money wasn't the issue. The exposure she needed to catch the eye of potential clients was.

"So what is the news with Reynolds?"

Ivy's posture wilted. "Apparently, you were right. I lost the contract."

"How terrible."

Ter-ee-bul indeed, but she shrugged like it didn't matter.

"How was your father's funeral?"

And there was a topic she wanted to talk about even less than Reynolds. "Death be not proud, though some have called thee..."

"You are quoting poetry at me, Ivy. I want to know how you are feeling."

"I barely knew him."

Annalise raised her eyebrows but didn't push further. She picked up a black minidress with a deep-plunge neckline off the floor. One of the outfits Ivy walked in during last fall's fashion week. Annalise tossed it at her. "Wear this. It makes you look like a goddess."

Ivy stepped in the dress and zippered the side. She gave her reflection one more look and walked to her kitchen to check the mail. She picked up the stack and shuffled through it until her gaze connected with a familiar return address. New York University.

Last winter, she'd happened upon a course catalog—the sheer thickness of it something to behold—and spent three consecutive nights perusing the selection of classes, highlighting her favorites, picturing herself in one of those lecture halls with a fresh notebook and a brand-new gel pen. She imagined the professor's imparting knowledge filling her back up again, replacing all that had been stolen over the past ten years. She imagined herself as a person with substance, someone who could do something besides model. The idea became so enticing that Ivy got on their website, filled out the application, and now her one and only backup plan had sent a reply.

She held the small package, its size doing little to still the sudden bout of nerves inside her stomach. Annalise's heels clicked across the hardwood floor. Ivy turned away from her friend and blocked the letter. Nobody knew she'd applied. Not even Annalise.

Her friend walked to the kitchen island and buried her nose in the rose petals.

Ivy's thumb twitched over the envelope's seal. Should she open it?

She bit her lip. If she didn't open it now, she'd think about it all evening. She couldn't risk a muddled brain. Not tonight. Not with Clara Vans in attendance. Taking a shaky breath, she slipped her finger beneath the flap. She unfolded the letter with trembling fingers and blinked at the typed words. It opened with a polite thank you for her application and ended with an even politer rejection.

She hadn't gotten in. The university had rejected her.

"What are you doing over there so secretively?"

Ivy hid the letter behind her back.

"Come on, Ivy. We do not want to be late." Annalise stepped in front of the door, an amused smile drawing up the corners of her mouth. "In the words of our main man, Bruce-y, forget what is bothering you and show me your sexy face."

Show me your sexy face.

Bruce's motto. Her life's purpose. A sudden surge of anger pushed against Ivy's despondency. She crumpled the letter in a tight fist and shoved the paper ball down the sink. She flipped on the garbage disposal. The blades growled and gurgled as they shredded the paper into soggy confetti.

"An interesting way to recycle." Annalise opened the door. "Are you out of garbage bags?"

Ivy plucked her purse off the counter, strode past her friend, and did the only thing she was any good at. She put on her sexy face.

4

Ivy followed Annalise past the crowded line of club-goers, her shoulders back, hips swaying as a balmy nighttime breeze caressed her skin. The women in line swiveled their heads to watch her and Annalise pass. Several men whistled. Ivy let their attention fuel her waning confidence, because that's exactly what she needed if she was going to impress Clara Vans. They stopped in front of the velvet rope where two familiar bouncers stood guarding the entrance.

"Good evening ladies. You here to enjoy the launch party?"

"Ventino's new line of purses?" Annalise quipped. "What's not to enjoy?"

The taller bouncer unclipped the rope and swept his gorilla hand toward the entrance, his attention moving up Ivy's legs as she stepped past.

The muffled beat of dance music throbbed through the heavy door. As soon as the bouncer swung it open, the music spilled out into the night and pulsed through Ivy like the deep thud of jungle drums. More fuel.

He offered his elbow. "Allow me to escort you to the back room."

She took his arm, Annalise took his other, and together, they moved with him through the throng. Their escort stopped in front of an open room filled with purse-lined tables and a crowd Ivy knew well. Men dressed in Armani, women clad in the latest and greatest fashion trends, all standing in small cliques, holding drinks and hiding personal agendas behind pretense and gossip. She understood the rules and subtle nuances. She'd played the game since she was fourteen.

"Have fun," the bouncer said before turning to leave.

Ivy smiled her thanks, then leaned close to Annalise so she could be heard over the music. "Is Gary coming?"

Gary was Annalise's quasi-boyfriend and a successful photographer.

The two had met at a photo shoot for Ralph Lauren in the Dominican Republic a couple of winters ago. Annalise pointed toward one of the tables. "He's over there."

"Do you see Clara Vans anywhere?" Ivy asked.

"You aren't wasting any time, are you?"

"Let's just say I didn't come to look at purses." Ivy scanned the crowd. "I need a drink. I'd offer to get you something, but I'm sure Gary will take care of you." Gary always took care of Annalise. He took care of all his models, using his under-the-table connections to feed a whole host of habits, the most popular being cocaine and diet pills. Annalise partook of both. Ivy, neither. She'd seen firsthand what addiction had done to her mother. She squeezed her friend's hand before making her way to the bar and sliding onto one of the leather stools.

A man dressed in a business suit claimed the seat beside her. He leaned his elbows on the bar top and looked at her with open interest. Ivy feigned naivety. Losing her contract. NYU's rejection. All of it melted away. Here was something she was good at.

A bartender approached. "What can I get you, beautiful?"

"An apple martini, please."

He nodded and went to work.

Ivy reached for her purse, a premeditated action. Just as expected, the man beside her put his hand on her forearm. "Allow me."

She looked up with wide eyes, pretending to notice him for the first time. He looked a few years younger than her father and every bit as handsome. "You sure?"

"For you? Anything."

She shifted her weight, mirroring his posture.

The bartender placed her martini in front of her. The man dipped into his wallet and handed over a bill. "Gin and tonic."

That's when Ivy noticed it. A hint of a tan line circling his left ring finger. She blinked, then brought the martini to her lips.

"I recognize you," he said.

She ran her fingers over her necklace. "You do?"

"You're the woman on those makeup commercials. You have to be." The bartender slid the man's gin and tonic across the bar top. He took a sip, ice clinking together in his glass. The flush in his face told Ivy it wasn't his first drink. "Am I right?"

Unfortunately, he wouldn't be for very much longer. "You are."

He whistled. "You're even more stunning in person than you are on television."

The words tickled her ego. This man would empty his wallet just to sit beside her for the rest of the night. If she let him, he'd buy her roses and jewelry and perfume. All because he wanted her. He burned with it. She could see the desire in his eyes. She brought her chin to the top of her knuckles and flashed her dimple.

"What do you say we dance when you finish that drink?"

"I don't usually dance with strangers."

He leaned one elbow on the bar and swiveled his chair toward hers. "What if I told you my name—would that help?"

"It might."

He leaned closer. "Brian."

Ivy took another long drink. His leg brushed against hers, but she didn't pull away. "You want to dance with me, Brian?"

His eyelids fluttered. "Uh-huh."

She traced her finger around the outside of her martini glass.

He watched her movement. "What do you say?"

"Here's what I have to say." She set her hand on his knee and paused, listening to the catch in his breath. Disgust blistered beneath her skin. "Get your ring out of your pocket and put it back on your finger."

He drew away, his mouth hanging open.

"Be a man, Brian." She picked up her drink. "Go home to your wife." Resisting the urge to knee him where it hurt, she sauntered back to the private room and found one of Bruce's assistants standing off to the side. A breath of fresh air in a room full of clichés. Maya was a perpetual wallflower, which probably explained why she tugged at Ivy's heartstrings.

Ivy walked over and offered a friendly smile. "Hi, Maya."

Maya melted with relief. "Ivy!"

"Let me guess—Bruce asked you to make an appearance?"

"He wanted me to keep an eye out."

Ivy drank the last of her martini. "For promising new clients, no doubt."

"I really don't like these parties," Maya said, fidgeting with her scarf.

Her dislike was painfully obvious, but what Maya lacked in social acuity she more than made up for in hard work and kindness. "You know," Ivy said out of the corner of her mouth, bending her knees a bit to compensate for their height difference, "if you decided to call it a night, I don't think Bruce would be any wiser."

"Really?"

"I wouldn't say anything." Ivy plucked the slice of apple from the rim of her glass. "Besides, Bruce has plenty of clients already."

Maya darted a few glances around the room, then hitched her purse strap over her shoulder. "I do want to catch up on some episodes of *The Bachelorette.*"

"I'll be curious to know what you think of her latest decision."

"Will do. Thanks, Ivy!" Maya gave her a side hug, then wove through the crowd until she fell out of sight.

When Ivy turned around, she spotted Clara Vans at one of the purse tables. Taking a delicate bite of her apple slice, she set her martini glass on a table and made her way over, selecting a zebra-print handbag from the collection. "Ventino is a genius."

Clara looked up from the black clutch she held out in front of her. "Isn't he?"

"I did some work for one of his collections a couple years ago."

"Did you?"

Ivy held out her hand. "My name's Ivy Clark."

"Oh yes. You're one of Bruce's girls, aren't you?"

She nodded as a bartender entered the room, a tray full of champagne flutes balanced on the palm of his hand. Several people raised their drinks in gratitude. Ventino himself nodded his thanks at the bartender before catching Ivy's eye, a lazy smile spreading across his face. The two of them had a fling a while back. According to Annalise, Ivy had broken Ventino's heart. Obviously, Ventino didn't hold a grudge. And unlike that creepazoid Brian, he wasn't married. She smiled back before refocusing on Clara.

"Bruce is wonderful," Clara said.

"He is." She set down the zebra bag, gathering her courage. "I absolutely adore the direction you've taken *Friction.* I've been in several issues in the past. I've always admired the magazine's vision, but even more since you came on board."

Clara picked up a red leather purse and held it beneath her nose. "This is exquisite."

"In fact, I was talking to Bruce the other day about how much I'd love to do some more work if you ever—"

"Ms. Vans, just the woman we were looking for!"

Ivy turned to her left, toward the voice booming over the music. Charles Creighton, another hotshot agent, escorted the most exotic-looking girl Ivy had ever seen. She couldn't be a day over sixteen, yet she held a glass of wine like it was a natural extension of her body.

Clara abandoned the purse.

Creighton spun the girl around, like she was up for bid. The apple martini soured in Ivy's stomach. "I'd like you to meet Gabriela Gerbasi. She's been in almost every fashion magazine across Europe. She's a sensation in Milan and Paris. I'm telling you, Clara, people are in love with her."

The girl took a drink of her wine and had the audacity to look bored.

Ivy shifted. She used to be the one editors drooled over. The one her agent paraded around clubs like a trophy. But it hadn't lasted. That high that came with being loved by the world? It didn't last at all.

Creighton turned to Ivy, as if noticing her for the first time. "Iris, how are you?

"It's Ivy."

"Right, Ivy. How's Bruce?" The two were longstanding competitors. Several times early in Ivy's career, when she was the promising one, Creighton had made her under-the-table offers—swearing to take her career places her uncle never could. Maybe she should have taken him up on them. Or maybe it wouldn't have made a difference.

"Fine, thank you." Her words fell like icicles.

"I heard about losing that contract with Reynolds. You really ought to be more careful with your reputation. O'Banion said you were downright argumentative."

Ivy blanched. Downright argumentative? O'Banion was slandering her name. A simple suggestion was hardly argumentative. She shot a furtive glance at Clara. "O'Banion exaggerates."

"No need to get riled up. It wasn't because of him that you lost the contract. It's just the nature of this industry. New faces are always flooding the market. Competition is especially fierce at the moment. Wouldn't you say, Clara?"

Clara didn't seem to hear a word. She was too busy salivating over Creighton's Brazilian-looking commodity. "I'd love to talk about getting her an editorial, Charles. She's exactly the right fit for my magazine."

Creighton kissed Gabriela's cheek and took Clara's hand. "Let's have a drink, shall we?" He led Clara away, abandoning Ivy with the girl, who sipped her wine and rummaged through the purses as if she hadn't understood a word that had been spoken. Maybe she hadn't. Ivy had gone through the same thing abroad. Bruce auctioning her off in foreign languages, always fishing for the highest bidder.

The emptiness she'd tried to tuck away all evening ripped open inside her chest. She searched the room for Annalise. Instead, she found Luis Ventino. He leaned against a high table, surrounded by three women, but he stared at her. She moved to the drinks the bartender had dropped off, picked up a flute, and took a long sip. When the champagne was all gone, Ivy strutted toward Ventino and fought against the empty chasm the only way she knew how.

5

Cool air greeted Davis as soon as he stepped inside his darkened apartment. An early morning run along the beach with a buddy, followed by a solo ocean swim, and he still couldn't divert his thoughts from last night's dream—about funerals, overexposed photographs, and a pair of haunting eyes. The funeral had been a week ago, so why the dream now? He flipped on the light switch and tossed his keys. They clattered, skidded, and came to a halt in front of his answering machine.

His stomach grumbled. He pushed sweaty hair up his forehead and ran his hand down the front of his face, scruff scratching at his palms. He hadn't gone grocery shopping in a good two weeks, but he did have some leftover Frogmore stew and pecan pie that he'd picked up from Fried Greens after his slow-pitch softball game last night. That beat a bowl of cereal any day.

Hopping on alternating feet, he yanked off his running shoes. They clunked onto the welcome mat. He shuffled into the kitchen, washed his hands, and pulled out the stew. He opened the container and placed it inside the microwave, but when he hit Start, nothing happened. Well, great. How was he supposed to eat without a microwave? He checked the plug, his stomach snarling.

"I know. I know. You're hungry."

Davis turned in place, searching for something oven-proof, and found a flashing red light on his answering machine instead. He pushed the button and pulled open a skinny cupboard between his refrigerator and stove. Grandma Eleanor had helped him unpack his things when he moved in a couple of years ago. He had no idea where she'd put his baking sheets. Or if he even had any.

"Hey, Davis, it's your favorite aunt."

He paused his search at the sound of Marilyn's voice. She sounded okay—definitely not upbeat, but not despondent either. Over the past week, whenever he stopped by for a visit, she'd seemed understandably adrift.

"So I have something I'd like to run past you. It's an idea I had awhile ago, before..." Her words fell away. Over the past six months, she'd spent her time caring for James, helping him fight and then accept a sickness that descended and destroyed with the quickness and ferocity of a raging wildfire. "Anyway, I've decided I'm going to put together an advertising campaign—something to market my new line of wedding gowns."

He opened another cupboard and smiled. Aunt Marilyn thrived at her boutique. She was making quite a name for herself. Blushing brides all across the Lowcountry came to Something New to try on her dresses. A campaign sounded like the perfect distraction—something to occupy her time as she transitioned into the realities of widowhood.

"Remember my friend Joan Calloway? She's a fashion editor for *Southern Brides* magazine. She contacted me a few weeks ago, asking to do an editorial spread featuring my dresses. I couldn't commit then, but now I can. She thinks they're quirky and fresh."

He pulled out a plastic bowl and a misplaced corkscrew and reached into the back of the cupboard, his palm moving over empty space and the grain of unfinished wood, then caught something promising. Something that felt ovenproof. He brought it out. "Aha!"

"Anyway, I was hoping you might consider being my photographer."

The smile slid from his face.

"Now please don't get mad, but I mentioned your name to Joan. She called me back a little while ago raving about you. Apparently, she looked up some of your work online."

Davis went to the sink and rinsed the dust from the ceramic dish.

"She wants to meet with me tomorrow for dinner to go over the details of the photo shoot we're going to do next week. I told her you probably wouldn't be there. But Davis"—she let out a long breath, a note of desperation in the sigh—"this is important and there isn't any other photographer I want to work with. Or one I trust so implicitly. Besides, I think it could be a fun experience. Stop by and we can talk about it, okay?"

A loud beep swallowed Marilyn's farewell. Davis tore off a paper towel and wiped the dish dry, his mind no longer on the food.

Sunlight dappled through the leaves of the large oak trees lining Marilyn's street, speckling the colonial houses with pinkish gold. Davis caught sight of his aunt trimming the confederate jasmine climbing up her trellis as he pulled down her long drive and parked in front of the three-car garage. He didn't want to disappoint his aunt, but there was no getting around it. He made a vow two years ago, and a fun experience, as Marilyn had called it, was not a strong enough reason to break it.

Letting out a deep breath, Davis stepped outside into a heat that was already starting to swelter, despite the early hour. Usually the full brunt of summer's wrath held out until July, but June was proving to be an exceptionally nasty piece of work. He shut his door.

Marilyn set down her pruning shears and waved, her face barely visible beneath her floppy hat.

Davis cut through the lawn and met her in front of the butterfly bushes. "Hard at work already?" He surveyed her flower garden, which had grown more expansive throughout the years. The powdery-fresh fragrance of the crepe myrtle with its fuchsia popcorn trusses and the sweetness of the purple four o'clocks perfumed the air. When his kid sister Sara was young, she loved helping Marilyn water and prune and pull weeds. She loved chasing the butterflies that flitted and floated around the bushes too.

"You know what they say about early birds." Wisps of sweat-dampened hair escaped from beneath her hat and stuck to her neck. She pulled off her gloves and her hat, revealing a messy bun and cheeks pinked by the heat. "Did you get my message?"

Davis scratched his jaw. "I did."

She held up her hand. "Now before you say anything, I think you should know what you'd be saying no to. Sara and I were up late last night, brainstorming ways to make the campaign into something bigger. And we came up with a charity fashion show. It'd be a great way to highlight my dresses, bring some excitement to Greenbrier, and raise money for a good cause."

His curiosity piqued. "What's the cause?"

Marilyn's face lit up. "You know that new art program Sara's been talking about? I'm hoping we could raise enough funds to bring that program to Greenbrier's community college. We'd have all the proceeds from the fashion show, along with twenty percent of the sales I make from now until next year."

Davis blinked, completely unprepared. Marilyn's suggestion undid his resolve, tangling his motivations into a knot that was impossible to tease apart. A couple of months ago, Grandfather had read about it in the newspaper—some leading-edge art program for the visually impaired, founded by Frank Calvin Boritz, a world-renowned painter who also happened to be blind. Part of Davis wanted to jump in and say yes, of course. Anything for Sara. But the other part of him resisted. How could he tell that he wasn't merely jumping on the first excuse to take up his camera again?

Marilyn looked up at him, hesitant and hopeful. "Thoughts?"

He scratched his jaw, watching as a Carolina wren hopped along the alabaster branch of the crepe myrtle. It stopped, cleaned its plumage, then spread its wings and flew away. "If I say yes, what would I be getting myself into?"

"You'd do the editorial shoot for Joan. After that, I'd want you to do some photographs for advertisements—a brochure, maybe even some billboard space along the highway. And then, of course, I'd need you for the fashion show. Not just to shoot pictures, but to help organize it. You know much more about this stuff than I do."

Too much. He knew too much.

His aunt reached out and touched his arm, as if sensing his thoughts. "It's time to put that knowledge to good use, right?"

Davis stuck his thumbs through his belt loops and chewed over the proposition. He had vowed to himself that he was done with photography. He had no business taking up his camera when Sara could no longer take up her paintbrushes. But what if picking up his camera again meant giving his sister back a piece of what she'd lost? a piece of what he'd taken?

"Joan's convinced my bridal wear is going to be the next big thing. I'm not sure about that, but I already know your pictures are going to bring in customers. You're brilliant, Davis."

He let the praise bounce away. He didn't need to hear it. His ego had inflated enough last time. "How long of a commitment are we talking about?"

"A couple months, give or take a few weeks."

A couple months. He could reinstate his vow after that, right? Sure, he'd be doing photography again, but this time it wouldn't be about him or his selfish desires. It would be about helping Sara. Besides, it was wedding photography in South Carolina, a world apart from high fashion in New York. He let out his breath and made a quick decision. "Okay."

"You'll do it?"

Ignoring the tightening in his stomach, he stuck out his hand. "What's my first assignment, boss?"

Marilyn squeezed his hand. "Dinner tomorrow with me and Joan—she's very eager to get going. Then you can pick Ivy up at the airport when she arrives, hopefully in a few days. It might be a good idea for you two to get better acquainted. It's good to build a certain amount of rapport with your model, right?"

"My model?"

"I spoke with Bruce. She's going to be the new face for my bridal wear line." A thousand tangled emotions twitched inside Marilyn's smile. "Ivy's coming home."

6

The door flew open and crashed against the wall behind it. Ivy popped up from the couch like a jack-in-the-box springing from its hiding place. A stab of pain shot through her head. Her hands flung to her tangled mass of hair as she sucked air through her teeth.

What in the world?

"What were you thinking?" The door slammed shut. "Please, enlighten me, because I'd sure love to know what goes on in that head of yours."

She cringed and clasped her head tighter, cradling the source of her misery with trembling hands. Opening one eye, she found her uncle, pressed and dressed, pacing in her kitchen. Her sluggish mind tried to comprehend why, but she couldn't pin down anything except the obvious. He had no right to barge into her apartment. "Haven't you heard of a little courtesy called knocking?"

"I knocked. You didn't answer."

She pushed the jungle of tangles from her eyes. Her stomach gurgled—only not from hunger. She placed her hands on the leather cushion to steady herself.

Bruce stared at the vase of roses on her counter, then eyed the rest of her things—the dried and framed flowers hanging on her wall; others bundled together in bouquets, hung upside down on hooks where her keys should be; stacks of books—poetry, classics, even a few mass market romance novels—spilling off her bookshelf; and the snow globes she kept on her end tables. The sudden desire to fling her body over her private items trumped the pain dissecting her brain. Bruce might be her uncle, but he was still a man, and she preferred to keep men out of her private space. She stood from the couch and swayed.

"Desperation doesn't suit you, Ivy. You look awful."

Desperation? That's what he thought? "Look, you need to—" A fresh stab of pain sliced through her words. She closed one eye and tried again. "You need to get out of my apartment."

"On the contrary, this apartment is leased under my agency, which makes it mine." He fished a key from his pocket and dangled it in the air, proving his point. "I can't believe how unprofessional you were last night."

She palmed her head. "I want you to leave."

"Are you hearing a word I'm saying?"

"Only me and the rest of New York City." She took a step forward, but something snagged on the Persian rug. One of her heels was still strapped around her ankle. Stomach protesting, she bent over and freed herself. "How was I unprofessional? And how do you know anything about last night?" Maya left early, and as far as Ivy could tell, none of Bruce's other minions had been in attendance. She squinted at the clock above her stove. Ten in the morning. Even in the modeling industry, the gossip mill didn't turn that fast.

"Flirting with Luis Ventino? Are you insane?"

"We had fun." The parts she remembered anyway. "Is that a crime now?"

"You've had fun with Ventino before."

"And?"

"He's more smitten now than he was then."

Oh, she knew. She could tell last night how smitten he was. He hadn't laid eyes on anybody but her. Not even the gorgeous young Gabriela. What did Clara Vans matter, or anybody else, when she had the undivided adoration of the CEO of Ventino handbags?

"And given your track record with men, you're bound to tear his heart out by next week and officially burn all your bridges."

"It was a little harmless flirting."

"Not to Ventino it wasn't." Bruce pulled at his jaw and shook his head.

Her fingers turned cold. So did her heart. She'd lost her contract—her only sure thing. Fashion editors didn't want her anymore, at least not Clara. And in a few months, she'd be a twenty-five-year-old freelance model with no prospects. She'd gone from the runways of Milan and Paris and London to this.

Ivy closed her eyes, fighting against her growing sense of desperation. Who was she without modeling? And why did she feel as if she'd lived a thousand lifetimes when she'd barely lived one? She rubbed circles into her pounding temples. When she opened her eyes, she spotted an envelope on her sofa table. The one from NYU. A listlessness oozed through her body, weighting her arms until they sank by her sides like a pair of matching anchors.

"I want your butt at the agency in thirty minutes." Bruce walked to the door and flung it open. "Thirty minutes. I have a job for you."

Twenty-seven minutes, three bottles of water, and four Advil later, Ivy walked through the front doors of the Olsen Modeling Agency—a hub of energy, even at ten thirty on a Friday morning. Despite the dull thumping in the base of her skull, Ivy smiled. Bruce had a job for her. Everything was going to be fine. She walked up to the front desk, heels clicking against white marble flooring. "Hey, Maya, did you get to watch last week's episode of *The Bachelorette*?"

Maya looked up from her work, bright-eyed and fresh-faced. "I can't believe Drew got a rose. How could she pick him over Jason?"

"I was just as puzzled as you, sister." Ivy glanced at her watch. "Is Bruce ready for me?"

"He said he didn't want to be bothered until—"

A hum of excitement interrupted Maya's words. Vera Morrell—the newest and hottest face on the market—strutted down the hall, bookended by another of Bruce's personal assistants and the agency's summer intern—

temporary gofer and agent-wannabe. They each wore a Bluetooth, scrolled through their iPhones, and fussed over Vera as they exited the building. Neither one gave Ivy a second look.

"I guess he's ready for you now," Maya said kindly.

Squaring her shoulders, Ivy marched down the hall, knocked once, then swung open the door to Bruce's office.

He tore his crossed feet from the top of his desk, scattering loose papers onto the floor, sat upright in his chair, and hung up the phone. "What do you think you're doing?"

Apparently, he didn't like having his personal space barged into any more than she did. "Right on time. Exactly like you taught me." She held out her wrist and pointed to her watch. "Just trying to maintain my professional reputation, Bruce."

"Sit down."

"You said you have a job for me."

He set his elbows on top of some papers and steepled his fingers.

"Well?" She scooted onto one of the chairs facing his desk.

"Your mother called me last night."

Ivy's heart squeezed. Surely he didn't mean Renee. Because she'd disappeared several weeks ago, shortly after learning the full extent of James's illness. The timing of her disappearance from the rehab facility was no coincidence. Even after all these years, the grip James had on her mother's heart was unwavering. "My mom is AWOL."

Bruce waved his hand. "You know who I mean."

"What does Marilyn have to do with my career?" She'd never wanted Ivy to get involved in the industry in the first place.

"It has to do with her bridal boutique in Greenbrier—Something New."

Ivy crossed her arms and leaned back. Where exactly was he going with this?

"She designs her own line of wedding gowns. I guess she's starting to make quite a name for herself. Ellie Chan—that new pop singer—wore one of Marilyn's gowns in her wedding last year and now everybody wants to see what all the fuss is about."

"How exciting."

Bruce picked up the pen near his elbow and gave it a few clicks. "She wants you to be the face of her new advertising campaign. I said you'd do it."

"You can't be serious."

"Why not?"

"Wedding dresses? You want me to model wedding dresses for Marilyn?" She tipped her head back and laughed, only the notes came out warped. "Please tell me you see the irony."

"It's a good idea. She's got an editorial shoot lined up with *Southern Brides* magazine and several other jobs after that."

"Why would Marilyn want me?"

Bruce shrugged. "Does it matter?"

Ivy shook her head. Go back to Greenbrier? Work with Marilyn? Model wedding dresses, of all things? The idea was beyond ludicrous. "Send me on some go-sees. I'll get other jobs."

Bruce dropped his pen. "Ivy…"

"What do you want me to do, Bruce? Dye my hair? Lose weight? I'll do whatever it takes." To get jobs. To win the public's approval. She'd do anything.

"There's nothing you can do, Ivy. You're getting older, and younger models are flooding the market. It's the way this industry works. You know that."

She hated the softness in his voice. She didn't want his pity; she wanted his confidence. "You're not even trying."

"Nobody wants a twenty-five-year-old model at their go-sees. Especially not one who is losing it."

"I don't turn twenty-five for a few more months, and I'm not losing it. Send me to Europe. Or Tokyo. I don't care. I'll even go to Toronto. But I'm not going anywhere near Greenbrier." The last thing she needed to do was cuddle up with her past.

"You've already done those circuits. Twice. And I don't have time to baby-sit."

"Baby-sit?"

"Your interactions with Ventino aside, you got wasted at a party in front of some the industry's top professionals and you represent my name." Bruce pointed to his chest. "Charles Creighton called me to report that you were wild and out of control and, quote, 'had a tongue like a viper.'"

He thought she was wild and out of control because she had a few drinks and spoke her mind? Never mind the models strung out on coke, like Annalise, or the ones flashing the paparazzi, like Vera Morrell. She pinched the bridge of her nose. She felt like a moldy bag of cheese tossed in the trash because she'd reached her expiration date. "Why don't you say what this is really about?"

"I don't know what you're talking about."

She brought her hands to her lap. "Your brother's dead, so you no longer have to do him any favors. He didn't want me around, so you took me away, and now you don't have to bother anymore."

"Don't be ridiculous."

"I'm being ridiculous? He hasn't even been buried two weeks and you're already trying to get rid of me."

Bruce shook his head, like he was disgusted by her accusation. "This was never about your dad."

"What was it about then?" But even as she asked the question, Ivy already knew the answer. It was about Bruce. It was always about him and how much profit he could make off her. Well, he'd made plenty. He'd wrung her dry. He'd taken everything. Her soul included.

"You've had a ten-year career and enough money in savings to set you up comfortably for a long time to come. You should count your blessings."

Ivy laughed. "My blessings?"

"Do you know how long models usually last in this industry from the time they sign with an agency? Six weeks. Six weeks, Ivy. Most of them don't make it into a single editorial. They walk a few runways and that's it." Bruce leaned back in his chair. "You've been around for a decade."

And it wasn't enough. At least not enough to be remembered. That ever-elusive door into the supermodel realm—where age mattered much less than fame and name recognition—still remained out of reach. She'd thought, after a year with Reynolds Cosmetics, she'd reached the threshold. But now, with that ripped away, her future spilled into a giant abyss—one she couldn't see into no matter how hard she tried. She gripped the arms of her chair and stared at the wall, annoyed at the thickness crowding her throat.

"I didn't do anybody any favors," Bruce said.

"Just yourself, right? I've lost my usefulness, so now it's time to chuck me."

"You're sitting in my office. Obviously I haven't chucked you."

"You're exiling me to Podunk, South Carolina. Same thing."

"There aren't any other options, kid. You need to get your head on straight. I need an excuse to get you out of New York before you break Ventino's heart. And I hate to break it to you, Ivy, but nobody else is making any offers."

7

The indistinct chatter of dinner conversation circled the room as Davis looked at the menu without really seeing it. Joan Calloway, a woman with spiky copper hair and lime green glasses, sat across from him. Marilyn sat to his left. Joan worked out of Charleston, the headquarters for *Southern Brides.* She met Marilyn and Davis halfway, in a little town called Sutton Creek, and now they sat in a small Sicilian diner, ready to talk about the editorial. Joan set her menu down. "I am so thrilled you are going to do the shoot, Davis. As soon as I saw your work, I fell in love."

The waitress saved him from attempting a response. "Have all y'all decided what you're going to eat tonight?" she asked with a friendly smile.

Joan handed over her menu. "I'll have the orange and fennel salad."

The waitress turned to Marilyn.

"The same, please."

Davis picked the first thing he found. "How about the eggplant caponata?"

"Sure thing." The young lady took all three menus and left to punch in their orders.

"Let's talk about the shoot, shall we?" Joan pushed her glasses up the bridge of her nose. "The current fashion trend right now is quirky and chic. Which is exactly the kind of dress your aunt makes. But as you well know, fashion is fickle. I need to capture this trend before things change.

"I'm thinking a four- to six-picture spread. I'm thinking big contrast. Historic South meets contemporary brides." Joan used her hands when she spoke, bracketing the air as if framing an imaginary caption. "I'm friends with Candace Lipowitz, the manager of the old Primrose Plantation in Greenbrier. She's agreed to meet with you Sunday morning to give you a private tour. That way you can check out the location and get a storyboard together for me. We need to get this photo shoot done pronto if we have any chance of running it in the August issue."

Davis blinked. It was as if somebody had picked him out of the warm sun and tossed him into a pool, no chance to dip in his toes. One minute he was the maintenance man at Cornerstone Church, and the next he was sitting with a fashion editor for a major bridal magazine, listening as she rattled off all sorts of familiar details, and he couldn't get a word in edgewise.

"When is our model due to arrive?" Joan asked.

Marilyn sipped sweet tea through a straw. "Ivy's flight arrives on Saturday."

"Never in a million years did I think somebody like Ivy Clark would shoot for my magazine. And you, my photographer? This is going to be the best editorial we've ever done." She reached across the table and gripped Marilyn's hand. "This is going to bring your bridal wear line into the public eye, honey. I wouldn't be surprised if brides come calling from all across America. And you, young man"—Joan kept Marilyn's hand pinned beneath hers but turned her eyes on Davis—"you'd better free up your schedule. I know more work offers will come."

Her words might as well have been a clap of thunder over his head. The question he couldn't shake since yesterday blinked in his mind's eye like a flashing sign.

What was he doing?

Marilyn patted his forearm with her unoccupied hand. "It's going to be the perfect jumping-off point for our campaign. Just think how much money we'll raise for the art program. Sara will be thrilled."

His aunt knew exactly what words to use to distill his rising doubt. "Do I need to find hair and makeup people?"

"I've got it all arranged, honey. You just need to worry about the vision."

Right, the vision. Something on which he used to thrive. But it had been almost two years and the only vision he'd explored during that time was helping Sara acclimate to her new normal. Now, all of a sudden, he needed to adopt Joan's vision. Well, what if he couldn't? Perhaps, in his attempt to bury his passion, he'd lost his gift. There was a very real possibility that Davis wasn't good anymore.

"I'm convinced this is going to be brilliant. Remember, Sunday morning you're to meet Candace for the private tour of the plantation, and if you could get me the storyboard by Tuesday, that would be great."

The waitress reappeared, holding three plates of food. She set them down one by one. Joan picked up her fork and stabbed some greens. "Until then, it looks like there's only one thing for you to do."

He cleared his throat. "What's that?"

"Get out that camera and practice."

Davis sat in the middle of his living room, surrounded by the items he'd brought up from his basement storage closet. He pulled his Mamiya 645 from its case and grazed the digital back with his fingers. He'd bought the camera as a gift to himself, right before the *Vogue* photo shoot. He'd only used it that one time. He set it down and reached for the Nikon D2X—the cool weight familiar in his hands. How many fashion shows had he shot with that camera? He pulled the strap over his head and toyed with the zoom.

Leaving the camera dangling around his neck, he scooted himself around to examine the other odds and ends surrounding him. Firewire cable. Various attachable lenses. The Broncolor Impact and different-sized lighting stands. A minitripod, gaffer tape, elastic bands, polarizers to fit his lenses. Davis had worried he wouldn't remember what everything was or how to use it all. He worried that two years might be too long. He ran his hand over the silky surface of a diffusion screen.

He'd worried for nothing.

Letting out a deep breath, he repacked the small items inside his gadget box, folded up the light stands and umbrellas, and slid them carefully into the carrying case. He put everything away until all that remained was the Nikon hanging around his neck—fully charged, black and smooth, resting against his chest. He walked to his sliding patio door and stepped out onto the third-story balcony.

His apartment complex overlooked Bay View Golf Course to the right, nature trails to the left, and a creek that divided them. In the distance, the sun dipped closer to the horizon, throwing sparkles over the creek and outlining a heron in pinks and oranges. Davis brought the camera to his eye and peered through the viewfinder. He pressed the shutter. His heart did a funny sort of pirouette as the camera captured the image.

He inhaled the humid evening air. How many times had his father taken him hiking or mountain climbing when they lived in Telluride? How many times had they walked mountain trails, searching for the right moment to capture God's creation? They'd seen so many wonders on those walks—elk, mountain goats, a bright-purple flower growing up from a patch of snow. A million and one sunsets and sunrises, all captured and cataloged in his memory.

Dad used to say that God gift-wrapped His creation for the world. But in the hustle and bustle of day-to-day living, people didn't stop to unwrap the gift.

"That's why it's up to you to keep your eyes open, Davis. All the time, keep those eyes open. Search for those moments." Dad wasn't exceptionally talented with the camera. His passion for the craft stood out more than his mastery, which is why he worked maintenance. Making a living off photography had never been an option for his father.

But Davis? He was different.

"God gave you a special eye for His beauty. You see things the rest of us don't," Dad would tell him. *"It's an important gift. So you keep those eyes open, son. You capture His beauty and then you share it with the world. Because this*

world's hurting, Davis. They're lost and dying and searching for something special. God wants you to help them see it."

Davis's throat tightened at the memories. *I failed, Dad.*

He hadn't captured God's beauty. He'd captured the world's. Instead of sharing grace and truth, he publicized sensuality and lust. He hadn't just buried his gift in the sand; he'd made it into an idol. He'd used it for his own glory and, in the process, caused irrevocable damage. He dropped his chin to his chest.

Help me find a way back, Lord. Show me how to become that kid again, the one in the woods who took pictures for You.

The prayer felt hopeless. He wasn't a little kid. He was a man. A man who'd made mistakes—not accidents, but choices. Willful choices. The kind that proved how unfit he was to do anything with photography but mess up.

8

Marilyn's mind refused to settle. She spent the night turning over in her giant bed, catching the faint yet jarring scent of James's expensive cologne on his pillow, staring at the clock until a restless sleep eventually caught and released her much too quickly. One minute the clock read 1:27 and the next it read 4:32, only she didn't feel as though she'd fallen asleep at all. She forced herself to stay in bed until 4:58 then gave up altogether.

By a quarter past seven, she had prepared the guest apartment that she and James had added over their garage three years ago—changing sheets, vacuuming the floor, scrubbing an already spotless bathroom, even sanitizing the refrigerator in the kitchenette. She'd taken her morning speed walk with Nancy, a friend from book club. She'd read from her Bible, spent time in prayer, eaten breakfast, balanced her checkbook, and showered.

Sara wasn't even awake yet.

Now Marilyn sat in the middle of her bed with Georgia, her white Pomeranian, in her lap, a conglomeration of photographs and magazine cutouts that she'd collected throughout the years spread in front of her. Marilyn picked up a glossy four by six and brushed her thumb over Ivy's skinny legs, jeans rolled halfway up her shins as she sat in a pedi chair and looked down at her feet soaking in the foot bath. It was her first weekend visit, when God let loose His holy shout and tipped Marilyn's world on its axis. It was a visit that never would have happened if not for her morbid curiosity.

But what woman wouldn't have been curious?

Discovering her husband of fourteen years not only had a mistress but a child with that mistress? A cruel twist of fate. One that had her questioning the God she worshiped with an increasing sense of devotion over the years. What woman in that situation wouldn't want to at least see the child?

No matter how much James resisted, no matter how much her parents cautioned, Marilyn could not let it go. Her husband had a daughter. She could forgive him his infidelity, as hard as that was to do, but she could not forgive him for so easily dismissing his flesh and blood. So she insisted with an insistence that frayed their tenuous marriage—the first time she'd ever really insisted upon anything—and miraculously she got her way.

Ivy came. James hid in his office. And Marilyn fell in love.

Sixteen years had passed between then and now, yet she could still remember the way her stomach felt as she led Ivy up the stairs into one of the guest bedrooms. She could remember the uncertainty of Ivy's movements, the way her large eyes seemed to observe and absorb everything. She was so shy, so quiet as Marilyn helped her unpack the clothes and toothbrush from her Cinderella backpack.

"I promise I'm not a wicked stepmother." A nervous laugh followed Marilyn's words, one that sounded much too loud in the silence. She hadn't expected such overwhelming feelings. Was still processing them, in fact. She cleared her throat and tried again. "Have you ever gotten a pedicure?"

Ivy looked at the deep rouge nail polish on her toenails, chipped and worn, and shook her head. Marilyn wondered if Ivy painted them herself or if Ivy's mother had—Renee, the other woman.

Marilyn scratched at a blemish on the bedpost. "Would you like to get one?"

Ivy nodded.

So that's what they did.

Ivy picked out a bubblegum-pink polish, and the Vietnamese pedicurist even glued gemstones on her big toenails in the shape of a heart. She didn't say much beyond "Yes, please" and "No, thank you," but it didn't matter. The way she smiled down at her feet, spreading and wiggling her toes as the gemstones caught the light, filled Marilyn with nonsensical joy. Perhaps there was grace to be found in this mess after all.

When they arrived home, their Gullah maid had the entire house smelling like jambalaya, and James sat out in the great room watching a baseball game. As soon as he saw them, his relaxed posture went rigid. He shut off the television and stood.

"James," Marilyn said, stopping him before he could make his exit, "look at Ivy's toenails. Aren't they pretty?"

James ran a finger beneath his collar. "They look nice."

Had he taken the time to look at his daughter's face, he would have seen the blush spreading across her cheeks. He would have seen the way she leaned toward him like a flower hungry for the sun.

But he didn't look.

As Ivy watched him disappear into his office, her hopeful expression melting away, a nearly irrepressible urge came over Marilyn. She wanted to gather Ivy into her arms and hug away the hurt. But that might make her uncomfortable, and Marilyn didn't want to make Ivy uncomfortable. So instead she said, "His work keeps him very busy."

At the time, it was her subtle attempt to assure Ivy that it wasn't her; it was James. He was the problem. Now, with sixteen years of wisdom in her stead, she heard the words for what they were—a weak excuse. Words she wished she could take back.

A soft knock sounded on her door, pulling her from the reverie. Georgia lifted her head off Marilyn's knee and let out a yip. Marilyn quickly swept the photographs into a pile and placed them back inside a cherry wood box meant for recipes.

The housekeeper stuck her head inside. "Good morning, Marilyn."

"Good morning, Annie."

"The guest apartment looks mighty clean."

"I may have tidied up a bit."

Annie smiled knowingly. "Would you like me to bring some flowers up?"

Marilyn closed the lid to the box and scooted to the edge of the bed.

"That's okay. I have some time before I have to leave for the boutique. I can put something together."

She went out to the garden and gathered a bouquet of rhododendrons. They weren't indigenous to the South. They required more tending and care than the others. But Marilyn grew them anyway. She had for fourteen years—ever since she found out they were Ivy's favorite.

Davis twisted off the outside water valve and rolled up the hose. The ladies' bathroom had a leaky pipe under the right-side sink that needed tightening, and after that, he'd check out the oak tree jutting over the parking lot. Pastor Voss suspected a lightning strike last week and worried that some of the branches had snapped loose. Davis looped his arm through the rolled hose, hoisted it onto his shoulder, made his way to the church's storage shed, and told himself he wasn't stalling. If a tree limb crushed somebody's car during tomorrow's service, he'd never forgive himself.

He kicked open the shed door and ran into a wall of stifling heat. Beads of sweat gathered and rolled between his shoulder blades as he stepped inside the darkened shed. He'd hung the hose on a rusted hook next to the riding lawn mower and was wading through the inferno toward his toolbox when a rap on the opened door grabbed his attention.

"Davis, you in here?"

He peered through the semidarkness and spotted Pastor Voss outlined in the sun-drenched doorway, flyaway reddish white hair curled and kinked from the humidity. Davis grabbed the toolbox, made his way through the obstacle course, and stepped outside. The eighty-degree temperature greeted him like a cool fan.

"I thought I saw you out my office window." Pastor Voss fanned himself with his worn-out Atlanta Braves baseball hat, the wrinkles lining his face running deeper than usual.

"Everything okay?"

"Just the regular worries and wears. God's way of teaching this old man some long-suffering patience."

Davis could guess at one of the wears. His daughter, Trudy Piper. No matter how many times the poor man preached against loose tongues, his youngest daughter kept right on gabbing—fanning local gossip into flame. "You're not usually around on Saturday mornings," Davis said.

"I'm organizing a prayer vigil for Twila Welch this afternoon."

Sara gave twelve-year-old Twila free piano lessons. Her mother, Annie, cleaned Aunt Marilyn's house every Saturday and Tuesday. Davis tightened his grip on the toolbox handle and made his way through grass that needed mowing, toward the church's back door. "How's the chemo working?"

"We're not sure yet. Any chance you can make it to the vigil? She can use all the prayer she can get."

If only Pastor Voss had asked him sooner. Like yesterday, before he'd agreed to pick up Ivy from the airport. Davis opened the door and waited for Pastor Voss to pass through. "I wish I could, but I promised my aunt I'd pick up her stepdaughter from the airport."

"That tall, pretty gal?"

He stepped inside the church's back door, thankful the air-conditioning unit was still faithfully chugging away. "That's the one."

Pastor Voss needled the side of Davis's face with an observant stare. "You okay?"

A simple yet loaded question. One he didn't know the answer to. "I'm not sure."

"Want to talk about it?"

He stepped into the lobby. "Marilyn asked me to help her out with a special project."

"I'm sure she could use the distraction."

"You haven't heard what the project is yet."

"Oh?"

"A campaign for her bridal wear line. I'm going to be taking pictures again."

Pastor Voss pulled on his ear lobe.

"Marilyn wants to end the campaign with a charity fashion show. All proceeds go toward an art program for blind students."

"Ah."

"It's something I have to do." For Sara. If only he didn't have to break his vow to do it.

"And Marilyn asked her stepdaughter to do the modeling?"

"Yep." He kept picturing Ivy's face and the way it had looked at the funeral, before she caught him staring. Every time he closed his eyes, that's what he saw. And every time it left him with a niggling feeling, like he was missing something and needed to look harder. "I can't get her out of my head."

"That's understandable. She's quite a beauty."

Frustration pressed against him. This wasn't about her looks. He groped for an explanation, unsure how to proceed. "I've known plenty of women just as beautiful as Ivy, Pastor, and none of them got into my head like this. This isn't about her looks."

"What's it about then?"

"I don't know. I think I'm just turned around. This world I'm stepping back into, it's like eating food that leaves you hungrier."

"And Ivy belongs to that world?"

"Ivy *is* that world."

Pastor Voss took off his hat, scratched his hair, and recapped his head, his expression a mask of compassion. "Trying to fill our bellies with food that makes us hungrier is an exhausting way to live, don't you think? Sounds to me like that young gal could use a proper meal. Living water. The bread of life."

Davis shifted. The tools jangled in the metal box.

"You're free from that world, Davis."

"Yes sir."

"It's a good place to be, isn't it?"

Davis nodded.

Pastor Voss squeezed his shoulder. "Maybe God wants to show Ivy Clark the same freedom."

9

Ivy leaned against a wall beside one of the airport's exits, reading her weatherworn copy of *Sailing Alone Around the Room.* Who better to distract her from the impending car ride from Hilton Head to Greenbrier than Billy Collins? Of all the contemporary poets, he was by far her favorite. His brilliance with irony, the way he could make the mundane fascinating or strip bare the mysterious never ceased to charm her. And right now she needed to be charmed or at least distracted. Awkwardness ballooned inside her chest. What could she and Marilyn possibly talk about on the fifty-minute ride home?

A conveyer belt rattled and hummed to life, setting into motion a sparse cluster of travelers. Ivy turned another page of her book when the doors slid open, letting in a gust of soupy air and Davis Knight, of all people—the man who stared at her through the funeral service and brought her a sandwich during the luncheon afterward. He walked with sure strides through the doors, unknowingly passing her as she leaned against the wall, and searched the travelers surrounding the conveyer belt. An army duffel bag came around the carousel. A heavyset man wearing combat boots stepped forward to claim it. A white, circular tote followed, shadowed by a matching pair of maroon suitcases. The balloon that had expanded inside Ivy's chest popped and flew away. Marilyn's nephew she could handle.

She put Billy in her purse and grabbed the handle of her expandable rolling suitcase, courtesy of Diane von Furstenberg's signature design, and rolled it over to her unexpected chauffeur. "And here I thought the drive would be boring."

He turned around, a day's worth of stubble covering his strong jaw, and nodded in greeting. "I didn't think we'd see each other again."

"In person, you mean?" A grin crawled across her lips. If he followed her career, as he'd admitted to doing outside Marilyn's home, he'd see her in magazines, advertisements, catalogs.

A faint pink tinged his cheeks as he motioned toward her carry-on. "Is that all your luggage?"

"I'm a proficient packer. A by-product of world travel." She swept her hand toward the sliding doors and stepped behind him. "I'll follow you out."

"Can I take your suitcase?"

She handed it over, brushing her hand against his as she did.

He ignored the contact and headed toward the exit.

Ivy studied him. A full head of short, dark blond hair. Broad shoulders tapering to a narrow waist. And then there'd been his face—the epitome of a surfer boy. He might be younger than her usual taste, but this was Greenbrier. She'd have to compromise a little.

Her grin came back. Maybe her exile to South Carolina wouldn't be so horrible after all. How could it be—with a delicious distraction like Davis Knight?

The side of Davis's face tingled from Ivy's teasing stare. He ignored her perusal and focused on leading her to his Jeep, Pastor Voss's words playing through his mind. He tried to brush them aside, but they refused to be brushed.

God, if You want to show Ivy freedom, You and I both know I'm not the guy for the job.

He snuck a peek over his shoulder. Wearing sunglasses much too large for her face, her lips turned up into a smirk.

And anyway, I'm not so sure she wants freeing. She looks pretty comfortable to me.

But she hadn't at the funeral.

No matter how hard he tried, he couldn't get that picture out of his head.

The glare of the sun bounced off the cement and hit him in the eye as he crossed the street beneath the pavilion. Squinting, he rolled her suitcase over the curb, opened the hatch of his Jeep Cherokee, and deposited Ivy's meager luggage into the back of his car. Either she wasn't planning to stay long or she really was a packing expert. He shut the trunk and opened her door.

Her heels clicked a slow rhythm against the pavement as she walked toward him, swaying her hips in a slow-motion runway strut. "And they say chivalry is dead." She stepped in front of him and tipped her glasses. "Well, they haven't met you, have they, Mr. Knight?"

He swallowed, annoyed at his body's response.

See her.

The whisper caught Davis off guard. See her? How could anyone *not* see her? She was a woman everyone noticed, especially men. Yet on the tail end of his thoughts came the echo of words spoken long ago.

"You see things the rest of us don't. It's an important gift."

His father's words.

Unsure what to do with them, Davis walked around the back of his Jeep and climbed behind the wheel. The engine rolled over a couple of times before coming to life.

"So, are you Marilyn's gofer, or do I flatter myself into thinking you offered to come get me? Since you're a fan and all."

"Marilyn had to be at the boutique. She asked me to give you a ride." He backed out of the parking space, pulled onto the road, and turned north. The silver cross hanging from his rearview mirror swayed and fractured a beam of sunlight.

Ivy clucked her tongue. "First Esme, now you."

"Who's Esme?"

"Some old lady on the plane who kept talking about the 'good Lord.'" Ivy touched the necklace. "It's an interesting choice of car décor."

Davis looked at her sideways. "Are you a believer?"

"A believer in what—God?"

"What else?"

She gave the necklace one more turn and brought her hand into her lap. "There's a whole arsenal of what-elses."

"Like?"

"Money. Fame. Beauty. Buddha." She ticked each one off on her fingers.

"Is that what you believe in—a man?"

"Jesus was a man."

He couldn't help it. He laughed. Young Ivy, the religious philosopher. "Fully man and fully God. A great mystery of the faith. I might be wrong, but Buddha never claimed to be God, did he?"

"Your point?"

"My point is that it seems silly to worship somebody who's a fallible human—like me and like you."

Her forehead puckered.

The tiny crease had him looking closer. He wanted to know what it meant. "Are you really a Buddhist?"

"No, I'm not a Buddhist. But I hung out with one once." She rolled down her window. The wind swirled strands of ponytailed hair around her bare shoulders. "It was very enlightening."

The tone of her voice dripped with not-so-hidden meaning. He shifted in his seat. "Are you always like this?"

"Like what?"

He searched through his lexicon for the appropriate word and settled on come-hither. It made her mouth turn up into an amused smile. He turned on his blinker and merged onto the highway. Green foliage whizzed past their opened windows as sultry air fanned through the car. The smell of sea salt mingled with the coconut car freshener he'd stuck under his seat before heading to the airport. "Allow me to clarify my initial question. Are you a believer in God?"

"Yes."

His heart lifted. "Really?"

"Do I think there's a Creator out there somewhere in the cosmos? Yes. Do I think this Creator, or God, as you call him or her or it, gives two lollipop licks about little old me? No." She frowned, as if she'd given away too much and wanted to take it back, then slipped off her shoes and set one perfectly manicured foot on his dashboard. "I don't generally philosophize with men about religion, Dave. It's not my area of expertise."

She tossed her words like baited hooks. Any other man would bite—ask what her expertise was. Davis avoided the worms. He could guess just fine. "Can I ask you a question?"

"You just did."

"Cute." He curled his elbow over the black rubber where the window had disappeared, holding the steering wheel with two fingers. "Why did you agree to model for my aunt?"

She twisted a strand of hair around her finger. "It's a job."

"Somebody like you probably has a million job opportunities to choose from. Why would you choose this one?" A few weeks ago she couldn't get away fast enough—even admitted to running—and now she was back?

"It's just one editorial shoot."

"Marilyn has bigger plans than one editorial shoot."

Her head swiveled toward him like somebody had given it a forceful spin.

Davis frowned. Didn't Bruce tell Ivy what Marilyn wanted from her? But before he could ask, his car lurched. He grabbed the steering wheel with both hands. Ivy tore her foot from the dash. The car sputtered, sputtered again, then died in the middle of the highway. Davis didn't put much stock into signs, but surely this wasn't a good one.

Ivy ground the ball of her high-heeled shoe against the gravel. A breeze swept down the road, blowing its hot breath against her body. As she looked beyond the highway, to the wildflowers swaying and fluttering in the wind, she found herself wondering what it might be like—to be one of those flowers, loved and cared for by something as immense as the sun.

The urge to sprint across the road and dance with them swelled inside her chest. Not a club dance, but a free dance, with her arms and limbs wild and loose and bursting with joy. But she couldn't run across the street like a child. Not with Davis pacing on the shoulder of the highway, slightly out of earshot, his phone against his ear and his thumbnail stuck between his teeth. He didn't act like a normal man. Instead of looking at her with desire, he looked at her as if she were made of fine print and required reading glasses. Plus, he asked too many questions. It made her feel old and tired and annoyed. She held her arms out like wings and lifted her face to the sun.

If she could fly, where would she go?

Her hands dropped to her side, slapping against the outside of her thighs. She wasn't a bird. Or a bat. Or a Pegasus. Or any other creature with wings. Or with petals, for that matter. She was stuck. With her agent hundreds of miles away in New York City—a man who hadn't mentioned anything beyond a simple editorial spread in *Southern Brides* magazine. He owed her an explanation. She stepped onto the road, toward the Jeep Cherokee resting in between the right lane and the grassy shoulder, its hazards flashing like two orange strobe lights. She opened the passenger-side door, dug through her purse, and dialed Bruce's mobile on her cell. He didn't answer. She hung up on his voice mail and tried the agency. Maya's voice greeted her after the second ring.

"Good afternoon. Olsen Modeling Agency."

"Hey, Maya, it's Ivy. Can you put me through to my uncle, please?"

"I'm sorry, Ivy. He's gone for the day. Do you want me to take a message?"

Ivy swallowed the growl rising up her throat. It wasn't Maya's fault that Bruce had sent her on an assignment blind. "If you speak with him, will you have him call me, please? It's important." She said good-bye, texted Bruce on his cell, claiming an emergency, and tossed her phone back into her purse.

Her uncle deserved to be strangled. Instead, the sun pummeled the side of her face like she was the one who'd done something wrong. She put up her hand to shade herself and turned toward Davis, who was still on the phone with his thumbnail in his mouth. How long did it take to call for a towing service?

A car flew past without slowing. Davis pocketed his phone and jogged toward her. She imagined him shirtless, with a surfboard, and made a mental note to invite him to the beach. "Do you surf?"

"Do I what?"

"Surf." She brought her hands out to her side and pretended to dodge a few waves. "You know, like in the ocean."

His eyebrows drew together.

"No? You should learn."

"Okaaay." He rattled his head, as if shaking away her suggestion. "I called Ludd's. They're a repair shop in Greenbrier. Somebody is headed out to pick us up." There was something about the way he said *somebody.*

"You know who this somebody is going to be?"

"The owner's son."

"And you don't like him because…?"

"I didn't say I didn't like him."

"You didn't have to. I made an inference based on the scowl I see before me."

"I like him fine. It's just…" He brought his hand to the back of his neck and shook his head, like it didn't matter.

"It's just what?"

"He used to date my sister."

Davis's sister. White blond hair and sunflower dresses. She used to skip a lot. Ivy remembered her more clearly than Davis, since Sara was much closer to Ivy's age. By the time Ivy came to live with James and Marilyn permanently, Davis had already gone off to college. "I remember her. Sara, right?"

He nodded.

Ivy dug through her memory. She didn't recall seeing her at the funeral. Just Marilyn and Davis. But then Ivy didn't have a keen radar for women. "So this guy broke Sara's heart and you're playing the whole protective big brother gig?" A dull pain hugged her middle. When had a man ever protected her like that? "This ought to be interesting."

"What?"

"The car ride." Another car drove past, only this one slowed a little, like it couldn't decide if it should stop and help or keep going. "How long until I meet the heartbreaker?"

"Forty-five, fifty minutes. And his name is Jordan." Davis tapped the tire with the toe of his shoe. "I can't believe my car broke down."

She eyed the vehicle, unable to join Davis in his disbelief. The thing looked exactly like the kind of car that would break down. A semi drove by, followed by an RV. She fiddled with the rubber lining of the passenger side window, then leaned into her palm. "So what should we do, Davis? Fifty minutes is a long time."

"We could talk."

"About what? God? Politics? The meaning of life?" What did someone like her have to say about topics like that? Nothing worthy of hearing. "That's not what I had in mind."

He pulled at his jaw.

"Do I make you nervous?" she asked.

"No."

"Liar."

"You don't make me nervous. You make me curious."

"Well, that's a first. And what, exactly, are you curious about?"

"About who you are." He held out his hand and flicked it up and down, motioning toward her body. "Underneath all this."

Underneath all this? This, as in, her hair and her legs and her face? She removed her hand from the car. She wasn't anything underneath all this. All this was it. She turned south, gazing down the length of the highway, and spotted a red sports car in the distance. "It's pointless waiting for a tow truck out in this heat when we don't have to, don't you think?" She stepped around him and his broken-down Jeep, brought herself into full view of the passerby, and stuck out her thumb.

"What do you think you're doing?"

"Hitchhiking."

"Don't be stupid."

She stuck her thumb out farther. "Trust me, Dave."

The red car slowed.

Davis grabbed her arm and waved the car away with his other hand.

"You lost us a ride."

He released her quickly and stepped back. "For all you know, that guy could have been a serial killer."

"A serial killer? Here?" The threat seemed statistically impossible. "You're paranoid."

"Probably." The set of his jaw stiffened. His eyes flashed, then dimmed. "But I'm not going to be responsible for putting you in danger."

An intriguing reaction, but the chirp of her cell phone prevented her from examining it further. Judging by the ringtone, her dear uncle was calling.

Davis moseyed past the shoulder and sat beneath the dense foliage of green, attempting to find some relief from the sun. He stared at the poppies and cornflowers decorating the stretch of land between the road leading north and the one headed south. Even though he'd chosen a location far enough away to give Ivy her privacy, he couldn't help but catch snatches of her end of the conversation.

She tapped her foot against the ground, her hand and, thank goodness, her thumb safely tucked inside the pocket of her navy blue shorts. A woman like her had no business hitchhiking. He dug the soles of his shoes into the grass and draped his elbows around his knees, wishing his father's words would leave him alone.

"I considered it an emergency!" Ivy's raised voice interrupted a chorus of birds.

Talking to Bruce, no doubt. Probably demanding the first flight back to New York as soon as Davis snapped the final picture of the editorial shoot. He wiped at the sweat beading along his temple and checked his watch. He needed to get them to Greenbrier in one piece, her to the boutique, and his car to the shop, all before his grandparents' anniversary dinner. And he'd have to suffer through a forty-minute car ride with Jordan Ludd, a kid who claimed to love Sara, but left her the first minute something went wrong. A heavy weight settled in his stomach. He had no right to be angry with Jordan. Not when the blame for Sara's heartbreak lay, ultimately, at his own feet.

"And you're convinced this is going to give me exposure?" Ivy toed the grass, her tan legs impossibly long. She turned her back to Davis, taking her voice with her. After a moment, she pulled the phone from her ear.

He let go of his knees. "Everything okay?" he called.

"Oh, just dandy."

"Want to talk about it?"

She pivoted around. "You're very into talking."

"You don't want to stay, do you?"

She closed the gap between them, cocked her hip, and placed her hand on her waist. She had gone and parked herself right in front of him. Davis kept his gaze trained on her face, even if it meant crooking his neck at an uncomfortable angle. "You remember me as a kid, right?"

He nodded.

"Did I look very happy to you?"

No, she hadn't. She'd looked sad. And lonely. The same way she looked at the funeral. He plucked a few clovers from the ground. "I think you should stay."

"Thirty minutes ago you couldn't believe I'd taken the job. Now you expect me to stay?"

"I don't expect you to stay. I just think you should. It might be good for you." He set his hands behind him, stretched his legs in front, and crossed one leg over the other, as if his relaxed position might detract from the inherent conflict of his statement. He had no doubt that Greenbrier could be good for Ivy, but he also knew her presence there would do nothing but blur the careful lines he'd drawn around his life. "I wasn't challenging your motives, by the way. I was only curious about them. You admitted to running away last time you were here, and now you've come back for a job you don't need."

Her expression twitched.

Or did she? He knew better than most how quickly the tide could change for a model working in high fashion. Was it changing for Ivy? He tossed the clovers at the ground. "Well, it doesn't matter. Your uncle is right about the exposure. Marilyn's wedding dress line is going to take off. Brides already come to her boutique from across the Lowcountry."

"You're an expert on wedding fashion?" She sat beside him. "That's an odd hobby for a man like you."

For a man like him? Surely Ivy knew he'd been a photographer once.

"Don't look so worried, Dave. Bruce assured me that my time will be well spent." She leaned close and tucked her next words into his ear. "Looks like I'll be sticking around. For now, at least. Lucky you."

His Adam's apple twitched. Yeah. Lucky him.

10

During the funeral, Ivy hadn't had the chance to take in much of Greenbrier. She'd been in town only one day, and given the circumstances, she'd been a little distracted. Something about seeing the man responsible for her life lowered into the ground had turned her off toward exploration. Now, however, with nothing but dread keeping her company, she sought out the diversion.

She straightened and craned her neck around Davis, who blocked the majority of her view. Spending forty minutes squished between him and Jordan Ludd, who didn't seem any more comfortable with Davis than Davis seemed with him, had lost its intrigue after the second mile. She'd tried flirting with the young man in an attempt to rile Davis, but she might as well flirt with a pile of bricks, and all Davis did was stare out the window, his jaw pulsing like a heartbeat. She chalked up the kid's lack of interest to his equal lack of IQ, but she could find no excuse to explain Davis's indifference. The whole ride left her with a bruised ego and sticky from the less-than-impressive air conditioner.

Davis leaned back in the seat, granting her access to the world outside the cramped cab of the tow truck. "Ivy needs to be dropped off at Something New before we go to the shop."

Jordan mumbled his reply, or more like grunted, and turned through a roundabout showcasing a hibiscus-framed stone heron spouting water from its beak. The island town was much the same, with manicured lawns surrounding antebellum homes, the kind that made Ivy feel as though they'd time-warped into the nineteenth century. Like any minute she might hear cannon fire in the distance or see Confederate soldiers strapped with muskets marching down the street to the waving of women's handkerchiefs.

The truck pulled onto a lopsided street called Palmetto Boulevard. Lopsided because shops adorned only one side. The sun peeked over the row of multitiered brick buildings and cast elongated shadows across the cobblestones—fat, black arms reaching toward the palm-tree dotted white shore. Jordan stopped a few blocks down, in front of a black awning with white lettering.

Something New.

The boutique Marilyn had opened ten years ago, the year Ivy left for New York City permanently, stuck out more than the others. Couture was not something Greenbrier knew well, but somehow, someway, her stepmother made it work. A sheen of sweat slicked Ivy's palms. Marilyn was inside. Bruce had warned Ivy, over the phone, to behave. He'd reminded her that Marilyn was a paying client, and this was her chance to get back on track. To let things settle in New York City while she made waves down south. Good waves. She took a deep breath and wiped her palms against her shorts. She'd dealt with many clients throughout her career. Marilyn didn't have to be any different. Ivy only needed to go inside, ask about the time frame and details for this particular assignment, and find a place to stay while she served her sentence.

Davis opened the door and stepped onto the sidewalk. Ivy unpeeled the backs of her thighs from the vinyl and scooted off the seat to join him. The ocean air smelled so different in South Carolina than it did on Staten Island. Even the sky looked different, as if somebody had flipped a brightness switch and made it bluer. And the street wasn't just clean, it was take-your-shoes-off clean. No litter by the curbs. No cigarette butts. Not even a sidewalk crack for the cigarette butts to fall into, if there were any. The perfection of it unnerved her. Having grown up in Chicago, then moving on to places like New York and Paris, Ivy preferred a little dirt and grit beneath her feet.

Davis walked around to the back of the truck, where he'd wedged her luggage, uncorked her suitcase, and handed it over. "As soon as my car's fixed, I can give you and Marilyn a lift to the house."

The house. Ivy didn't like the way he said that. Like it was the only one on the island. Like he expected her to stay there. "Marilyn doesn't have a car?"

"She rides her bike to work."

"Her bike?" Ivy hitched her purse strap higher up her shoulder. "A Schwinn or a Harley?" Somehow, she couldn't picture Marilyn on either.

Davis smiled. A genuine, unguarded smile that showed off slightly crooked teeth and dimples the shape of parentheses. "Definitely not a Harley." He glanced over his shoulder at Jordan, then pointed westward. "I'll be two blocks that way, on Peterson Street, if you need me. It shouldn't take long. You should check out the strip if you get bored."

"All by my lonesome?"

His dimples disappeared. "I'll see you later."

She watched him get into the truck, battling a listlessness she didn't want to feel. Men usually liked her presence, yet Davis seemed unimpressed. Was Bruce right? Was she losing it? She filled her lungs and narrowed her eyes at the truck as it drove away, pulling Davis's Jeep Cherokee after it. Mr. Knight was not beyond seduction. No man was. She'd snag his attention, and she'd do it in less than a week. She'd prove to herself that she still had it.

Ivy turned toward Something New and pushed through the front door. A peal of bells sounded overhead and a whoosh of cool air and light jazz greeted her. She stepped onto polished mahogany that looked more like glass than wood and found herself facing a deep-set boutique, decorated by mannequins clad in white gowns, posing in front of brightly lit three-way mirrors.

The clicking of heels sliced through her reluctant appreciation. Marilyn walked toward her dressed in a tailored cream-colored business suit, a measuring tape in one hand and pins in the other. Except for the gray in her roots and some extra wrinkles by her eyes, she looked much the same. Maybe not the ravishing beauty Mom had been, but pretty enough to make

Ivy wonder why James had done what he did. She pushed the thoughts away and returned Marilyn's smile.

Her smile.

How could the woman smile at Ivy like that—as if she truly meant it? It defied any shred of logic and left Ivy as off kilter as it had back then. Surely she had ulterior motives.

"How are you?" Marilyn's voice came out smooth and soft, flavored with just the right amount of southern drawl. "Davis called to tell me about the car."

Ivy shrugged.

Silence crept in between them and stood its ground. The jazz music did little to alleviate it. Ivy fidgeted with her hands and searched for a way to begin. Any one of her questions would suffice. *How long do you need me here? What's involved? Why are you paying so much money to have me? Why in the world do you want to hang my face in your boutique?*

Okay, maybe not that last one.

A stranger's voice broke through the awkwardness. "My daughter's all ready, Marilyn." A middle-aged woman with salt-and-pepper curls and peach lipstick came out from behind one of the three-way mirrors, holding a bottle of Snapple in her hand. "Oh, sorry. I didn't know you were with somebo..." Her voice trailed off as slowly as her mouth opened, then froze in place. It was as if somebody had jabbed the slow motion button before hitting pause.

Marilyn ignored the woman's odd reaction. "How beautiful does she look?"

The woman peeled her attention away from Ivy, blinked, then shifted her Snapple to her other hand. "Like the belle of the ball. She thinks this is the one."

"Oh, how exciting. Tell her I'll be back in two seconds."

The woman nodded and hurried behind her mirrored hiding place.

Two seconds wasn't very long. Ivy better use it well. "Bruce told me you'd fill in the details for me, as far as what's expected."

"I was hoping we could sit down and talk about it later tonight."

"What's tonight?"

"I'm making dinner for Mom and Dad at the house. They're celebrating their fifty-third wedding anniversary. I was hoping Rose—if you remember, that's Davis's mom—would still be in town, but she and her husband had to get back to work. You're welcome to join us if you want."

The bastard child joining the widow and her parents to celebrate fifty-three years of fidelity? Somehow, that was a bit too ironic for Ivy's taste.

"Davis and Sara will be there. You remember Sara? I was hoping we could get together afterward and talk about the campaign. I'm sure you and Davis discussed some of the details on your way here, but you probably still have questions."

"Why would Davis and I discuss the campaign?"

Marilyn frowned. "Didn't he tell you?"

"Tell me what?"

"Davis is your photographer."

Ivy smiled like Marilyn was telling a fantastic joke. But Marilyn didn't smile back.

Wait a minute. Davis was going to photograph her? How ridiculous. She shook her head. Almost stuck her fingers in her ear to clear it out. No. She had to have heard wrong. Misunderstood somehow. "I'm sorry—did you say Davis will be my photographer?"

"Yes."

The softly spoken word scratched like sandpaper. There was no way Davis Knight would be her photographer. She didn't care how well Marilyn paid or how much exposure Bruce promised. She couldn't risk botched-up photos splayed in an editorial spread, even if it was *Southern Brides,* all so he could experiment with a hobby. Not when her career was on the line. She couldn't believe the fashion editor of the magazine would hire an amateur. Nothing against Davis. But what did he know about fashion photography?

Marilyn's quick assurance about her nephew's brilliance did nothing to settle the doubts pinging through Ivy's mind. Davis had probably snapped pictures of Marilyn's dog at some Sunday afternoon picnic and she'd fallen in love. All fine and dandy, except casual picture-taking did not make a person an expert in photography—especially fashion photography. Ivy needed these pictures to make waves, and without an experienced photographer, they wouldn't even make a ripple. Or worse, they'd drill holes in the bottom of her boat and sink her altogether.

Ivy marched up the street, spotted a street sign that read Peterson, and turned the corner. The cobblestone turned into ordinary cement and the row of multicolored awnings disappeared. She squinted down the length of the road, searching for a sign for Ludd's Auto, and found it sandwiched between a pawn shop and a car wash. The tail end of the Jeep Cherokee jutted outside the opened garage and a pair of feet poked out from the vehicle's underside. She peered inside a window and spotted Davis, sitting in a plastic chair, tapping his foot against oil-stained cement, arms crossed over his chest. She stepped through the garage and through the side door.

Davis looked up, and they shared some sort of electrically charged face-off—a stare down in the middle of a filthy repair shop. She crooked her finger and beckoned him to join her. But he didn't come. At least not to her. He stood and pushed out the front doors, jerking his head for her to follow. The subtlety of his actions spoke volumes. She heard his message loud and clear: Davis Knight would not be led.

He leaned against the stucco with his hands shoved inside the pockets of his cargo shorts. "Done at the boutique already?"

"I found out some interesting news."

"Okay."

"Marilyn says you're going to be my photographer." Ivy waited for him to laugh. No such luck. "Call me crazy, but what do you know about fashion photography?"

He made a face—like her question was a sour lemon.

"I'm flattered, Davis, that you've followed my career." She stepped closer. "But if this is about taking pictures of me, you don't have to go through Marilyn to do it."

He didn't step away, but something inside him seemed to retreat. He cocked his head. "Aren't you tired?"

"Tired?" It was a left-field question.

"This act of yours. Because I don't think it's you."

She crossed her arms, as if doing so might hide away whatever Davis saw. Did he really think a fifty-minute car ride and some shared memories made him an expert on Ivy Clark? He didn't have a clue what was her and what wasn't. "You think because you've followed my career and maybe you know some stuff about wedding dresses that you're qualified to take pictures for a national magazine?"

"Trust me, I'm not any more thrilled about the idea than you are."

"Then why are you doing it?"

"I have my reasons."

"Thanks for being so specific."

The corner of his mouth twitched "What are you so worried about? That I'll take awful photos and ruin your career?"

"Actually, yes, you hit the hammer right on the head."

"It's a nail."

"What?"

"You hit the nail on its head. Not the hammer."

"What are your qualifications? And if you say anything about being hired for local birthday parties, I might roll my eyes."

"I was a fashion photographer in New York for a few years."

A mosquito buzzed by her nose. She swatted it away. What Davis was saying didn't make any sense. "People aren't fashion photographers in New York for a few years." He made it sound like a hobby.

"Not normal people, no. I'm not claiming to be normal."

"Why'd you leave?"

He scratched the back of his head. "It's complicated."

It didn't sound complicated to her. He obviously couldn't hack it in New York, so he'd come back here to lick his wounds, and now the well-being of her entire career rested in the hands of a wannabe. "Can I see your portfolio? Maybe a website? Something to help me decide if I should get myself into this."

"Aren't you already into this?"

"I want to see your work."

"I don't have anything to show you."

"How doesn't a photographer have anything to show?"

"I don't have anything to show because I'm not a photographer. At least not anymore. I haven't taken pictures for almost two years."

"This keeps getting better."

A black truck on monster wheels rolled down Peterson Street. The leathery-faced man behind the steering wheel smiled and waved at Davis, then turned his beast into the car wash. The mosquito came back. Ivy batted her hand around her hair. "If you haven't taken a picture in almost two years, why in the world would Marilyn give you the job?"

"Because. When Marilyn gets an idea in her head, nobody can stop her. Not even me."

She pressed her fingertips into her temples. "I can't do this."

"Why not?"

"It would be fashion suicide." Modeling Marilyn's wedding dresses for her handsome but surely unqualified nephew? A guy who freely admitted to not being a photographer? Did Bruce know about this? She shook her head. No, of course he didn't know. Otherwise he never would have sent her to do something so amateurish.

"Look, Ivy. I know what you're thinking." He ran two broad hands down his face and looked at the sky. "You're thinking I don't know what I'm doing. But trust me, I was a good photographer."

"Just not good enough to make it in New York City."

"I was making it fine."

"Tell me what 'fine' means to you." Because a couple of test shoots with no-name models and some random pictures in a beginner's portfolio was not her definition of the word.

"Fine enough to make a living. Fine enough for my photos to make it into some magazines and on the cover of one."

"Which magazines—*Fishing Weekly*?"

"Vogue."

Her eyes widened. "I'm sorry. For a second there I thought you said *Vogue.*"

"You heard correctly."

"I don't believe you."

A teenager on a scooter whizzed past, zipping through street puddles that splashed water against Ivy's shoes. She stepped closer to the garage. So did Davis. "Why would I lie?"

"Why would you leave?" If his stuff had made the cover of a magazine like *Vogue,* then only a lunatic would leave. He'd just crested the peak from wannabe into stardom. Who would run away the minute all their dreams came true? "Then why haven't I ever heard of you?"

"Do you know the name of every fashion photographer in the industry?"

"The good ones."

"I was just starting to make a name for myself when I left, so there's no reason why you would have heard of me. And anyway, it was almost two years ago, which means I'm nothing but a vague memory. If that."

"I don't get it. You went to NYC to be a photographer?"

"Yes."

"That was a dream of yours or something?"

"At the time, yes."

"You started to get your foot in the door?" *Vogue* was a tad more than in the door. More like in the door, up the stairs, and into the master bedroom. "And then you left."

"Correct."

"Why?"

He took a deep breath, like he'd need all the oxygen he could get in order to do the story justice, but before he could say anything, Jordan Ludd trotted out of the garage, a set of keys dangling from his finger. "The transmission's shot."

Davis's face fell. "Seriously?"

"'Fraid so." Jordan held out the keys. "It'll take us a couple days to round up the parts and get it fixed for you, if that's what you want to do."

"I'm not buying a new car, so I guess that's my only option."

"In the meantime, you can use one of the spare cars we've got here." He pointed toward a blue Mazda in the parking lot. Rust had eaten through half its bumper and a large dent had taken care of the rest. "Just be easy on her."

Davis fished his wallet from the back pocket of his jeans. "What do I owe you?"

"We'll square up after your Cherokee's fixed." Jordan screwed up his face, like he wanted to say something but couldn't get it out. "How's, uh... How's, um..." His half-formed question surrendered to the humidity and fell at his feet. He shuffled his shoes as if wiping the words off his laces.

"She's fine."

Ivy's ears perked. She could only assume *she* was Sara.

Jordan bobbed his head, or more like his entire upper half. "That's good."

Davis took the keys.

Jordan mumbled his good-bye and returned to the garage. Ivy let out a low whistle, stuck her hands into the back pockets of her shorts, and leaned back on her heels. "Aren't people who hang crosses from their rearview mirrors supposed to be forgiving or something?"

"He's not the one who needs forgiving."

Odd comment, but she had more important questions that needed answering. "Where were we? Oh, right. You were just about to explain why you left."

He sighed. "I needed to get away from all the chaos. Somewhere where I could think."

"That's why you left—to think?"

"You're a model, Ivy. You're in the industry. It's an intoxicating world. You know how easy it is to lose yourself."

No, she didn't. She had no idea. How could she lose herself when there'd been nothing of herself to lose? "Most people take a vacation to think. They don't uproot and leave altogether."

"I didn't like the man I'd become."

"And who was that?"

"Let's just say I lost myself to the point of ugliness, and then something happened and God closed the door and brought me back here."

Oh, goodness gracious, God brought him back? "So God told you to stop photography, but now He's telling you to jump back in? To start taking pictures again?"

He lifted his shoulder. "I don't know."

She was opening old wounds, pressing too hard. She could tell by his face. She didn't want to, but she couldn't help herself. She needed to know why she should stay. Why she should trust her career to a man who hadn't taken a professional picture in almost seven hundred thirty days? "Can I ask you one more question?"

"Sure."

"If you don't like the man you became in New York City, what makes you think you'll be any different here?"

Davis didn't answer her question.

11

Marilyn, I can't stay here." The words came out dry. Standing in front of the looming home, staring up at two stories of brick and elongated windows, prickly emotions stirred beneath the surface.

At the age of eight, Ivy started staying in the cavernous home for one month out of every summer, fascinated at first by the vaulted ceilings, wide-set staircase, a butler's pantry, and the courtyard and marsh out back. It was so much different than her mother's downtown condo in Chicago, which had been chic and hip, but nothing at all compared to this. Ivy had gone like an obedient dog, her stomach hurting over what to wear or what to say should her father speak to her. Turned out, she worried for nothing. James hardly said a word.

"Sure you can." Marilyn took hold of Ivy's suitcase and walked toward the home. "We added a guest apartment a few years ago."

Ivy took off after her, ready to yank away her suitcase and call for that yellow cab again. She wasn't going in that house. This time she had a choice. "Marilyn."

She stopped in front of the porch and turned around, weariness and residual grief stretching her features. "Please, Ivy. I'd love for you to stay. This house is too big for two people."

"Two people?"

"Sara lives here. She's excited to see you again." Marilyn fiddled with the small cross on her necklace. Ivy frowned. She was seeing a lot of those lately. "She didn't get the chance to speak with you at the funeral."

Sweet of Sara, but they hadn't known each very well as kids and were nothing but strangers now. Ivy looked over her shoulder, toward the place where Davis's loaner car had been moments ago and wrinkled her nose at the sulfuric scent in the air. It came from the marsh out back. She'd never gotten used to it as a kid. "If I'm going to be here in Greenbrier, I'll need my own space."

"The guest apartment is its own space. Here, come with me and I'll show you." She lifted the carry-on suitcase by its handle and carried it across the lawn to the side of the garage. Ivy followed, her heels punching skinny holes into the ground.

Marilyn pointed at a white wooden staircase leading to the story above the three-car garage. "See? You won't even have to come into the house if you don't want. Although I hope you will. We have to discuss the campaign at some point, and I'm having that dinner party for Mom and Dad tonight. You're welcome to join us."

A laugh gurgled inside Ivy's chest but got stuck somewhere in her throat. She doubted Marilyn's parents felt the same way.

"I'd hate for you to stay in a hotel room while you're here." Marilyn bumped her suitcase up the stairs and opened the door. "We're just two blocks west of the beach and a block south of the country club. You can't beat the location."

Humidity pressed against the back of Ivy's neck. She wiped beads of sweat from her hairline when something itchy stung her forearm. She smacked at the spot. A mosquito splattered against her skin. She followed Marilyn up the stairs, but only to escape the heat. And the bugs. She expected a cavernous room and walls that echoed with memories, but when she stepped inside, that's not what she got.

Cool air clashed against her skin. An inviting four-poster bed covered in a white comforter beckoned from the opposite side of the room, which opened into a quaint kitchenette, a spacious bathroom, and a walk-in closet. White carpet covered the floor, and straight ahead, on top of a mirrored dresser, a bouquet of pink rhododendrons burst from a glass vase like an explosion of fireworks, their bright color magnified by the whiteness of the room. Rhododendrons were Ivy's favorite, but surely Marilyn didn't remember such an insignificant detail like that.

"You used to like flowers when you were younger. They aren't much, but I wanted you to know how appreciative I am that you're doing this." She deposited the suitcase near the door and twisted her fingers together. "I know this can't be easy."

Ivy bit her lip.

"I changed the sheets this morning and cleaned out the refrigerator, in case you wanted to use it."

"What happened to Bernice?" Good old Bernice, a Gullah woman who cooked and cleaned and washed Ivy's clothes when she came for her summer visits. She'd felt like Ivy's only friend, and she spoke with an accent so thick it could hardly be considered English. Seemed strange for Marilyn to do the cleaning with her around.

"She moved to Atlanta a while ago. Annie's our housekeeper now." Marilyn twisted her fingers some more. "Well, I'll let you get settled. Dinner's at six if you'd like to join us."

And that was that. Somehow, Ivy was staying.

As soon as Marilyn left, Ivy brought the flowers into the bathroom, removed them from the vase, dumped the water down the drain, and gathered the stems together with one hand and pulled out her hair band with the other. She wrapped the band around the stems and hung the flowers upside down near one of the windows, then got to work unpacking her stuff.

When she reached the bottom of her suitcase, she pulled out a snow globe. The only one she'd packed. The glass sphere felt cool and heavy in her hands. Turning it in a circle, snowflakes fluttered and swirled around the Eiffel Tower. Ivy remembered the first time she saw the famous landmark. Raymond had taken her there. He'd wined and dined her, then brought her to a fancy hotel. It had been her first fling. The first time a man looked her in the eyes and told her he loved her. The first time she experienced the euphoric high that came with being pursued.

She had been fourteen years old.

Ivy sank onto the bed and stared at the flowers. In a couple of days, the sun would dry them. They would be nothing more than beautiful dead petals.

Ivy opened the door that led to the rest of the house. She had to find Marilyn and tell her no, thanks. They could talk about the details of the campaign tomorrow morning. An anniversary celebration was a bit much, especially one for Marshall and Eleanor. Marilyn might kid herself into thinking they wanted to see her, but Ivy knew better.

The door creaked as she stepped out onto the landing and descended a short staircase into the hallway of the second floor. Silence rattled through the house and settled like an anvil inside her body. She hated it. Give her dance clubs. Give her music. Give her distraction. Anything but silence. The front door opened below her. A dog yipped and paws skittered across the hardwood.

"Dad, Mom! Happy anniversary!"

So much for finding Marilyn before the guests of honor arrived.

Ivy came to the edge of the staircase, the smell of butter and seafood making her mouth water. She hadn't eaten anything since breakfast but a bag of pretzels on the plane. She attempted to peek down the stairs, but all she could see without bringing herself into view was a small white dog jumping on legs.

"Down, Georgia!"

The white dog circled Marilyn's feet and plopped near her heel.

"The food smells wonderful, honey. You shouldn't have gone to so much trouble." The voice belonged to Eleanor. She sounded the same.

"It's your fifty-third wedding anniversary, Mom. Of course I went to so much trouble."

Ivy put her foot on the first step.

"Please tell me it's not true."

She gripped the banister and stopped. That voice belonged to Marshall. He sounded the same too.

"What is it you want me to tell you?" Marilyn's voice came out as stiff as an overstarched dress shirt.

"That you didn't invite that girl into this house."

The sharp words hurled Ivy into the past. She was a little girl all over again, overhearing a conversation she didn't want to overhear—only that one had been between Marilyn and James.

"That girl is your daughter, James."

"I'm not comfortable having her in this house," he replied. *"And if you say you are, then you're lying. She was a mistake, Marilyn."*

Ivy ground her teeth. She refused to let those long-ago words hurt her. Refused to let them matter. So what if her father hadn't wanted her? Hundreds of other men had since then.

"Please, Marshall, let's not get into this tonight." Eleanor put her hand on his arm. "Not on our anniversary."

"It was one thing to have her visit when James was living, but he's dead. There's no reason to have her here. Especially not under this roof. Do you know what people will say?"

"I don't care what people will say, Dad."

"I don't understand this obsession you have with her. You are my daughter, and I will not stand by and watch you torture yourself."

"It isn't an obsession."

Eleanor's feet shuffled. "Please don't get worked up, dear. Remember what Doc said about your heart."

So the old codger had a faulty heart. There was something to be said about karma.

"My heart's fine, El. And Marilyn, of course it's an obsession. You're inviting painful memories inside to stay. Just like before. You refuse to keep the past in the past. James repented and wanted to forget, only you never let him. You insisted she come."

So it was Marilyn who arranged her summer visits. Ivy had always suspected, but this was the first time she'd heard those suspicions confirmed.

"Dad, Ivy was part of James's life, whether he chose her or not. She's his daughter, for crying out loud. His daughter. I couldn't let him ignore that."

"But James is no longer here. You did what you could. Now it's time to drop it."

"I want her here."

"This is ridiculous. If you want her to model your dresses, then fine. Let her. We all know she's gorgeous. But bringing her into your home? There's no reason for that."

Marilyn sighed. "I don't expect you to understand."

"That girl does not belong in this house. I won't have her influencing my grandchildren."

"Influencing your grandchildren? Dad, Davis and Sara aren't little kids anymore. They are both adults and so am I. I'm sorry, but this is my house and you'll just have to respect my wishes."

"She's not your daughter, sweetheart. As much as you might wish—"

"That's enough!" Marilyn's sharp words slapped across Marshall's baritone.

Silence settled like an unwanted houseguest. Ivy could relate. She pressed her fist against her stomach. As a child, she had remained hidden, pretended not to hear. She wouldn't pretend anymore. She wouldn't run away. Maybe she'd take Marilyn up on the dinner invite after all and let Marshall boil in his awkwardness.

She loosened her grip on the banister and walked down the stairs. "Marshall. Eleanor. I didn't know I'd elicit so much heated discussion. And on your anniversary too."

Marshall's eyes flickered toward the staircase. Eleanor's mouth dropped open. Marilyn's face whitened. "Ivy, I don't know what you overhead, but—"

She held up her hand to stop Marilyn's apology, turned to Marshall and addressed the severe set of his bushy eyebrows. "Congratulations on fifty-three years of marriage. Fidelity is a wonderful thing to celebrate."

He scowled.

A smile spread across Ivy's lips but stopped as a young woman walked into the room. Wispy blond hair. Ordinary face. Wrangler jeans. Simple T-shirt. Sara. Only she didn't twirl and dance like Ivy remembered. She walked beside a yellow Lab, clutching a leather harness strapped to the dog's body.

"Grandpa Marshall, Grandma Eleanor. Happy anniversary!" Her face lit up over the words, but not her eyes. They stared at nothing. Vacant. Unfocused. Ivy took a step back. What had happened to Sara?

"Your sister is blind," Ivy said, intercepting Davis as he came through the front door.

Georgia yipped at Davis as he paused halfway over the doorstep. What kind of greeting was that? He ran his hand down the front of his shirt and stepped all the way inside. He couldn't believe Ivy had actually accepted Marilyn's invitation to the party. How could he celebrate his grandparents' anniversary with Ivy in the room, the question she'd asked earlier echoing off the walls of his mind?

"What makes you think you'll be any different here?"

What, indeed?

"I'm surprised you're here," he said.

"I hadn't planned on it, but then Marshall opened his mouth and I couldn't help myself." She looked over her shoulder, through the foyer, then back toward him. "You didn't tell me she was blind."

She said it like Sara was engaged. Like it was something to be excited about. The tone made him bristle. "Does it matter?"

Her eyes widened. She leaned back. "Not to me, but it obviously does to you."

Of course it mattered. His sister, once a promising artist, couldn't paint or walk through art galleries without seeing darkness. Davis caught her once, paintbrushes gathered beneath her nose, like the smell of the bristles might bring shape and color to her sightless eyes. The memory still broke his heart.

Ivy snuck another glance over her shoulder. "She wasn't blind when we were kids."

Davis nudged away the jumping Georgia with his foot. "What's your point?"

"How does that happen?"

"If you're so curious, why don't you ask her?"

"That would be rude."

"And asking her brother behind her back isn't?"

"Curiosity isn't a sin." Her mouth curved into a smile. "You're curious about me, remember?"

He took a step away. Why did she have to turn everything he said around? His curiosity didn't stem from his attraction. His curiosity had everything to do with the sadness he spied in her unguarded moments when she thought nobody watched.

"Davis?"

Georgia scampered across the room. He turned at the sound of Marilyn's voice and found her standing beneath the crown molding at the end of the foyer. "I thought I heard you come in. Care to join us?"

Did he want to escape this conversation with Ivy? Yes. One hundred percent yes. He swept his hand toward Marilyn. "After you."

Ivy frowned but didn't argue.

He followed her into the dining room and found Sara at the dining table, her unfocused eyes staring toward the windows as she chatted with Grandma Eleanor. Faded evening sunlight lined the edge of her profile, illuminating her skin. Her guide dog lay at her feet. Resolve settled into his limbs. He had to do something—no matter how small—to help Sara. Even if it meant unpacking his camera in order to do it.

"Davis, honey, you look peaky. Are you feeling okay?"

He shrugged off Grandma Eleanor's comment and wrapped her in a hug.

"Of course he's not okay." Grandfather stood by the windows and drummed his fingers against the frame. "He's wasting his college education working maintenance at Cornerstone Church when he should be taking over for me."

Never mind the fact that Davis had no interest in hotels or investing or that he truly enjoyed the slow pace at Cornerstone Church. He let go of his grandmother. "I thought you and Pastor Voss were friends."

"What does that have to do with anything?"

"You think he likes that you're trying to steal me away from Cornerstone?"

"Anybody can fix a church."

Davis gritted his teeth, kissed Sara on the cheek and sat beside her, pretending not to notice as Ivy relaxed back in her seat with folded arms, watching the interplay between him and Grandfather with open interest.

"Come sit down, dear." Grandma Eleanor motioned to the head of the table.

Grandfather sat.

Marilyn passed around the greens and filled glasses with sweet tea. "I was thinking it might be a good idea for Ivy to go to the plantation with you tomorrow."

"Oh, I can go by myself." His answer came too quickly.

Sara held out her hand, palm up, waiting for her brother to take it. "Davis, are you going to say grace?"

Everybody bowed their heads. He spoke some stilted words to God, all too aware of Ivy's unbending head and probing stare. He said his amen and wrapped his fingers around his glass.

Lord, if You want me to see her as You do, I'm going to need some help.

Ivy stabbed a piece of lettuce with her fork. She crunched the bite between her teeth and ran her pinky along the crest of her bottom lip. "I'd love to go tomorrow. Thanks, Marilyn."

Discomfort weighted the room and didn't leave, not during the crab casserole and biscuits, not when Marilyn brought a french silk pie from the refrigerator, and not when talk turned to Something New and Marilyn's I Do bridal wear.

"I'm excited you're taking pictures again." Sara smiled a smile that was so uncalculated, so sincere, Davis had to look closer. How she could smile like that—especially about him and his camera—would never make sense.

Grandfather huffed. "He shouldn't be taking pictures."

Marilyn brought her fingers to her temples. "Dad, please, not tonight."

Davis swallowed his bite. "He's right, though."

Sara turned in Ivy's direction, her gaze landing a little left of her intended target. "He's amazing. Have you seen his work?"

Ivy circled the fork tongs around her half-eaten piece. "He told me he didn't have any work to show."

"I think Marilyn kept his magazine photos."

"I did!" Marilyn's chair scraped against polished wood. Davis held up his hand to stop her, but she ignored him and left the room.

"Tear sheets?" Ivy raised her eyebrows. "How professional."

He tightened his grip on the fork and pushed remnants of pie around the china. When Marilyn returned, she waved torn-out magazine pages in her hand and pushed them across the table while Grandfather muttered something under his breath.

Ivy took two of the sheets—one from *Harper's Bazaar* and the other from his last shoot for *Vogue*—the one featuring supermodel Clarissa Von

Steuben. The one that had fashion editors and agencies still calling from time to time. He watched her flip the pages over and study the other side, loathing the sliver of pride lodging in his chest. He hated that he cared what Ivy thought or that these tear sheets proved his worth in her eyes. Davis looked down at his plate. His worth didn't come from his photos or women or success.

Forgive me for forgetting it once. Don't let me forget it again.

"So I guess I don't have to worry anymore. I'm convinced."

He looked at Ivy across the table. "About what?"

She fanned herself with the magazine pages, something hungry glinting in the caramel of her eyes. "That you know exactly what you're doing."

If only he felt the same way.

12

Hot wind tangled through Ivy's hair. Early July in South Carolina was an awful time to drive around a rented car with a faulty air conditioner. Davis watched from the corner of his eye as she gathered it into a bundle and held it captive with one hand, stray wisps fluttering in her eyes. "Your grandfather's a charming man."

He pulled into the entrance of the Primrose Plantation. Before he left last night, Marilyn had taken him aside and told him about the conversation Ivy had overheard before dinner. It had made his chest ache, and as far as he knew, he hadn't inherited any of Grandfather's heart problems.

"I mean, seriously, charming."

"He's picky about who he likes." That was a gross understatement. Grandfather rarely approved of anybody, which meant Ivy didn't stand a chance.

"Well, he definitely likes me."

"I wouldn't let it upset you."

"Do I look upset?"

He turned from the road and stared at her arched eyebrows. No, she didn't. She looked bored or maybe untouchable. The ache in his chest returned. And with it, his father's words…

Yet when it came to the woman in his passenger seat, Davis wasn't sure Dad was right. He wasn't sure he knew what he saw at all. The brakes squealed as he pulled the borrowed Mazda up to the gate where a boy sat inside an entrance booth. He slumped in the window, his hair sticking up from the back of his head like a broken mattress spring, eyelids tottering halfway between opened and closed. Davis slung his elbow over the side of his door and leaned his head outside the car window. "We're here to see Mrs. Lipowitz."

The kid pushed a mop of bangs around his forehead. "She's out for the day."

"We're supposed to meet with her this morning." Joan had said Sunday, and today was Sunday. He needed a storyboard prepared by Tuesday, but he couldn't do that without seeing the place first.

"She called this morning." The kid yawned. "Some kind of family emergency."

"Do you know when she'll be back?"

"She didn't say."

Davis scratched the back of his neck, then plucked his phone from the console and checked for messages. There were none. "My name's Davis Knight. I'm doing a photo shoot for *Southern Brides* here on the property next week. We were supposed to meet with Mrs. Lipowitz today to tour the grounds and the home so we can prepare for the shoot."

Another yawn split the kid's mouth wide open; he didn't even try hiding it with his hand.

"Is there any way we could meet with somebody else?" Davis asked. "Somebody in charge?"

"Tour guide can show you around."

"Great. We'll do that."

"You'll have to wait till he gets here, and he don't do private tours."

"When will he get here?" Davis mashed the words through his teeth.

The kid looked at his watch. "Forty minutes."

"Okay, then. Could you let us inside and we'll wait for him there?"

"I'm not allowed to open the gate to the public till nine thirty."

By the time they made any leeway with this conversation, it would be half past ten. "Listen, we're not technically the public. We were supposed to meet with Mrs. Lipowitz, and she was going to give us a private tour, remember? I'm sure, if you called her, she'd confirm everything I'm saying."

"Sorry, mister, but I can't bother her right now. And I'm not allowed to let anybody in without special permission."

What did he need—a badge? He had special permission.

Ivy set her hand on Davis's knee and leaned her body across his lap.

He pressed back against the seat, away from the scent of lilacs in her hair. What did she think she was she doing, leaning over him like this?

"What do people call you, handsome?"

The kid's mouth dropped open, only this wasn't a yawn. He'd probably never seen a woman like Ivy Clark in his life, let alone heard one call him handsome. Davis would have felt sorry for the young man if Ivy hadn't gone and draped her body across his lap. The boy's Adam's apple bobbed in his throat. "Colton."

"It's a pleasure to meet you, Colton." She extended her arm toward Davis's window and offered her hand. Colton stared at it with round eyes. When it was obvious he couldn't, for whatever reason, reach his own hand out of the booth and shake Ivy's, she brought it down on the steering wheel. "Listen, Colt, I'm having a rotten morning. The air in this car doesn't work and my hair's all a mess. You know what would turn everything around?"

Colton did something with his head that looked like half nod, half shake.

"If you bent the rules a teensy tiny bit and let us in." She pinched at the air with her fingers. "I promise we'll be on our best behavior."

"Um, yeah, sure. I guess I could do that." A dazed-looking Colton reached for a button and the gate squeaked opened.

"I sure appreciate it, Colt. We'll make sure to tell the tour guide what a polite young man you are." Ivy removed her body from Davis's lap.

Shaking his head, he drove through before the kid regained his senses and changed his mind. "Poor Colton didn't stand a chance."

"Hey, everybody has to be good at something, right?" The faintest hint of something broken distorted her voice. It was a thousand times more intriguing than her winks or her touches or her smoldering stares.

Davis cocked his head. "That's your talent—enchanting young men?"

"They don't have to be young."

An odd weight plunked on top of his shoulders—it had nothing to do with Sara or photography and everything to do with Pastor Voss's words gathering inside his brain: *"Maybe God wants to show Ivy Clark the same freedom."* Davis was ninety-five percent sure Ivy didn't want to leave her chains. Ninety-five percent sure she didn't see them as shackles. But what about that other five percent? What if a piece of her—no matter how small—needed, maybe even wanted rescuing? The heaviness grew. And with it, that same pull, that same fascination he'd felt for Ivy when she was nothing but a ghost in Marilyn's home, roaming the halls. Barely there. "You don't have to resort to that to get a man's attention."

She lifted her shoulder. "It works for most men. At least, most normal men."

"The implication being I'm not normal, since I haven't fallen under your spell yet?"

" 'Yet' is the key word."

"You're underestimating me." This time when he got behind the camera, it wouldn't be about women or fame. It would be about capturing beauty—like Dad had taught him. The beauty of weddings and marriage, a lifetime commitment, an institution created by God. He pulled into a parking space and unbuckled his seat belt.

"You're underestimating me," she said.

"I think you underestimate yourself." His words came out quiet and gentle, but she flinched when he delivered them.

"You liked the plantation?" Marilyn asked as she zipped up the dress.

"It was fine." More like captivating, but Ivy wasn't in the mood to gush. Not when her head still spun from Davis's morning yo-yo act. One minute, annoyed. The next, cautious. And the minute after that, so tender it stirred up a longing she didn't want to feel—one that chafed like sandpaper. Annoyed. Cautious. Gentle. Annoyed. Cautious. Gentle. One-two-three. One-two-three. Until Ivy's head spun into a knotted spool of thread. What was wrong with him? Why couldn't he act like a normal guy?

In an attempt to set her thoughts aside, Ivy focused on the dress. The strapless sheath hugged her body and stopped short of her knees, the silk cool and smooth against her skin. Marilyn held out a pearl white shrug that matched the dress. Ivy slid her arms through and fit the garment over her shoulders. The high collar circled around the back of her neck like poppy petals, leading the eye down to her exposed clavicle, highlighting the honey-colored tone of her skin.

A dreamy look took hold of Marilyn's face as she studied Ivy's reflection in the mirror. Her mouth looked full of words, lots of them, but ever since last night's dinner their interactions had turned into a stilted waltz—leaderless and clumsy. The kind of dance that fumbled through the song and fizzled out before the music ended. Marilyn clasped her hands beneath her chin. "I'll go get your accessories."

Ivy pivoted in front of the mirror to see her back and ran her hands down her front. The dress fit like Marilyn had stitched Ivy inside it. For one uncensored moment, she imagined herself walking down a rose-covered aisle, the church filled with faceless people as she headed toward her faceless groom. She let the image fade to black, hating the pin-sized hole it left behind. Falling in love and staying in love were two totally different beasts. While Ivy had mastered the art of getting men to fall in love with her, she stayed clear of the latter, and a wedding day most definitely required the latter. She pulled her shoulders back in an attempt to repair the pinhole leak and searched for Marilyn. The stupid dress fit fine. So get her out of it already. Who cared about the accessories?

"You're a stunning bride."

A young lady with carrot-colored hair stared at Ivy's reflection, a spark of jealousy glinting in her almond-shaped eyes. "I could never wear a dress like that." She adjusted the dress draped over her forearm, her opulent diamond catching on some of the beading. "Those kind only look good on mannequins. Or people like you."

Ivy made a coquettish turn in front of the mirror. "You like it?"

"It's to die for." The redhead looked at Ivy's left hand. "Who's the lucky man?"

Ivy hid her ringless finger behind her back, a delicious idea drizzling over her thoughts. Just how fast did the rumor mill spin in a town the size of Greenbrier? Maybe she couldn't get into Davis's bloodstream like she got into most men's, but that didn't mean she couldn't get under his skin. She turned around. "Davis Knight."

The dress slipped down the girl's arm. "Shut the front door!"

"Do you know him?"

"Know him? Girl, every bachelorette in Greenbrier knows him. He doesn't exactly blend in, if you know what I mean. But then, neither do you." She repositioned the dress over her arm. "Name's Rachel Piper. My grandpa pastors the church where Davis works. The two of us went to school together. He graduated a year ahead of me. I didn't even know he was dating anybody."

"We haven't made any announcements yet. It's been a bit of a whirlwind romance."

"Well, I'll say. There's going to be a lot of broken hearts in Greenbrier when y'all decide to spill the beans."

A middle-aged woman with matching red hair waved from the back of the boutique.

Rachel rolled her eyes in an amused sort of way. "This is the twelfth dress I've tried on today. Mama's on a warpath to find me the best one in South Carolina. But I'm sure you know how that is."

The pinhole widened. No, Ivy didn't.

"Well, you go on and tell Davis congratulations for me. You two make a gorgeous couple." Rachel waved at Ivy's reflection and hurried toward her mother, who held up a beaded ivory dress like a winning lottery ticket.

The widening leak left Ivy feeling like a deflated air mattress. She glared at herself in the mirror. She needed to get out of this dress and blow herself back up again. Find something entertaining, something loud and exciting to fill up the empty space. She snuck a glance at Rachel and her mother, heads together in the back of the boutique, gushing over their latest find, Rachel's engagement ring refracting the light when a question whispered across Ivy's soul.

She could reinflate herself all she wanted, but who was going to fix the leak?

Her shoulders wilted.

Marilyn returned and Sara followed behind, as blind as she was yesterday. She held onto the harness wrapped around Sunny, her guide dog. The yellow Lab led her around the furniture and stopped in front of a cushy chair. Sara felt for the seat and sat down. "Marilyn said you look beautiful." She clasped a necklace in her lap. "I wish I could see you."

Unsure how to respond, Ivy placed her hand against her middle as Marilyn stood on tiptoe and pinned the birdcage veil with French netting to her hair. It was amazing how much the accessory completed the ensemble. Maybe Bruce was right. Wearing this dress at the Primrose Plantation with Davis behind the camera would make for some stunning photographs.

With the short veil fitted into place, Marilyn took the three-strand pearl necklace from Sara and fastened it behind Ivy's neck. Ivy slipped on the high heels and examined her reflection. In a few days, she'd have to play the role of blushing bride. A woman in love. She smiled big and wide—like happiness bubbled up from her insides and spilled over onto her outsides. It looked too forced. She'd have to keep practicing.

Marilyn stepped back. "Someday you're going to make a breathtaking bride."

Ivy's smile died.

Sara petted the top of Sunny's head. "Davis is late. I was supposed to meet with my tutor twenty minutes ago."

"Your tutor?"

"I'm learning to read Braille. Davis arranged it."

"You two seem close."

"I like to think so," Sara said.

"I'll be right back to get you out of this dress." Marilyn touched Ivy's elbow with cold fingers and excused herself to assist the mother-daughter duo—Big Red and Little Red—in the corner of the boutique.

"How did you like the plantation?" Sara asked.

"It was definitely beautiful."

"Grandfather used to take me there. The home had some amazing artwork. I remember one piece in particular. A Rembrandt. Oh, it was exquisite. And the gardens. I remember those too." Sara didn't just talk. She moved. Her whole body spoke.

"I think your brother loved it."

"I'm glad."

"So, Sara..." Ivy fidgeted, shifting her weight from one foot to the other. She wanted to know more about Sara's blindness. Like how it had come to be and why Davis refused to talk about it. She also wanted to know more about Davis himself. Like why somebody with his talent would quit. Or why he acted like a man suffering from multiple personalities. "Do you work here at Something New?"

"Sort of. I've helped Marilyn for a few months now. To be honest, I'm just starting to get used to this blindness thing. If a person can ever really get used to it."

Ivy blinked. Sara had opened the door and Ivy's curiosity was all too eager to clomp over the threshold. "How long have you...been this way?"

"Almost two years."

"What happened? I mean, how did it happen?"

Sara scratched Sunny's ear. "I fell down a flight of cement stairs and hit my head on the railing. When I woke up in the hospital, my vision was gone."

She told the story like one might read an overdone news article, like that one fall hadn't changed her life in a profound and irrevocable way. "Wow."

"Tell me about it. Most clumsy people deal with some bumps and bruises, the occasional spilled drink or broken vase. I'm an extreme case."

"What did you do...before?"

"I went to college at the university. I was going to major in art history. I wanted to be the next Mary Cassatt or maybe a curator. I could never decide." A frown sculpted her lips. She lifted her shoulders as if to shrug it away. "Now I get to pour my creative energy into music. I compose. I'm not very good, really, but it's an escape. When I play the piano, it's almost like I can see again."

Ivy fingered the pearls wrapped around her neck. "I'd like to hear you sometime."

The front doors of Something New flew open. A gust of heat swept across the floor and wrapped around Ivy's calves. Davis strode toward them, camera clanking against his chest, a frenzied look in his eye. Ivy adjusted her veil. For a moment, talking with Sara, she'd forgotten herself.

"Are you that desperate to see me?" she asked as he reached the mirror.

His eyelids fluttered as if her presence startled him. And she saw it. Finally. A glimpse of desire peeking out from his pupils. He liked the way she looked in this dress. He shook his head, as if to rattle himself from a daze, and returned his attention to Sara. "I can't believe I forgot about your tutoring session. I got into this storyboard thing for Joan and completely lost track of time."

"It's not a big deal. We can reschedule."

Davis looked pained. By his expression a person might think forgetting this one appointment was a matter of life or death.

Ivy pointed to his camera. "I like the new look."

He yanked the strap off his neck and clutched the camera at his side—like he'd been caught with incriminating evidence. Before Ivy could inquire or tease him over the strange reaction, Rachel Piper spotted Davis from across the boutique and flapped her arms like a distressed bird.

"Davis! It's bad luck to see the bride in her dress! Don't you know that?" Rachel looked at Ivy, who rolled her eyes as if to say *Silly groom*.

Davis's forehead wrinkled.

"Congratulations! I'm so happy for you," Rachel called.

Davis turned his wrinkled forehead toward Ivy. "Did you tell Rachel about the photo shoot?"

Ivy nodded. "Apparently she's very enthusiastic about it."

Marilyn returned and hooked her arm around Davis's elbow and motioned toward Ivy's reflection. "What do you think?"

He scratched the back of his neck. "It looks fine."

Sara laughed. Ivy couldn't help herself. She laughed too.

It seemed to make Davis's wrinkles scrunch closer together. "If we hurry, we can catch your tutor before she leaves."

"Why doesn't Ivy come?"

"I think she has work to do with Marilyn," Davis said.

Marilyn waved her hand. "Not at all. We're finished for today."

"Maybe we can grab a bite to eat afterward," Sara said, standing from her seat.

"That sounds like a great idea. Thanks for the invitation, Sara." Ivy smirked at Davis. "Your sister and I are going to be good friends. I can just feel it."

His eyes darkened—like thunderclouds rolling across blue sky. He shifted, the movement bringing something into Ivy's line of vision. An eleven-by-fourteen black-and-white photograph, framed and mounted on the wall behind Davis. Marilyn in a white dress, clasping onto the groom's arm. A man who epitomized handsome and confident. He flashed a charming, white-toothed smile at the camera and shielded his bride from showers of rice.

James. Her father.

The smirk on Ivy's face melted away. Never once had he smiled at her like that. Never once had he shielded her from anything. Now that he was in the ground, she'd never get the chance to ask him why.

13

Sara followed Sunny to the front doors of the tutoring center across from the marina, squished between Berry's Pizza Palace and Sunn and Swimm Water Sport Rental. The tutoring center taught it all. Foreign language. Braille. Sign language. Davis watched Sara disappear inside the building as the vinyl in the backseat squeaked and he glanced in the rearview mirror. Ivy hadn't spoken a word on the short drive to the marina. She'd sat as still as a statue in the back, gazing out the window.

Davis twirled his keys around his finger and stepped into the sunshine. He opened her door. While she joined him in the sun, he bent inside the car and pulled out his sketchbook. The one he'd used to draw up some ideas for the storyboard.

After his visit to Primrose, after seeing the architecture of the home, the rhythm and movement of the grounds, two years of pent-up creativity unleashed with a fury, cramping his mind with ideas. So he'd grabbed the sketchbook, picked up some bridal magazines from a convenience store, and let his vision ooze onto the paper.

He wanted to share his thoughts with Ivy. After all, she'd done more editorials than he had. Not only would her approval set his own insecurities at ease—insecurities that came with an extended absence from his craft—it would give them something safe to talk about while they waited for Sara to finish up in the tutoring center. He waved his sketchpad at her.

"What do you have there?" she said.

"Ideas. For the photo shoot."

"How exciting."

He ignored her dry tone. "I was hoping you could help me out. Give me some feedback."

"You want my opinion?"

"Why wouldn't I?"

"I'm the model. My opinion doesn't matter."

She was going to be the focal point of every photo. How didn't her opinion matter? He leaned against the car and squinted at her. "I'm not following your logic."

She batted her hand, as if to shoo away the entire conversation, and grabbed his Nikon from the backseat of the Mazda. "How about we ditch the sketchpad and do some practice shots down by the beach." She pulled the strap over her head and brought the camera to her eye. "Or I could take pictures of you. You're not too shabby to look at, you know."

Davis tucked the sketchpad under his arm.

"Smile for the camera, Davis. Show me sexy. Show me naughty." The shutter clicked several times. "Come on, at least show me something."

"Give it here, Ivy." He reached for the camera.

She stepped back.

He frowned.

"Ooh, frustrated. I like that. Give me more."

"Cut it out."

"More, Davis. I need more of you." *Click. Click.*

Her words unsettled him. "Come on."

She laughed, only the sound came out hollow. "Give me everything." *Click. Click. Click.* "Everything, Davis. Until nothing's left."

He caught her elbow with a gentle hand. "Hey."

She hid the camera behind her back.

He reached behind her and pried the camera away. Ivy stopped laughing. She stopped moving. All of a sudden, Davis felt her closeness. And his body responded.

Her chin tipped in invitation. But her eyes held him back. Twin pools of honey filled with a world of contradictions—depth and emptiness, pain and laughter, invitation and refusal, and behind all those incongruities, longing. One that could swallow him whole if he let it. A longing too big and too wide for him or anybody else to fill. It didn't just flicker like a candle; it raged like a forest fire. It made him step away.

One corner of her mouth quirked. "And here I thought you were going to kiss me."

He took another step back, hoping the distance might cool him down. "Let's say for a second I would have. What would that accomplish?"

"Why does it have to accomplish anything?"

He pushed his fingers through his hair. His kiss would be like a drop when she needed a downpour.

"It's okay to kiss me, Davis. Most men do."

"Would that make you happy—if I kissed you? Would that make everything better?"

"You think too hard." She slid her hands into the pockets of her shorts and took a step back herself. "Why does it have to make anything better? Why can't it just be fun?"

"Because I don't think it's fun for you. I don't think that's why you do this."

Her smile soured. "Okay, Dr. Knight, since you're psychoanalyzing me now, why do I do *this*? Whatever *this* is."

"I think you're looking for something in me that you're not going to get."

"Like?"

"Love."

She tilted her head back and let out a laugh. "Well, then, I guess I should thank you for your honesty. Now that I know you couldn't possibly love somebody like me, I'm free to expend my efforts elsewhere."

"I didn't say I couldn't love you. I'm saying I don't think my love would be enough."

She crossed her arms. "This is a bizarre conversation. All I wanted was a kiss and you turn it into love. Well, Dr. Knight, not one part of me is searching for that."

Her impassioned words pinched his heart. Who was she trying to convince, him or herself? "Ivy, I'm not trying to—"

"Davis!"

The familiar voice had him swallowing a groan. Violet Bogden, the marina manager's wife, waved from across the parking lot, wearing magenta capri pants and an excited smile. She bobbed across the uneven cement—half running, half walking, as a cloud overhead cast her pink body in shadow.

"How good to see you two here at the marina." She turned to Ivy and put her hand against her sun-splotched chest, dimpling her freckled skin. "I'm so sorry about the loss of your father. To have died so young. He was such a handsome, successful man."

Ivy's face froze into a beautifully chiseled ice sculpture.

Violet was undeterred. "To hear the delightful news after something so sad tickled me pink."

"You're definitely pink."

Ivy's deadpan comment would have made Davis chuckle, but he was too distracted by Violet's words. Delightful news? Surely she wasn't referencing the photo shoot. There was no reason for that to tickle her when she had nothing to do with it.

"You two will make such beautiful babies."

His confusion quadrupled. Babies? With Ivy? Davis pulled at his earlobe. "I'm sorry, but did you say *babies*?"

"I just got off the phone with Trudy Piper. She was at Something New this morning, helping her daughter Rachel pick out a wedding dress, and she told me the news."

Davis turned to Ivy. A hint of a smile thawed her frozen expression—like she'd tucked an amusing secret into one corner of her mouth.

"Mrs. Bogden, Ivy isn't pregnant. Or, I mean, if she is..." His attention traveled to Ivy's stomach. If she was pregnant, it had to be very early. "Well, if she is, it's not my child. We aren't… I mean, we haven't…" His cheeks burned. How had he gotten into this conversation?

Violet winked at Ivy. "He's such a gentleman."

Ivy nodded emphatically.

"So when's the big day? When are you two lovebirds tying the knot?"

Davis coughed. "Tying the what?"

"Getting married." She chuckled. "My, Davis, you sure are being bashful about this. People get married all the time. You should know, seeing how many future brides buy dresses from your auntie."

He flattened his palm over the crown of his head. "I'm not embarrassed. I'm confused. What makes you think Ivy and I are getting married?"

"I told you. Trudy called a bit ago to share the news."

"There must have been some sort of mix-up." Judging by Ivy's smile, she was the mix-up. Or at least the source of it. "Ivy and I aren't engaged. We're not even dating. She's in town because I'm doing a photo shoot with her for Marilyn."

"Oh." Violet deflated like a flyaway balloon. "I didn't know you modeled."

"I don't model. I'm going to take the pictures." He held up his camera as if that should clear up the misunderstanding. "I'm a photographer."

"Oh. A photographer. I didn't know." Her cheeks turned as red as his own felt. She stood there for an awkward moment, looking at the pair of them like she was waiting for someone to explain how her friend Trudy could have misled her so. When it became apparent that neither had an explanation to offer, she leaned back on the heels of her flip-flops. "Well, I hope you two enjoy the weather today."

"We will."

She nodded absently and headed toward the marina.

Davis watched her go. "Interesting little rumor. I wonder how it got started."

Ivy shrugged. "Small towns."

Right, except Greenbrier wasn't that small.

Marilyn hung the dress in the back room where it would wait until the photo shoot and ran her hands down the silky fabric. Ivy was finally back in Greenbrier, yet somehow the chasm between them felt wider than ever.

Lord, how much more does my heart have to bleed?

Marilyn headed back into the boutique. Her God was not cruel. She knew that in her head, but sometimes she couldn't stop the uncensored thoughts of her heart. No matter how hard she tried to squash them into oblivion with prayer and confession and obedience, the most she could manage was obscurity. They'd spent ten years lurking in the background and now Ivy's return had them creeping out of shadow. Surely God would not give her this love simply for the pain of it...right? That squeak of a word made Marilyn stop and squeeze her eyes shut.

I don't want to have these thoughts. Please make them go away.

When she opened her eyes, she found herself facing the large frame mounted on the wall behind the front desk—a picture of her and James on their wedding day. She'd caught Ivy staring at it earlier. The look on her face had brought back a memory so crystal and clear it might have been yesterday instead of twelve years. Ivy's fifth summer visit. Each year she came something more had died in her eyes—a piece of the little girl she should have been, and with the death came a distance Marilyn didn't know how to bridge.

The final day before Ivy would return to Chicago, Marilyn had invited her to go shopping at the mall, since all of Ivy's clothes seemed one size too small. Even her shoes. But Ivy declined, so Marilyn had gone on her own, guessing at Ivy's taste, and when she returned, she found Ivy sitting in the center of her bed, looking through a photo album.

"What do you have there?" Marilyn asked from the doorway.

Ivy hid the album behind her back.

Maybe Marilyn shouldn't have pressed, maybe she should have given Ivy the clothes and let it be, but the reaction left her curious. She stepped inside the room she'd decorated in pink and lace, set the shopping bags next to the dresser, and sat on the edge of the bed.

Slowly, Ivy brought out the white photo book.

It was Marilyn's wedding album, although she had no idea where Ivy had found it. Marilyn ran her hand over the leather and opened to a page with a photo of James, his hand wrapped around her waist as the two of them stood in front of a five-tiered wedding cake, smiling as though they'd never stop. She flipped another page, to a picture of her and James kissing on the dance floor.

"I hate him."

Startled, Marilyn looked up.

Ivy stared back at her, her bottom lip quivering even as she lifted her chin, as if waiting to be scolded. But Marilyn would never, because in truth, sometimes she hated him too. "Ivy..."

"I hate him." A single tear slipped down her cheek. "And I hate you." Before Marilyn could respond, Ivy scrambled off the bed and hurried out of the room.

She did not speak again that visit.

The harder Marilyn pushed Ivy to unload all that burdened her, the further she retreated into her cave and the worse the feeling in Marilyn's gut grew. After Ivy left, she tried calling Renee, but the line was disconnected. It wasn't until the Department of Children and Family Services removed Ivy from Renee's custody that Marilyn understood the full extent of Ivy's heartbreak. But by then, the shy eight-year-old girl who had first entered her heart and home was gone.

Marilyn blinked away the regret and the memories until the framed photograph of her and James came back into focus. She stared at the younger version of herself, amazed that she could have been so naive. That young woman had been filled with so much hope for the future. That young woman had known nothing of a barren womb or an unfaithful husband. That young woman had no idea that this was what her life would become.

I will redeem…

The whispered words rose out of the darkness. Marilyn clung to them with ferocity.

14

Ivy held the phone against her ear, her leg jiggling as she waited for some elaboration. There had to be more to the message. In the mirror's reflection, the makeup artist removed glass containers of foundation from a cheap-looking alligator purse and fielded Marilyn's questions. Ivy jabbed the power button, as if the sharpness of the motion might scrape away the too-short voice mail. Not from Bruce, who hadn't returned her phone call, but from one of Bruce's assistants.

"No jobs. Stay put. Finish your work for Marilyn."

Only finishing her work for Marilyn involved staying in Greenbrier, and after a couple of weeks, she already needed to get away. From the house and the pictures of James. From Davis and his yo-yo act. From the whispers and stares whenever she walked down the strip. Nobody knew her story in New York. When she walked down the overcrowded streets, she wasn't the illegitimate child. She was a woman who turned heads. Sure, people whispered, but they whispered things like "Do you think she's a model?" or "Did you see her legs?" Not "Such a sad way to come into this world."

Ivy threw her leg-jiggle into double time and pressed the three on her keypad. Speed dial for Annalise. If she couldn't get away, maybe a venting session would make her feel better. After the third ring, she got shuffled to voice mail. Didn't anybody answer their phone anymore? She tossed her cell onto the makeshift vanity.

"Mad at your phone?" The hairdresser's bracelets clanked together as she unwound a thick strand of Ivy's hair from a roller. The woman's jewelry had to weigh more than the woman herself. Rings on every finger. Bracelets dangling from skinny wrists. Nose ring. Eyebrow ring. Earrings. And not just studs, but great dangling pieces of silver that stretched her earlobes like pulled taffy.

Ivy forced her leg to stop. "Something like that."

The drone of conversation grated. She closed her eyes and took a deep breath. So the makeup artist carried her makeup in a tacky ripoff. So the hairstylist's jewelry weighed more than a baby elephant. As long they did their job, it didn't matter. The only thing that mattered was pouring her mounting frustration, and yes, her fear, into the photo shoot. Harness the energy. That's what Annalise taught her. The insecurity, the excitement, the nerves. Roll it all into a battery and let it power her with an energy the camera couldn't ignore.

Never mind Davis's bizarre behavior. Never mind NYU's rejection. Never mind her agent's neglect or her twenty-fifth birthday just over two months away. She'd make this her best photo shoot ever. She'd take pictures Bruce and nobody else could ignore.

Ivy opened her eyes.

Jewelry Lady removed the final roller and attacked her hair—pulling, tugging, and covering it in hairspray. A man had taken up residence in the chair next to her, examining his profile in the mirror as the makeup artist pounced on his face. High cheekbones, a prominent jaw, and eyes the color of midnight that smoldered beneath dark eyebrows—the kind that looked natural but were really waxed. Textbook gorgeous. So this must be her groom.

"Are you my wife?" He spoke with a faint accent.

Ivy stuck out her hand. "Only if you approve."

He leaned over the seat, uncaring of Purse Lady's work, and kissed her knuckles. "My name's Stefano. But most people call me Stefan."

"Are you from Italy?"

"*Benissimo, bella!* You recognize my accent. And here I thought I was getting better at hiding it."

"I have sensitive ears. How long have you been in the States?"

"Four years last week. So what do you think of my country?"

"Magnifico."

One side of Stefano's mouth curled. "We will have a happy life together then, no?"

Ivy returned his smile. They'd get along just fine.

Jewelry Lady finished. The freelance fashion stylist hired by *Southern Brides* led Ivy behind a private screen and went to work—dressing her, pinning in the veil, clasping the pearl necklace, straightening every crease, every wrinkle, until the dress hugged her body in all the right places, then returned Ivy to the mirror so Purse Lady could finish her makeup. Stefano was gone. Probably getting dressed.

When all was complete, Ivy stood staring at her reflection. The dress. The birdcage veil framing her face. Three-string pearls wrapped around her neck. Lipstick that matched the blood-red roses in her hand. The diamond ring glittering on her finger. Flawless. Perfect. Without fault. Like a bride who deserved to wear white.

Only Ivy knew the truth.

Focus. Davis only had three more hours to finish the shoot, and so far he didn't have one picture he wanted to use in the editorial. He clicked three shots. Stefan stared at Ivy like a piece of meat. Davis didn't know what he disliked more—Stefan's unoriginality or his hungry stare. This editorial was supposed to be about the first joyous step in a long-lasting journey. An honest story about a woman in love on her wedding day. A story he could take pride in when finished.

But something wasn't working.

The something was Stefan. He didn't fit the vision of a faithful husband who cherished his new bride. Davis didn't believe it and these pictures had to be believable. He snapped another picture and looked at the image on his screen. He couldn't ask for a replacement now. It was too late. Stefan was his groom. Ivy his bride.

Lord, help me focus. Help me direct. Help me capture the beauty of a wedding day.

He stepped away from the camera and pulled at his jaw. His stylist for the day jumped in and fussed over Ivy's and Stefan's clothes—dabbing away sweat, redoing makeup, straightening and readjusting. Davis looked behind him, toward his sister. She wore sunglasses and a wide-brimmed hat and used her hands while she talked to Marilyn. He needed these pictures to be brilliant. Not for his sake. But for Sara's. Because a portion of every dress sale Marilyn made would go to that new art program for the visually impaired, and beautiful pictures would bring buyers.

His stylist gave him a thumbs-up and stepped back. Jeff, an old friend who knew a thing or two about photography, moved a light diffuser in front of the window to soften the sunlight seeping through the glass. Davis looked through his viewfinder and frowned. He wanted to capture love, not lust. He looked over the top of his camera.

"Stefano, I need you to look at Ivy like she holds your heart in her hands. Like you cherish the very air she breathes. Look past what's on the outside. Look at her like you see something no one else can see." He ducked behind his camera, his cheeks suddenly warm, and waved his hand at Jeff, who shifted the diffuser to the left. "Ivy, just keep doing what you're doing."

Stefan grabbed Ivy's waist with one hand and set his other against the archway of the door. Davis rolled his eyes. He zoomed in closer to Ivy and took three steps to the right. If he only got Stefan's profile, then the look on his face wouldn't matter. Nobody would notice him. All eyes would be on Ivy in that dress.

Focusing all his energy, he shot the pictures and did exactly what he told Stefan to do. He looked past Ivy's angles. Past her lines. He looked past her smile and her forced laughter. He found something real behind the lens of his camera and captured pieces of a woman nobody else saw. Veracity behind perfection. Vulnerability hiding behind beauty. And beyond all that, deeper still, was a brokenness that pierced his heart and made him ache for hers.

Ivy ignored the thrumming of her heartbeat and the flush in her cheeks. She lavished her smiles and her laughter on the man who held her in his arms. Stefano. A man she knew. A man who didn't slice her open and expose her insides the way Davis did behind that camera.

She'd done a million shots in her lifetime, and never once had she felt so exposed. Or hot. They'd moved to the outdoor shots, and even as late afternoon melted into early evening, the days' heat refused to wane.

The camera clicked. Davis moved around them, telling Stefan to take her hand, Ivy to turn away and smile. She focused on Stefano's hand holding her palm—the warmth and smoothness of it. She focused on the flowers bursting from the ground—like orange and yellow fireworks exploding against a green sky. She focused on the silkiness of the dress against her skin. A group of tourists talking as they stopped to watch the action. She focused on putting everything into the pictures.

Stefano pulled her arm toward him. She landed softly against his body, her hand on his chest. He tipped up her chin, his eyes glowing with desire. Here was a man who made sense.

He bent toward her ear. "You are ravishing."

She cocked her head as if Stefan had told her an amusing secret.

A few more clicks and finally, "That's a wrap."

Ivy pushed off Stefan's chest, eager to get away. Not only because of the building pressure in her bladder, but because she needed a moment to gather her wits. She twisted her hand out Stefan's grasp and made a beeline toward the mansion.

Davis caught her elbow as she passed. "Hey. Are you okay?"

His touch against her skin did nothing to calm her. "Yeah, fine. Just need to use the rest room."

He let go.

Ivy focused on putting one foot in front of the other, searching for an explanation for her flustered emotions. Why this feeling of embarrassed nakedness when she'd lost all traces of modesty ten years ago? She took off her shoes one at a time without stopping and clawed at the pearls strangling her neck. She needed to breathe. She opened the front door of the Primrose mansion and pried herself loose from the shrug.

Her feet padded to the staircase. She gripped the banister, then crouched over her bag and swallowed the cool air. Was she having a panic attack? She'd never had one before, so she didn't really know what they felt like. Her phone vibrated against wood. She rummaged inside her purse and found a familiar New York number lighting her screen. The air whooshed out of her in a puff of relief. Bruce said he wouldn't call unless he got her a job. She hit Talk. "Bruce. It's you."

She cleared away the hysteria edging her voice, trying not to sound so shocked that her agent had called. "We finished the photo shoot. Do you have a job for me?" New York City's fashion week loomed around the corner. Maybe several designers wanted her to walk for them. She'd proven her market acceptance over the years. The public liked her. Maybe not as much as Alessandra Ambrosio or Gisele Bundchen, but enough.

"I'm not sure how to tell you this." He sounded far away or scrunched, like he'd squished his words through a pinhole.

Ivy gripped the phone with both hands and pressed it to the side of her face. "Bruce, I think we have a bad connection. Can you hear me?"

Silence.

"Bruce? Are you there?"

"It's Annalise, Ivy."

"Annalise? Bruce, what are you talking about?"

"She's dead."

15

Waves crashed against rock, spitting salt and sea into the air. The night enveloped Ivy like the giant towels Mom used to wrap around her body when she came shivering out of the pool as a little girl. Warm and soft. No streetlights shone from the strip. The only light came from the moon—a crescent sliver pinned against blackness—and a smattering of faraway stars—pinpricks of light that defused the dark like shimmering dust. These glimmers of white trickled from the sky and turned the surf into choppy bone.

Ivy didn't remember how she got there. She only knew she had her toes buried in the sand and her sandals dangling from her wrists and her arms wrapped around her shins. Compared to the immensity of the ocean melting toward the invisible horizon, she felt like a grain of sand. Or like one of the million glowing dust particles overhead.

Annalise is dead… James is dead… Annalise is dead… James is dead… You, Ivy Clark, are dead.

She hugged her knees tighter and expelled a rattling breath. How could Annalise be dead when she'd talked with her on the phone two days ago? How was James dead when for her entire life he'd always been there—not in the emotional, fatherly sense, but in the physical sense—several states down in South Carolina? One minute here, the next minute gone. Snuffed out like a candle flame. Death was a permanent, mysterious, unknowable beast to anyone on this side of it. And those who did know it had no way of letting those who didn't in on the secret.

What did it feel like to be dead?

Ivy released her shins and dug her fingers into the sand. Grainy and damp, it pushed underneath her nails. Was death much different than this?

She ground her knuckles into the earth. Sand scoured her skin. Marilyn used to say an afternoon at the beach beat a professional pedicure any day. Did the same apply to a person's hands? If she rubbed them hard enough into the ground, would they come up clean and new?

She closed her eyes and lay back against the shore. The waves crashed, then whispered. *Crash. Whisper. Crash. Whisper.* She breathed its rhythm, letting the push-pull of the ocean's heart caress her own. And when she opened her eyes, Davis Knight stood over her. Darkness shadowed his face, but the moon created the familiar silhouette Ivy would recognize anywhere.

"We've been looking all over for you." His words came out breathless, like he'd finished a fast sprint.

She sat up. "We?"

"Marilyn and Sara. Even Stefan. You disappeared."

"Can a person disappear?" In the dark. Or when she talked to Sara. When a person couldn't see her, did she still exist? It was a question without an answer, like the one about the tree falling in the forest, only hers wasn't about sound. It was about her. When nobody can see Ivy Clark, does Ivy Clark disappear? She fisted the sand and let the grains spill through her fingers.

Davis sat and draped his arms over his knees and peered, not at the ocean, but at her, his face the color of dark denim stitched with pale moon. "Ivy, what happened? Why did you leave like that?"

"Weren't we finished?"

"With the pictures, yes. But you hadn't signed the model release form and…" His voice slipped into the waves. He turned to the sea, the roaring crashing enormous sea. "I didn't get to thank you."

"For what?"

"For the photo shoot. You were magical."

Her—magical? She couldn't muster a laugh, though his words deserved it. That photo shoot had made her feel anything but magical. "Do you think, when we die, we turn into sand? Or maybe stars?"

He cocked his head.

"Like maybe"—Ivy lifted another handful of sand and let it spill to the ground—"James is in this sand." She crushed the remaining grains in her fist, then cast her gaze to the white-freckled black abyss overhead. "Or maybe he's up there, somewhere, in the stars."

Davis dropped his knees and sat crisscross applesauce.

Ivy smiled. Mom forbade the term "Indian-style." *"What's that supposed to mean, anyway, Ivy?"* she'd asked one evening while they painted each other's toenails—before Ivy's summer visits to Greenbrier, when life was still good. *"'Indian style'? I don't think people in India sit that way any more than people in America."*

"Mom, not India Indians. But Indians. You know." Ivy had started play-acting like one of the Lost Boys from Peter Pan, ending with her hand in the air and a deep-voiced *"How."*

Mom had clutched Ivy's shoulders and gave her a grown-up look. Like she wasn't six but twenty-six. *"What, dear daughter, are they teaching you in school?"*

Ivy exhaled the memory.

"I don't think your father's in the sand or in the stars."

"Where is he then?" She didn't have to ask. Davis hung a cross from his mirror. He thought he was in heaven. Or hell. Or maybe purgatory. Didn't Christians believe in purgatory? Or was that only Catholics? Who knew. Maybe the two were one and the same.

"Why are you out here thinking about the dead, Ivy?"

"Because nighttime makes me think of death." She looked over her shoulder at the strip. "Doesn't Greenbrier believe in streetlights?"

"Sea turtles."

"What?"

"It's nesting season. Female turtles come to the shore and lay eggs along the beach. Then, about three months later, the eggs hatch and the baby turtles make their way to the sea. The lights confuse them. Sometimes, instead of crawling to the sea, they'll crawl toward the lights and onto the road. So the mayor has a lights-out rule at nine o'clock. For the sea turtles."

Something about the story reverberated in a deep place, like the echo of a gong in the depths of her soul. She was a sea turtle. Only nobody had bothered to turn off the lights, not for her.

"Sometimes I think we're like sea turtles."

Ivy stared at Davis the mind reader. "How so?"

"It's like this world is one big distraction. A bunch of lights. So many of us are crawling in the wrong direction. Away from the sea. Sometimes we have to turn all that off to get ourselves headed the right way again."

"Is that why you left? New York City was your streetlight?"

"You could say that."

Her shoulders hunched. She felt old and weary. Like if somebody flipped her inside out, the beautiful part of her would disappear and the real her—the her on the inside—would be nothing but wrinkles and age spots and saggy skin.

She took a deep breath. Closed her fist around a handful of sand. "Annalise is dead." The cold words clashed against the humidity.

"Who's Annalise?"

"A friend." A mentor. A combination of the two. "When I first got to New York, I wasn't even fourteen. Bruce introduced us. We lived in the same apartment for a while with four other models, which is a bad idea, in case you're wondering. She was two years older than me, but it felt like a lifetime." Ivy combed the sand and piled it beneath her knees. "She took me under her wing. Showed me the ropes. Taught me what to say, how to act, who to trust." Ivy wouldn't have lasted two weeks without Annalise.

"Is that why you left tonight? You found out she died?"

"Bruce called. That right there should have tipped me off that something was wrong." Her muscles cramped with sudden and unexpected anger. Annalise sniffed coke and popped diet pills and guzzled Red Bull.

Ivy knew. Bruce knew. But neither said a word. Why should they? It was a normal part of the industry. "She collapsed at some nightclub. By the time the paramedics arrived, she was already dead. Supposedly, the culprit was heart failure."

"Heart failure for someone so young?"

"Cocaine pays no attention to age."

Davis let out a long breath. "Do you… I mean…"

"Don't worry, Davis. My drug of choice has always been men."

Her words must have stunned him into silence, because he didn't respond.

A grim feeling of satisfaction stole through her body. He would be disgusted now. He would judge her, maybe even hate her. He definitely wouldn't stick around and try to get to know her. "Hey, at least men are safe though, right? Oh, and free. Don't forget that. At least I stay in control. Annalise should have stuck to men."

"Ivy?"

The hairs on her arms prickled at the way he whispered her name—soft and sad with a whole world of tenderness tagged to the end. "What?"

"I'm sorry you're hurting."

She bit her lip. The tide crept closer to her feet. *Crash. Whisper. Crash. Whisper.* Was it her heart or the waves?

"If you want, I'll go to the funeral with you."

Her spirit lifted, but she squashed the warm relief before it could grow. Despite his last name, she couldn't afford to let Davis be her knight in shining armor. Knights didn't exist. Not in her world. "Not necessary, Dave. You're a sea turtle, remember? Going to New York would turn you in the wrong direction."

"Okay, but who's going to help you find the sea?"

The question undid her. She buried her face in her knees and let her tears ooze from closed eyes, thankful the night hid her anguish.

16

W*ho's going to help you find the sea?"*

Two days plus eight hundred miles, and those words still stuck inside Ivy's mind. As hard as she tried, she couldn't shake Davis's question. Or the way in which he'd asked it—buttery and light, melting over her, turning her soggy. It haunted her at night. Pestered her during the day. And funneled through her brain as she sat in a stiff chair inside a New York City funeral home, listening to Annalise's American cousin give the eulogy.

Her second funeral in a month.

Ivy shut her eyes. She wanted to respect her friend's passing. She wanted to rummage through memories and pluck out Annalise's smiles or the times they'd worked together, but her father's face stood guard in front of the memories like an unmoving sentry. As much as she wanted to remember Annalise, all she could picture was the face of a dead man.

James had loved Marilyn once, maybe even again. He'd loved her mother too—madly and passionately. Not long enough for Renee, but for a time. Before Ivy was born and even in her earliest memories, James used to fly all the way to Chicago, even when his business endeavors didn't call for it, just to be with her mother. Ivy wanted to deny it, but how could she? Her very existence proved their passion. Sure, that love had turned dysfunctional. Sure, the removal of that love had destroyed all the good things about her mother. But at least it had been there. The only one James had never loved was sitting in Ivy's chair. Wearing Ivy's skin. Replaying a nighttime beach memory while the heaviness on top of her chest caved against her lungs. He should have loved her most. She was his daughter. His own flesh and blood.

But he hadn't loved her at all.

She didn't miss James. She didn't mourn the loss of their relationship or the hope that one day they might have one. His death didn't bring the type of loss one might expect—tears and pain and regret. But it did leave an empty space. An unanswered question. One that only he could answer.

What made her so unlovable?

She'd never be able to ask him that.

A wave of laughter rippled through the crowd. Ivy forced herself to focus.

"I'm very sad to say good-bye to my one and only cousin. We can all agree she was beautiful and vivacious. She liked to have a good time. She lived and laughed, and although this world will miss her, although this world is dimmer without her, her spirit lives on. We can take comfort that she is in a better place."

Everybody clapped.

Ivy wanted to stand up and chuck her shoe at the man's head. Why did funerals always glorify the dead? Patch over the bad? *"She lived and she laughed"*? Never mind how she died, strung out at a club, her veins saturated in cocaine. Never mind any of that. She was in a better place now. Ivy wanted to throw up. She had enough bitterness gurgling like bile in her stomach to make it happen. Under whose authority was she in a better place? Just because some guy said it didn't make it true.

Nobody knew where Annalise was now.

A cold shiver twisted around Ivy's spine and clamped onto her jaw.

Davis, at least, didn't patch over grief with trite condolences. She'd much rather sit by him in the warm sand than in this room of familiar strangers. Anger swelled. No. She didn't need to sit by Davis; she needed to get away from him. And Greenbrier too. She brought her purse onto her lap and looked around the funeral home.

No Bruce.

He'd gone to his brother's funeral. He'd dragged her along. Yet he couldn't spare an hour of his day for his oldest client. Her lips tightened. It was time to pay her dear agent a visit.

"What are you doing here? You're supposed to be in Greenbrier."

Ivy threw her purse into the chair in front of Bruce's desk. "I had a funeral to attend. Or did you forget about Annalise already?"

He sat up straighter. "Of course I didn't forget."

"Then why are you here? Why aren't you at the funeral? She was your client for twelve years, Bruce. Twelve years! Doesn't that mean anything to you?"

"I went to the visitation. There wasn't a reason for me to go to the funeral too."

"You take two days out of your schedule and buy a plane ticket to go bury a brother you barely ever talked to. The least you could do was make an appearance for Annalise."

"Look, I would have gone. But I have an important meeting"—he yanked up his sleeve and looked at his watch—"in three minutes. One I couldn't reschedule."

"Every meeting can be rescheduled."

"But not every meeting should be." He settled back into this chair. "I know you and Annalise were close. I'm sorry she died."

"You'd be a lot sorrier if she'd been younger."

His eyes flashed. "You think me that callous?"

She pleaded the fifth. If she didn't have anything nice to say, she might as well not say anything at all. Mom had taught her that once. A long, long time ago.

Bruce tipped back in his seat and twirled a pen around the tip of his thumb. "Since you're here, how did the shoot go?"

"Fine."

"I spoke with Marilyn a few days ago. She seemed very happy with your work. Said she wants to do another photo shoot for some advertisements and then something about a fashion show."

"At least you're talking to one of us. You don't answer my phone calls anymore, Bruce."

"One phone call, Ivy. Let's not exaggerate. And what did you want to hear? That I can't find you any jobs?"

"You're not looking."

"Of course I am."

What would happen if he couldn't get her any work? "Maybe once the editorial comes out, you can show it to some wedding designers."

He stopped his pen spinning and laughed. "You specifically told me you didn't want to do any more of that kind of work."

"I do now." Anything to keep her away from Greenbrier. She couldn't go back to that suffocating heat and Marilyn's unnerving kindness and Davis's confusing scrutiny. Her mouth dried up. How could she go back? Davis was there. Davis was everywhere. Prodding. Poking. Digging. She had to get away, not return. Or else she wouldn't survive. "Some go-sees, Bruce. That's all I'm asking. Catalog. Commercial. It doesn't have to be Ralph Lauren or Calvin Klein. It can be anything. I don't care. Just get me some work."

"How long are you in town?"

"I don't know. I bought a one-way ticket."

"But you're going back."

She pressed her lips together and looked at the wall to her left, covered in pictures. Framed tear sheets from every designer and fashion magazine known to man. *Vogue. Harper's Bazaar. Elle.* Calvin Klein. Dolce and Gabbana. Armani. Christian Dior. Gucci. Valentino. Chanel.

The faces of Bruce's models stared back. Annalise's. Her own. They all looked the same. Every last one of them played a different rendition of sexy. The sudden urge to fly at the wall, to tear each frame from its nail and smash it against the ground overwhelmed her. She felt like a feral cat—wild and dangerous.

Bruce plopped his elbows on his desk and let out a much-too-long, much-too-loud sigh. "You can't promise a client your time then back out because you're bored."

"I'm not bored."

He clicked the tip of the pen with his thumb. It clacked like an old-fashioned typewriter. She wanted to yank it out of his grip and stab it into the photo right over his head, the one of her posing for Calvin Klein jeans. She was sixteen. Thin as a rail. Ravishingly beautiful. Bruce had been so proud of that shot. And yet Ivy remembered feeling hollow. Like her outsides were growing sharper and more defined while her insides faded completely away. And nobody cared. Nobody even noticed.

"Here's what we're going to do." He removed his elbows from the desk. "I'll get you some go-sees. I have some of my models going to a few over the next couple of weeks. You'll go to those, and then I'll get you a ticket and you'll fly back to Greenbrier and follow through with your commitment. When you're all finished there, we can talk about your next career move."

He stood from his chair. "I'll follow you out. You can speak with Maya about the go-sees." He went to the door and opened it wide. "She'll give you the addresses and the details."

Ivy blinked. "You're kicking me out?"

"I have a meeting scheduled with a new model." He tapped his wristwatch. "Remember? I'm already two minutes late, and you know I hate to keep my clients waiting." He took her arm and steered her toward the hallway. She had no choice but to walk. So she did, Bruce trailing her heels. She marched down the hall and stepped into the brightly lit lobby.

A lanky man was there, with graying hair and a pointed Adam's apple, sitting in one of the seats with his ankle crossed over his knee. And next to him, a girl. Long. Gangly. Platinum blond hair hanging halfway down her back. Exotic green eyes. She didn't look a day older than twelve.

Bruce clapped his large hands. "Luke, Tatiana, so sorry to keep you waiting. Why don't you come on back to my office?"

Ivy whipped around and faced her uncle. "She's your new model?"

"She's stunning, isn't she? Get a look at those eyes." Bruce didn't lower his voice. He spoke loud enough for the girl to hear. Tatiana's smooth cheeks blossomed with color. Shy but pleased. "I found her at a modeling convention—in Boston, of all places."

He found her? This girl wasn't a penny or a stray puppy. "She's a kid."

"She's thirteen. Not much younger than you when you started."

Ivy's insides exploded, a violent eruption of emotion. Snippets of memory flashed through her mind like a strobe light in a nightclub. They danced in broken fragments, then gathered into one vivid memory—stronger than all the rest.

A year after a social worker had showed up on her doorstep and took her away from her mother. Her sixth day in New York City. Uncle Bruce introduced her to a photographer—a chain-smoking stranger who spoke in sharp monosyllables, ordering her into poses while heat from the bright lights assaulted her eyes. The dam of tears that had built over the eleven months she lived in James's house, the unwanted daughter waiting for her mother to get clean and come to her rescue, bowed, then snapped. She spilled into a puddle of sobs on the floor. The photographer cursed. Bruce picked her up and took hold of her scrawny arms. She'd wanted to collapse against his chest. She'd wanted him to hug her, smooth her hair, tell her everything would be okay. Instead, he cuffed her under the chin and smiled. So handsome it took her breath away. He looked exactly like her father. "You were born with beauty, kid. Something most girls would kill for. I've seen your potential since you were eight years old. You want to be a model, don't you? You want to stay here with me, right?"

What was her other option? Go live with her dad and Marilyn—a man who didn't want her and a woman who wasn't her mom? No. Never. She wiped her eyes and gave him an earnest nod.

"Well, then. All the stuff going on in here?" He patted his chest. "It doesn't matter. Nobody cares as long as you look beautiful for the camera. You do that and everybody will fall in love with you. You do that, and you'll be staying in New York City for a long time. You'll have it made, kid."

Yeah. Ten more years of Bruce's pep talks and she sure had it made.

Luke stood. Tatiana did too, looking excited and nervous and shy, her eyes filled with wonder as she took in the elaborate surroundings. Ivy could see all the emotions playing across her face, every last one, and pretty soon, Bruce would tell her to shut them away. To bury them, because nobody cared. Nobody ever cared. But maybe Luke did.

Bruce walked down the hall, whistling.

The girl's father made to follow.

"Is she your daughter?" Ivy asked.

"Yes." Luke's word came out slow. Unsure.

"Do you love her?"

His eyebrows furrowed. "What kind of question is that?"

Bruce stopped whistling and did an about-face. "Ivy, what are you doing?"

"Do you love your daughter?"

Luke's confusion gave way to indignation. "Of course I love her."

"Then don't let her do this." She turned to Tatiana and told her what James and her mother and Bruce should have told Ivy years ago. "Be a kid, Tatiana. Enjoy your life. Laugh and play and climb trees. The world doesn't need another sex symbol."

Bruce grabbed Ivy's elbow. "Thank you for that eloquent speech." He smiled at Luke, then the girl—as if to reassure them—turned Ivy sharply and marched her to the front door. "If you weren't my niece, I'd drop you right now."

"Aren't I lucky. To have such an understanding, compassionate uncle." She breathed the belligerent words in his face and stomped out of his office.

17

Sweat trickled between Davis's shoulder blades and down his face as he pounded the hammer against the shingles of Cornerstone Church's roof. They'd need a new one soon. His temporary patch jobs during hurricane season only helped so much. The late morning's brightness lost its edge, offering a brief respite from the heat. But the humidity remained. The sun must have slid behind a cloud.

Davis shifted a few feet over and resumed his pounding, hoping enough whacks with his hammer would tire the chaotic thoughts tumbling through his mind. Surely a morning of hard work would sweat the chaos right out of him. The brightness reclaimed its potency and pressed hot fingers against his back. The cloud, apparently, was not a large one.

"Are you upset with that roof?" The voice of Pastor Voss halted Davis's hammer in backswing. He looked over the church's rusty gutters—which would also need fixing sooner rather than later. Pastor Voss stood in front of a flower bush, clutching two bottles of Snapple in one hand, shielding his face like a visor with the other. "It's a hundred degrees down here. I hate to think what it's like up there. Why don't you come down and take a break?"

Davis brought down the hammer. A couple of weeks after his evening in the sand next to Ivy, and his mind had yet to regain equilibrium. Time and distance didn't help. Sweating didn't either. Would talking? The hammer clattered against the roof. He shuffled toward the ladder and clanked his way down the metal rungs.

Pastor Voss met him at the bottom and handed him a sweaty bottle of tea. Davis twisted off the cap and took a long swig. The cold sweetness soothed his parched throat.

"I think the whole of Greenbrier heard you whapping away at that thing." Pastor Voss nodded toward the front doors of the church as the air-conditioning unit rattled to life. "Let's go inside and drink these. I need a break from sermon prep. It's going in circles."

Davis followed, unsticking his sweat-soaked shirt from his chest and mopping his brow. When he stepped inside the church lobby, the cool air crashed against his skin.

A chuckle rumbled from Pastor Voss as he turned into a narrow hallway. "So, Davis, my youngest daughter seems to think you're engaged. You need me to perform the ceremony?"

"Ha. Ha."

"If I don't laugh at her antics, I'll cry. Don't feel much like crying today."

Davis followed him to his small office, where books of every size and color wrestled for space on the bookshelves. Some lost the battle and ended up on the floor or stacked in crooked piles on the desk. Pastor Voss settled into a brick red chair. Davis eased to the edge of the chair's twin, careful not to get his sweat all over the cushion.

"If you can believe it, your grandfather invited me for a round of golf this morning. Doc warned him the heat would give him a heart attack. I think the man's nuts."

"He's nuts for golf, all right." Davis took another long drink.

Pastor Voss did the same and pulled the glass bottle away with a crisp, "Ahh." He set it on the small end table squished between the two chairs. "So what's bothering you?"

"What do you mean?"

"All last week you brooded, and now you're beating my roof to death. Something's on your mind and I think you ought to let it out."

Davis tried to hold a grin on his face, keep things light, but his lips slipped into something that felt more like a grimace. "Is this going to be a therapy session?"

"If that's what it takes to keep you from tearing down my church."

If he needed therapy, he could have called Jerry, a buddy on his slow-pitch softball team who was a licensed therapist. But what good would any of that do? Talking wouldn't save Ivy from the pain she'd displayed all those nights ago. Talking wouldn't erase the past or the desire accumulating in his chest. He pushed air from his lungs and tapped his heel against the carpeted floor. "I'm not sure where to start."

"At the beginning is usually best."

A beginning implied his problems didn't all melt together. Davis searched the ceiling, like the heart of the matter pulsed somewhere in the tile. "When Sara was two, Mom took her pacifier away. A month later, Sara got bronchitis and couldn't sleep. So Mom gave the pacifier back. She tried to explain to Sara that she couldn't have it back forever, just for a little while, until she got better. It was harder the second time Mom took it away. Sara fought for it longer."

A crease folded itself between Pastor Voss's eyebrows.

Davis bent over his knees and stuck his hands in his hair. "I feel like an idiot for picking up my camera again." Words built in his lungs—lots and lots of them. And on an exhale, before he could stop himself, they gushed out.

"The only reason I agreed to do this work for Marilyn is because of Sara and that art program, but now I can't stop thinking about my camera or Ivy. She left a couple of weeks ago, and we have no idea if she's coming back. Life would be easier if she didn't come back, but the thought of not seeing her again depresses me, and that, in and of itself, is problematic. I promised Marilyn I'd finish this project, which means taking more pictures, and my editorial will come out in *Southern Brides* any day now."

Winded from his fast-paced monologue, Davis took a deep breath and looked up at Pastor Voss. But Pastor Voss didn't move, except for his eyelids, which blinked like drips from a leaky faucet. "That's a lot that needed to get out."

And Davis didn't feel one ounce better for it. He slapped his hands against the armrests. "I should get back outside and nail down the rest of those shingles."

Pastor Voss set his hand over Davis's. "Those shingles aren't going anywhere."

Neither was this conversation.

"Why are you worried about your editorial coming out in that magazine? Did the pictures not turn out as you hoped?"

"No, actually, they turned out better than I'd hoped." When he turned them into Joan Calloway two days after the shoot, she had gushed. Davis looked over Pastor Voss's desk at the large black-and-white photograph mounted on the wall. Not Jesus or the cross, like a person might expect. But a little boy inside a barn. Light shone through the slats. The small kid crouched near the ground, peeking through to the world outside. The photographer had captured the lines and angles of warped wood in precisely the right way.

"So what's the problem, Davis?"

"My grandfather thinks it's ridiculous that I'm taking pictures again. He thinks the charity angle is a lame excuse to indulge myself." In Davis's weaker moments, he worried his grandfather was right.

Pastor Voss took a sip from his bottle.

"But I'm not." Davis reached for his Snapple lid and rolled it in his fingers. "Am I?"

"Did you pray before you made your decision?"

"Yes."

"And you felt God nudging you to do this?"

God nudging him? Davis wasn't sure what that felt like, especially since two years ago, he would have sworn God never wanted him to touch a camera again. Not after what happened. "It felt like something I should do, if that's what you mean."

"Then what are you worried about?"

"I'm worried I won't be able to stop this time. When the campaign ends. Or that the process would be even more painful the second time around, like with Sara and her pacifier."

"Why should you stop?"

"You know why." Davis flicked the bottle cap toward the trash can near the door. It bounced off the rim and landed inside.

"Why did Ivy go back to New York?"

"Her friend died. She left for the funeral."

"Poor girl."

Davis examined the floor. "Did you ever meet her as a kid?"

"Can't say that I did."

"She's so much different now. But also sort of the same." Five years of high fashion in New York City had turned Davis into a shadow of his former self, and he'd gone there as an adult. Not at the impressionable age of fourteen. "When I look at her, I can see her chains, but how is she supposed to find freedom when she's in love with them?"

"Don't mistake love for need. Everybody needs to hold on to something. Sounds like that gal's holding on to the wrong thing."

Davis scratched his jaw. "I just can't imagine her accepting anything we might have to offer."

"That's the great thing about God, Davis. Her acceptance isn't up to you. All you can do is show His love, share His truth, and let Jesus take care of the rest."

"But you don't know what she's like. You haven't seen how she acts toward me." His skin flushed as he remembered her body draped over his in the car when she finagled their way into the Primrose Plantation. Her winks. Her coy smiles. Her not-so-subtle touches. "I'm not so sure God wants me spending time with somebody like her."

"Jesus hung out with tax collectors and prostitutes."

"Yeah, but did the prostitutes ever come on to Him?" Davis's insides squirmed. How could he help Pastor Voss understand? He drained the rest of his drink and wiped his palms on his shorts. "Do you have things in your past you're not proud of? Things that make you feel ashamed?"

"That's what makes Christ's death on the cross so personal."

A frown tugged at Davis's mouth. "This model, Ivy, she's like a ghost. She's like a walking memory of that time in my life, reminding me why I shouldn't be doing this."

"Well, son, you know what they say about ghosts."

"What?"

"Eventually, we all have to face them."

Ivy lay on her couch as the air conditioner hummed to the silence. She adjusted the cool washcloth over her face. After returning from her fifth morning of go-sees, she'd pulled down all the shades in her apartment, hoping to conquer the headache throbbing in her temples.

They couldn't have gone worse if she'd showed up in Marilyn's pink pajamas and a shiny zit in the center of her forehead. She'd been surrounded by teenagers. Beautiful, perfect teenagers. Not only had she felt like a grandmother, she couldn't stop replaying the scene she'd caused in Bruce's office. She'd lived the last two weeks in a state of dread, going wherever Maya told her to go, avoiding Bruce for fear he would finally drop her. She obviously wasn't an asset to him anymore. He had a hundred other models making him money. He didn't need her.

Her stomach had tangled into such knots that she hadn't even bothered going to the last go-see. Instead, she'd escaped to her apartment, hoping to float in a state of quiet nothingness. Hoping the darkness would squeeze everything else away. But worry followed her. If Bruce left her, if he told her to hit the road… Ivy shuddered. No, she couldn't even think of it. She needed to rest before driving to the airport. She needed to rally before returning to Greenbrier.

Because she would return.

Not because Bruce told her to, though that was certainly reason enough. Not because she'd given her word. But because that's all she had left. A wedding campaign in Greenbrier, South Carolina. She'd give that last remaining pinch of hope everything she had.

A knock sounded at her door.

Ivy wedged herself between the cushion and couch and pretended not to hear. With her lights off, maybe whoever it was would take a hint and go away.

Tap, tap, tap.

She set her hands over the cloth and pressed the dampness against her face. *Go away.*

Tap, tap. "Ivy, you in there? Open up. I need to speak with you."

She flew from the cushions like a cork popping from a champagne bottle. The cloth dropped from her eyes. The strap of her tank top fell off her shoulder. She straightened it. Turned in a frantic circle, straightening pillows and running a trembling hand through her hair. Why was Bruce here? He never came, except for that one time—the morning he'd banished her to Greenbrier and then he hadn't bothered with knocking.

Tap, tap, tap. "Ivy?"

Please, no... Please, no... Please, no...

She repeated the mantra inside her head. *Don't let this be it.* Bruce couldn't let her go. She was his niece. Flesh and blood. That had to mean something. James's face flashed in her mind, reminding her that no, it didn't have to mean anything. She pushed her knuckles into her stomach and opened the door.

Bruce paced in the hall. As soon as the door opened all the way, Ivy stepped back and he paced right over her threshold.

"Why is it so dark in here?" He marched to the windows and pulled up the blinds.

Ivy squinted against the onslaught of brightness.

His gaze took in her bare toes, rolled up her body, and stopped at her eyes. "You look like death."

She managed a weak smile. "Thanks."

He smacked something against her kitchen counter. It connected with a crinkled envelope and knocked it into the air. NYU's emblem twisted and turned as the envelope fluttered to the ground. Ivy reached over and snagged it midfall, before Bruce could lay eyes on the return address. Why hadn't she thrown it away or ground it up in the garbage disposal along with the rejection letter? She tucked it into the back pocket of her shorts and looked at the object in Bruce's hand. A rolled-up magazine. He tossed it onto the island. It plopped, then unrolled itself. *Southern Brides.*

Joan must have sent Bruce an early copy.

"I should be livid with you after the stunt you pulled with Tatiana and Luke."

She stepped forward. "I know. That was completely messed up. I'm so sorry. After everything you've done for me, I should have never done that."

"You're right about that."

"I'm so sorry, Bruce. Really, truly sorry." She'd grovel until kingdom come if it meant keeping her agent.

"Would you quit apologizing?" He flung open the magazine and jabbed his finger at the pictures. Her and Stefan surrounded by flowers. "Take a look at that. Just look at it."

Every last drop of moisture in her mouth evaporated. She stepped toward the opened magazine like it was a snake with bared fangs. When she looked, her heart plummeted. She stared with accumulating dread at the pictures. At the Ivy Davis had captured with his camera. She didn't recognize her at all. That Ivy looked like a stranger, a woman hiding too many secrets. A woman with too much vulnerability behind her smile. It wasn't like any picture she'd ever taken. It was one hundred percent horrible.

"Oh no. Bruce..." He would fire her now. Of course he would. He'd given her two weeks of go-sees with no results and now he would let her go. Wish her well. She was done.

"These are brilliant!"

She looked up at her uncle. "What?"

"Absolutely brilliant." Bruce laughed, then started pacing again. Ivy looked at the pictures. Were they seeing the same ones? Was Bruce losing his eye? She squinted, but as hard as she tried, she couldn't see any brilliance in them. "We're going to have to postpone your flight. I'll arrange for you to fly back tomorrow evening so you can finish your work with Marilyn. And you will finish it, Ivy. You'll take more pictures with Davis, and you'll convince him to come back to New York City with you."

"Hold up, Bruce, you're losing me. What's going on?"

"A rep from Vera Wang called. I spoke with her last week at a fashion gala and told her about you and this shoot. I sent her the pictures this morning and she wants you. Vera Wang wants you."

Ivy's mind spun. She placed her hand on the counter to keep her knees steady. "Wait...what?"

"I've set up a meeting tomorrow morning. This rep, Juliette, wants to see you in person. They're starting a big campaign for their spring dress line at the end of September, right after the fashion show you're doing for Marilyn. She wants you, and she wants Davis Knight."

Gravity disappeared. She actually had to expend effort to keep her limbs from floating over her head. A laugh bubbled up her throat and tumbled out her mouth.

Bruce squished her face between his palms and kissed her forehead. "Just when I think you're done, Ivy. Just when I think you're finished, you go and pull something like this."

Ivy swelled beneath his praise. Absolutely swelled. Bruce loved her. She wasn't losing her usefulness at all. She would finish her work with Marilyn, polish up that smile—that smile she hated but Vera Wang loved—and return to New York to do the biggest photo shoot of her life. To do something that might finally give her the staying power she needed.

"Now all you have to do is convince Davis. You can do that, right?"

Bruce's words popped her ballooning joy. Convince Davis to come with her to New York City? Gravity came back in a resounding swoosh. She was pretty sure she couldn't convince Davis to do anything. Especially not something like this.

18

Bells tinkled overhead as Davis opened the front door of Something New. Benny Goodman's "Sing, Sing, Sing" tapered into the slower-paced "String of Pearls" by Glenn Miller. Trombone and clarinet trickled from hidden speakers and swirled with Marilyn's vanilla-peach air freshener. As her nephew, Davis knew the name of every musician—possibly every song—from the Big Band era. The woman had a secret collection of Duke Ellington posters tacked to the walls in her basement and still did laundry to Ella Fitzgerald singing on an antique phonograph.

Davis shoved a rolled-up copy of *Southern Brides* into the back pocket of his cargo shorts. He wanted to show it to Marilyn on the off chance she hadn't bought herself a copy as soon as it hit stores this morning. If she happened to shed some light on Ivy's extended absence while he was there, then so be it. That's not why he was coming. He stepped farther inside the boutique and spotted not just one but three copies of *Southern Brides* arranged like a fan on top of a short glass table to the right of the checkout counter. He imagined his own copy wilting in his back pocket. So much for his excuse.

Marilyn bustled around a large rack of dresses, half-swallowed by two puffy ensembles draped over one arm. She used her free hand to squish down tulle and chiffon and smiled at him over the fluff. "Davis, I didn't know you were stopping by. Did you see what came out today?"

He took the magazine from its hiding place and gave it a pathetic wave.

"Isn't it wonderful?" Her heels clicked in tune with the music as she closed the gap between them. "Joan sent me a copy yesterday morning, and already two people have brought the magazine in to say how good the spread looks."

Davis relieved her of the dresses. He preferred to see Marilyn's face when he talked to her. "You're busy."

The flush in her cheeks shaved years off her face. This was exactly what she needed. She'd said she wanted a distraction from her loss, which on most days was hard to spot but present nonetheless—occasionally manifesting itself through a vacant stare or a flightiness uncharacteristic to his aunt. Well, he'd helped deliver that distraction. He should feel good about that.

"I've had two phone calls from potential clients who found me because of the magazine. And another from a web guy who wanted to know if I'd be interested in taking my store online. Can you believe that?" She looked over her shoulder at a stocky girl with mousy brown hair twirling in front of the mirrors, talking to Sara. "And Becky-Sue Bruckle told me she's not leaving without a dress."

He squinted one eye. He remembered Becky-Sue. "She graduated with Sara, didn't she? Twin sister named Stacy?"

"Sweethearts, both of them. Becky-Sue got engaged last week to Jonas Ludd. You know Jonas. He's Jordan's older brother."

Davis frowned. Just what Sara needed—a reminder of the man who broke her heart. He looked over Marilyn's head, toward his sister and Sunny, who sat by her side. She held several veils as she spoke with Becky-Sue.

"How's Sara doing?"

"Excited about the editorial. She's made me describe every picture at least a half a dozen times." Marilyn smiled like a proud mother. She would have been an excellent one. "Eager for our meeting tonight."

Meeting? He wrinkled his forehead.

"You haven't forgotten, have you? We're getting together to talk about the fashion show. We need to get a move on if we want to have it at the end of September. That's already less than two months away."

"Oh, right." He bit his cheek and shifted his weight from heel to ball. It had been almost two and a half weeks. Was Ivy not coming back? "Do you know...are we going to...?"

"Please don't say you're bailing, Davis. We need all the help we can get. Sara and I don't have a clue what we're doing."

"I'll be there." He'd like to know if Ivy would be there too, but he didn't know how to ask without sounding overly invested, so he let the question evaporate and motioned toward Becky-Sue. "Am I taking these over there?"

Marilyn waved her hand and led the way. When he got near the mirrors, he hung the dresses on a set of ornate hooks and put his arm around Sara.

She jumped and dropped the veils.

"Davis!" Becky-Sue stopped twirling. "How are you?"

Sara swatted his arm. "You scared me half to death."

"I'm good, Becky-Sue. How are you?"

She did a little bunny hop toward him and nearly stabbed his nose with her engagement ring. "I'm engaged!"

He patted the top of Sunny's head. "Congratulations."

"She's a little excited about it," Sara murmured from the corner of her mouth.

"So it would seem."

Marilyn stepped onto the stage and started buttoning the back of the dress. Becky-Sue could hardly stand still. She was like a four-year-old in a grown-up body, which could be mistaken as a side effect of engagement to anyone who didn't already know Becky-Sue. But this was just how she always was. In fact, he'd heard Sara joke that while in utero, Becky-Sue must have snatched all the exuberant genes while Stacy got stuck with the serious ones.

"I still can't get over it. I mean, four months ago, Stacy and I went on a blind date with Jonas and his brother, and now here I am with this ring on my finger. It's hard to believe, isn't it?"

Sara's expression gave an odd sort of twitch at the mention of Jonas's brother. Davis grimaced at Becky-Sue in the mirror. She must have caught the look, because she reined in her excitement. "Stacy and Jordan are only friends now, of course. They're not romantic or anything. In fact, Stacy thinks Jordan's still in love with you, Sara."

Davis's grimace grew more pronounced. If he was standing closer, he'd nudge Becky-Sue in the rib with his elbow.

Sara fiddled with the hem of her T-shirt. "I hope he finds a nice girl and settles down. Your sister's a nice girl, Becky-Sue."

Becky-Sue ran her hand down the pleats of her dress, then clasped them in front of her middle. She flashed Davis a full-cheeked grin. "I heard congratulations are in order for you too."

He bit back a groan. Of all the people Ivy could have told about the false engagement, why did it have to be Rachel Piper—the town gossip's daughter?

"Stacy heard from our cousin Lucy, who's friends with Rachel, that you're engaged to a model." She brought her hands to her chin. "Rachel said your fiancée has legs up to here."

Marilyn finished the last button and laughed. "Davis? Engaged to Ivy?"

The groan escaped. "It's a rumor, Becky-Sue. I'm not engaged."

"Oh, really?" Her face fell, like he was wrong somehow. "Because Stacy said that Lucy said that Rachel said she heard it straight from the horse's mouth."

"I think I'd know for certain if I were engaged or not, don't you?"

Becky-Sue blushed.

Sara bent over and patted around the floor for the fallen veils. He came down by her side to help. "Be nice," she whispered.

"Aren't I always?"

Marilyn grabbed one of the dresses Davis had hung on the set of hooks. "Let's try one of these on, Becky-Sue. I think a halter will flatter you more than the strapless."

Becky-Sue let out an excited squeak and followed Marilyn into the dressing rooms.

Davis stood.

"Engaged to Ivy?" Sara asked, taking the veils from Davis. "How did that rumor start?"

"How do you think?"

"She's coming back today, you know."

"She is?"

His sister cocked her head as if deciphering the lilt of his question. At least she couldn't see the burn in his cheeks. "She called Marilyn this morning. She had an important meeting, but she said she'd be back tonight to help us organize the fashion show."

Ivy was coming back. He would see her tonight.

Sara stuck one of the veils in her hair. "It will be fun to see her again, won't it?"

"I think Marilyn's eager to have her back." It was a safe answer, a half truth. Because in all honesty, so was Davis.

Ivy pulled her suitcase from Marilyn's trunk and tried not to breathe through her nose. The smell of marsh saturated the evening air. Extra pungent. Yuck. After a fifty-minute car ride from the airport, in which Marilyn bombarded her with questions in an attempt to combat the silence, Ivy yearned for her white room above the garage. Maybe some relaxing music while she soaked in the tub and read some more of Billy Collins, but the soothing thought flitted away.

After her Vera Wang meeting with Juliette, Ivy knew one thing: the livelihood of her career hinged upon Davis. If she had any chance of taking him back to New York, she needed to spend time with him, which meant sitting in on the fashion show–planning session. A few days ago, she had been determined to avoid him. Today, her future depended on their closeness. If foreboding had a smell, she imagined it would smell like that marsh—a complete appetite stealer.

She trudged to the porch with coiled muscles and opened the front door. The smell of fried chicken and a barking white Georgia greeted her. She plunked her suitcase onto the travertine stone flooring and moved out of the way so Marilyn could come in. The stairs whispered Ivy's name, but her tiredness would have to wait. She had more important things to do, like sit inside a house she hated and figure out why Davis left New York City. There had to be more to it than not liking the man he'd become. Maybe if she could unravel that particular mystery, she could figure out how to approach him about returning.

Marilyn shut out the heat and crouched to pet the frantic dog yipping at her feet. She left the luggage near the steps and made her way to the kitchen. Ivy followed and found Sara sitting on a high stool in front of the island, bouncing a tennis ball to Sunny. A slight woman with a dark braid swinging down her back stood on tiptoe and attacked the top of the stainless steel refrigerator with a feather duster. A bowl of banana pudding sat next to a vase filled with white oleanders, and the loud whirring of a blender drowned out the sound of dog nails skittering across wood. Davis stood behind the blender, sporting bronzed muscles in a hunter green T-shirt and golden hair that wasn't as short as she remembered, holding the power button as ice cream and milk swirled and mixed.

The entire scene unnerved her. She'd stepped into the front cover of *Family Living.* Blenders and milkshakes? Fetch with the family pets while the maid whistled a tune? This was new. This was foreign.

Davis stopped the blender and smiled. "You're back."

The lady with the feather duster turned around, the apple red Lee press-ons capping her fingernails deluging Ivy with a sudden and unexpected ache. Her mother had a habit of filling Ivy's Christmas stocking with Lee press-ons when she was a little girl. Renee had called last week after checking herself back into the rehab facility. As much as Ivy wanted to hope, she knew better. Her mother could never manage more than thirty days of sobriety.

"My daughter's idea of a manicure." The woman with the feather duster brought her hands behind her back, her freckled cheeks turning pink.

Marilyn plopped her keys on the counter. "Annie, this is my stepdaughter, Ivy. Ivy, this is my housekeeper and friend, Annie."

Annie smiled a shy, gap-toothed smile.

Sunny deposited the slobbery tennis ball onto Sara's lap. She picked it up and tossed it toward the foyer. Both dogs scampered away, nails scratching against the floor. "It's nice to have you home."

Ivy's heart cramped over the word. *Home.* It floated in the air like a soap bubble. She imagined reaching out her finger and popping it. This place wasn't home back then, and it couldn't be home now. She was here to do a job. Not play house.

Marilyn walked to the refrigerator and opened the door.

Davis uncapped the Hershey's syrup and squeezed a ribbon of black into the blender. "Be careful, Aunt Mare. Last time I opened that thing, I got attacked by all the Tupperware. You have enough meals in there to last a lifetime."

"People from church keep bringing them to me." Marilyn pulled out a Saran-wrapped dish of potato salad and set it next to the pudding. "If it doesn't stop soon, Pastor Voss will have to intervene on my behalf or I will drown in fried chicken."

Annie hurried into the adjoining room, brandishing her feather duster. The kitchen opened into a smaller version of a living room, not to be mistaken for the great room across the foyer. It was a cozy space filled with a striped sofa bookended by two old-fashioned easy chairs. Ivy used to sit in there as a little girl, curled up like a cat in a corner of the sofa. She doodled silly pictures while Bernice cooked dinner and sang West African soul music. It was a safe room, one James never visited.

Ivy slapped her hand against the countertop. She had enough uncomfortable silence in the car. She didn't need more of it now. "Let's get this show on the road, shall we? What are we talking about? A charity show? I've walked for a few of those before. One for AIDS, another for breast cancer. What's this one for—malaria?"

"An art program for the blind and visually impaired," Davis said.

Ivy looked at Sara. "Oh."

Marilyn removed spoons and a stack of small porcelain bowls from a drawer, spooned some banana pudding into one, and slid it over to Sara. She dipped her fingertip into the creamy top and let Sunny have a taste. "Davis wants to bring the program to Greenbrier's community college. I think I might be the only student."

Marilyn plopped a dollop of potato salad into her bowl and pushed it around with a fork. "You're our expert, Ivy. Where do we start?"

All eyes turned in her direction. Ivy sagged beneath their appraisal. What did she know about captaining a charity event? She was just a model. "Well..." She sifted through her memory and plucked out the charity shows she'd walked for in the past. "First, you want to figure out how you're going to raise money. Do you want to charge an admission fee? Auction off dresses?"

"I was thinking an admission fee," Marilyn said.

"If you really want to raise money, you could ask local businesses to donate packages for auction in exchange for free advertising. Anything wedding related. Maybe honeymoon prizes or floral packages. That sort of thing."

Marilyn beamed. "That's a great idea."

A ribbon of warmth swirled through Ivy's chest. "The next thing is figuring out a venue. You'll want to find a place that has a lot of space. A room for the models to change in and out of outfits. Something with a stage for them to walk on. Room for guests." She picked at the underside of the countertop and snuck a glance at Davis. "I bet we could find one together."

He shrugged.

"I need to take notes. Where's a pen when you need one?" Marilyn held up a finger. "Don't say anything important while I'm gone." She pushed away from the counter and left the room.

Sara tossed the tennis ball again.

Davis toyed with the power button on the blender. "I know I already said it, but I'm sorry about your friend."

His softened voice made her think of that night. And his question. *"Who's going to help you find the sea?"* She blinked away the memory. Vera Wang was her sea, and if Davis really wanted to help her, he could. "Everybody's gotta die sometime, right?"

He gave her a long look and offered her a bowl of pudding. Ivy ignored the rumble in her stomach and waved the food away. She couldn't afford to gain a single ounce. Nothing about her appearance between now and the Vera Wang photo shoot could change.

The dogs settled at Sara's feet. "How was your time in New York?" she asked.

"It was something." Ivy tapped a fingernail against the countertop, searching for a way to keep the conversation headed in the right direction. "You should go there sometime. You'd like it."

"I'm more of a small-town girl."

Davis clipped the end of Sara's words with the whirring of the blender. He let go of the button, removed the pitcher, and filled four tall glasses with milkshake.

Ivy examined the tick in his jaw. "It's good for small-town folk to get out and visit a big city. Enlarges your world, you know?"

"I've been there. Once." Sara ran her hand over the granite countertop. "I went when Davis lived there."

Cha-ching! "Really?"

Davis scooted a glass in front of Sara, then sent one sliding in Ivy's direction. "Did you have a nice flight?"

She ignored his attempted distraction and kept her focus on Sara. "How long ago was that?"

"A couple years."

"I saw some nasty thunderstorms on the radar. Did you hit any turbulence?"

"Nothing too traumatic, but thanks for the concern, Dave." Ignoring the glint in his eye, Ivy turned back to Sara and twisted the cold glass in a circle. "So tell me what you thought of the Big Apple."

Sara bit her lip. "It wasn't really my scene."

"Was it your brother's?"

"I didn't belong there any more than Sara did," he said.

Before Ivy could respond, Marilyn swept into the room, holding up a spiral notebook and a ballpoint pen. "Okay, what did I miss?"

"We were talking about Sara's trip to New York City."

Marilyn stopped, her attention twitching to Davis.

All right, something was definitely going on.

"Excuse us for a second." Davis took Ivy's elbow and guided her into the foyer like a naughty child before letting go of her arm. "What are you doing?"

She rubbed the swatch of skin his hand had touched, wondering what he might say if she came straight out and explained her dilemma. Would he agree to come back to New York with her? She studied the hard set of his jaw. No, definitely not. He didn't like her enough to agree. At least not yet.

"Just trying to figure out why New York City is such a hot-button topic in this house."

"Why?"

"Can't a girl be curious?"

"The subject's off limits."

"Don't you know, Davis, that when you tell a girl something's off limits, it only makes her want to push harder?" She raised her eyebrows. "Would you ever go back?"

He didn't answer.

"For a little while? Temporarily?"

"No."

"You offered to go to Annalise's funeral with me, and that was in New York."

"That was different."

"How so?"

He ran his hand down his face. "It's the lights when I need the sea, remember?"

Ivy tapped her chin. "Sara and I are living in the same house, which means we'll be spending a lot of time together. We're bound to get close." She crossed her fingers in front of her face. "Almost like sisters. And sisters talk, Dave. They tell each other things."

His eyes narrowed. "You can play all you want with me, Ivy. I can handle it. But please leave Sara out of this."

Marilyn poked her head into the foyer. "Everything okay?"

Davis shoved his hands into the back pockets of his cargoes. "Everything's fine. We're just straightening some things out."

"Are they all straightened?" Marilyn wagged her pen at them. "Because I'd sure like to dive in."

He turned to Ivy with smoldering eyes. "I don't know. Is everything straightened?"

She didn't wither. Not even a tiny bit. "As straight as can be."

19

Davis fanned the front of his shirt against his chest and stared at the building, an architectural island sitting in the middle of an expansive lawn, shaded by Spanish moss and live oaks. So far this afternoon, he and Ivy had visited two potential venues for the fashion show: the Greenbrier Community Center on the north end of the island and a warehouse-turned-convention-center on the eastern edge of the business district. Ivy hadn't approved of either. Davis let go of his shirt, took off his Colorado Rockies cap, and scratched the top of his head. "What do you think?"

She squinted against the sun. "What is it?"

"It's a theater now, but during the War of Northern Aggression"—he bracketed the words with his fingers—"it used to be an orphanage."

"The war of what?"

"It's what my Grandfather calls the Civil War. This lady, Betsy Crestledown, was the wife of a wealthy-merchant-turned-general. When her husband died of infection, she built this as an orphanage to accommodate the growing population of orphans during and after the war."

"Quite a woman."

"A local hero." Davis recapped his head and walked along the azalea-lined cement path, looking at Ivy from the corner of his eye. They got off to a rocky start last night, but once they rejoined Marilyn and Sara, Ivy had dropped her obsession with New York City and stuck to all things fashion show. In fact, he'd seen a side to Ivy he wasn't sure many people saw—a light in her eyes that shone brighter the more she lost herself in the planning. One that had already flickered to life several times this morning.

He stopped in front of the large double doors and wrapped his fingers around the brass handle. "In case I forget to thank you, you were really great last night with the fashion show stuff."

Pink tinged her cheeks. "It's not rocket science."

He smiled. Ivy embarrassed? This was new. "Maybe not, but I would have taken one look at the community center and put down a deposit." Who but Ivy would know the models needed more room to change in and out of clothes?

Her blush deepened.

Davis's smile widened as he opened the heavy door and spotted a man leaning back in a swivel chair—the kind of guy who could be thirty or sixty and neither would be that surprising. One of his boots tore a page of a golf magazine as he pulled them off the welcome desk and examined Ivy.

"Why, hel-lo."

Ivy smiled—actually smiled—at the grease ball. Davis stepped in front of her and blocked the man's impolite perusal. The guy leaned over the desk and stuck out his hand, craning his head until he found Ivy's legs. "Name's Duncan. What can I do for y'all today?"

Davis shook Duncan's hand, squeezing a little harder than necessary. "We'd like a tour of the facilities. We're looking to do a fashion show here in Greenbrier at the end of September and need a place to do it."

Duncan relaxed back in his seat, crossed his ankle over his knee, and kept his beady stare on Ivy. "You came to the right place. We host beauty pageants here every June." He uncrossed his leg and looped his thumbs inside the front pockets of his jeans. "I'd bet my shrimpin' boat you're that model everybody's talking about."

Ivy stepped around Davis and propped her elbow on the high desk. "Your shrimping boat is safe."

Davis's stomach flexed involuntarily. He wanted to yank her back and tell her to quit it. He wanted the Ivy who blushed at his compliment, not the one who flirted with perverts.

"Well, I'll be darned. I never met an honest-to-goodness model before." Duncan swiped a set of keys from a drawer and came out of his chair, his full height a hair short of Ivy's nose. "Give me a sec. I'll go round back and let you in the auditorium." He looked Ivy up and down once more, let out a low whistle, and disappeared into a dimly lit hallway.

Ivy set her chin in one hand and drummed the desktop with her other. "Charming fellow."

"You shouldn't encourage men like him."

"Men like him?"

"Duncan. Stefan. That kid at the plantation."

"What kind of men should I encourage then, Dave?"

He opened his mouth to answer, but the auditorium doors jangled, clicked, and flung open. Duncan stood on the other side, whistling as he stuck a key in a switch plate and turned on the lights. "Come on in. Feel free to look at the back rooms if y'all have a mind to."

Ivy walked past Davis and moseyed down the carpeted aisle, gazing from the seating to the stage to the lights overhead. "Does this place have a decent sound system?"

"Sure does."

She stopped in front of the stage. "We could set up a small runway down the center aisle here. It wouldn't be hard." She clicked her manicured nail against the wood, then used the side stairs to walk onto the stage, swaying her hips like the runway already existed. She looked over her shoulder and crooked her finger at Davis. "You coming?"

Duncan let out another whistle. "You wouldn't have to ask me twice."

Davis followed Ivy backstage as she walked from room to room, pausing in certain corners. He rubbed the back of his neck, trying to distract himself from his disproportionate annoyance. Her flirting with Duncan and Duncan's greasy response should perhaps irritate him, not make him want to punch the guy in the face. He cleared his throat. "That was really sweet of you, asking Sara to organize the music."

"Don't patronize your sister."

He pulled his chin back. Patronize Sara? "How'd you come up with that?"

"She knows music, doesn't she?"

"Yes."

"Then there was nothing sweet about it." She ran her hand up a red velvet curtain hanging from the ceiling.

He shifted his weight. The floorboards creaked beneath his cross-trainers. "They're counting on you to help run this thing."

"Uh-oh. Mistake number one. Do you want to warn them or should I?"

"The show's not until the end of September. It's the beginning of August."

She held onto the curtain and looked over her shoulder. "What's your point, Dave?"

"Are you going to stick around?"

"I said I would, didn't I?"

Confusion spun into spools of doubt. Why would Ivy stay in Greenbrier unless something was in it for her? "I don't understand why you'd want to stay."

"I'd rather not have to get on a plane every time Marilyn wants us to do another shoot."

Davis narrowed his eyes. He wanted to believe her. He really did. But she answered too quickly and looked away too soon, which could only mean she had other reasons for staying. Reasons that could change as quick as the tides. Reasons that could leave Sara and Marilyn in the lurch. "I don't want to see my aunt or my sister get hurt."

Ivy let go of the red velvet. "What are you implying?"

"I just don't want you to make promises you're not going to keep."

She looked him in the face, her eyes honeyed steel. "I keep my promises."

"Good. I'm glad." Davis filled his lungs with air and stepped closer, trying not to acknowledge the charge in the atmosphere. He might be attracted to Ivy, but he knew better than to act on it. The last thing she needed was another man coming on to her, seeing her looks without bothering to look for the Ivy underneath. "Since you're sticking around, I was thinking..."

"Uh-oh. Mistake number two."

"Do you want to be friends?"

The corner of her mouth quirked. "Do I want to be friends?"

"Yeah."

She crossed her arms. "What if I want to be more?"

"There isn't more to have."

"I'm not big on making friends, Dave." She studied him beneath arched eyebrows. The air vents rattled and swayed the curtain in a slow back-and-forth rhythm. "But maybe I'll make an exception with you."

A sharp whistle sounded from the back of the auditorium. Davis stepped around the curtain, onto the stage, and found Duncan hadn't moved from his spot next to the doors. "Y'all made up your mind yet?"

Davis shifted the curtains and looked at Ivy, who gave the place one last look and smiled. He cupped his hand near his mouth. "We'll take it."

Duncan waved them off the stage and stuck his key into the light switch. Darkness flooded the auditorium. "Then come on out front and we can talk out the details."

Davis used the light from the opened doors to maneuver his way off the stage, helped Ivy down, and quickly let go of her waist. Even in the dark, he could see the divot in the center of her forehead. He meandered up the aisle and focused on keeping things light. "What's wrong? You don't want to be friends with me?"

"It's not that."

"What is it then?"

"It's about the pictures you took."

He couldn't help himself. He laughed. "You don't like them?"

They stepped through the doors, out into the lobby, and joined Duncan at the desk.

"Bruce says they're good. Designers say they're good. What I think doesn't matter."

"It matters to me."

"That's sweet, Dave, but beside the point."

"What's the point?"

"A guy with your talent doesn't belong here in Podunk, South Carolina. No offense, Dunc." She cast a look at the man rummaging through desk drawers.

"None taken, darlin'."

"Bruce could get you jobs in New York City." Ivy snapped her fingers. "Like that."

Here she was going on about New York City again. "I'm not looking for jobs."

"Why not?"

"I already told you. I'm only doing this temporarily."

"I've worked with a lot of photographers in my career, and not one of them comes close to touching your passion. You loved every second of that photo shoot, and if you tell me you didn't, you're a liar."

Duncan twirled a set of keys around his finger, watching the exchange unfold. Davis turned his back to him. "Why do you care what I do or don't do with my camera?"

"Because I think it's a sin to waste that kind of talent. I don't get why you'd want to. Or why you feel you have to."

A sin? Since when was Ivy concerned with sin? "I asked you to drop this last night."

"You didn't ask me. You told me."

His muscles coiled. "We're here to find a venue for the show. Let's stick to that."

"Hey, you're the one who wanted to be friends, Dave. Isn't this what friends do? Open up or whatever? Push each other to be all they can be?"

"That's the army."

Duncan rapped his knuckles on the desk. "When's your shindig?"

"Last Saturday in September. The twenty-fifth."

Duncan flipped a page of a pocket calendar. "It's open, but we're filling up fast. If you want to reserve the day, we need a down payment ASAP. A check written out to Betsy Crestledown Theater."

"You don't take credit cards?" Davis asked.

"No sirree. Only checks or cash."

"I'll have to bring one later." And pray nobody reserved the spot before then.

Duncan circled his finger in the air at Ivy. "Why don't she bring it in?"

Davis narrowed his eyes.

"Sure, Duncan." Ivy gave Davis an "at least he acts like a normal man" look. "I wouldn't mind seeing you again. I wouldn't mind one bit."

Georgia panted at Ivy's feet, tiny paws scuttling against the floor as Ivy approached Marilyn's bedroom door and knocked.

"Yes?"

Ivy spoke to the wood. "We found a venue."

"Oh, Ivy, that's great!" A pause. Some shuffling. "Hold on a sec. I'm getting dressed. I'll be right out and we can talk."

"I don't need to talk. I just need a check so we can hold a reservation at the theater."

"Betsy Crestledown?"

"Yeah."

"Perfect! Checks are in the desk in James's office. Go ahead and write one out and I'll be down in a minute to sign it."

Her father's office? Georgia licked Ivy's ankle. She nudged the dog away and headed down the stairs.

It's only an office, and he was just a man.

She strode through the foyer, through the small room adjoining the kitchen, and stopped in front of the french double doors—James's hiding place. As a kid, she'd known better than to enter.

She flexed her fingers and nudged the door. The hinges groaned. Inside, with the shades drawn, the air felt still. Untouched. Tomblike. As if nobody had entered since James had breathed his last. She flicked the light switch, expecting cobwebs, but found polished wood instead. She took five quick steps to the desk and found the checkbook beneath the lamp. She grabbed the lone pen stranded in the middle of an unmarked desk calendar and began writing, but the pen didn't cooperate. It stopped working before she could scrawl the dollar amount. She shook it and tried again. No luck.

Taking a deep breath, she pulled open the top drawer and rummaged past notebooks, manila files, a stapler, paper clips, an old pocketknife. No pens. She shut the drawer and opened the one beneath it, expecting more of the same.

Instead, she found a heavy wooden box with a hinged lid stained cherry red. It looked like the kind of thing that held memories. And it belonged to her father. Her heart throbbed. Should she peek inside? And if she did, would the contents throw her off balance or crumble her foundation?

Baseball cards would do nothing. Pictures of James as a child might make her a little wobbly. Love letters between him and Marilyn, or worse, love letters between him and Mom? That would toss her somewhere on the high end of the Richter scale.

Curiosity won out. Ivy ran trembling fingers over the warm wood, then removed the box from the drawer. She lifted the lid and inhaled the scent of cedar. A shadow darkened the inside so that all she could see were muted papers.

Photographs?

She reached in, removed the bundle clumped together by a rubber band, and turned the pictures right side up. What she saw made the air swoosh out of her lungs. Ivy plopped down on the swivel chair.

They were pictures all right, but not of James or Marilyn or Ivy's mother. They were pictures of her—Polaroids, black-and-whites, wallet-sized school pictures, candids, even a whole stack of magazine tear-outs. All of Ivy. Her heart thudded inside her chest, pulsed in her ears. How had he gotten them and why did he have them?

She untwined the rubber band and flipped through the stack. When she reached her second-grade picture—a photo of her sporting lopsided bangs due to an experiment with Mom's salon scissors—she turned it over and found her mother's familiar handwriting.

Ivy. 7 years old. 2nd Grade.

She turned over the rest, brushing her fingers over the bubbly scrawls. Purple pen. Red pen. An occasional black Sharpie. Mom had sent these. So did that mean James asked for them? Ivy spread the magazine tear-outs on the desk. No writing, but somebody had taken care to cut them out nice and straight. She tried to picture James in his office, wielding a scissors as he flipped through *Elle* or *Cosmo*. Even though it was impossible to imagine, here was the evidence. In a box. In her father's desk.

What did it mean?

A pocket of warmth expanded inside her rib cage. She pressed her hand against the unfamiliar feeling. Hope stirred like the fluttering of bird wings, slowly at first, then fast and feather light. She flipped through the pictures again, slower this time, stopping at the ones Marilyn had snapped—Ivy in a pedicure chair the first time she visited, a somber-faced Ivy with a giant plate of lobster in front of her, another of the two of them together—Marilyn smiling wide, one arm around Ivy's shoulder, the other holding out the camera with the beach in the background. It was a smile that didn't make sense, a smile Ivy never quite trusted. As she continued flipping, she tried to imagine James tucking each photograph away in this box, pulling them out late at night, when Marilyn slept, brushing his thumb across her face.

Had James loved her after all?

The wings fluttered harder, faster. He had to, right? This was proof that he at least had cared about her. Why else would he bother cutting all these out and bundling them together?

Three quick knocks tapped against the office door. "Did you find the checks?"

Ivy jumped from the chair and swiped the pictures into a messy pile.

Marilyn stopped midstep, her gray blond hair wet from her after-work shower, lips frozen in a crooked pose—as if stuck between a smile and an uh-oh. She stared at the opened box and the photographs scattered beneath Ivy's arm.

Ivy stuffed them in the box haphazardly. "Sorry. I didn't mean— I wasn't looking— I, I needed a pen."

Marilyn's hands fidgeted. "Do you need me to sign the check?"

"Oh. Yeah." Ivy scooted the check forward.

Marilyn removed a pen from a cup on top of the file cabinet.

A whole cup full of them.

How hadn't Ivy seen them earlier? Besides, who put a pen cup on a filing cabinet instead of a desk? Marilyn scratched her signature along the line. When she finished, she handed over the check and wiped her palms down her yoga pants. "I hope you aren't upset with me."

"Upset with you?"

Her attention flickered toward the box. "If your mother minded sending me the photos, she never said so."

The bird wings stuttered. "What?"

"Neither did Bruce's assistant. She promised it wasn't a problem"—Marilyn pointed at the tear sheets—"sending me copies of those magazines."

A cold fist tightened inside Ivy's gut. She wanted to shake her head. Plug her ears. Undo Marilyn's words—words that tore away the burgeoning hope that had only second before been filling her up. "This is your box?"

Marilyn's brow crinkled, and then, as if her faux pas dawned with the slowness of a morning sunrise, her face drained of all color. "You thought...?"

Ivy looked at the floor. Yes. Of course she did.

"Oh, Ivy."

Ivy snatched up the box. "Can I have it?"

"I'm so sorry."

"Can I?"

Marilyn's eyelids fluttered. "Sure. Of course."

Ivy tucked the box under her arm, swept past Marilyn, and took the stairs two at a time. She hurried down the hall, flung open the door to her makeshift apartment, and slammed the box on the dresser. Her own personal reminder. Her North Star, guiding her to the truth. James never loved her. Of course he hadn't.

She went into the bathroom and turned on the water. Maybe a scalding-hot bath would strip away the idiotic longing sloshing through her body. She uncrumpled the check from her fist, walked to her nightstand, and shut it inside her Billy Collins poetry book. She could deliver it tomorrow. Right now, she didn't much feel like enduring Duncan's beady stare. She sat on the edge of the bed and bent over her knees.

Why Marilyn? Of all the people who should care, why was it her?

20

How do they train a dog to read?"

Sara laughed, a refreshing sound in light of the past few days. Greenbrier and its lack of distraction made Ivy stir-crazy. So did Davis's disappearance. She hadn't seen him in three days. Not since their afternoon spent venue shopping or that same evening, when Ivy found Marilyn's box and made a ridiculous assumption.

"Sunny can't read words. He reads cues. People. Situations. He listens."

"Sara, he's sitting and looking at the crosswalk sign like he can read it."

The orange Don't Walk flashed to a white Walk. Sunny lifted his rear off the curb and led Sara across the street. Weren't dogs supposed to be color-blind? Ivy stared after them, a bit in awe of the canine, then hurried to follow before the light turned green—the only light along a crowded Palmetto Boulevard.

"So, Frogmore stew? I have to tell you, it doesn't sound too appetizing."

"You can't come to Greenbrier and not have a proper Lowcountry boil."

"You promise there aren't any frogs in it?"

Sara traced an *X* over her chest. "Cross my heart and hope to die."

"I'm going to make a guess and say it's not low calorie."

Sara laughed again. "Not exactly. But one southern meal won't kill you."

Kill her? No. Make her bloated? Possibly. It was a risk she couldn't take. Not with the shoot for Marilyn's brochure on Monday. But when Sara asked her to lunch, Ivy couldn't say no. Nor did she want to. Not only did she enjoy spending time with Sara—an odd sort of discovery—but she could use the time to her advantage and do a little Davis excavation, see if she couldn't dig up a little something to help her along in her quest. "I haven't seen your brother in a few days. Have you talked to him lately?"

"I bumped into him this morning while I was rehearsing some songs at church. Sounds like Cornerstone's keeping him busy. The air-conditioning unit broke down on Thursday, and he's trying to install new cabinets in the nursery before tomorrow's service."

Right. Rehearsal. Sara led the singing every other Sunday. Maybe Ivy ought to rehearse with her. She couldn't carry a tune, but at least she'd run into Davis. She needed to find a way to broach the subject of New York City again. The Vera Wang shoot was less than two months away, and besides Davis's bizarre offer of friendship, she'd made zero progress. "I hope he's ready for Monday's shoot."

Sara and Sunny walked along the brick sidewalk, under the awning of Gizmo's Art Gallery and past large cement flowerpots. Ivy matched her stride and opened her mouth to keep the conversation rolling, but her skin prickled in a familiar way, a way that said, "Hey, somebody's watching you." She swiveled around in search of the looker and found a familiar man, only he wasn't staring at Ivy. He was watching Sara. It was the guy who came to the rescue with his tow truck when she and Davis found themselves stranded on the side of the highway. He stood motionless across the street as a gaggle of camera-clad, Hawaiian-shirt-wearing tourists stepped around him. What was his name again? J-something.

He didn't stop staring until Ivy caught his attention with a wave. He averted his gaze, but not before Ivy caught the look in his eyes, one she knew well—desire. Her curiosity bubbled and frothed. Why would a man break up with a woman he still wanted? Mr. Mechanic jogged across the street and disappeared inside a shop, its display window blooming with every color of flower imaginable.

Ivy caught up to Sara and took her arm.

Sara stopped, skimming nothing in particular with unfocused eyes. "Something wrong?"

"Mind if we take a quick detour before lunch?" Ivy led them beneath the shop's awning.

"A detour?"

"This thought popped into my head. Wouldn't it be fun if our models carried flowers when they walked down the runway? It'll highlight the dresses, don't you think? And we need to round up some fun packages for the auction. What bride wouldn't bid for a killer deal on flowers for her wedding? Mind if we take a quick peek inside a flower shop?"

Sara bit her lip.

"Do you have a problem with flowers?"

"What flower shop is it?"

Ivy bent backward so she could read the sign. "ZuZu's Petals."

"Oh."

"Is there something wrong with that flower shop?"

"Mrs. Ludd owns ZuZu's Petals."

Ludd, that was it! Jordan Ludd.

"She's Pastor Voss's older daughter."

Ivy's simmering curiosity turned into a roiling boil. "You don't like her?"

"It's not that." Sara fidgeted with Sunny's harness. "I used to date her son."

"So you broke his heart and now his mama hates you?" Best to play dumb.

"Not exactly."

Ivy tugged Sara's arm. "C'mon, Sara, nobody could hate you. She might not even be working."

Sara resisted. Ivy tugged harder. Sunny did a back-and-forth dance on his paws. Ivy wondered what cues the animal was reading now. "No, really Ivy. I'm not comfortable going in there. You go without me. We'll wait outside."

"Don't be silly. Mrs. Ludd knows you, so that means she loves you. She might say no to me, but she won't say no to you." Ivy looked in the window. Over tops of the flowers, Jordan spoke to a plump strawberry-haired woman snipping leaves off flower stems. "We should have flowers for the fashion show. I'm sure of it."

Sara pulled her sunglasses over her eyes. "Okay, fine."

Triumphant, Ivy opened the glass door and stepped inside. Mrs. Ludd and Jordan stopped talking as Sara shuffled in with Sunny—her hair tangled into its usual wispy ponytail, wearing no makeup and a pale yellow top that did nothing for her. Ivy was certain Sara didn't turn men's heads, not ever. But Jordan gawked like she was the most beautiful woman in the room.

Mrs. Ludd's scissors clattered against the counter. "If you aren't a sight for sore eyes standing in my store."

Ivy grimaced at the woman's choice of words. Sore eyes? Really?

Sara stayed by the door and gave a small wave. "Hi, Mrs. Ludd."

Mrs. Ludd gave Jordan a sharp nudge—one that seemed to say, *Go on and say something.* But Ivy knew frozen when she saw it, and Jordan was definitely frozen. She stepped forward and offered her hand. "My name's Ivy Clark."

Mrs. Ludd gave it a firm, friendly shake. "You're the gal my sister keeps jabbering about. She and her daughter saw you at Marilyn's boutique a while back when they were shopping for a wedding dress."

"Oh, right." So Big Red was Mrs. Ludd's sister. Thanks to her and her friend Pinky from the marina, word spread fast in Greenbrier. Maybe Ivy could recruit them for a little charity show publicity. "I'm not sure if you heard or not, but Marilyn's organizing a charity fashion show on the twenty-fifth of September."

Mrs. Ludd's round face brightened. "Is she really?"

"And truly..."

"Oh, honey, this town'll eat that right up."

"That's what we're hoping. Since it's a bridal show, we'd like somebody to put floral arrangements together for our models in exchange for some free publicity for your store. And if you really want to go above and beyond, you could auction some flower packages for a guest or two."

Mrs. Ludd looked over her shoulder and slanted her eyebrows at Jordan. Except for the subtle rise and fall of his chest, he hadn't moved at all. His eyes remained fixed on Sara, who stayed by the door, clutching Sunny's harness and shuffling her feet, lost in a world of blindness.

"Jordan, honey, could you go get me my calendar?"

The color drained from Sara's face.

Jordan unstuck his feet from the floor and disappeared into the back room. Nobody spoke. Ivy looked at Sara, who kept her head down. Ivy looked at Mrs. Ludd, who stared at Sara. It was all so weird. Ivy needed to figure out their story, because all she knew from Davis was that the two used to date. Jordan returned and handed his mom a planner.

Ivy slipped her hands in the back pockets of her shorts and rocked on her heels. "So, Jordan, do a lot of cars break down in September? We'd love your help with the show."

Sara bumped into the door. The bell jangled.

Jordan's attention volleyed from Sara to Ivy. "I'm not sure."

"You've got a strong voice. You could emcee for us. Read off the dress designs. Accessories. Shoes. I bet you'd be fabulous."

Jordan blushed. "I'm not too good with words."

"Okay then." Ivy turned to Sara, hoping to draw her into the conversation. "What do you think, Sara? Maybe he could head up the cleaning crew. We'll need help cleaning when we're all finished."

"I... I'm not sure." She placed a hand over her stomach, like she might be ill. "I'm sorry, I need to get some fresh air." She tightened her grip around Sunny's harness and hurried out the door.

Jordan didn't go after her. He stood with arms dangling by his sides.

Mrs. Ludd looked up from her calendar. "My calendar's clear, honey. You tell Marilyn we'd love to help in any way we can." She glanced at her son, annoyance flickering across her brow. "Jordan can help too."

Ivy searched the street, looking one way, then another. A lanky man wearing a large belt buckle and cowboy boots escorted a multipierced woman up the sidewalk. Ivy waited until they passed, then stepped over the curb to get a better look. She needed to find Sara and apologize. She shouldn't have thrust Jordan on her like that, especially not if he'd broken her heart once before. But where could Sara be?

Ivy walked down the sidewalk toward Charlie's Crab Hut, the place they were supposed to eat lunch before Ivy derailed the plans. A block and a half later, she spotted the furry backside of Sunny in the distance across the street, beyond a row of palm trees, off the boardwalk, sitting in the sand beside a woman with a thin ponytail on a wooden bench.

A blue truck marked with a silver F-150 rumbled pass. Ivy crossed the street, made her way through the sandy grass, and sat beside Sara. "Hey."

Gentle waves hissed against the beach, and frothy whiteness receded in ripples out to the sea. The hot breeze danced wisps of hair around Sara's face as she twirled a loose thread from her shirt around her finger until the tip turned red. "Did you know he was in there when you brought me inside?"

"Yes."

"Why did you do that?"

Sara's softly spoken question pinched the small hollow beneath Ivy's breastbone. Because she had wanted to know if Jordan loved Sara and if Sara loved him back. Maybe curiosity was a sin. "I'm not sure."

Sara unwound the thread. "Do you think I wanted him to see me like this?"

"What do you mean, 'like this'?"

She motioned to her person. "I don't even know if my outfit matches."

"He doesn't care about that."

A doubtful puff of air brushed past Sara's lips.

"You can't see the way he looks at you. I can. And trust me on this, Sara, the man's in love." Ivy leaned back, her shoulder blades biting into the wood. "What I can't decipher is how you feel about him."

Sara's ears turned red.

"You love him too, don't you?"

Sara went back to work twirling the thread around her finger. Her non-answer was really all the answer Ivy needed. She considered passing along her mother's warning. Even sixteen years later, Ivy could still feel Mom's fingers digging into her little-girl shoulders. Still see the dark circles beneath Mom's eyes. *"Never fall in love, Ivy. Nothing good can come of it."* Maybe the words in and of themselves wouldn't have left such a lasting impression if Ivy hadn't witnessed the truth of them. With every one of James's rejections, Ivy's mom had slipped further and further away until there was nothing left at all. "Why did he break up with you?"

Sara scratched Sunny's ears. "He didn't break up with me."

"But your brother said—"

"I know what Davis thinks, but he made an assumption and I didn't bother to fix it."

"Poor guy."

"Who—Davis?"

"No, Jordan. He's lovesick. Trust me, I know that look well."

"I'm sure you do." Sara unraveled the thread and let it float away on the breeze. "Davis says you're very beautiful."

Ivy frowned. If Davis thought she was so beautiful, why did he treat her like a leper one minute and a broken toy the next? Why did he offer his friendship when she offered him more? She toed the sand. "Men have no problem falling in lust with me, but they get over it in a month or two." Ivy looked out at the choppy surf, then back to Sara. "It's been how long since you and Jordan broke up? And he still looks at you like he wants to drop down on his knee and propose."

"I'm sure you're exaggerating."

"I promise I'm not."

Sara sighed. "It's better this way."

"For who?"

"Him. He deserves better."

Better in what sense—the physical? Sara might not be a ravishing beauty, or even a beauty at all, but there was something about her—a lightness and a joy—that made her more appealing than any of the models Ivy had known in New York. It might have taken her a little while to notice, but Ivy saw it now. Sara was beautiful, and it had nothing to do with her appearance. The revelation caused something to shift in Ivy's core. She tried to laugh, but the sound barely dented the air. "Sara, I don't know how any man could do better than you."

"Davis! What are you doing here?" Grandfather gripped the end of his driver and rested the club against the turf of the country club's driving range.

Doc Armstrong, a longtime family friend, swung an iron and sent a ball sailing toward a distant yard marker—a shot that would have been straight down the fairway if a fairway existed. Meanwhile, Pastor Voss hacked at his Titleist. It shot a line through green grass and fizzled short of fifty yards. He grabbed his back. "This is why I don't like golf."

Doc set up another ball. "You're pulling your head."

"I'm pulling everything." Pastor Voss rubbed his lower back. "And I'm too old for this."

"You're younger than I am," Grandfather said.

Davis grinned. The three of them reminded him of the characters in that movie with Walter Matthau—*Grumpy Old Men.* "I wanted to run something by you."

"Have you changed your mind?" Grandfather flexed his fingers inside his white golf glove and exchanged his driver for a three wood. "Going to quit that job at the church and finally put your college degree to good use?"

"Hey now," Pastor Voss said, massaging his back, "don't be putting that idea into his head. What would my church do without him?" He turned to look at Davis. "How are those cabinets coming, by the way?"

"Finished an hour ago, and I haven't changed my mind, Grandfather. This isn't about that."

Grandfather harrumphed. "What is it then?"

Doc took another graceful swing. The ball sailed into the air and out of sight.

"I'm helping Marilyn round up some honeymoon and wedding packages to auction at the fashion show." Davis closed his eyes. *Here goes nothing.* "I wanted to ask if you'd chip in."

"Chip in how?"

"Put together some honeymoon packages for auction. You have an in with five-star hotels and resorts all across the country. It'd help us raise money." If Grandfather agreed, it would be a huge moneymaker.

Doc spit on the end of his club and rubbed it with his thumb. "A fashion show?"

"A charity event. All proceeds will go toward funding an art program at the community college."

"Oh, right. I've been hearing talk." Doc's face split into a grin. "Speaking of talk, congratulations on your engagement." He elbowed Davis and shot him a wink. "I hear your fiancé is quite the looker."

Grandfather's club clattered into his bag. "What's that?"

Davis groaned.

"Just a silly rumor, Marshall," Doc said.

"Started by my daughter, it would seem," Pastor Voss said. "I suppose another sermon on gossip's in order."

"Your daughter didn't start it, Pastor Voss." Davis was pretty sure the blame for that lay on Ivy, whom he'd see again in two more days for their next photo shoot. He shouldn't feel so eager.

Doc started to chuckle. "I'm sure there are worse rumors than being engaged to Ivy Clark."

Something like a growl rumbled from Grandfather's chest. "That girl is nothing but trouble."

"You don't even know her," Davis said.

"I know enough to warn you against getting mixed up with her kind."

Tension settled in Davis's jaw. "What kind is that?"

"Don't play stupid. She's a regular Jezebel."

Doc Armstrong waved his club between them. "No fistfights on the driving range, gentlemen. Marshall, I know you think you're tough for an old codger, but a fight with your grandson will do your heart in, I'm afraid."

Grandfather tapped his chest. "My heart's fine."

If his definition for "fine" was cold and hard, then yes, it was.

Pastor Voss unzipped a pouch in his golf bag and pulled out a bottled water. "The child's lost, Marshall. She needs a Savior, not an old man heaping judgment on her shoulders."

Davis nodded vehemently. "Exactly."

"Whatever she needs won't change who she is."

The water bottle crinkled as Pastor Voss untwisted the cap. "A little faith can bring about a world of change."

"Spin it however you'd like, you can't make a silk purse out of a sow's ear."

"Jesus turned water to wine," Pastor Voss replied.

Davis ground his teeth. This conversation would spin in circles until the crickets started chirping. Pastor Voss might have time to stand around debating theology with Grandfather, but Davis didn't. He needed to check on the air-conditioning unit one more time before tomorrow's service, then get home and prepare his equipment and his heart for another photo shoot on Monday. "I came here to ask if you'd help out with the show. You might not approve of my part in it, but you love Sara and she loves painting. So are you in or out?"

Grandfather studied the head of his three wood. "If I say yes, will you consider helping out at the office?" He wiggled the head of his club behind the ball and spread his feet into position. "Men my age retired fifteen years ago, but here I am."

"We haven't retired yet." Doc Armstrong opened a bag of sunflower seeds and poured some into Pastor Voss's waiting hand.

"Exactly my point." Grandfather swung. The ball flew into the air, slicing a hair to the left. "You two are pups compared to me."

"Pups?" Pastor Voss laughed. "I'll be seventy next month."

Davis gritted his teeth. James had had a posse of men lined up, all capable and eager to fill in the spot James would leave when he became too sick to work. Grandfather stuck around, not because he had to, but because he was too controlling to leave. It would be no different if Davis took over. "You know my answer."

"Come on, Marshall. Help the boy out," Doc said, popping a few seeds into his mouth. "It's for a good cause."

Grandfather pulled a meticulously folded handkerchief from the back pocket of his golf pants and mopped his brow. "Fine, Davis. If you think this is going to brighten Sara's life, then all right. I just hope you remember my generosity when I'm too riddled with arthritis to work and my business has nobody to manage it."

21

Thick morning mist hovered over the ground as Marilyn walked through her backyard toward her place of refuge, coffee mug in hand, Bible and journal tucked beneath her arm. Some of the fog pockets were so thick it was like walking through a cloud. Marilyn closed her eyes and let the smell and sounds of the marsh guide her. Last night, she'd spent the late evening hours stargazing and hadn't bothered to bring in her rocking chair. It would be nice to start the week in the same place—her and God—as the sun rose up from the horizon and broke apart the fog.

As soon as she stepped onto the dock, though, she discovered the chair was already occupied. Ivy sat with one leg tucked beneath her, the other draped over an armrest, her long hair pulled high in a messy bun. Marilyn paused for a moment, mesmerized by the intense way Ivy read from the book she held in her hands. The two had barely spoken since Marilyn caught Ivy looking at the pictures she'd stowed away in James's desk. That little-girl longing Marilyn had seen in Ivy's eyes still ripped at her heart.

James, you were such a fool.

The entire encounter had added an extra layer of awkwardness to their relationship—another barrier Marilyn couldn't figure out how to breach. Better to leave Ivy in peace than attempt a stilted conversation that would only call attention to the wall that stood between them. She had taken a step away when Ivy turned a page and let out a sigh so long and heartfelt that Marilyn couldn't help herself.

"What are you reading?" she asked.

Ivy brought her bare foot onto the dock and blinked at Marilyn. She placed her finger inside the book to hold her spot. "I, um, borrowed it from the bookcase in the living room. I hope that's okay."

"Of course." Marilyn stepped closer and caught a glimpse of the title.

Walden by Henry David Thoreau—the opposite of light reading. "I've tried reading that one several times. Could never manage to get past page ten. You looked like you were enjoying it though."

"I can never tell if he's a poet or a scientist." Ivy looked down at the paperback in her hand and smiled. Although the gesture wasn't meant for Marilyn, it still drew her closer. There was a depth to Ivy people rarely saw. James certainly had never bothered to look. "One minute he's personifying plants and the next he's classifying them."

"You'd make a great literature professor."

The comment seemed to be the wrong one, because Ivy's posture stiffened.

Marilyn scrambled for something to say before Ivy retreated altogether, praying substance into the moment so she could grab on tight and hold it close. "What did you think about your first taste of Frogmore stew?"

"Heavy."

"It's an acquired taste." Marilyn took a sip of her coffee, which was no longer hot but lukewarm. If only she'd brought an extra cup for Ivy. "You and Sara seem to be getting along."

"She's easy to get along with." Ivy's attention flitted to the Bible and journal tucked beneath Marilyn's arm. "You still do that?"

"Every morning."

Ivy nodded, stood. "Well, I don't want to get in your way."

"You aren't in my way." The words came out too fast, too eager.

Ivy shrugged awkwardly, and in Marilyn's desperation to prolong the inevitable, she blurted the first question that came to mind. "How's your mother doing?"

The regret was swift. If Ivy's eyes had shutters, they would have slammed shut. Marilyn had broached a taboo topic. Ivy never talked about Renee, not here, not with her. "She's fine."

And with that, Ivy walked away, disappearing into the mist that had yet to break apart.

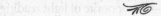

Davis might not have liked Stefan the model, but at least he had been a nice buffer during their first photo shoot. This second time around, Davis had no buffer. This time it was only Ivy—in a long ivory gown that hugged her body before flaring outward at her knees. Her hair fell like silky waves flowing down her back, pinned behind her ear on one side by a single large rose.

He snapped several pictures and swallowed, trying to ignore the heat in his stomach, the familiar sensation of tingling nerves as he captured the perfect angle. He tried to find neutral ground where this was just a camera and Ivy was just a girl. He reminded himself not to get too invested, because the more invested he became, the more pain he'd experience later, when the campaign ended and he returned his equipment to the basement where it belonged.

But who was he kidding? The camera wasn't just a camera—it was a passion that had stolen so much. And Ivy wasn't just a girl—she was the woman stuck in his thoughts, no matter how hard he tried to unstick her.

He was enjoying this too much.

Ivy pivoted her body and looked over her shoulder, eyes smoldering. He snapped the photo, moved three steps to the left, and snapped two more. Everything and everybody else—the lights, the props, the staging, the makeup artist, Marilyn, his friend who was acting as his assistant—fell away. Disappeared. Until all that existed were he and she and the rhythm and flow of the pictures. The two of them moved like a choreographed dance. She'd move, he'd step. She'd smile, he'd snap. Again and again until the battery of his camera flashed a warning and his friend Jeff yawned and fumbled with a light stand.

Davis pulled the camera away from his face. Ivy set down her bouquet of roses, her gaze unwavering.

"Did you get it?" Marilyn's voice. But he couldn't look away from Ivy.

"Yes." He swallowed.

"I haven't seen your eyes this bright in a long time, Davis. Makes me happy to see it." Marilyn squeezed his elbow. "It's like you were made for this."

Davis switched off the camera. The shoot was over.

Heat circled her neck like a heavy collar. It wouldn't go away, no matter how hard she fanned her clavicle. Davis had spent the last several hours looking at her like the world had transformed into a tunnel, with him on one end and her on the other and nothing in between. She was all that mattered. It was the first time he'd shown any hint of desire. And she wanted more of it.

Ivy slipped off her heels and pushed open the door of the changing room in Marilyn's boutique. Davis was still in the back near the mirrors where they'd done the photo shoot. Only he wasn't alone. His buddy folded up umbrellas and light stands while the man she sought leaned over a table and fiddled with a piece of paper—probably the model release form.

She stood in the doorway, watching.

Davis set the pen down and helped dismantle the set. Jeff noticed her first. He smiled and fumbled a diffusion screen when he saw her. She smiled back, but wished she didn't have to. She'd rather he wasn't here. Davis handed Jeff another piece of equipment. He wedged it beneath his arm and walked to the front, his smile too big, his face too red.

"You sure were something else today." Jeff opened the door. The equipment lodged beneath his arm slipped. He jerked and caught it, the door smacking him in the rear. When he righted himself, his face had turned pickled beet.

"Thank you." Ivy walked over to give him a hand, then approached Davis, who stuffed a tripod into an oblong duffel bag. Her feet made no sound as she walked toward him. She sat on the table, one leg crossed over the other, bobbing her foot in a slow, lazy circle, palms resting on the table's edge as she watched him bag more equipment. When he turned around he stutter stepped, as if her presence had startled him.

"Hey."

His one-word greeting echoed in the high-ceilinged room. The boutique had worked well for the photo shoot. Lots of space. Windows. Natural lighting. She hopped off the table and closed the gap between them. He stood in place, confusion expanding in his eyes the closer she got, filling her with determination. She didn't want his confusion. She wanted his ardor. She wanted to drink it up, saturate herself in it. Before he could blink, she slid her hand around the back of his neck and brushed her lips against his.

He yanked her arm away and stepped back. "What are you doing?"

"Celebrating."

"That isn't how I celebrate."

"No?"

He wanted her. She could see it in his eyes. She could tell by the way he kept moving away, as though he didn't trust himself to be close to her. So why didn't he take her already? "You mean you never kissed any of the models you photographed in New York?"

"The next time I kiss a girl, it won't be because I want her."

"Why will you kiss her, then?"

"Because I love her."

Her heart shriveled. *"Because I love her."* Ivy wanted to reach inside her chest and rip the pain away—this raging, pulsing pain that burned like a furnace and never seemed to extinguish. She didn't need Davis's passion. And she definitely didn't need his love. She made to turn away, but he grabbed her elbow.

"I'm not a toy, Ivy."

"Did I imply that you were?"

His eyes narrowed. "What are you after?"

"I don't know what you mean."

"With me. Sara said you two went to lunch on Saturday. She said you asked a lot of questions about me."

"Can't a girl be curious?"

"What do you want to know?"

"Nothing." More like everything. Like why he left New York. Why he refused to go back. What would entice him to return. If she asked him, would he? For her? She looked down at his hand wrapped around her elbow. There was no way of knowing unless she asked. She looked up and met his eyes, the question creeping to the tip of her tongue. "Davis…"

The door swung open. Jeff walked inside the boutique, empty handed and whistling.

Ivy tried stepping away.

But Davis didn't let go of her arm. "Tell me what you were going to say."

She looked into the depths of his blue eyes and shook her head. When Jeff wasn't in the room jangling equipment and she had a better grip on her emotions, after she was sure Davis wouldn't reject her—then she'd ask him.

22

What do you think?" A young woman with peacock-feather earrings and jet black hair held up a long-sleeved beaded wedding dress and draped it across her front, chunky bangle bracelets sliding and clacking toward her elbow.

Ivy stepped closer to the wall. She was supposed to meet Sara and go over music ideas, not dole out fashion advice to bohemian strangers. "I don't work here."

"You're Marilyn's daughter, aren't you? And a model. Fashion sense is in your blood."

"I'm not Marilyn's daughter."

"She sure talks about you like you are." The woman poked her leather sandal out from beneath the bottom of the wedding dress and examined the glint of light off the beads in one of the boutique's many mirrors. "Be honest. What do you think?"

Ivy bit her thumbnail. The woman had fabulous arms. Tanned and toned, but not overly muscular. Why would she want to cover them up? Ivy stepped up to one of the racks and pulled out a different dress—a sleeveless gown that wrapped over one shoulder.

"You okay over there, Arabella?" Marilyn called, pinning a long veil onto a mannequin.

"Fine, Mare. Your daughter's helping me out."

Ivy took the sleeved dress from the black-haired woman a little more forcefully than intended and returned it to the rack.

The woman hitched her oversized purse over her arm and extended her hand. "Arabella Armstrong. No relation to the biker-turned-villain or the astronaut. But I am related to Doc. You know Doc, I'm sure. Everybody does."

"No, I don't." Ivy shook Arabella's hand. "I'm Ivy Clark."

Arabella squeezed her palm like a quick, strong heartbeat. "Not Olsen?"

"I told you, Marilyn's not my mom." Renee Clark was her mother, and Ivy had never once considered taking James's last name. She shoved the shoulder-strap dress at Arabella. "When's your wedding?"

"No wedding planned yet. No man, either. But that ain't stopping this gal from having her fun." Arabella wiggled thick black eyebrows. "When Prince Charming shows up, the perfect wedding dress will be one less thing to worry about, you know?"

Ivy didn't know. She didn't believe in Prince Charming.

Arabella saluted and made her way toward the dressing rooms, peasant skirt fluttering around her ankles. Ivy pushed her face against the windowed front door and peered down the street, willing Sara to materialize. Last night it had seemed Sara needed some reassurance regarding her music selections, and since Ivy needed to resume the Davis Knight excavation, she'd started over Frogmore stew, meeting up was a win-win.

Sara came into view, struggling with a box in one hand, holding Sunny's harness with the other. Ivy met her at the door and relieved her of the heavy bundle.

"Sorry I'm late. We lost track of time at the tutoring center. I'm finally starting to get the hang of Braille. I never thought I'd say it, but it's kind of exciting."

Ivy brought the box to the leather sofa by the display window and set it on the ground. "Haven't you heard of an iPod?" she said, rummaging through dusty record jackets. "I didn't even know cassette tapes and record albums existed anymore." She pulled out a CD case. "Even these are endangered species."

"I have a lot of songs on my laptop, but there's something about holding the music in my hands. And besides, we Knights never throw anything away." Sara crouched low and patted the ground for the box. Her fingers brushed against Ivy's. "Marilyn loves Big Band music. I was thinking we'd go that route. Classy and wedding-ish, but also high energy."

"Sounds perfect."

"Like Count Basie. Have you heard 'One O'Clock Jump'?"

"Nope."

"It's a blue CD case with black lettering." Sara stood and gave a soft-toned command to Sunny who led her to the register. She fumbled around underneath the counter and came back with a CD player, stopping when her toe touched the box. She let her fingers walk the wall until she found the outlet, plugged in the player, and held out her hand for Ivy to hand her the correct CD.

"What's up with the rubber bands?" Ivy asked. There was at least one strapped around every single CD case. Some had as many as ten.

"I'm trying to come up with a system so I know which CD is which, but I haven't perfected it yet." Sara removed three rubber bands and slid the CD into place. When the music came out of the speakers, Sara tapped her foot to the beat.

"Oh, can all y'all turn that up? Best song ever." Arabella had stepped out from the dressing room and did an odd sort of wiggle with her body. Ivy's insides warmed. Not because of the dance, but because of the dress. Ivy had chosen well. It looked amazing. "Gotta love Bing Crosby," Arabella said.

Sara turned up the music. "It's Count Basie, Bella."

"Toe-may-toe, toe-mah-toe."

"More like tomato, rutabaga," Sara mumbled.

Ivy laughed.

Arabella did another wiggle, then gave Ivy two thumbs up. "Are you a fashionista or what? This is the dress. I'm putting it on permanent hold, and maybe my Prince Charming will find me soon so I can move out of Doc's house. A girl my age shouldn't be living with her daddy." She hitched her thumb toward Ivy. "Mare, what are you paying your girl?"

Marilyn winked from across the boutique. "Not enough."

Ivy looked at the floor, her cheeks warm.

"I heard the funniest rumor from Lena Bully—horrible last name, isn't it? We were in line at Gumbo's Grocer, both of us buying pickles, when she tells me Davis is engaged. But that's not what got me laughing. She hands her pickles to the clerk and says he's engaged to his cousin. And I said, well, this wouldn't be the first time two cousins got married. But then I thought, No, Davis wouldn't propose to his cousin."

"Ivy isn't our cousin." Sara pushed aside a stack of cassette tapes bundled together. "At least not by blood."

"It's a rumor, anyway," Ivy said. One she started to get under Davis's skin. She had no idea it would eventually get under her own.

"Well, that's a relief. My friend Connie—you remember Connie, don't you?" Arabella turned from the mirror and pointed her words at Sara. "Davis's old sweetheart? She would never say it, but if she got wind that Davis had dropped down on one knee for another woman, she'd be flat-out devastated."

Ivy's attention perked. Davis's old sweetheart?

The song ended.

Marilyn shuffled Arabella into the dressing room.

Another song came and went. The CD spun inside the player. Arabella came back out, dressed in her regular clothes, and stopped in front of a display case of necklaces. Hangers scraped against metal as a customer browsed around the far side of the boutique.

Sara tucked a strand of limp hair behind her ear. "Do you like my brother?"

"Like him?"

"I'm trying to figure out why you started that rumor. Is it because you have feelings for him? Were you trying to prove something?"

"I started the rumor because I was bored." Ivy crossed one leg over the other and bobbed her foot. Arabella's comment about Davis's old flame had flung the door to Ivy's curiosity wide open. "Does your brother ever date?"

"You mean girls?"

"Well, he doesn't date men, does he?" Although that *would* explain his lack of interest.

Arabella laughed, slowly turning a display case of necklaces. "If Davis is gay, then he sure fooled Connie."

"Davis is not gay," Sara said, adjusting extra large rubber bands wrapped around an old album. "Please don't start that rumor."

Arabella clasped a rhinestone choker around her neck. "Hey, you have a birthday coming up, don't you?"

Sara put the album in the box. "Over a month away, but Marilyn's already planning a surprise party for me. You can come if you want."

Arabella unclasped the necklace. "It's at my restaurant, honey."

"How is it a surprise if you know about it?" Ivy asked.

"This is Greenbrier. Secrets don't exist. But people like to pretend they do." Arabella brought her white-framed sunglasses over her eyes. "Sara, you make sure Marilyn keeps that dress on hold for me. I'll never find anything more perfect."

"Will do."

Arabella wiggled her fingers and stepped out of the boutique.

Sara held up another CD. "Is this Ella Fitzgerald?"

"Yes." Ivy tucked her hair behind her ear. "So, this Connie woman. What's she like?"

"She goes to our church and writes for the *Greenbrier Tribune.*"

"And she's still in love with your brother?"

"I'm sure Arabella was exaggerating. They dated a while ago."

Ivy wondered how much digging she could get away with before Sara's suspicion reached its threshold. She watched as Sara swapped CDs from the player, returned Count Basie to his case, and wrapped it with three rubber bands. "Who does your brother date these days?"

"He doesn't really."

Ivy laughed. "A good-looking bachelor like Davis? Of course he does."

"As far as I know, he hasn't dated anyone since he came home from New York."

Ivy's jaw dropped. "You mean to tell me he hasn't dated in two years?"

Sara shrugged. "Not that I know of."

Ivy scooted to the edge of her seat, remembering the hot-and-cold game she and Mom used to play. Hot. She was getting very, very hot. "I don't understand why he left. I mean, he's amazing at photography and he just got that job with *Vogue.*"

Sara dropped the CD into the box. "It's a long story."

Something clicked like two puzzle pieces coming together—Sara's blindness. Davis returning. "He came back to take care of you, didn't he?" That sounded one hundred percent Davis. Only he would throw away his career and abandon his dreams for his beloved sister.

Sara's fingers wrestled in her lap.

"It's okay. You can tell me," Ivy said.

"Maybe you should ask him. It's more his story than mine anymore." Sara sighed. "He and I see my blindness differently. At least we do now."

"What do you mean?"

"He thinks it's an affliction. I've come to see some blessing in it."

The words roused Ivy's skepticism. "Blessing?"

"Don't get me wrong. It's not easy. In fact, I have plenty of moments when I still hate it. There are times I miss seeing so badly that I don't want to face a dark world one more day." Sara pulled a rubber band onto her wrist and stretched it with her thumb. "But good has come out of it too."

Ivy shook her head. What good could come out of Sara losing her eyesight? "I don't understand."

"Before, when I could see"—Sara stretched the rubber band farther—"I had everything planned out. I knew exactly where I was headed. After college, I'd spend some time in France. Study watercolor. Gain some experience and move back to Greenbrier. Rent the studio above an art gallery in Hilton Head and sell my pieces there. The owner already loved my work and promised to show it." Sara recited her long-ago plans without inflection.

"But you lost all of that. Blindness stole everything." Ivy failed to see the blessing.

"I know. I was angry for a long time. I lashed out and blamed a lot of people. I said a lot of hurtful things." Sara's brow wrinkled. "For the first time in my life, I wasn't comfortable here anymore."

"Here?"

"This world. I longed to see. I longed to paint. And then I realized..." Sara stopped stretching the rubber band.

Ivy scooted to the edge of the couch. What? What did she realize?

"This world was never meant to be comfortable. It was never meant to feel like home. It took darkness to show me truth."

"What truth?"

"I will see again. One day, I'll open my eyes and I'll see Jesus. I'll see my Savior." Sara's face radiated with a determination, an assurance Ivy had never seen before. "He's saving my sight for that day. When I'm finally home."

Goose bumps crawled up Ivy's arms. *Home.* The word reverberated inside her like a giant gong, echoing in the empty places of her soul. Sara said that word with such conviction, as if she held it to her chest with a white-knuckled grip.

"It's brought about other things too. Like starting to teach piano lessons. I never would have done that if I could see, which means I never would have met Twila—one of my students. I never would have considered becoming a music teacher either." Sara set her hands on her knees. "And strangely enough, I see people better this way."

"See people better?" How was that possible?

"The physical doesn't get in the way."

Sara's face shone like the moon reflecting the sun. It radiated an assurance and a simplicity more beautiful than any pose or any look Ivy could ever give a camera. Somehow, Sara's beauty worked from the inside out. Ivy nudged the box of music with her toe. She should be putting together a plan of attack, a strategy for getting Davis to New York. But her mind couldn't focus. It kept repeating that one word—*home.* The kind of home Sara talked about was a home Ivy had never known.

23

Charlie's Crab Hut overflowed with chatter and the smell of seafood, especially at noon hour. Davis slid a saltshaker back and forth across the table, volleying it from palm to palm like a hockey puck. Sara gave her order to Becky-Sue Bruckle, who was working very hard to catch the dim lighting with her engagement ring.

Sara stopped midsentence and addressed him. "You okay?"

He sent the saltshaker sliding toward the pepper. It hit the wall, tottered, but remained standing. "I'm good." This, of course, was a lie. He was tired. Last night the same two words hovered over his sleep—*see her.* He'd tossed and turned, his thoughts forming pictures in his mind, a whole photo album of Ivy Clark—broken Ivy at James's funeral, untouchable Ivy at the luncheon afterward, tearful Ivy on the beach, hungry Ivy when she tried kissing him after the last photo shoot. Once he finished with the pictures, his thoughts turned to his camera, and right when he was on the cusp of sleep, they reeled him two years into the past like a kick to the groin and the whole thing started all over again. He plucked a menu from the caddy. "I'll take the shrimp and grits. Heavy on the gravy."

Becky-Sue didn't write anything down. "Got it. I'll be right back with your drinks."

As soon as she left, Sara spread her napkin on her lap. "Davis, are you sure you're okay?"

"Yeah, sure. Maybe a little tired." He folded his hand on the table. "Now, do I flatter myself into thinking you simply wanted to eat lunch with your big brother or is there something specific on the agenda?"

"Both."

"Okay."

Sara's face lit up. "Ivy and I sat in Something New for almost two hours yesterday listening to Benny Goodman. Can you believe she'd never heard of him before? She thinks I made some really good choices for the fashion show."

So Ivy was the agenda. Davis's unease doubled. As much as he wanted to give Ivy the benefit of the doubt, he couldn't quite shake the feeling that she was after something. That she had a reason for hanging around Greenbrier, one that was bigger than boredom or convenience.

"Do you know she's walked in over fifty fashion shows? Can you believe that? She's been to almost every place on the map. Russia. Tokyo. Australia. She thinks that if we do a good job getting the word out, this show could turn into something really big. Well, big for Greenbrier anyway."

"Sara, you should be careful."

She dipped her chin. "Be careful about what?"

"I don't want you to get too attached to Ivy." Sara loved too easily, gave her heart too readily. He didn't want to see her get hurt. Especially not as a result of his photography.

"I like her."

"She's going to leave as soon as the show is over." He grabbed the saltshaker again and resumed his volleying. "I think she's after something—from me in particular."

"Maybe she genuinely likes you. Did you ever think about that?"

Nothing about her kiss had been genuine. "I doubt it."

"I think she likes you, Davis. I really do. I mean, yesterday she was asking about what kind of women you've dated."

His wariness quadrupled. Ivy was digging and using Sara as her shovel. "Do me a favor, Sara. Next time Ivy asks about my love life, defer her questions to me. I don't want you getting dragged into the middle of this, whatever this is."

Sara petted the top of Sunny's head. He panted by her chair, probably overheated from the cramped restaurant. Davis continued his saltshaker hockey game, lost in thought, until Becky-Sue set two tall glasses of iced tea, extra sweet, on the table, placing Sara's at her fingertips. "Your food will be out in a couple minutes. Enjoy your drinks."

"Thanks, Becky," Sara said.

Davis peeled the paper away from his straw and poked it through the ice. He wrapped his fingers around the glass, cool and damp from condensation, and took a long pull from the straw.

"Something about her makes me sad," Sara said.

Davis took another drink. So Sara had noticed it too.

"I asked her about her childhood last night. She didn't have much to say."

"That's because she didn't have much of a childhood." At least not from what Davis could gather.

"I know. Don't you think that's sad?"

Of course he did. It agitated faults in his chest that were better left intact. It made him want to reach out his arms and save her. But Ivy gave no indication that she wanted to be saved. And even if she had, his arms weren't sufficient.

"Remember how you, me, and Dad would go hiking in the mountains when we lived in Telluride? Or how, when we moved here, Grandpa took us sailing and Jet Skiing? We'd dig for clams with no shoes on or chase fireflies out on the dock and pretend gators were going to bite off our toes."

Davis smiled. He couldn't help it. "Grandma Eleanor told you that story about her cousin who lost his pinky toe to a giant crab, and you wouldn't swim in the marsh for two years."

"I like my pinky toes." Sara reached her hand across the table and felt for his knuckles. "Ivy never had a childhood like that, Davis. She didn't get to run on the beach or collect seashells or squish her feet into pluff mud."

"What's your point?"

"We should give her some of those experiences."

"Sara, she's twenty-four years old."

"So? Who says you have to be a kid to have childlike fun? C'mon, Davis.

Shouldn't Ivy get to experience awe? The kind we felt as kids, when we looked at the sunset or pried open a clamshell or found a nest of sea turtles." She squeezed his hand. "Let's help her feel awe. Let's help her see God's beauty."

Sara's words sounded so much like Dad's. So much so that they hurt.

Becky-Sue set two plates in front of them. Shrimp and gravy for Davis. Fried chicken for Sara. "You two need anything else? Drink refills? An extra side of gravy?"

"No, we're good. Thanks."

Sara felt for her fork. She picked it up and scooped some mashed potatoes. Davis watched, amazed. His sister had come so far—especially in the past year. She was almost as independent as she'd been before the accident. She chewed her food and swallowed. "Grandpa says there's a new moon tomorrow."

Davis shoved a bite of shrimp into his mouth.

"You know what that means, don't you?"

"Spring tide."

"The perfect time for some old-fashioned crabbing."

Davis watched Ivy take in the scenery, strands of hair feathering her bare shoulders. Her gaze extended past the courtyard in Marilyn's backyard to the dock that led out to the salt marsh. The wide mud path had morphed into a sparkling waterway. "As a kid, I never understood where all the water came from."

"Just wait until it recedes." Two small buckets clanked in Sara's right hand while her left held on to Sunny's harness. Jeans rolled and cuffed halfway up her calves as her flip-flops slapped against the soles of her feet. The image she created elicited long-ago memories, before New York and blindness had stolen their dreams. "Creates a fun current for boaters."

"And we're going to catch crabs?" Skepticism and a tinge of fear formed Ivy's words.

Davis readjusted his grip on the container of crab bait and the net he'd rummaged from Marilyn's storage shed and fought off the smile creeping across his lips. "Don't look so nervous, Clark. They won't bite." He'd come for Sara. She was determined to give Ivy a childhood experience, and he refused to leave his sister alone with Ivy Clark on a dock near the water—not only in danger physically, but emotionally too. "I was more concerned with the pinching."

"C'mon. You can't bail now." Davis thumped Ivy on the back. "You're holding the peaches." He followed Sara and Sunny toward the edge of the dock, determined to keep things light. The wooden slats swayed along with the water, reeds growing underneath and sticking through the cracks like feet ticklers. He looked over his shoulder. Ivy had stopped short of the dock, clutching a brown paper sack with three ripe peaches tucked inside.

"Uh, Dave, not sure if you remember the Primrose Plantation or not, but didn't the tour guide say something about alligators in the marshes that surrounded the rice plantation?"

"I promise I won't let any gators get you."

Birds chirped behind her. The sun played peekaboo between the pines on the other side of the marsh as Davis padded along the sun-warmed wood. The water splashed and gurgled over hidden pluff mud, diluting the sulfuric odor. Nature surrounded Ivy on three sides, turning her into a reluctant peninsula. Davis removed his Nikon from the knapsack he'd slung over his shoulder. He itched to turn it on and capture the image, but this had nothing to do with raising money for an art program. And hardly anyone carried around a real camera anymore. He certainly didn't. So what excuse did he have for bringing it?

Sara used her bare foot to feel for the edge of the dock, found it, then sat down and dipped her toes into the water, creating a decoration of ripples over its surface. Sunny plopped onto his hind quarters beside her. Davis set the bait down.

"Uh, Sara…" Ivy straddled the dock, one foot on grass, the other on wood. "You do know we're about to pull crabs out of that water, don't you?"

Sara jerked her toes up and yelped.

Ivy lunged forward, as if she might save his sister from a giant toe-eating blue crab.

Davis laughed.

Sara plunked her feet back in. "Lucky for me, they prefer smellier bait."

With hesitant steps, Ivy joined them. She looked over Davis's shoulder, inside the container, then lurched back, cupping her hand over her mouth and nose. "What in the world is that?"

"Chicken necks and fish heads."

She pressed her other hand against her stomach. "So glad I asked."

"The crabs love 'em." He reached inside the container, scooped up a fish head, and tied it to the end of the string Sara had pulled from her bucket.

Ivy looked away. "Remind me why we're doing this again."

"Because it's fun," Sara said. "We haven't gone crabbing in forever. We used to do it almost every spring tide as kids, didn't we, Davis?"

He finished his handiwork. "Sounds about right." With a nine-year gap between them, Sara lived the bulk of her childhood in South Carolina, while Davis had lived the majority of his in Telluride. He was sixteen when he became a southerner, which meant he couldn't muster the same level of nostalgia or enthusiasm as his sister.

"And now what? You have a strong urge to recreate the past?" Ivy scrunched her nose at the bait container.

"We thought you might as well enjoy yourself while you're here." Sara splashed her toes and petted Sunny's head. The dog lay beside her, eyes half-closed as he leaned into Sara's scratching.

"I'm more of a 'find my enjoyment at a bookstore' kinda girl. Or a club. Not so much into nature." She swatted at a mosquito on her shin and missed.

Crouching on one knee, his other bent at a right angle, Davis felt in the back pocket of his board shorts, pulled out a swiss army knife, and cut some of the string. He tied the end of it on a dowel and tossed the line over the dock. It plunked into the water with a small splash and sunk with the weight of the bait.

"Um, Sara," Ivy said, "now might be the time to take your feet out of the water."

Sara brought her feet onto the dock and sat with crossed legs. "If it makes you feel better. But trust me, the crabs won't care about my toes with those little delicacies down there."

Ivy set the peaches in Sara's lap and sat down. "How will we know if we catch one?"

"If there's a tug on the line, we'll bring it up and see." Sara unharnessed Sunny and gave him a couple pats. "You're off the clock, boy. Davis will look out for me."

Heaviness gathered on top of Davis's shoulders and pressed him onto the dock. How could his sister have such confidence in him after his failure to look out for her in the past? He pushed the memories away, attached five more strings to dowels, tied the bait, and dropped them overboard until the dock looked like a long wooden insect with spindly white legs standing on water.

He washed off his hands and sat by Ivy's side as a light breeze rippled over the marsh. The sweetness of honeysuckle and wild mint rode the breeze's coattails, stirring Ivy's lilac perfume. It was a smell he was growing accustomed to.

"So what do we do now?"

Sara opened the brown sack, pulled out a peach, and offered it to the air. "We wait."

Davis took the fruit and bit into its fuzzy flesh, filling his mouth with peach juice and sweetness. He couldn't help shaking his head. Three grown-ups perched on a dock like school kids. What was he doing? He took another bite as the fluttering of butterfly wings captured his attention. Two beautifully patterned monarchs tangoed in midair, swooping and swirling over the water, one chasing the other as it tried to get away. Sara loved butterflies. She used to chase them in their backyard in Colorado. Sunny sat up, ears perked, like he had a mind to jump in after them.

Sara cocked her head and handed the second peach to Ivy. "Did we catch something?"

"Sunny's about to. He found two butterflies."

Sara took out the last peach and brought it beneath her nose. "Tell me about them."

Davis swallowed another bite. "Orange and black. One's larger than the other."

His sister closed her eyes as if gathering the details and painting a picture in her mind.

He leaned forward, desperate to help her paint it. "One's chasing the other. The other one's playing hard to get, but the big one isn't giving up. They're sort of swooping over the water and Sunny wants to taste them."

Sara pulled Sunny back. "I love butterflies."

He didn't miss the longing in her voice. It pinged around inside his chest like a loose pinball. *I'd give her my eyes if I could, Lord.*

The sun dipped behind the pines and cast yellow and pink sparkles over the water's surface. Sadness flickered across Ivy's brow as the butterflies fluttered close, around her head, then swooped back toward the water. He sure would like to know what she was thinking.

"I'm glad God's like those butterflies and not like that crab bait," Sara said.

Davis took another bite of his peach and wiped at the juice dribbling down his chin.

Ivy raised an eyebrow. "You're glad God's not like a bloody chicken neck?"

He chuckled.

"I'm glad God doesn't plunk Himself into the water and wait for us to find Him. I'm glad He chases us like that butterfly."

Ivy frowned.

The larger butterfly twirled with the smaller, but the smaller twisted away with a flutter of wings and lifted higher into the air. Davis fiddled with the camera strapped around his neck. Did Ivy know God pursued her?

"He loves us too much to leave it up to us to catch His scent. Right, Davis?"

He tipped his face toward the sun. Sara was right. God loved Ivy too much to let her languish in a world of empty dreams. But she ran so fast. And like that smaller butterfly, she didn't want to be caught.

"Fear not, for I have redeemed you," Sara said. "I have called you by name, you are mine."

Ivy tore her gaze from the winged insects and turned her eyes toward his, as if he'd spoken those words instead of Sara. The look on her face pinched a spot inside his chest. *You are His, Ivy. Not mine. Not Bruce's. Not the world's. But His. Do you know that?*

He bit the inside of his cheek. How could she when nobody had ever shown her God's love? Not her father. Certainly not the men who treated her like an object.

Ivy blinked several times, breaking their stare. "Where'd you hear that, Sara?"

"From God."

A seed of a smile planted in the corner of Ivy's mouth. "The two of you speak, huh?"

"He speaks to everyone."

The smile didn't germinate. "Trust me, Sara. God doesn't speak to people like me."

"Yes, He does. All you have to do is pick up the Bible and listen." Sara tilted her head toward the sky. "That verse was from the book of Isaiah."

The skin between Ivy's eyebrows puckered.

One of the strings jerked.

Tossing the remainder of his peach in the water, Davis pushed himself up to crouching and wound the string around the dowel. "Ivy, could you get the net?"

Sara came to her knees. "Did we catch one?"

"We caught something," Davis said, pulling up the line.

Ivy grabbed the net resting near the basket as a blue crab came into view.

"Bring it underneath it so we can scoop it up."

She looked at the net gripped in her hand, then at the spastic crab. "Are you crazy?"

"It's fun, Ivy, I promise," Sara urged.

Ivy took a hesitant step forward and reached out the net. The crab plopped inside. Ivy squealed. The angry crustacean snapped its pincers. The net bobbed and jerked in her hands. "Davis!" She held it out from her body, like she might fling the whole thing into the water. Smiling, he tied another fish head to the string and returned it to the bottom of the marsh. Then he rescued her. He took the net and reached inside.

Ivy yelped and squeezed her eyelids shut. "Oh my goodness, what are you doing? You're going to lose a finger."

"Checking to see the sex." Davis held the flailing crab in his hand the way Grandfather had taught him, so he wouldn't get pinched. A male. He plunked it inside the bucket just as another string jerked. He reeled it in, only this time it was a female, so he returned it to the water. "We don't want to keep the females. Not if we want to keep eating crab."

On the third catch, he set the crab on top of the wooden planks. The animal scuttled along the wood. Sunny squirmed as Sara held him back. Ivy jumped behind Davis and gripped the thin fabric of his T-shirt.

Davis laughed. Sara joined. Before the crab scuttled too far, he scooped it up and put it in the bucket. Ivy let go of his shirt. When both buckets were filled and the bait was gone, Davis balled the string and stuffed it in his pocket.

"Now what?" Ivy asked.

"Now we eat."

"Phew, I'm hot." Sara wiped her forehead and put Sunny's harness back on. "I don't know about you, but I could use a swim." And before he could object, before he could stop her, she gave Sunny a command and both of them jumped off the end of the dock, where the water was deepest.

Ivy gasped.

Davis stepped to the edge of the dock, but quicker than he could dive in after her, Sara resurfaced, giggling and treading water as she held on to Sunny's neck. "Aren't you two hot?"

His fear morphed into a jolt of unexpected playfulness.

Ivy came to his side. "Do something before she gets eaten by an alligator."

He hid his smile and peeked over the edge. "The gators around here are pretty small."

"Says the man who's not in the marsh. Are you nuts?" She flapped her arm toward Sara. "Your sister can't see."

Davis looked at Sara, laughing with Sunny, surrounded by sparkling water. He pulled his camera off his neck and set it on the dock. "You want me to go get her?"

"I don't want you to stand here and talk about it, that's for sure."

A slow grin took hold of his lips.

Ivy took a step back. "What?"

"Why don't you come with me?" And before she could protest, before she could take one more step away, he grabbed her around the waist and jumped in.

24

Steam rose from the shower as Ivy peeled off wet, mucky clothes and let them splat in a small pile in the corner of the bathroom. She stepped underneath the stream and watched black mud and gunk rinse from her legs and swirl around the drain. She'd never been so filthy or smelly in her life. She'd never had so much fun either. Maybe if she'd known how enjoyable crabbing could be, she would have listened to Marilyn's encouragement all those years ago and joined the neighborhood kids. Ivy closed her eyes and let the spray cover her face, trying to forget the feel of Davis's strong arms wrapped around her waist in the water and the low baritone of his laughter as she tried not to panic at the thought of crabs pinching her toes and alligators hiding in the reeds.

She didn't know what was more disconcerting—the slick, foul-smelling mud sucking off one of her favorite sandals, or the way her insides wobbled when Davis pulled her out of it. She batted away her emotions and moved her focus to Vera Wang. She kept her mind centered on high fashion as she cleaned, shampooed, and toweled herself dry. The air conditioner rattled and blew from the vent near her feet, prickling her skin. She wrapped herself in a thin cotton robe and rubbed her arms.

I have called you by name, you are Mine.

The words came uninvited, making her heart beat like a bass drum in the pit of her stomach. What would it feel like to belong to somebody as big as God, to hear the creator of the universe call her, Ivy Clark, by name? She picked up her wide-toothed comb and got to work detangling her hair. If only she could comb away the useless wish knotting in her chest. God wanted people like Sara—innocent and sweet and pure. God didn't want people like

Ivy. With a mistress for a mother and an adulterer for a father. Someone who'd given away her virginity at the eager age of fourteen. Someone with scars and pockmarks staining her insides. She knew enough about Sara's faith to know God wouldn't want anything to do with someone like her.

Her cell phone chirped in the other room. Ivy padded across marble flooring onto plush carpet and swiped it off the nightstand.

Bruce.

She answered on the second ring.

"How's my favorite niece?"

His only niece.

"Tell me, how are things going? Has Davis agreed to come back yet?"

His question dropped like an anchor through her body. "I'm working on it."

"You'd better work faster. I talked to Juliette yesterday to agree on some dates. Sounds like she's more obsessed with having Davis than she is about having you."

"Gee, that's nice to hear."

"Just keeping it real. Do you think he'll come back to do the shoot? Should I talk to him? Or maybe put him in contact with Jul—"

"No!"

Silence.

Ivy flushed. She hadn't meant to sound so dramatic, but that was exactly the wrong thing to do. "Trust me, Bruce, this is a sensitive matter. If you call him or Juliette calls him, he'll never agree. Just let me work on it, okay?"

"But you can convince him, right?"

Ivy grabbed onto the tie of her robe, her skin warm with the memory of Davis's hand holding hers, yanking her from the mud, laughing as Sunny shook and sprayed them both with mucky swamp water. The knotted wish in her chest pulled tighter. She'd planned on going crabbing because Davis was going, and in order to convince him to return to New York, she had to spend time with him. What she hadn't planned on was enjoying herself so much. She bit her thumbnail.

"Ivy? You there?"

"Yeah, I can convince him."

"Good. Start working that magic of yours. The quicker the better. You only have a month and a half before the Vera Wang shoot."

Her stomach turned a cartwheel. She nodded into the phone, then spotted something white tucked beneath the door that led into the hallway. She walked over and picked it up, the card crisp and heavy in her hands. She frowned at the *For You* scrawled in untidy letters across the front. "Hey, Bruce, since I have your ear, let's talk about fashion week."

"It's in a month."

"I know. Who am I walking for?"

He sighed. "Ivy, you're not walking this year."

"Why not?"

"Nobody wants you."

She set the card on the dresser.

"Look, don't focus on that, okay? Focus on Vera Wang. That's your ticket."

Ticket for what—another contract, an opened door? And then the shoot would wrap and then what? She'd be scrambling for another job, holding on even tighter. Soon she would turn twenty-five. And after that, twenty-six. Time kept marching onward. What was she supposed to do when it all ended? All of a sudden, it felt so futile. Like catching wind in a jar.

She mumbled a lame good-bye and set the phone in between the mysterious card and the new bouquet of flowers Marilyn brought her on Monday. So far, Ivy had three bouquets wrapped and hanging upside down in her room. Drying and dying. She ran her finger over the smooth curve of her Eiffel Tower snow globe, then spread her fingers over top of Marilyn's cedar box. The one she'd foolishly hoped belonged to her father.

Ivy blinked at the card, then got to work opening it up. Inside, she found a short note written in a childlike scrawl.

"Fear not, for I have redeemed you; I have called you by name, you are mine." Isaiah 43:1. God wrote these words for you, Ivy.
Love, Sara.

Redeemed.

The first time Ivy heard that word was after her first day of second grade. Alarmed when Mom didn't meet her at the bus stop like she usually did, she'd raced up seven flights of stairs, too worried to wait for the elevator, and found her mother in her pajamas, sitting in the corner of the couch with her knees drawn to her chest, tears streaming down her cheeks as she watched a beefy black man in a fancy black suit speak from their television set.

"You are redeemed! He can redeem! He will redeem!"

The more amens and hallelujahs that chorused from the crowd, the more guttural his voice became, and every time he used that word, Mama's tears ran quicker. *Redeem.* Ivy sat on the couch by her mom, rubbing her back, handing her tissues until the box was empty and the man was finished and a commercial about Kentucky Fried Chicken took over the screen. It wasn't until later, after her mother was tucked into bed, that Ivy found the word in the dictionary.

Redeem: to buy back; to gain or regain possession of.

Her little-girl self wasn't sure why a word like that would make Mama cry. All she knew was that the longer James stayed away, the sadder her mother became. And he hadn't visited in a long, long time.

Ivy tucked Sara's card inside Marilyn's box. She closed her eyes, wanting darkness. Instead, the image of two butterflies swooped behind her lids. Try as she might, she couldn't get them out of her head.

Young women of all shapes and sizes lined the front wall of Something New. Ivy sat in a chair sandwiched between two empty ones as Davis and Marilyn mingled. Ivy crossed her arms and legs and tapped an impatient rhythm against the floor. She had suggested putting an ad in the paper, calling for local models to walk in the show. Why hire out professionals for a local charity event? It would cost unnecessary money. Anyway, the more they could involve the people of Greenbrier, the more people would attend.

One small problem.

They only needed seven models, and half the town had showed up. At least the female half. And if there were any diamonds in the rough, they hid themselves well. She scowled at an old woman sporting gray roots, bubblegum pink lipstick, a tattooed anklet, and a pair of aquamarine clogs. Seriously? Did the woman really think they'd dress her in one of Marilyn's bridal gowns and send her stumbling down the runway?

Davis listened to a short blonde jabbering in his ear. She stood between a familiar young redhead—the girl Ivy had used to start the engagement rumor—and the bohemian Arabella. As if sensing her stare, Davis looked at her. His smile came with ease. Hers, not so much. He waved a temporary good-bye at the trio of women and took the seat next to hers.

"So guess what? Rachel Piper's fiancée is Kipper Manning, an anchorman for the local news. She said she might be able to get him to run a story about the fashion show. And Connie West, she's that blonde over there, wants to meet us tonight at the oyster roast and run a story in the *Greenbrier Tribune.* I think they just want to be in the show, but hey, if it gets the word out, we'll take it, right?"

Connie West—as in Davis's old sweetheart? No wonder the blonde was eying Ivy so suspiciously.

"Hey, you okay?"

She would be once she convinced him to go to New York with her. Two days after Bruce's phone call and his warning still echoed through her mind. Vera Wang wanted Davis more than her. Ivy needed him to come. "We shouldn't have put an ad in the paper. It was a stupid idea."

Arabella waved from across the room—shiny black hair hanging straight down her back, fingernails painted lime green, athletic build, killer arms. Maybe thirty, give or take a few years. Ivy tucked the tip of her pen beneath her chin and looked closer. Nice jaw line. Not a gorgeous face, but then most models didn't have gorgeous faces so much as interesting ones. Ivy was an exception. Arabella obviously loved wedding dresses. She'd never make it in New York, but what about a fashion show in Greenbrier?

"Over half these women look like grandmas," she mumbled.

"It's Greenbrier's first fashion show. Can you blame them for wanting to be a part of it?"

Ivy flicked her pen at Arabella. "What do you think about her?"

"She lives with her father—Doc Armstrong—in one of those big antebellum homes off the strip. Kitchen manager for Hoppin' John's Café. Nice. A little quirky. I think she'd be a good model for you."

"I like her face." Ivy scanned the rest of the women. Young. Old. Somewhere in between. Sneaking not-so-subtle glances in her direction, all twittering with excitement. And why—because they wanted to be models for a day? Didn't they realize? One small-town fashion show—or even a big city one—wouldn't change a thing. At the end of the day, they'd still be the same.

"Ivy?"

"What?"

"Seriously…are you okay?"

The events from their crabbing adventure on Thursday slurped through her memory. *"God speaks to everyone… Nobody wants you… Juliette's more obsessed with having Davis than you… God speaks to everyone… God wrote those words for you...*" She shook the words away and attempted to rally. "Never been better."

"You want to go outside? Get some fresh air?"

His questions and the compassionate way he asked them make her want to pull out her hair. She didn't need sweet and concerned. Those emotions wouldn't get him to New York. "Fresh air isn't what I need, Dave."

He pulled at his jaw—tan and scruffy from a day-old beard. "Did something happen over the last couple days? I mean, you were actually having a good time on Thursday, or at least it seemed like it. But now you look like you're either going to punch me in the face or get sick."

"Thanks."

"Come on, Ivy. What's bothering you?"

"Did you think a day of playing in the mud would make everything better?" She stood. "Jumping in the marsh and watching butterflies and listening to your sister quote the Bible isn't going to fix me, okay?"

He touched her elbow. "Ivy, wait..."

She jerked away.

He held up his hands, showing her his palms. "I want to know why you're upset."

There was no way she could explain it to him when she couldn't tease it apart herself. Her mood was the result of a whole jumble of things—Bruce's phone call, Sara's card, Marilyn's flowers, Davis treating her like a lady when they both knew she didn't deserve it—for heaven's sake, why couldn't he act like a normal guy?—Annalise dying, that stupid box of pictures. If only one of those things had gone differently, maybe she wouldn't be in such a rotten mood today. She wanted to spill all the if-onlys onto the floor and stamp them with her feet. But she couldn't. And treating Davis like a heel wouldn't solve a thing.

She rubbed the back of her neck, then ran her fingers through her hair. "Ignore me. I'm tired. I have a headache. And I don't like the idea of turning all these women away. We only need seven models."

His face softened. "You won't crush their world by turning them away. They're just fixing to have some fun and chew the fat. That's all."

She looked at all the smiling, excited women. Had she ever, even once, looked that way on a go-see? Ivy shook her head and looked at the ground. No. Not once. Getting turned away might not crush them, but it had always crushed her.

25

Davis straightened the collar of his polo shirt and opened the front door of Marilyn's home. He came to pick up Sara and Ivy for the oyster roast. Joe Bodgen had one every year in mid-August at the marina, before the kids of Greenbrier went back to school. Davis promised to meet Connie there and discuss the fashion show so she could run a story in the paper. Between that and stealing some time on the evening news, this fashion show might actually turn into a pretty big deal.

Preparing himself for Ivy's dark mood, he stepped inside the foyer as two long legs appeared at the top of the stairs. A few steps later and the rest of Ivy came into view. All five feet ten inches of her. Wearing dark khaki shorts cuffed at the hem and a flowy-looking white top that dipped over one of her shoulders. Her hair was pulled up into a messy bun, she wore long navy blue earrings, and she carried a pair of shoes in either hand. "Your sister's sick."

Worry had him stepping forward.

Ivy held up her arms. "Whoa there, Fido. No need to pop a blood vessel. It's a minor head cold. Probably from that swim in the marsh." She descended the final stair. "Marilyn made soup and brought home an entire medicine aisle from Walmart."

He relaxed for a second before realizing what this meant. An evening alone with Ivy? He wasn't sure he was up for that particular challenge.

"So that leaves me and you." She winked, but something in her voice fell flat. She said and did the usual thing, but with an emptiness that tugged at his heartstrings. Whatever was bothering her this morning was still bothering her now. "Do you prefer your women shorter than you?"

"Say again?"

She held up a pair of flats in one hand, a pair of strappy wedged sandals that would add at least three inches to her height in the other, her brow cocked with a hint of challenge.

"What, you think I'm afraid to look you in the eye?"

"I'm sure a man of your stature isn't used to it."

A smile pulled in his cheek. She thought she had him all figured out. "Just because I'm not used to it doesn't mean I mind it."

"Ooh. I like a man with confidence."

"Put on your shoes, Clark."

"All right, wedges it is." She set the flats by the closet and stepped into the others, wrapping and tying the straps around her ankles.

Davis waited for her to finish, then opened the door. "Ready for your first oyster roast?"

She took his elbow. "I've been ready my whole life."

As they approached the marina they passed several people. A few men waved at Davis before gawking at Ivy. Even the women watched and whispered. Far worse than the stares, however, was the way Ivy responded to them, like she believed what they implied—that she was nothing more than a pair of great legs. Davis broadened his shoulders and straightened his spine as if making himself bigger might block Ivy from view. He should never have picked the wedges. With a tightening jaw, he led her through the crowd. Smoke, beer, and seafood mingled in the humidity as they stepped up to the oblong fire grate.

"So is there any special trick to eating an oyster at an oyster roast as opposed to a restaurant?"

"I think the same rules apply." He pointed to the table past the grate, lined with lemon juice, malt vinegar, Tabasco sauce, sweet pickles, and saltines, and shuffled Ivy into the line. The crowd nudged him from behind, squishing him closer, so only a thin strip of air separated his body from hers—a thin strip that hummed with electricity.

Settle down, Knight. She needs a friend, not another admirer.

If only the self-talk would erase his attraction. Taking in a deep breath, Davis looked at the boats and yachts lining the wharf, rocking in the gentle waves of the Atlantic. "You ever gone sailing, Ivy?"

"Not technically."

"How do you 'not technically' go sailing?"

"I've been on a sailboat for a few photo shoots, but none of those boats technically took to the water and sailed."

"We should fix that." Maybe later tonight he'd take her out, help Sara along in her quest to give Ivy more of a childhood. There was nothing like the vastness of the sea or the power of the wind or the chirping of friendly dolphins to magnify the splendor of God's creation. He ordered a bucket of oysters from Joe, helped Ivy pick out some condiments, and found Connie sitting at an empty picnic table. He led Ivy through the crowd and took a seat.

"Connie, this is my friend Ivy Clark. Ivy, this is Connie West. She writes for the *Greenbrier Tribune.*" He hadn't had a chance to introduce them during tryouts. Ivy had picked Arabella, Rachel Piper, and five other girls to walk in the show before claiming a headache and driving Marilyn's Lincoln Navigator home.

"Hello, Ivy." Connie's cheeks dimpled with a smile. "You already know my two best friends, Rachel and Arabella."

Davis used his knife to pry open one of the shells and tried not to cringe at the bittersweet tone of Connie's voice. Apparently, she harbored some hard feelings about not getting picked.

"The town's going crazy over the pair of you. Engaged cousins." She clucked her tongue. "How about that for a front-page story?"

"We're not cousins—"

"It's a rumor—"

Davis and Ivy spoke at the same time.

Connie's smile tightened. She set her chin in her hand. "I figured. Davis has always been more interested in intellectual types."

The clamshell he'd been working on popped open and flew over Ivy's head. He narrowed his eyes at Connie. "Ivy's plenty intellectual."

Connie batted her hand. "I didn't mean it as an insult, Davis."

Ivy stared with heavily lidded eyes—either unimpressed or bored with Connie's games.

Davis shifted forward in his seat, ready to get the interview over with. "So about the fashion show. All proceeds are going to help fund an art program at the community college, one for blind or visually impaired students. I'm hoping the event will draw a big crowd."

"Don't put the cart before the horse, Davis." Connie pulled out a digital recorder from her purse and wiggled it in the air. "I was sorry to hear about your father's passing, Ivy. I ran a story about him last year. The county hospital would never have a children's wing if not for his time and donation."

Ivy's face drained of color.

Connie didn't seem to notice. She was in full-blown reporter mode. "Not only did he pay for it, he visited the children several times. I interviewed the mayor's daughter who was there battling a severe case of pneumonia, and she talked about him like he was some kind of hero. He must have been a wonderful father."

Davis glared at Connie. He hadn't set this up to talk about James.

Ivy didn't say a word.

By the time he turned around to see why, she was on her feet, marching toward the parking lot, fists clenched at her sides.

The slamming door cracked like thunder. Ivy stalked through the foyer, Davis trailing her steps as she stomped into the kitchen and found Marilyn, humming as she rearranged a bouquet of flowers. All Ivy's anger toward James—years and years of it—gathered like steam in a kettle.

"Why am I here?" Each pain-laced word whipped the next.

Marilyn stopped, a flower falling from her hand into the sink.

Davis touched her arm. "Ivy…"

She shrugged him away. "Why did you ask me to come here?"

Marilyn's forehead knitted into a tangle of lines and wrinkles. Her attention flitted to Davis before landing back on Ivy. "Because…I…I needed a model."

"So you asked me?" Ivy flung her hand against her chest. "There are a million models out there. Any one of them could have sufficed."

"I didn't want any of them. I wanted you."

"I'm not your daughter."

Marilyn's shoulders deflated. "I know."

"So what is this, then? Am I a pity project for you—Marilyn the Martyr? Because if that's what this is, I don't want your pity."

Marilyn's face drained of color. "You've never been a project."

"He visited the children several times… She talked about him like he was some kind of hero… He visited the children several times…" Ivy looked down at her hands: her father's pinkies, her mother's palms. How could Marilyn even stand to look at her? "All those years he would come to us—to her—and you let him back into your bed."

Davis stepped forward. "Ivy, that's enough—"

Marilyn held up her hand, shushing his protest.

The steam of emotions pushed against Ivy's throat—an accumulation of suppressed hurt and hatred. "He might not have loved me, but it sure didn't seem like he loved you much either."

"Ivy."

"Davis, please go." Marilyn's voice cracked.

He stood in place, unmoving. Until Marilyn said his name again and his retreating footsteps echoed in the cavernous room.

"Why did you take him back?"

"He apologized."

"And that made everything better?"

"No, of course not." Marilyn pressed her fingers against her lips and looked out the sliding glass door that led to the courtyard. "I didn't want to forgive him. You have no idea how much I didn't want to, but every time I packed my bags, I felt God telling me to stay, even if I couldn't always love him."

"He slept with another woman. He cheated on you."

"He was sorry."

"Yeah." Ivy swallowed the tremor in her voice. "He was sorry about me."

Marilyn shook her head. "That's not what I meant."

"But it's true."

They were words Marilyn couldn't negate, no matter how much it looked as though they tortured her. James not only didn't love Ivy, her very existence inconvenienced him.

"He visited the children several times… She talked about him like he was some kind of hero… He visited the children several times…"

Ivy's eyes blurred. She pressed her lips together, gathering Connie's words to her chest, wrapping them around her wounds like dirty bandages. "What's wrong with me?"

"Sweetheart, there is nothing wrong with you."

"Then how could he love those kids when he never looked at me for more than a second?"

"What kids?"

"The kids at the hospital."

"Oh, Ivy…"

She turned from Marilyn's sympathy. She didn't want it.

Marilyn touched her shoulder.

Ivy wrapped her arms around her waist and pulled away. And then Marilyn's touch was gone, and Ivy felt so alone—with her grief, with her thoughts, with the truth.

Her father wasn't a villain. Because villains didn't write checks to good causes. Villains didn't spend time with sick kids in hospitals. Ivy had no idea what to do with this new information. She had no idea what to do with him. Knowing he loved her mother and Marilyn was bad enough, but knowing he visited the mayor's daughter? Knowing he spent time with kids who were no more than strangers? It made his rejection so much less about him and so much more about her.

"Visiting those children was nothing more than an act of penance at the end of a dying man's life. He was driven by guilt, not love. And a desire to be needed."

I needed him.

The words hung like stagnant air in her lungs. She couldn't speak them. She couldn't give them a voice.

"Ivy, if you found out James loved you, would that make a difference? Would it fix whatever's broken?"

Ivy turned around.

"If we could bring your father back from the dead, and you could ask him these questions, would you find whatever it is you're looking for?"

Silence followed the question. It was much, much too heavy.

Marilyn reached for Ivy's arm, but Ivy shivered and withdrew.

"He was a man. A flawed, broken, selfish man who didn't know what he had even when you were right under his nose. He failed me and he failed you. Neither of us will get what we're looking for from him." With pinched eyes, Marilyn turned around and walked away.

Ivy stared at the empty counter. Marilyn was right. All the answers in the world. They wouldn't be enough. They'd be too little, too late.

Davis rocked on the front porch swing, swatting mosquitoes as waterlogged clouds rolled across the horizon and Ivy's sharp accusations rolled through his mind. A tropical storm hit the North Carolina coast last week, and another was scheduled to reach land somewhere along Georgia in a few days.

He wrapped his fingers around the wooden armrest and let the creak of the springs and the croaking of bullfrogs sing him a Lowcountry lullaby. A breeze thick with humidity rustled the Spanish moss hanging from the ancient oak towering at the edge of Marilyn's lawn.

For the past couple of years, James had siphoned a generous portion of his money into the building and maintenance of the children's wing at the county hospital, but Davis had no idea the man visited the place. It didn't seem like something James would do, but then Davis never really knew him that well. Sure, they attended the same family functions and on occasion ate family dinners together, but that did not lend itself to really knowing a person. Besides the obvious—good looks, corporate success, and Grandfather's favor—he never understood what Aunt Marilyn saw in the guy.

Now Ivy was inside, taking out whatever anger she felt toward James on Marilyn. His aunt didn't deserve to play the scapegoat. But Ivy sure didn't deserve to get landed with a father like James. Davis closed his eyes and leaned his head back against the rocker, conjuring an image of her ashen face on the drive from the marina. The white patches along her knuckles as she pressed her fingers onto the window ledge.

The front door opened, followed by the shutting of the storm door. The cushion beside him sank and the swing squeaked. A cold hand patted his knee. He opened one eye and spotted Marilyn's familiar wedding band.

"That girl's in a world of hurt," she said.

He crossed his ankles. "What about you?"

"I'll be fine." But even as she said it, tears gathered in her eyes.

They swung in silence, questions building in Davis's mind as Marilyn stared down the long drive, out into the empty street. The heat had swept the neighbors off their porches and inside to cooler air. Or maybe they were all at the oyster roast. "Marilyn?"

"Yes?"

"Why did you invite Ivy down here?"

She didn't answer at first. In fact, she waited so long Davis wondered if she would answer at all. But then, "The minute I first laid eyes on Ivy was the minute God taught me I didn't have to bear a child to have a child."

"What do you mean?"

Her brow furrowed. "For reasons I'll never know, I fell in love with a daughter that belonged to another woman. I know it doesn't make any sense. It drives your grandfather crazy, and a lot of the time, I have no idea what God is up to, but…" She held up her hands, palms facing the sky, and let out a long sigh. Like finishing her thought was too tiring. Or maybe too confusing. "I wish James would have had more time. I wish I could have gotten Ivy here before he died. I wish he would have reached out and tried to contact her in New York."

"Why didn't he?"

"He was afraid."

"Of what?"

"His past. Her rejection. A million and one other things, I'm sure. I think he thought he'd lost the right to reconcile with Ivy a long time ago, so he didn't try. I sure wish he would have." Marilyn batted her hand as if to shoo it all away. "You know what your Grandma Eleanor would say."

" 'If wishes were horses, beggars would ride.' "

She caught a stray tear on her knuckle. "I should have thought up this whole wedding dress campaign while James was still alive and gotten Ivy down here whether he thought he deserved it or not."

"From what I know of Ivy, I don't think she would have come."

Marilyn set her hand against her chest. "I don't know, Davis. I can't explain it. With him gone, I want her here. It feels right."

His skin prickled. He couldn't explain it either, but Marilyn's words resonated. It did feel right. "Aunt Marilyn?"

"Yes?"

"Do you think she'll be okay?"

She patted his knee again. "I hope so. But right now, it sure doesn't feel like it."

Ivy set her hand on top of Marilyn's box and stared into the heavy, ornate mirror. Her perfect reflection mocked her.

Who was she?

Closing her eyes, she tossed around descriptors inside the darkness. Model. Beautiful. Alluring. Desirable. But they all fell victim to gravity, falling to the ground like a handful of rocks. She sank to the floor, wrapped her arms around her legs, and tried to picture the James she thought she knew visiting sick children at the hospital.

"What do I do with you now?"

Was it possible to be a lousy father but a decent man? Did being a decent man matter—did it balance the scales—when you were the daughter? She hugged her knees tighter, trying to block the memories, but they slithered closer, wrapping around her mind and squeezing until she was no longer sitting on the floor of her temporary apartment but crouched in the bedroom of her childhood condominium, knobby knees pressing into her mattress, horns blaring from the Chicago street outside her window, a crisp, autumn breeze whapping at her blinds.

Mom shouted in the hallway. *"I might as well kill myself and get it over with!"*

Ivy catapulted across the room and stuck her face to the crack between the door and wall, her little-girl heart punching bruises against her chest. Mom wouldn't kill herself. She couldn't. Mom was all Ivy had in the world. Nobody loved her better or even at all. She wanted to sprint into the hallway and beg James to pay attention to her mother. To kiss her. To love her. To do whatever he needed to do to take those words away.

Instead, he grabbed Mom's wrist. *"Keep your voice down, Renee. Do you want your daughter to hear you?"*

"Your daughter! Do you hear yourself? She's yours too, James. She's ours. We made her together, yet you act like she doesn't exist. Doesn't she mean any-

thing to you? Don't I mean anything to you?" Mom wrenched her hand away from him and stumbled out of sight.

There was a loud crash, like glass smashing into teeny tiny pieces.

Ivy flung open the door and flew out into the hallway. Mom didn't have many rules. One of them, however, was staying in her bedroom anytime James came to visit. But Ivy couldn't obey that rule. Not now. She rounded the corner and found them squaring off, Mom with a knife clutched to her chest. The sharpened blade made Ivy's breath come too quick.

"Don't be stupid, Renee. Put the knife down."

"Cutting out my heart isn't stupid. Not when you've already done it!"

Ivy clamped her hands over her ears. She hated when her mother got this way. Whenever she drank from the bottles in the locked cupboard, she turned into a different person. And whenever her father stayed away for long stretches of time, her mother took to drinking from those bottles. The last time he'd come had been the beginning of Ivy's summer break, which meant Mom had been taking drinks from the cupboard a lot lately.

James stepped closer—a slow, hesitant step. *"You're drunk, Renee. You're not thinking straight."*

"You used to love me. You used to want me. You used to burn with passion for me. I want to know what changed. Do you love Marilyn more than me?"

"She's my wife."

Ivy pressed her hands tighter against her ears. She wanted to rewind. Make him take it back. Make him promise he didn't mean it. Couldn't he see that if he would simply promise his love everything would be better?

Her mother let out a frantic laugh. Ivy closed her eyes, counted backward from ten. Her school guidance counselor had come to her third-grade classroom the week before and had told Ivy and her classmates that counting backward from ten helped most things. She reached seven when a door slammed. James stood in front of her. It was the closest he'd ever been.

"Go to your room. I'm going to get your mother." And then he left.

Every bone in Ivy's body wanted to chase them both down the stairs.

Because what if James gave up before he found her and Ivy was left all alone? Instead, she obeyed her father. She ran to her bedroom closet and shut the door, wondering if eight-year-olds could have heart attacks. Ivy scooted to the very back—until her thin shoulder blades met the cool wall—and buried her face in her knees. She rocked back and forth, back and forth, counting backward from ten a hundred times over.

Nobody came for her until the next morning.

The closet door opened and there stood Mom, all the light snuffed from her eyes, as if her insides and her outsides had gotten separated when she ran out of the condo, and James had returned with her outsides but had forgotten all about her insides.

After that day, he never came back to Chicago.

And Mom's insides stayed away for good.

There were no more late-night kitchen dances or rainy-day puddle stomping. This new version of her mother didn't like to sing in the shower or paint toenails. Some days she didn't even like to get out of bed. And when the bottles in the locked cupboard no longer satisfied, she started giving herself shots in her arms until she wasted away to skin and bone. Ivy spent five long years taking care of her mother's shell until the Department of Children and Family Services showed up and took her to Greenbrier.

Ivy had promised herself she would never let James destroy her the way he had destroyed Mom. Nobody would. When it came to men, she would be the one in control. She held the cards. They were at her mercy. She was taking from them. And as long as she took from them, they couldn't touch her.

But it was all a lie.

Every man Ivy had taken from left a stain that couldn't be scrubbed away. The long line started with James, then Bruce, then Raymond, and every one after. Each had stripped a piece of flesh from her heart until all that remained was a cold, hard stone.

Shuddering, Ivy tore herself from the memories. She rose from the floor and set both hands on the dresser, taking in deep breaths until her knees stopped shaking. She flipped open the box, removed Sara's card and brushed a finger over the words.

"Fear not, for I have redeemed you; I have called you by name, you are mine." Isaiah 43:1. God wrote these words for you, Ivy.
Love, Sara.

When she closed her eyes, she didn't see her mother's tear-streaked face as she watched a television preacher, but two butterflies swooping over sparkling water. Maybe James wasn't all bad. But he wasn't a butterfly. He hadn't pursued her mother. He hadn't pursued Ivy either. Nobody had. She slipped the card inside with the pictures and slid the box beside the mirror, beneath a bouquet of dead flowers.

Marilyn watched as Ivy reversed the car out of the driveway and drove down the street. Earlier, Ivy had rebuffed her invitation to church before asking to borrow the car. Marilyn didn't know where Ivy was headed, nor did she know what repelled Ivy more—going to church or spending time together. Probably both. Once again, Marilyn found herself having no clue what to do—push Ivy to open up and risk widening the chasm between them or give her space and risk appearing as though she didn't care, when that was far from the truth.

Lord, what am I supposed to do?

The question was met with silence and the memory of Ivy's hurt face from the night before. Marilyn had gone to bed wanting to strangle her husband. Only James was dead, leaving her alone with a handful of conflicting emotions and nowhere to sling them. Sighing, she turned away from the large window and headed up the stairs toward Sara's bedroom. Last night, a cold had put Sara to bed early, which meant she had missed yesterday's confrontation.

Marilyn stopped in front of the open door and placed her hand on the doorframe. Sara stood in front of her dresser, combing tangles out of her hair with quick, jerky strokes before setting to work on a french braid. Unnoticed in the doorway, Marilyn watched. After Sara's accident, so many well-intentioned people had offered her words of hope—that God would heal her, that she would see again—as if that was a given. It was the same hope people had offered Marilyn all those years ago. Story upon story of women who had struggled through infertility and ended up with a child on the other side.

"God is good. It'll happen," they had told her.

As if God's goodness depended upon whether or not He answered prayers the way people wanted Him to answer. The hard truth was that sometimes He didn't. He hadn't rescued Marilyn from her infertility, and He hadn't rescued Sara from her blindness. But that didn't negate His goodness. It just meant He had different plans.

Sara wrapped a hair band around the end of her braid, then unzipped a cosmetic bag sitting on top of her dresser. She removed a CoverGirl compact, flipped it open, and brought it beneath her nose, as if breathing in the scent. Marilyn cocked her head. Sara used to wear a touch of makeup before the accident—a hint of blush and a thin layer of mascara on her long, pale lashes. Afterward, however, she hadn't bothered with it at all.

Slowly, meticulously, Sara brushed powder onto her cheeks. She pulled a stick of mascara from the bag, twisted it open, and touched the tip of the wand as if feeling for moisture. Using her fingers to find her eyelashes, she brushed the applicator over them. A bit of black smudged her lid. Marilyn stepped forward, wondering if she should offer to help. But then, without warning, Sara heaved the applicator across the room.

It clattered against the wall and fell.

"Good arm."

Sara spun around.

Marilyn walked inside and picked up the mascara, unsure if Sara's puffy eyes were a result of crying or her cold. "Would you like some help?"

"I'm fine," she snapped.

Marilyn drew back at the sharp words.

Sara moved to the bed, her shoulders sagging. She sat on the edge and tucked her hands between her knees.

That's when Marilyn noticed it—a photo album splayed atop Sara's pillow. Marilyn joined Sara on the bed and ran her finger over one of the photographs. A picture of Jordan and Sara at a church picnic, Jordan's arm draped over Sara's shoulder as they squinted happily at the camera. Marilyn remembered the day. It was several years ago, one of Sara and Jordan's first dates. Her niece hadn't been able to stop smiling. "You don't see very many photo albums anymore. Everyone's pictures are on their phones."

"I don't even know why I still have it. They're nothing but glossy pieces of paper to me now."

Marilyn frowned. Sara had come a long way these past two years. She had forgiven Davis. She was learning to handle her blindness. She was even learning to be thankful in the midst of it. But that didn't mean her longing to see had disappeared. Or that she didn't have bad days like everybody else.

"Sorry for snapping," she said.

"It's okay."

"Being sick makes everything else feel worse. Especially this blind thing."

"You know what I've learned?"

"What?"

"Anytime I'm sick or overtired, I don't let myself think too much about my circumstances. Feeling rotten has a way of making the whole world seem darker, you know? Better to let bad days be bad days and trust that they'll pass." Marilyn placed the mascara into Sara's palm. "Why the makeup? I haven't seen you wear it since before..."

"The accident?"

"Yeah."

Sara turned the mascara over in her hand. "If life would have turned out differently, today would have marked my four-year anniversary with Jordan." Sara closed her fist around the mascara and shook her head. "I guess I wanted to feel like a girl again. Not a blind girl, but a girl. If that makes any sense."

Marilyn set her hand on Sara's knee.

"I keep waiting for life to get easier."

Marilyn laughed. The sound escaped as nothing more than a puff of breath. Easy was not a word that described their lives. "Here, face me."

Sara turned and sat cross-legged on the bed.

Marilyn gently wiped the smudge of black away with the pad of her thumb, took the mascara from Sara, and twisted it open. "Look up."

"Aunt Mare, do you ever wish you'd had a different life? Something not so…hard?"

Marilyn finished Sara's right upper lashes and paused before moving on to the left. "Sometimes. But then the hard is what makes us who we are. The hard is usually what God uses to draw us closer." And what if God came down and offered her a different life? If she'd never walked the path of infertility or knew about her husband's infidelity and had three grown children with grandchildren on the way—what would have become of Ivy? "If I have to choose between what's easy or what will bring me closer to Him, I pray my choice will be Him."

"That's a scary prayer."

"Tell me about it."

A hint of a smile pulled up the corner of Sara's mouth. "But you pray it anyway."

"On my brave days. Not so much my bad ones. Now look up."

Sara pointed her gaze back up at the ceiling.

Marilyn finished Sara's other eye, then leaned back to examine her handiwork. "You know what else I've learned?"

Sara blinked a few times as if getting used to the feel of mascara on her eyelashes again.

She twisted the mascara shut and looked at her niece. "God's not in the business of pampering His children. He's in the business of perfecting them."

26

A woman in white greeted Ivy at the counter. "May I help you, ma'am?"

Ma'am? The name made Ivy feel ancient, something she didn't need to feel. Not when she already felt like she'd lived a million lifetimes. This morning when Marilyn invited her to church, Ivy declined and instead came to visit the place her father helped build—the children's wing of the Beaufort County Hospital. For whatever reason, she needed to see it. "My name's Ivy Clark." She wiped her hands down the thighs of her jeans. "I'm…I'm Mr. Olsen's daughter."

The woman's face brightened then dimmed. "I was so sorry to hear about his passing. He was a wonderful man."

So she'd heard. "Is it okay if I look around? I mean, is that allowed in a hospital?"

The nurse smiled. "We have a plaque at the end of the hall with your father's name on it."

"Great. Thanks." Ivy turned from the counter and shuffled down the corridor, which was quiet and mostly empty, except for muted television chatter and an elderly doctor reviewing a chart. She wandered to the plaque at the end of the hall, but the sound of laughter floating from one of the rooms made her pause.

Ivy peeked inside the room. A young girl—maybe eleven or twelve—with no hair and large dark eyes nestled inside a painfully thin face lay in bed, smiling at Jordan Ludd. He sat there with a shy smile and grease-stained hands.

"Jordan?" His name escaped before she could take it back.

He looked up from the girl's bed and spotted Ivy, his cheeks blushing their usual shade of crimson. He took off his hat and wrung it in his hands. "Mornin', Ivy."

No "What are you doing here?" Just a simple hello. Ivy tried to look at him, but her attention kept pulling toward the little girl. She sat up in bed, swimming in a hospital gown, surrounded by flowers and stuffed animals and balloons. Despite her ill health, there was a brightness to her that spread throughout the room.

"Hi," the girl said.

Ivy was struck by a sudden inexplicable bout of shyness. "Hello."

"My name's Twila." The girl sat up straighter, the bed squeaking beneath her, her eyes growing bigger the longer she stared. "What's your name?"

"Ivy."

"Are you a model?" Twila brought her fingers to her scalp, where her hair should have been.

"Yes." Ivy flicked a glance at Jordan. "What are you doing here?"

He stood in the corner with his brown hair matted against his head. "Twila's a member of my granddad's church. The two of us like to keep company on Sundays."

"My dad helped build this wing." Ivy had no idea why she blurted the words. Jordan hadn't asked. She looked at the girl. Did Twila know her father? Did he visit her before he died like he'd visited the mayor's daughter? She shook the questions away and asked the one that mattered far more than the others. "Are you okay?"

"My last round of chemo made me really sick, but I'm doing a little better now." She bit her fingernail. "How do you and Jordan know each other?"

"I'm friends with Sara Knight."

"Really? I love Sara. She gives me piano lessons."

Jordan's forehead turned the same color as his cheeks.

"And my mom cleans her house," Twila added.

"Is your mom Annie?"

Twila nodded. "Are you really a model?" she asked again.

Ivy held up her hand in a Girl Scout's pledge. "I'm the real deal."

"I wish I could be a model." She pointed to a stack of preteen magazines on her nightstand. The newest teen heartthrob and his ridiculous haircut plastered the cover of the top magazine and right beneath that, a picture of a young beauty—probably the same age as Tatiana, Bruce's newest obsession. "But I'm not pretty enough." She smiled down into her sheets and touched the nape of her neck. "I don't have any hair, and even if I did, I don't look like you."

A muscle in Ivy's chest pinched. She wanted to rip up those magazines—the ones that made a girl like Twila think she was anything less than perfect—and light them on fire. She wanted to wipe Twila's longing away. Tell her the beauty she wanted didn't exist. Or if it did, didn't last. She wanted to tell Twila that if anybody in this room was beautiful, it wasn't Ivy. "I know somebody who's a million times more beautiful than I am."

Twila's eyes widened, like Ivy's words weren't possible. "Who?"

"You know her."

"I do?"

"Yep. And so does Jordan." Sara's face swam in her thoughts. One hundred percent plain, but full of life and smiles and joy. If Twila was going to pin her admiration on somebody, let it be her. "Sara Knight. Your piano instructor."

Twila leaned forward. "Jordan and Sara used to be sweethearts."

"So I've heard."

A nurse knocked on the opened door and came inside, holding a tray of food and some pills. "Time for Miss Twila to eat some lunch and have a rest."

Jordan put his hat back on his head and tapped Twila on the nose. "I'll be back later, sprite. I'll even bring you more magazines if you want."

She settled back into bed and looked at Ivy. "Will you come?"

Ivy couldn't stay today. She was meeting with Sara and Marilyn to iron out some other random details for the show. But something about Twila made her heart want to say yes, and her heart never, ever wanted to say yes. "Can I come another time?"

"I get to go home tomorrow. But next time I have piano lessons with Sara, you could listen. I'm not very good, but I'm not very bad either."

"I'd like that."

Twila smiled back and waved good-bye.

Ivy followed Jordan past the nurse and into the corridor, where she pulled him to a stop by his shirt sleeve. "Cancer?"

"Leukemia. She's been fighting for a long time now."

Ivy frowned. "Do her a favor and don't buy anymore of those magazines."

"Oh." Jordan's eyelids fluttered a bit, like he didn't understand why Ivy would make such a suggestion. "Okay."

"Does Sara visit?"

He looked down at his shoes. "I think so."

"Jordan?"

He grunted.

"Do you still love her?"

Jordan shuffled his feet.

Ivy looped her thumb into the front pocket of her jeans. Davis didn't want her meddling in Sara's business, especially where Jordan was concerned. But he didn't know what was going on between these two, and whatever assumptions he'd made about Jordan were false. Let Davis get upset. She'd deal with the consequences later. "Look, Jordan, I know you think she doesn't, but Sara still loves you."

More feet shuffling.

"You should come to her birthday party next month. It's supposed to be a surprise, but she already knows about it."

"I'm not sure she'd want me there."

"I'm sure she would."

He looked up from the gray-speckled linoleum.

"Come on. Haven't you read any fairy tales?" She cocked her head and smiled. "Take up your sword, man. Chase after her. It's time to rescue your damsel."

"Rescue her from who?"

"Herself."

Hoppin' John's Café hid at the tail end of Palmetto Boulevard, behind a row of overgrown hedges and several oaks—the kind with twisted limbs and gnarled branches. Ivy stood in front of the hedges, waiting for Davis, who promised to meet her ten minutes ago so they could talk to Arabella about catering lunch for the fashion show.

Ivy stepped onto the brick sidewalk, looking both ways for a blond male with broad shoulders and impossibly blue eyes. She hadn't spoken to him in two days, since her embarrassing outburst on Saturday. Her nerves twisted. She didn't want him to bring that up. She didn't want him to psychoanalyze her unwarranted anger toward Marilyn. Instead, she wanted to speak with him about an idea, one that had formulated after yesterday's hospital visit.

Twila wanted to be a model. Davis was a photographer. Why couldn't he give the little girl a photo shoot? She looked both ways again, but still no Davis. Didn't he know it was rude to be late? Not to mention unprofessional. Ivy looked up at the darkening sky. The weather report called for rain, but so far, the clouds had yet to unzip.

Somebody tapped her shoulder.

Ivy turned around.

Davis stood behind her, his eyes hidden behind a pair of sunglasses, his increasingly shaggy hair mussed from the wind. His sudden appearance shot a blip of energy through her body. "Where'd you come from?"

"I've been waiting inside." He flashed a row of faintly crooked white teeth. "You look fidgety." He stepped to the side so she could join him on the wooden planks leading to the café's front doors. "Everything okay?"

"You mean, am I over Saturday's temper tantrum?"

He took off his sunglasses. "If that's what you want to call it."

"I'm getting there."

Davis reached for the brass handle and opened the door. A plume of cool air washed over Ivy's face and shoulders. She stepped inside to the twang of country music and a friendly faced teenager.

"Hi, Davis! Welcome to Hoppin' John's." The hostess motioned around the restaurant, drawing Ivy's attention to the walls, which were covered—almost floor to ceiling—with photographs, posters, wooden signs, even a large gaudy painting of what appeared to be a lady with a missing hand.

"Hi, Bonnie," Davis said. "We're here to talk to Arabella about catering for the fashion show. Is she around?"

"I'll go get her."

As soon as Bonnie disappeared behind the bar, Davis bent toward Ivy's ear. "Don't judge the food by the decorations."

Ivy nodded toward the painting. "What is that?"

"A portrait of Arabella's mother."

Ivy scrunched her nose. "What happened to her hand?"

"Lost it to a gator."

"Shut up."

"No joke. She went crabbing in the marsh when she was little. They jumped in afterward and a gator got a hold of her and tore it right off."

She slapped his bicep. "You are a horrible liar."

Davis smirked. "You're right. I'm not even sure that's Arabella's mom." He cocked his head at the painted woman. "And I don't think she's missing a hand. I think it's the angle."

"Really?" Ivy tilted her head slowly as if trying to see it, then shrugged. "So I have a proposition for you."

The lighthearted set of his eyebrows disappeared.

"Is a proposition from me really that bad?"

"Depends what it's about."

"It's about Annie Welch's daughter."

"Twila?"

Ivy nodded.

"How do you know Twila?"

The restaurant's twangy country music turned feminine. "I met her at the hospital yesterday. In the children's wing."

"Oh."

"Don't worry, I'm not going to freak out again. So James cared more about kids he didn't know than his own daughter. Big deal, right?"

"What does your proposition have to do with Twila?"

"For whatever reason, she wants to be a model."

A man walked inside the restaurant. Davis touched Ivy's elbow. She stepped forward to let him by.

"I was thinking. Maybe you could take pictures of her. Give the girl her own photo shoot. Something fun to take her mind off her illness."

"I'm not sure."

"Why not? Davis, your photos are brilliant. And honest." Ivy thought of the editorial in *Southern Brides.* She'd hated it at first, but after further examination, she could see what had appealed to Juliette. The photos weren't fake. They were real. Almost too real. "You could make Twila feel beautiful. You could make her feel special."

He squinted his eyes and stared at the ceiling, as if considering her words. Then the hostess returned with Arabella. "How are two of my favorite people?" Bella didn't give them time to respond. "Connie told me she's running your fashion story soon."

Ivy scrunched her nose at the memory of Connie West. She'd be happy never to see her again. The door opened behind them. Ivy stepped closer to the bar as the hostess greeted the customers and led them to one of the many booths lining the windowed walls.

"It's supposed to come out next Sunday," Davis said. "I talked to Kipper

Manning too. He's going to give us some time on the air. Seems like this event's really going to take off."

Arabella twirled a chunky bracelet around her wrist. "Marilyn's happy you're taking pictures again."

"Just temporarily. Until the show's over."

Ivy frowned. Davis couldn't stop once the show was over. Not only for the sake of her career and future, but for his too. What she said earlier—she wasn't blowing smoke. He was truly talented. He had no business squandering that talent. Getting him to fall back in love with photography would be good for her, sure, but it would also be good for him. And everybody else who benefited from his pictures, like Twila.

A swarthy-looking Italian poked his head out from a swinging door leading into the back and rapped the wall with his palm. "Telephone call on line two, Bella. Some emergency with the order we sent out to Bay View Golf Course a while ago."

Arabella blew a strand of hair from her eyes. "I'll be right back. We'll talk details about the show." She hurried around the bar and disappeared into the back room.

Ivy took advantage of the interruption. "So what do you say?"

"About what?"

"Taking pictures. Of Twila."

"I don't know..."

"What's not to know?"

"Ivy, I'm only doing this as a temporary thing—to help Marilyn and to raise money for the art program. I can't start taking pictures of kids with cancer."

Frustration knotted her muscles. Davis's hesitancy made no sense. He was a good guy and this was a good thing to do. "Why not—because it'll make you realize how much you love photography? I don't understand why that would be such a frightening thing."

"I don't understand why you're pushing so hard." He cocked his head. "What does it matter to you if I fall in love with photography again?"

Ivy looked away. Did he suspect about New York or Vera Wang? And if not, shouldn't she get it over with already and tell him since she'd have to eventually? She slid her hands into her back pockets. No, now wasn't the time. Sure, she needed to get him to New York, but this Twila thing had nothing to do with Vera Wang and everything to do with Davis and his ability to capture what other people failed to see. In this case, Twila's beauty. If she told him about Vera Wang now, he'd assume she was using Twila's photography session as a ploy to get him to New York. "Can't I do anything without ulterior motives?"

She kept her expression neutral, innocent. This wasn't about Vera Wang. It wasn't. Let him look as deep as he wanted, he'd find nothing but the truth.

His cell phone rang.

Davis fished the phone from his pocket. "'Lo, Davis Knight."

Muffled words sounded from the other end.

"When?" Davis's brow furrowed. "Is she going to be okay?"

Ivy leaned closer. Was who going to be okay?

"Where is she now?" He turned toward the door. "I'll be right there." He stuck his phone into his back pocket.

"What happened? What's wrong?"

"It's Sara. She's hurt."

27

Davis strode into Doc's living room with Ivy trailing and found Marilyn sitting on the sofa. Grandfather paced in front of her, hands clasped behind his back while Jordan Ludd, of all people, stood off to the side and in front of an unused fireplace. He had no idea why either man was there, but Davis ignored them both and looked at his aunt. "Where is she?"

Marilyn stood up and wrapped him in a hug. "Doc's with her right now in one of his examination rooms. She's going to be fine, Davis. I didn't mean to worry you. I was having lunch with your grandfather when we got the call from Jordan. I didn't know how bad it was." She glared at Grandfather. "Dad, will you stop pacing like a maniac?"

"A phone call from Jordan?" Davis said.

The man in question moved in the periphery of Davis's vision, disheveled hair sticking straight up as if he'd run his hands through it one too many times.

"Why were you and Sara together?" Davis didn't mean for it to come out so rude.

Grandfather stopped and gave Jordan a beady stare. "Same question I asked."

"I wanted to talk to her." He twisted his hat. "Clear some things up."

"Good for you, Jordan," Ivy said.

Davis rounded on her. "Were you behind this?"

She lifted her chin, like she didn't care that she'd touched off a fire.

"I told you to stay out of it. You don't even know what happened."

Her eyes flashed. "Neither do you."

Grandfather rocked forward on the balls of his shoes and turned his disapproving stare on Ivy. "You, young lady, have no right meddling in affairs you know nothing about. I don't even know why you're here."

"She's here because I asked her to come," Davis said. And whether Grandfather wanted to believe it or not, Ivy cared about Sara. Davis turned to Jordan. "How did she get hurt?"

"I don't know. I surprised her. I mean, she didn't expect me to come to the boutique. We went for a walk. Just the two of us." Jordan started to turn red. "I mean, without Sunny." He looked at Ivy. She nodded for him to continue. "And she tripped on some stairs and fell."

Jordan's words painted a scene that was much too familiar. A painful, shameful memory Davis wished didn't exist. He sat down next to Marilyn, hating himself all over again.

Doc Armstrong came out of an adjoining room and into the living area, a stethoscope hanging around his golf shirt. "Sara's going to be fine, everybody. I gave her a brace for her sprained wrist, a couple stitches on her elbow. There are no signs of a concussion, but you'll want to keep an eye on her tonight in case she shows any symptoms. Marshall, you can stop worrying my carpet bald."

"Yes, please," Marilyn said.

"I gave her some Tylenol for the pain and asked her to rest for a bit. She can go home as soon as you want to take her. In the meantime, she's asked to speak with Jordan."

Jordan stuck his hat in the back pocket of his jeans and, without waiting for extra permission, walked into Sara's room. Davis narrowed his eyes after him, then turned to Ivy. "Why is he getting involved with Sara? What did you tell him?"

"The truth."

"Which is what?"

"Your sister's in love with him."

"Ivy, you have no idea what you're talking about. Jordan broke up with her. When he found out her condition was permanent, he left her and broke her heart, and now you're opening old wounds."

Ivy blew out her breath. "I swear, sometimes you're more blind than your sister."

He caught a glimpse of Marilyn's private grin. "What are you talking about?"

"Didn't you see his face? Jordan's in love with your sister."

"Some love. He left her the minute things got tough."

"No, he didn't. She left him."

He smiled an incredulous smile, because Ivy didn't know what she was talking about. Sara didn't leave Jordan. She was too in love with him to leave him. "Why would she do that? She was devastated after they broke up."

"Same reason lots of people do stuff." She crossed her arms and raised her eyebrows. He crossed his arms and raised his eyebrows right back, waiting for Ivy to enlighten him. She sighed. "Fear."

His eyebrows lifted higher.

"She felt like she wasn't good enough for him. She was afraid of tying him down to somebody with a disability."

"A disability she shouldn't even have," Grandfather boomed.

Marilyn shifted to the front of her seat. "Dad, that's enough."

"I won't hold back the truth. Tough love, Marilyn. You and I both know that Davis has no business picking up his camera again."

"Your grandson is a phenomenal photographer," Ivy said.

"Irresponsible is what he is. And look what his tomfoolery led to!" Grandfather huffed and shooed his hand. "If you would have come back to work for me after college like I suggested, none of this would have happened."

Hatred rose like bile in Davis's throat. He hated Grandfather's words, hated even more that they were true. "And become like James? You know, Grandfather, he was the only person you ever approved of, and look what a great guy he turned out to be." Davis regretted the rash words as soon as they left.

Ivy stiffened.

Marilyn deflated like a loose balloon whirling out of air.

Grandfather straightened to his full height. "James made a mistake. One mistake." Grandfather pointed his stare at Ivy. "One he admitted to and turned from. Why are you so determined to crucify the man for it?"

Davis imagined the words plunging into Ivy's heart and twisting. Couldn't Grandfather see how much damage those words caused? He put his hand on the small of Ivy's back, willing her to look at him. *Don't listen to him, Ivy. You weren't a mistake. Not to God.* But she didn't look. She was too busy blinking at the carpet.

Doc held up his hands as if to calm an increasingly agitated Grandfather. "Nobody's crucifying anybody. Take a deep breath before I have to get out the nitroglycerin."

"You're wrong. James made more than one mistake." Davis looked at Marilyn, sitting like a rag doll in the chair. He didn't want to hurt her by attacking the man she'd stuck beside, but he could apologize later. Right now, he needed Ivy to hear something. "The biggest of which was ignoring his own daughter. So no offense, Grandfather, but your approval means very little."

Davis stomped out the door. Ivy stared after him. She had no idea what Marshall had been talking about. She couldn't fathom how Davis's photography had anything to do with Sara's blindness, but she was determined to find out. She followed Davis's exit and found him sitting on the porch stoop, his cotton shirt outlining well-toned back muscles.

A strange feeling tingled behind her confusion—something she'd never felt. It bubbled the first time Davis stepped in front of her, then spilled over when he'd placed his hand on her back. Nobody had ever stuck up for her like that before. Never. It made the joints in her knees feel all tingly and weak.

Settle down, Ivy. He was just angry at the old man.

"So that was kind of intense."

No answer. He didn't even turn and look at her.

The porch floor creaked as she crept closer and sat by his side. "Don't get me wrong, Dave, your brooding is sexy and all, but Sara's alive. She had a small fall. No permanent damage."

He set his elbows on his knees and dug his hands into his hair.

Not the reaction she'd expected. So now what? She wasn't exactly the maternal, comforting type. Her comfort came in a different form. "Are you going to tell me what your grandfather meant by blaming Sara's blindness on your...what did he call it...tomfoolery?"

Davis turned his agonized face toward her, cupping his cheek with his palm. "He meant exactly what he said. Sara can't see because of me."

"How is that possible?"

"It's a long story."

"Well, you're in luck." Ivy tapped the top of her wrist, where a watch would be if she were wearing one. "My next counseling session isn't scheduled for another thirty minutes."

A ghost of smile pulled at the corner of his mouth.

"C'mon, Davis, don't you know it's beneficial to get things out?"

He took a long, slow breath, his brow furrowing deeper with every second that ticked past. He swallowed. Then spoke. "When my photos landed on the cover of *Vogue,* I was convinced I'd be the next Richard Warren."

"Lofty."

"Yeah, I know." He shook his head. "Anyway, I invited Sara to come celebrate with me. Flew her out and everything. Clubbing it up in New York? It wasn't her. She'd lived all of two places, both of them small towns—Telluride, Colorado, and Greenbrier, South Carolina.

"As soon as she arrived, I could tell she didn't want to be there. She wasn't comfortable with my world, which made me defensive. That first night, we were supposed to go to a party at one of the clubs. Some big shot from *Elle* was going to be there, and he'd promised me ten minutes of his time. But Sara didn't want to go. I told her I didn't fly her out to New York to sit on my couch. She told me she didn't recognize me anymore. I told her she needed to loosen up. The argument made us late, the icy roads even later. I was in a huge hurry because I didn't want to miss out on meeting with the guy from *Elle,* and Sara was moving so slow it almost felt deliberate.

"We had to walk down some stairs to get to the club. I grabbed her arm and started pulling her along. A few steps in, she slipped on some ice, fell the rest of the way down, and hit her head on the cement."

Ivy covered her mouth with her hand.

Moisture gathered in Davis's eyes. "She was in a coma for two days, and when she woke up, she could see nothing but blackness."

"Davis…"

"It was my fault. I made her come with me. If I wouldn't have been so focused on schmoozing with that hotshot, if I wasn't so determined to show Sara what a big deal I'd become, then she never would have fallen." He turned away and scuffed his shoe against a piece of gravel. "I didn't just lose myself in New York City, Ivy. I became a different person. I got so obsessed with chasing glory and success that I didn't even know who I was anymore or what I stood for. I lost my temper with Sara, and because of that, I have to live with the fact that she can't see. She can't do what she loves. I'm not sure I'll ever be able to forgive myself."

No wonder he left New York. No wonder he quit photography.

"This show. Raising money for that art program. I'm only doing it for Sara. I promised myself I'd never pick up a camera again, not when she can't paint. I hate going back on my word, but maybe this is my chance to give her back something she loves."

"Well then, that settles it." Ivy curled her fingers around her knees,

Bruce's phone call lurking in the back of her mind. She hated herself for such opportunistic thinking, but what other choice did she have? Ivy was a model. Take that away and she was nothing. Here was a solution that wouldn't just benefit her, but Sara too. Getting that art program to Greenbrier meant her friend could paint again. And once Sara could paint again, maybe, just maybe, Davis would come back to New York. "We're going to make this fashion show the biggest event this town has ever seen."

28

The radio crackled as Davis clanked down the ladder and mopped his brow. Three weeks spent outside during the tail end of South Carolina's hottest month—first splitting and replanting hostas in Cornerstone's front lawn, then replacing the church's roof alongside several volunteers—and he could feel the sun soaking into his skin, turning it a few shades darker than his usual tan.

Davis stepped beneath the shade of a walnut tree and pulled a cold bottle of lemonade from his minicooler, twisted off the cap, and took a long swig. The radio crackled again. He nudged it with his booted toe, sat down in the grass, and fiddled with the antennas. A deep southern drawl broke through the static—Greenbrier's Big Bubba in the Morning.

"We're kicking off Labor Day weekend with a little Diamond Rio and fireworks at nine o'clock. We've got a great lineup for this year's festival. Hope to see y'all there, folks. And in case you've been living under a rock for the past two weeks, don't forget to find the booth selling tickets to Greenbrier's first fashion show, showcasing our very own Marilyn Olsen, her wedding dresses, and the ever-lovely Ivy Clark. You mighta seen her around in, say…I don't know…*Vogue* magazine. It's gonna be great, y'all. End of this month. September twenty-fifth. Mark your calendars. Oh, and did I mention I'm emceeing the event? I think I might have a couple times."

More like a couple hundred…

Davis leaned against the tree trunk, unwrapped his sandwich, and took a bite. The roof had consumed the majority of the past fourteen days. He had very little to do with the buzz surrounding the fashion show. That was all Ivy. His admiration for her swelled. So did an odd sort of ache. He hadn't seen her for an entire week, and even before then, ever since he unloaded his past out on the Doc's front porch, their time together was sporadic. Like on-again, off-again rain. Tantalizing, but never sticking around long enough to rinse away the heat.

He'd see her tonight, though...

Davis washed his bite down with lemonade and plopped his elbows on raised knees. Ivy had gone above and beyond, throwing herself into the planning, dipping her hand into every aspect of the show. She found dressers, hair stylists, makeup artists. Finalized music choices with Sara and food choices with Arabella. Even convinced Grandma Eleanor to take entry fees at the door. She recruited Big Bubba in the Morning to emcee the event, designed programs, hung posters, and invited industry professionals—like Joan Calloway from *Southern Brides.* She worked like a frenzied woman on a mission. Like her life's breath depended on the show. Like something chased her. Davis knew what it felt like to run. It's why he went to New York in the first place, trying to escape the pain and anger that refused to leave after losing his dad and being uprooted from Telluride in the middle of his junior year.

Whatever her motives, her hard work paid off. The entire event had ballooned into something much bigger than Davis could have imagined. He took another bite and rubbed at his forehead as a familiar cherry red Volkswagen Beetle—the old kind—rattled into Cornerstone's parking lot and pulled next to his Jeep. Pastor Voss stepped out, a carryout bag from Fried Greens gripped in one hand.

"If I'd known you'd be here today, I would have gotten you something." Pastor Voss came into the shade, his Braves cap in its usual position, and eased himself into the grass with a groan. The bag crinkled as he pulled out one of Davis's favorites. "I've been fixing for a 'mater sandwich all day. You want half?"

Davis waved his ham and cheese. "I'll make do."

"I talked to one of the volunteers this morning, and he said you finished the roof yesterday."

"I didn't want to call in the troops for a couple more nails." Davis finished off his sandwich, brushed the crumbs from his hands, and drained his lemonade. "So why are you here? I thought you helped set up for the festival every year."

"I have a few more nails to pound myself. Sunday's sermon isn't cooperating."

"Ah."

"Jonas and Jordan are taking my place at the festival. Two pairs of young hands are better than mine."

Jordan. Davis might not have seen Ivy as much as he'd like these past few weeks, but he'd seen quite a bit of the pastor's grandson. It seemed, wherever Sara was, he was right there next to her. "Did Jordan tell you I humbled myself and apologized?"

"For…?"

"Treating him like a heel. Making assumptions. Did you know my sister broke it off with him? All this time I had it turned around."

"You were just being a protective older brother."

Davis tossed the empty bottle inside his cooler and touched the strap of his camera, rolled up on the grass. He caught himself snapping pictures when he didn't need to. Candid shots. Uncensored moments of honesty. His favorite kind. Like his sister when she sat at the piano bench. Or Marilyn laughing when she dripped ice cream on her blouse. And once, on the strip, he snapped a picture of Ivy watching a father swinging hands with a curly haired little girl.

"You going to the festival?"

"Ivy and I are selling tickets there tonight for the fashion show. We have our own booth and everything. Kipper Manning is coming to interview us for a spot on the Sunday evening news." Davis let go of his camera strap and stood. Now wasn't the time for pictures. Now was time to finish the roof. He reached out his hand and helped Pastor Voss get to his feet. "Well, I better get to work if I want to make it to the booth on time." Davis turned to the ladder and climbed the first rung.

"You seem to be in better spirits lately, Davis."

He paused, gripping the shiny metal between his fingers. Pastor Voss was right. He'd shared his past with Ivy Clark, and somehow he didn't feel quite so heavy.

Early evening and already hordes of people stuffed themselves into the festival. Kids waited in lines for rides. Here and there blobs of teenage boys threw saltwater taffy at teenage girls. Adults crowded beneath beer tents while harassed-looking mothers tried to rein in overstimulated toddlers.

Their booth to sell tickets sat along the marina, squished between a Gullah woman selling baskets and an artist drawing caricatures, all three stations capped by the tops of boat sails flapping in the wind. Davis twisted around in all directions, looking past and through the throng of people. Ivy would arrive any second. Not wanting to appear overeager, he got to work spreading out the pamphlets he'd received from the foundation in charge of the art program.

He noticed her fragrance first.

Fresh lilacs—like the big bushes Mom planted along the side of their duplex in Telluride. He could bury his nose in the scent and never come out again. When he looked up, he noticed other things too. Like the way the breeze tousled her hair. The way the sun cast a golden brown glow on her shoulders. The melted butter of her eyes. After seven days of not seeing her, he had a hard time looking away.

Ivy set her purse underneath a table inside the booth. "Hey, stranger."

Clearing his throat, Davis grunted a hello, then feigned interest in the programs Ivy had designed, scolding his heart for thrumming so fast.

"Took your sister to get a manicure today. You like?" She wiggled her fingers over the program Davis gripped like a lifesaver, showing off apple red nails. "Wanted to look fresh. I've never been on a small-town news station before."

He ignored her hand and flipped the program over. "Have you printed a lot of these?"

"More than a lot. I snagged us a deal from the Staples guy."

"They look great."

A group of young wide-eyed girls approached the booth. "Excuse me, miss, have you really been on the cover of *Vogue*?" one of them asked Ivy.

"I really have."

The girl who asked the question nudged some of the others with her elbow, as if to say, "I told you so." They covered their mouths with their hands—shy-like—and twittered.

"You girls coming to the fashion show?" Davis asked.

More twittering.

He didn't speak tween girl. He had no idea if that was a yes or a no. "The tickets are ten dollars. All proceeds go to funding an art program for blind students at the community college." He handed over one of his pamphlets. "If you come, you'd be helping a really great cause."

The girls blinked at his offering—like he was the one speaking a foreign language—then swiveled their heads to Ivy, who untucked tickets from an envelope and fanned them in her hand. "Why don't you come and watch? Maybe you can get a head start on finding your dream wedding dress."

Without hesitating, they fished inside pockets and purses, pulled out money, exchanged ten dollar bills for tickets, and moved to a different booth—one selling mood rings and bangle bracelets.

"You're better at this than I am," Davis said.

Ivy blushed. "It's not that hard."

"You don't give yourself enough credit, you know that?"

She fiddled with the ticket envelope, her attention flicking to the crowd when a smile exploded across her face—one so sincere and excited, Davis wasn't sure Ivy had ever looked more beautiful. She waved her hands over her head. "Twila! Hey, Twila, over here!"

Twila sat in a wheelchair, a blanket outlining the sharpness of her knees. Annie noticed Ivy first and pushed her daughter through the crowd. The girl's large eyes grew wider, overwhelming her thin face as she adjusted the pink bandanna wrapped around her head. She returned Ivy's wave—flinging her hand back and forth. The scattered times he had seen Ivy over the past three weeks, she always brought up Twila and a potential photo shoot. Davis listened but couldn't bring himself to commit. If he did something like that, how would he ever be able to put his camera away again?

Annie stopped in front of them and wiped at sweat forming along her hairline. Ivy leaned over the booth. "Where've you been, girl? You skipped Sara's piano lesson on Monday."

Twila fiddled with a loose thread on her blanket. The odd combination of her bloated face and her pencil-thin neck gave her the appearance of a bobble head. "More doctor appointments."

Ivy's smile lost some of its spunk.

Annie rubbed her daughter's shoulder.

"Hey, Twila, you know Sara's brother, right?" Ivy said. "He's the one who took those pictures of me for that wedding magazine."

Oh boy.

Twila let go of the thread, her pale lashes fluttering. "I see you at church sometime. You're there a lot."

He tipped his head. "I think we've met a time or two, Twila."

"Davis is a great photographer. I bet if you asked him real nice, he'd take pictures of you. Like your own personal photo shoot."

Twila leaned forward. "My own photo shoot? Really?"

The ball of tension in Davis's stomach unraveled like twine, threading through his limbs. How could he say no to her—this girl who was barely there in her thinness, her dark eyes sparkling with an anticipation that drowned out her sickness. He cast a grimace at Ivy. "I wouldn't be able to do it this weekend. We're going to be pretty busy here at the booth."

"I bet we could do it next weekend," Ivy offered.

Twila looked over her shoulder, at her mother. "Can I? Next weekend?"

"If Davis has time, honey."

Davis slipped his hands into his pockets. Ivy had backed him into a corner. He'd take pictures of Twila next weekend and he'd fall in love—with the girl, with his camera, with a life that could have been his if he hadn't proven how undeserving he was.

29

The fading sunlight dipped toward the horizon, shooting orange rays through the gaps in the Ferris wheel. The scents of bug spray and brine rode the tail end of a warm breeze that whipped sails and rippled the tide. Davis ushered Ivy through the throng, his hand grazing the small of her back. The heat of his almost-there fingers sent a current of warmth through her belly. She passed through a clot of people scoping out a good spot to watch the fireworks and came out in a clear patch of unpopulated marina.

Davis stood behind her with a somber face.

Ivy frowned. Ever since Twila and Annie visited their booth, Davis had straddled the conversation—one ear in, the other ear off in la-la land. Ivy had ended up taking over the majority of the ticket sales while he nodded mindlessly and handed out the pamphlets explaining how the art program worked. Maybe she'd gone too far, putting Davis on the spot with Twila like that. "Are you mad at me?" she asked.

"For what?"

"The whole Twila thing."

He took off his baseball cap, scratched his matted-down hair, and fitted the cap back over his head, twisting the bill so it pointed backward. He looked like a cute college student, not a full-grown man. "You just want to help a sick little girl. How can I be mad at you about that?"

A worm of guilt wiggled in the pit of her stomach. Davis was right. She did want to help Twila. See her smile. Make her eyes sparkle. Just like she wanted to help Sara. But she also needed to get Davis to New York City. She hitched her purse strap over her shoulder and dug her nails into the leather. "Should we go find Sara and Marilyn? I haven't seen fireworks since my summer visits as a kid, and we both know how long ago those were."

The corners of his eyes crinkled—sad little lines fanning out toward his temples. For some reason, her confession troubled him. He looked at his watch. "We have some time. We could go on a ride first, if you wanted."

"A ride?" She grinned. "You mean those things all the kids are getting on?"

He tucked his hands into his pockets. "Sure. We can be kids."

Ivy looked past a lane of light-up games lined with tacky stuffed animals and pointed to a large, roundish metal contraption sporting a long tail of kids and teenagers. "What's that one?"

"Tilt-A-Whirl."

"What does it do?"

He set his palm against his chest. "It breaks my heart that you don't know." He stepped closer, an enticing five o'clock shadow darkening his jaw. "It spins really, really fast and makes you stick to a wall."

"Seriously?"

"I never joke about Tilt-A-Whirls."

Her smile grew bigger.

"That's what you want to ride?"

"Who doesn't want to stick to a wall?"

"I should have known you wouldn't pick the Ferris wheel." He steered her toward the Tilt-A-Whirl line and deposited her at the end. "You want some cotton candy while we wait?"

Ivy shrugged. "Never had it."

Davis shook his head, like it was all too much. "You hold our spot. I'll be right back." He dug his wallet from his pocket and melted into the sea of bodies.

She swiveled her head, following Davis with her gaze, an unfamiliar feeling of lightness stealing through her body. First crabbing in the marsh? Now cotton candy and a Tilt-A-Whirl, followed by fireworks on the beach? If she wasn't careful, Davis and Greenbrier might do a number on her heart.

She placed her hand over the spot, as if to make sure they hadn't already, when hot breath tickled her ear.

"Hey, sweet darlin'."

She spun around, coming face to face with a man she didn't recognize. He wore a smirk and a red hat with Gamecocks written across the front. He had the distinct bearing of a man who was once handsome and fit in his high school glory days but had lost his six-pack and chiseled jaw to beer and potato chips. He took a long swig from his plastic cup, then wiped his mouth with the back of his hand. "Do I know you?" she asked.

"You should."

Ivy rolled her eyes at the lame pickup line. She knew drunk when she saw it, and this man was clearly beyond. She made to move away from him. The Tilt-a-Whirl would have to wait. But he stepped in front of her and held up his cup, foamy liquid sloshing over the side. "Hey now, let's not be so hasty. Why don't you let me introduce myself?"

Ivy crossed her arms. "Okay. What's your name?"

"Now that's the spirit." He tottered closer, his body reeking of stale beer.

Ivy leaned away.

"Name's Doyle Flanning, retired quarterback of the Greenbrier Gremlins, the only one to ever lead his team to back-to-back state championships."

"Impressive."

He stepped closer, his head wobbling a bit on his neck. "Don't think I don't hear the sarcasm in your tone. Because I do, Ivy Clark. I hear it loud and clear."

A shiver skittered its way up her spine. It wasn't so much that he knew her name—since most people in Greenbrier seemed to—as it was the look in his eye when he said it—half lustful, half contemptuous. She glanced around Doyle's large frame, searching for Davis. "Well, it was nice meeting you, Doyle. I should probably find my date."

He snagged her elbow before she could walk away. "Where you off to so fast? We haven't even finished our conversation yet."

"Maybe you haven't." Ivy yanked her arm from his grip. "But I have."

He reached out again, but before he could make contact, familiar hands shoved Doyle back. He stumbled backward, then popped up awfully quick for a man his size. "Hey now, was that really necessary?"

Davis stepped in front of her. "Looked to me like the lady didn't want to be touched."

Ivy couldn't seem to find her voice, and not because of creepy-boy Doyle. Guys had touched her like that since she was fourteen. This was just the first time somebody got angry about it.

"You can get lost or I can make you get lost. Your choice, buddy."

"Think you're a tough guy, huh?" Doyle raised his cup into the air, beer splattering his forearm, and took several steps backward. "To Ivy Clark. A beautiful face. A gorgeous body. And an empty heart. Women like you get off on teasing men like me."

Davis lurched at him.

Doyle brought down his cup and stumbled away.

But his words stayed behind. They hung in the air, taunting her with the truth. Beautiful and empty. That was her.

When the final fireworks boomed over the marina and the smoke hovered over the ocean like mist, Davis's aunt and sister got up from the quilt. Marilyn shook sand from the fabric and folded it into squares. "You coming with us, Ivy?"

Ivy stared at the waves. "I'm going to stay here."

Marilyn looked at Davis. Even with the faint light of a slivered moon, he could see his aunt's raised eyebrows. All through the show, while he described each firework to Sara, Ivy hadn't made a sound. Not a single appreciative ooh or aah. Davis shrugged, though he suspected the reason for her melancholy. "I can take her home."

"You sure?"

"Of course."

Sara clapped her hands against her thighs. "Thanks for helping me enjoy the show."

Davis wrapped her in a hug. "Anytime."

He kissed Marilyn on the cheek and watched as she and Sara shuffled along with the thinning crowd toward the darkened boardwalk. Davis dug his toes into the sand, remembering a night similar to this one. Alone with Ivy. On the beach. When she'd told him her friend died of a cocaine overdose and he'd watched her cry. Davis nudged aside his flip-flops and joined her in the sand.

"Not impressed with the fireworks?" he asked.

She lifted her shoulders. He looked at her through the night, wishing he could see inside her mind and read her thoughts. "Ivy, please tell me you don't believe a word Doyle Flanning said about you. Sara's known him since high school. He's twice divorced with at least one restraining order."

"You think he was lying?"

"I think he was drunk."

"So you don't think anything he said was true?"

"Not one bit."

She turned her face toward his. "Even the part about being beautiful?"

His skin flushed. Okay, so that part had been true. In fact, with the glow of the moon spilling over her bare shoulders and the ocean breeze ruffling her hair, Davis wasn't sure he'd ever seen a woman more beautiful. Or broken.

"Trust me, Davis, Doyle knew what he was talking about."

The words riled him. He wanted to kneel in the sand, grab her face, make her see. But somehow, he didn't think his touch was what she needed. "Doyle doesn't know you."

"Neither do you." The breeze blew a strand of hair in her face. Ivy peeled it from her cheek and brushed it away. "He was right. I tease men. I like to be wanted. It feels good."

"God wants you."

Ivy released a hollow laugh and wrapped her arms around her knees. "Come on."

"I'm serious. He wants you more than any man ever has or ever could."

"In case you forgot, my dad was married to another woman the night I was conceived. I might not know much about Christianity, but I know enough. Adultery is a sin and my life is the result. I was messed up from the beginning."

"I don't think you were messed up; I think the situation you were born into was. But you know something? God has a way of taking messed-up situations and flipping them on their heads."

"Oh yeah? Give me one example."

"Turning an executioner's cross into a symbol of hope."

Ivy hugged her knees tighter and looked out at the surf.

"Trust me, God wants you."

"You're wrong."

"I promise I'm not."

"You don't get it. I'm not clean, Davis. I'm about as far away from clean as a person can get."

"He'll forgive you."

She shook her head. "If God hasn't forgiven somebody like you, what chance is there for someone like me?"

He leaned back. What did she mean, if God hadn't forgiven somebody like him?

"Ivy, God has forgiven me."

She looked at him with eyes that crashed like the waves. "You don't live like it."

30

Ivy's phone buzzed against her thigh. She snuck it from her pocket and peeked at the display. One new message. Bruce. Her gut twisted. The man went from ignoring her phone calls to leaving a message a day—always the same. *"I need to give Juliette an answer, Ivy. We're running out of time here. Is Davis in or out? For your sake and mine, he better be in."*

She prodded the phone with her finger. How long would he let her ignore him? He was Bruce Olsen, after all. Her uncle, yes. But also one of the most influential modeling agents in New York City. He wasn't accustomed to waiting.

"Everything okay?" Davis asked.

With his camera hanging around his neck, his face looked the exact opposite of her unease. After a week of tiptoeing around one another, the air between them was finally starting to normalize. Their night on the beach after the fireworks last weekend had flipped some sort of invisible uncertainty switch that threw them both into awkwardness. She still wasn't sure what to do with a man who rejected her advances and then went on to tell her about God's love with a conviction that puzzled her.

"Ivy?"

"Of course I'm all right." She stepped onto the rickety porch of Twila's home and winked at the frail girl wrapped inside a blanket in her wheelchair, despite the humid warmth of late morning. Before Bruce's phone call, she'd been more than okay. Twila had loved every minute of the photo shoot.

Davis turned the wheelchair around and clunked it up the steps.

Twila laughed, her heart-dotted kerchief fluttering in the breeze like a boat sail.

Ivy's heart lifted. She'd been right to talk Davis into this. Right to indulge Twila. Birds chirped from the trees as the sun rose toward its peak, the air filled with just the right combination of magnolia and sulfur—a scent she was growing to love.

She cast a secretive glance at Davis. Golden sunrays highlighted his profile. Smooth forehead—unwrinkled and relaxed. Blond hair recently trimmed. "You're glad you did this, aren't you?"

"I guess I owe you thanks." He gave Ivy a reluctant grin, then twirled Twila around on her wheelchair. "And thank you, young lady. For giving me one of the most enjoyable experiences behind a camera I've ever had. You are truly an inspiration."

Twila blushed.

So did Ivy.

The front door squeaked open. Annie stepped onto the porch, the screen door whapping shut behind her. "How'd it go?"

"Oh, Mama, it was so much fun!" The girl bounced in her chair. She seemed so much healthier today. It lifted Ivy's spirits. "And Ivy gave me a free ticket to the fashion show! She said I can come backstage and everything."

Annie's smile didn't match the pinch in her eyebrows.

"Is that okay?" Ivy asked. "I guess I should have checked with you first."

Davis rolled Twila inside the home.

When the little girl was out of earshot, Annie scratched her elbow and leaned closer to Ivy. "The doctors stopped Twila's chemo treatments."

No wonder she looked better. "That's not a good thing?"

"They want to build her strength. My sister got tested and we found out she's a match. I think we might be doing a bone marrow transplant real soon."

All of a sudden, the air felt thick. Unbreathable. "Is it safe?"

Annie's eyes filled with tears. "It's sort of like a Hail Mary pass, you know?"

Those words would not leave Ivy's head. Not on the drive home and not when Davis walked her to her door, the consummate gentleman. She didn't stop talking the entire way. Maybe, if she talked long enough and fast enough, Annie's news about Twila wouldn't have time to settle over her heart.

"The fashion show's in two weeks and we really don't have that much to do. I mean, we have to do the fitting with the models, and I should probably teach them to walk. I can make some calls. Confirm things with Arabella. Make sure everybody who promised to auction off packages is still willing. That sort of thing. But other than that, I think we're good to go."

She inhaled and kept going. "Then there's Sara's surprise party. I promised your aunt I'd help her organize it. So I'll keep busy doing that too. Marilyn said your mom would be coming to town for it. When do you think you'll have those pictures ready, by the way?"

Davis blinked.

Ivy fidgeted. What was taking him so long to answer?

He tilted his head to one side, a world of concern etched on his face. "Are you okay?"

"Of course I'm okay. Why wouldn't I be all right?"

"It's just…I heard what Annie said about Twila."

Ivy swallowed.

"I'm sure she'll be okay," Davis said.

Ivy shooed his words away with her hand. "Of course. I know that." She grabbed the door handle, suddenly too hot to be outside. This was a silly conversation anyway.

"Ivy?"

She twisted the handle.

"When's the last time you were really happy?"

The question caught her off guard. So did the quick answer formulating in her memory. "The last time my mom hugged me." She let go of the handle, hating the lump lodging itself in her throat. It had before that fateful day—when James brought Mom's shell back but forgot the rest of her. "Nobody's held me like that in a really long time."

Davis stepped forward and wrapped her in a hug. Nothing lustful. Nothing desirous. Just a sweet, gentle embrace. Somehow she loved and hated it all at the same time.

Ivy leaned over the counter of Something New, relishing the quiet as she flipped through the Polaroids of the models in their dresses. Davis had taken them yesterday, and somewhere in the middle of all that tulle, he'd shared with Ivy that he was finally finished editing Twila's pictures. A week and a half after their miniature photo shoot and Davis was ready to share the end result. Ivy couldn't wait to see them.

She slid the sturdy Polaroids through her fingers and replayed the words Davis spoke before leaving. *"You've been invaluable, Ivy. No way we could have done this without your help."* She nuzzled the praise, bringing it close, recalling last weekend and the runway tutorial she'd given the models. How hard they all laughed when Arabella tripped in her heels. By the end of the evening, her stomach muscles ached from laughing so hard.

Then there was all the time she'd spent with Marilyn, planning Sara's surprise party—scheduled for tomorrow evening. Not to mention the two days Marilyn got sick and asked Ivy to run the boutique. It felt better than she could have imagined, working alongside Sara, helping future brides find the perfect dress. Ivy cocked her head at a picture of Rachel in a calf-length gown, eggshell white with lots of tulle. Lila, another one of their models, had tried it on first, only it didn't look right on her curvy frame. Ivy asked Rachel to try it on instead. Not only did it look great, but Rachel ended up buying it for her wedding.

Ivy's phone buzzed against the countertop. She entered her password and listened to Bruce's voice message.

"Did you fall off the face of the planet or what? Look, Juliette called yesterday. The photo shoot's scheduled for the first of October. Nine o'clock. That's a week and a half away, Ivy. I told her you'd be there. Davis too. He is coming, isn't he? He better be. Call me, will you?"

The message should have caused panic. Turmoil. Anxiety. Because she wasn't at all sure Davis would go with her to New York after the show. Sure, Sara would have her art program, but that didn't mean Davis would be comfortable stepping back into high fashion photography. In all likelihood, she would fail. He wouldn't take pictures for Vera Wang, and somewhere along the line, that reality no longer terrified her. The closer she grew to Sara, the more she helped at Something New, the more comfortable she became with Marilyn, the more time she spent with Twila…

Ivy pressed End on her cell phone and tossed it in her purse. Maybe NYU was wrong about her. Maybe she was good for something other than modeling after all.

Ivy had stepped inside a lot of men's apartments through the years, but none made her as nervous as this. She cleared her throat, smoothed out imaginary wrinkles in her blouse, and knocked on the door of apartment number 302. The door swung open before she finished her second knock. Without saying hello, Davis took her hand, pulled her through a sparse living room, and plunked her in front of a kitchen table splattered with an array of black-and-whites.

She picked up an eight-by-ten of Twila dipping her toes into the marsh. He'd captured the sparkle in her eyes perfectly. Ivy set it down, picked up another, then rested her hand against her collarbone. "Davis, they're stunning."

"You think?"

Tears welled in her eyes, but she blinked them back. "I know."

Davis smiled a smile that brought out his dimples. "Hey, you want some breakfast? I'm a master at chocolate chip pancakes. I'm not too shabby at sausage and grits either."

"Hmm, none of that sounds too good for a girl's figure."

"They're good for the soul though."

Her phone buzzed in her purse.

She gritted her teeth. Probably Bruce, and she couldn't avoid him forever. Eventually, she'd have to tell him that she'd failed her mission and deal with the consequences. Without giving herself time to reconsider, she dug out the vibrating device and held it to her ear. "Calling me before nine on a Wednesday morning? I should be flattered."

"Ivy? Is that you?"

The female voice did not belong to her uncle. Ivy pulled the phone away from her ear and looked at the screen. "Marilyn? Is everything okay?"

"I'm not sure."

Ivy hated the way those words made her stomach drop.

"A gentleman from the Betsy Crestledown Theater called. Someone told him about the advertisements we ran in the newspaper." Marilyn paused. "Ivy, he says nobody ever booked the theater for the fashion show. He's saying they have a junior theater production scheduled for that day."

The photograph slipped from her fingers and fluttered to her feet. "That's impossible."

"That's what I said. But he's adamant that he never received a deposit."

31

Ivy thumped up the stairs to her apartment, her hand clamping and releasing the wood railing like an angry heartbeat. There had to be a mistake—of course she'd sent in the deposit. She racked her brain, forcing her memory into submission. She and Davis had gone to the theater and decided it would make an excellent venue. She'd told him she'd take care of the deposit, got a check from Marilyn, and then…

Her heart thudded in tune with the pounding stairs. Then she found Marilyn's box. The one she thought belonged to James.

"I'm sure you sent it in, Ivy."

She held onto Davis's words, wanting them to be true. They had to be true. She didn't forget to send the check. She couldn't have. She was worrying for nothing. Somebody at the theater messed up. Not her. She and Davis would drive over there and clear everything up.

But what if she never sent it?

Of course you forgot to send the check. It wouldn't surprise Bruce. It wouldn't surprise anyone. Who were you kidding, trying to organize something as important as a charity event? Stick with what you're good at, honey. Men. Modeling. Vera Wang…

Shaking her head, Ivy flung open the door and stepped onto the white carpet. She trekked to her bedside nightstand and opened the drawer. Even if they could get another place on short notice, so many tickets had already been sold. Advertisements in the paper. Industry people invited. All of them would head to the Crestledown Theater, only they'd find a junior theater production instead of a fashion show. She rummaged through the drawer, pulling out a book of stamps, a receipt spotted with dried tea, a crinkled envelope, and…

Sailing Alone Around the Room by Billy Collins.

Her stomach puckered with dread. She hadn't read it in a long time. Instead, she'd taken to choosing from the large bookshelf in Marilyn's living room.

Davis stood over her, staring as she sat on the edge of her bed. "Ivy?"

She held the book out from her body, opened it up, and turned it over.

A folded check floated to the floor.

Davis bent over and picked up the check, unfolded it, and blinked at the blue-penned words—*Pay to the order of the Betsy Crestledown Theater.*

It was official. They'd lost the venue. Was it possible to find another place with less than a week to go?

Ivy tossed her head back and laughed. "Oh, this is too good."

He scrunched his forehead, unsure why she was laughing.

"Why do you look so surprised, Dave? I'm sure not." She took the check from his hand and flung it aside. It swept the air—back and forth, back and forth—then landed on the carpet. "Of course I didn't send it in. Did you expect anything different?"

Davis ignored the odd behavior and scrambled for a solution. Maybe if they put their heads together and worked really fast, all their hard work might not be lost. Surely they could find a way to fix this.

Ivy crossed one leg over the other and fanned her face with a white envelope. When she looked at him, something about her expression had changed. The softness he'd been seeing more and more of over the past few weeks was replaced by the same smile she gave men like Duncan and Stefan, her eyes smoldering.

"We should go." He stepped toward the door and scratched the back of his head. "Maybe if we talk to somebody at the community center..."

She set the envelope on her nightstand. "I want you to take pictures of me again."

"We just lost our venue."

"No other photographer has made me feel the way you make me feel. And I've had lots of photographers." She stood and sauntered toward her dresser. "You make me feel alive, Davis."

Her words escaped like velvet—smooth and soft. He pressed his tongue against the roof of his mouth, blood glugging through his veins.

"I think I make you feel alive too." She traced figure eights over one of her snow globes and met his gaze in the reflection of her mirror. "Let's go to New York. We could organize events way bigger than this. Raise enough money for the art program like this." She snapped her fingers.

He swallowed, hating the way her seductive tones muddled his thoughts. What was she playing at? This wasn't the Ivy he'd grown to admire. This was the old Ivy. The Ivy who wielded seduction like a sharpened blade. They were supposed to be beyond that. "Why are we talking about New York?"

She lifted her thin shoulder, something brewing deep inside her eyes. But before he could figure out what, she looked away from the mirror and picked up the snow globe—one of Paris and the Eiffel Tower. She passed it from one hand to the other. "It looks beautiful, doesn't it? So strong and sturdy."

His mind screamed at him to step out the door. Flee. But his body wouldn't listen. "Ivy, what's going on right now?"

She turned around, lifted the globe into the air and let go. It crashed to the floor, and instead of bouncing or thudding like he expected, it burst into pieces. Tiny, fragmented scraps of glass that sprayed his flip-flops. He stepped out of the way and stared. Her expression would have been indifferent, if not for the pain he saw in her eyes. "But it's nothing more than water and thin glass."

He looked down at the broken pieces, the stain of water soaking into the carpet. Heat exploded in his chest. "What—you think that's you? A snow globe?" His attention swiveled to the dried flowers hanging on either side of the mirror. "Is that what you want to be?"

"I can be whatever you want me to be."

"How about this?" Before he could stop himself, he closed the gap between them, glass crunching with every step, dug his fingers into her hair, and forced her to look at him. "You're not a snow globe. Or those dead flowers. You're not empty. You're not dead. You're a person. A living, breathing human being."

Her lips softened. She leaned forward.

Ignoring the way his body responded, he tightened his grip and looked into her eyes—at the thin rings of golden iris circling her pupils. And inside those pupils, an entire universe of desperation and hurt. "You might be able to hide yourself from the world, Ivy, but you can't hide from Him. He sees you. He sees all of you."

Before her brokenness could consume him, he let go of her and walked out the door.

As soon as Davis came around the side of the house, he spotted a slate gray Toyota Prius in Marilyn's driveway. The only person he knew who owned a Prius was Mom, but he was picking her up from the airport this afternoon. And anyway, hers was green, not slate gray.

He quickened his stride, stepped onto the front porch, and swung open the door to an empty, cool foyer. Georgia scurried around the corner to greet him as he wiped his shoes on the welcome mat and walked to the kitchen. Annie stood by the sink, humming a tuneless melody as she dropped mint leaves into a pitcher of sweet tea and stirred the concoction with a wooden spoon.

"Annie, I didn't know you worked on Wednesdays."

Annie blushed. "Marilyn's letting me work more hours to help pay the bills."

Right. Twila's procedure was tomorrow. "Do you know who's visiting?"

"Short, tiny woman with spiky hair." She let go of the spoon and pantomimed the haircut around her head. "Looking for you and Marilyn."

"Me?" Who did he know with spiky hair and a Prius? "Is Marilyn here?"

"She's running around, setting up for the party."

Of course, and he should be helping. Davis looked through the kitchen door toward the formal living room. "Where's the woman?"

"I had her sit out back in the courtyard." She turned over two tall glasses from the cupboard, filled them with ice, poured the tea, and picked them up. "Follow me."

Davis didn't follow. At least not right away. He needed to tell Sara and Marilyn about losing the venue. He needed to come up with a game plan before all their hard work went to waste. He needed to unpeel the memory of Ivy's hot skin from his fingers.

Annie elbowed the sliding door open. "Are you coming?"

Adjusting the collar of his shirt, he followed Annie outside onto the marbled courtyard, back into the heat. Ice clinked in the glasses. Annie set them on the patio table. The spiky-haired woman turned in the wicker sofa.

Davis recognized the cat-eye glasses first. It was the editor from *Southern Brides*. "Joan? What brings you here?"

Joan thanked Annie, picked up a glass, took a sip of the tea, then closed her eyes and let out a soft moan. "I could bathe in this stuff and never get sick of it."

A chorus of birds twittered in the walnut trees lining the walk. An itchy sting pricked at his calf. Davis slapped at the spot without looking. Stupid mosquitoes.

Joan touched the glass to her cheek. "Have a seat, Davis. We have lots to talk about."

Lots to talk about? Davis leaned toward the door. He didn't have time for Joan.

As if reading his hesitancy, she waved her hand toward the wicker chair opposite the sofa. "Your aunt will be here soon. I called her on my way down. I'm traveling to Savannah for a bridal expo and thought I'd stop in for a visit."

The door slid open. Annie reappeared with a tray bearing a pitcher of sweet tea and a plate of pinwheel cookies. She set it on the table, pulled a lighter from the pocket of her oversized jeans, and lit the citronella candles that cornered the courtyard. They did little to assuage the bugs.

Davis scratched his thigh. "You wanted to talk to me specifically?"

Joan bobbed her head and grabbed a cookie. "I'm dying for you to do another photo shoot for my magazine. The last one was absolutely enchanting. You have no idea how many compliments we've received about the spread."

Okay, what was going on? First Ivy invited him to New York, and now Joan wanted him to do another job. Either God wasn't completely opposed to him doing photography or the devil didn't mess around. He picked up his own glass of tea; the condensation cool against his palm.

"I would love to do an editorial in a sailboat. I keep picturing a bride at the wheel, her groom at the stern as they sail into happily ever after." She bracketed empty air with her hands, as if envisioning a panoramic view of her story. "I want you to bring the vision to life, Davis. I don't know any other photographer who can tell a story like you."

Surely lots of others could. He took another drink, the cool sweetness soothing his parched throat.

"What do you say?"

He looked down at his shoes, praying for an answer. Maybe one of those God-nudges Pastor Voss had talked about. All he felt was humidity. And bugs. He swatted at another mosquito. Two years ago he'd been so certain God was telling him to put away his camera. But what about the nature photography he did as a kid with his father on the trails of the Rocky Mountains? Or the pictures he'd taken of Twila? He had no idea where fashion fell in comparison to those things, but weddings? Those were God-glorifying.

"Davis? You still with me?" Joan perched herself on the edge of the sofa and refilled her glass just as the patio doors slid open. He turned, hoping for Marilyn, but spotted Sara, the birthday girl, holding Sunny's harness, sunglasses covering her eyes. Davis's burgeoning yes faded away. He had no right to do what he loved. "I'm sorry, but I can't."

Joan's face fell. "You can't?"

Sunny led Sara to the empty chair beside his.

"When this fashion show is over"—if they could still make it happen—"I'll no longer be taking pictures."

Joan's cell phone suddenly belted Aretha Franklin. She rummaged through her bag and fished it out, Aretha's voice interrupting the birds. "Sorry about this." She brought the phone to her ear. "Joan Calloway speaking."

She straightened, then held up her finger, indicating she'd just be a moment. Speaking into the receiver, she stood and paced toward the far end of the courtyard, lost behind a towering line of hydrangeas.

"Marilyn called and told me the news," Sara said. "Did Crestledown make a mistake?"

Davis took a deep breath. "We forgot to send in the deposit."

Sara frowned. The two of them sat in silence for a moment until Joan came around the corner. "That was your aunt. She got caught up at Something New, so I'm going to meet her there for a quick word." She picked up her purse and dug out a business card. "Please, Davis, think about it some more before saying no." She handed him her card, took one more cookie from the tray, and disappeared around the house.

"Think about what?" Sara asked.

"She wants me to do another photo shoot for her."

"That's great!"

"I'm not doing it."

Sara shook her head. "I wish you'd take pictures again."

"What do you think I'm doing?"

"A favor for me and Marilyn. And then it'll be back to your strange act of penance for what happened two years ago. You should say yes to her, Davis."

He gritted his teeth. Sara had no idea how easy it would be or how much he wanted to. "I can't."

"So that's it, then? You're just going to keep punishing yourself?"

"Somebody should!" The words exploded from his mouth, making his sister jump. He could see and she couldn't. Where was God's justice? "You're blind because of me, Sara."

She winced.

Davis buried his head in his hands. He couldn't get over it. As hard as he tried and as much as he prayed, he couldn't let it go. Maybe Sara didn't blame him for it anymore, but she had once. And ironically, life was almost easier when she did. Her blame, at least, felt like a tiny piece of vindication. He had no idea what to do with her forgiveness. "You deserve to see."

"Oh, come on, Davis, I don't deserve anything."

"Yes, you do." Sara hadn't done anything wrong. She'd been completely innocent. It should have happened to him. "Why did it happen to you?"

"Maybe you messed up."

The accusation stung, no matter how true.

"Or maybe I did. Or maybe neither one of us did. Who knows why."

He dragged his hands down his face and peeked at his sister, sitting with her arms propped on the armrests, Sunny by her side. Davis had no idea what God wanted him to do. He thought he knew. For a while. Stop taking pictures. Get away from New York City. Be in Greenbrier. But now he felt lost and confused. His heart ached to take up his camera. His mind screamed to put it away. He didn't deserve to take pictures. The proof sat two feet away from him. "I know you've forgiven me, Sara. For what happened. But I haven't yet. I don't know if I ever will."

"Will you stop playing God already?"

Her words startled him, and her expression. It was fierce, much more like Ivy than Sara.

"It doesn't matter if I forgive you. It doesn't even matter if you forgive you. What matters, Davis, is that God already has. So stop wearing your past like a pair of handcuffs." She stood. Sunny too. "You made a mistake, freaked yourself out, and instead of getting back up again, you threw the baby out with the bathwater. And you know what?" She jiggled Sunny's harness. The dog led her to the sliding door and she flung it open. "It's a crying shame." She stepped into the house and left him alone with the rising heat.

32

Three quick knocks sounded on Ivy's door. She stopped, her powder brush frozen by her cheek. If that was Davis, she didn't want to answer. She was much too embarrassed over the way she'd acted a little bit ago.

Whoever it was knocked again. "Ivy? Are you in there?"

Sara.

Ivy gave her other cheek a quick swipe of bronzer and made her way to the door. As soon as she opened it, Sara marched inside with Sunny. Something about her posture actually reminded Ivy of Marshall, and Sara never reminded Ivy of Marshall. "My brother is such an idiot."

Ivy raised her eyebrows. "What happened?"

"He happened."

"You're going to have to be a little more specific."

"Joan Calloway came over. She wanted Davis to do another photo shoot for *Southern Brides,* but he, of course, said no."

That's because he was probably having flashbacks of her terrible attempt to get him to New York. Ivy stripped off her top and selected something sexier from her closet.

Sara walked farther inside, faithful Sunny by her side.

"Wait!" Ivy yelled.

Sara froze. "What?"

"There's glass on the floor. I don't want Sunny to cut his paws." Ivy pulled the halter top over her head and grabbed the DustBuster from underneath her bed.

"Why is there glass on the floor?"

"Um...I dropped one of my snow globes." Ivy made a quick job of sucking up the glass.

Sara dropped Sunny's harness and started to pace.

Ivy turned off the vacuum cleaner. "Why is Davis an idiot for telling Joan no?"

"Because I know he wants to do it. I can tell. But he's determined to punish himself, and as long as he does, none of us will ever move on."

"He told me about what happened."

"I know I said some really awful things in the beginning. But we can't change what happened. I'm over it. I just wish he'd get over it too."

Ivy wasn't sure that was something a person could just get over. The story was pretty awful. And as much as she wished she could console Davis with words like *It wasn't your fault,* the truth was, it sort of was. "He feels guilty."

"I know."

"It's kind of sweet, if you think about it. He won't do photography because he loves you so much, Sara." Ivy slipped into a pair of wedges and sprayed a tiny spritz of perfume onto the inside of her wrist. "I've never had anybody love me like that."

Certainly not James. Not even her mother. Renee might have loved Ivy, but not enough to fight for her. Not enough to get clean and come back for her.

Sara stopped her pacing. "Are you blind?"

Ivy pulled her chin back, unsure how to respond to that particular question, especially coming from Sara. "What do you mean?"

"Is Marilyn invisible to you?"

Ivy blinked several times. Then she batted away the words. She didn't have time to contemplate them, not now. She needed to find Duncan and see if there was any way she could get their venue back.

Davis sank into the empty pew. Stiff, but welcoming. Betsy Crestledown Theater was booked. He tried to fix the mistake, but the damage was irreparable. He'd spent the remainder of the morning scrambling from one large building to the next. The community center—booked. Abandoned warehouse on Fifty-third Avenue—safety hazard. Greenbrier's country club—not even close to the right layout and way too expensive.

The cool, darkened air of the sanctuary bathed his skin—salty from a morning of sweating. Literally and figuratively. They had come too far to cancel now. He clasped his hands between his knees and bowed his head. While he'd meant to pray for a venue, his mind turned to Sara and the things she'd said about forgiveness.

A door opened, followed by a whoosh of air. Davis opened his eyes and placed his hands beneath his knees. The pew groaned. He didn't need to look to know who sat down next to him. "Morning, Pastor Voss."

"Aren't you supposed to be getting ready for your sister's surprise party?"

"That and a million other things."

"Want to talk about it?"

"Life feels a little chaotic right now is all." More like shredded and torn, when hours earlier everything felt so ordered and certain. He scuffed one shoe over the other. "Do you think I'm 'playing God'?"

"I'm not sure what you mean."

"Sara thinks I am." He stared at the hymnal rack. "You know everything that happened a couple years ago? She says forgiving myself doesn't matter. But that's ludicrous. Of course it matters." He came to the edge of the pew. "Right?"

Pastor Voss scratched his chin. "Maybe what Sara meant was that as far as forgiveness and the kingdom goes, our feelings don't mean anything."

Confused. He was very, very confused.

"The minute you confess your sin, God removes it completely. 'As far as the east is from the west.' I don't want to be presumptuous, but I've always assumed you've done that."

"A million times over."

Pastor Voss chuckled. "Once is all it takes."

Davis mulled over the words.

"Annie Welch told me about your photo shoot with Twila. That was mighty fine of you, Davis."

"We lost the venue for our show today." Davis put his elbows on his knees. "Sorry for changing the subject. It's just…if we don't find another venue, like *today,* we'll have to cancel everything." He frowned. Saying the words out loud made them so much more real.

"Why don't you use the church?"

He looked at Pastor Voss, sitting calmly, examining the light fixtures and twiddling his thumbs, like he hadn't just thrown Davis a much-needed bone. He glanced at the pulpit. Wide and deep, leading into a generously sized aisle. He twisted around and examined the rest of the sanctuary. Enough seating to fit five hundred people. He imagined the lobby outside the doors. Spacious. Welcoming. "You wouldn't mind?"

"Sometimes God answers prayers fast. Sometimes slow. Sometimes not at all. Looks like you caught Him on a fast day." Pastor Voss smiled and spread his hands. "You are more than welcome to use the church, Davis. Lord knows it wouldn't be standing if not for all your work."

Davis blinked, amazed at the ease with which his problem disappeared. He wanted to jump out of the pew and find Ivy. Tell her the good news. Her mistake didn't matter after all. Sure, they'd have to get some information to the press and make some phone calls, but between the four of them, they could get it done.

"So was that all that was bothering you—forgiveness and a venue?"

"Yes." Davis shook his head. "I don't know." He rubbed the back of his neck and peered up at the ceiling. "I don't know what to do about photography anymore. This lady, Joan Calloway—she's a fashion editor for *Southern Brides*—she wants me to take more pictures for her. Earlier, I told her no, which is what upset Sara."

A dull ache pounded in Davis's temples. He tried massaging it away. His emotions had run the gamut and it wasn't even noon, and most of those emotions were tied up in Ivy Clark. At what point did she start meaning so much to him? Somehow, he'd let her tear open a seam of longing and stir it into flame. He wanted to hold her and shake her, protect her and get away from her all at the same time. "My sister's not the only one who wants me to take pictures again."

"No?"

"I never would have taken those pictures of Twila if Ivy hadn't cornered me." For whatever reason, Ivy genuinely cared—not just about this fashion show and helping him raise money for the art program, but about him and his photography. A groan stirred from the depth of his belly. "God wanted me to *see her* and somehow I ended up falling in love with her." The words tumbled out before he could take them back. Hearing his own voice speak them out loud set his ears on fire.

Pastor Voss continued to examine the light fixtures, thumbs twiddling, like Davis hadn't just paraded his naked heart around the sanctuary. "That certainly makes things interesting, doesn't it?"

Davis rubbed his eyes with the heel of his palms. Interesting? More like catastrophic. Ivy lived in New York City. She belonged in the industry of high fashion modeling, a world he refused to be a part of ever again. Forget Romeo falling in love with Juliet. This was a hundred times worse.

Pastor Voss cleared his throat. "Romance aside, do you want to take pictures again?"

"Does what I want matter in light of what's right?"

"Right according to whom?"

Davis stopped his eye rubbing.

"You know the story of the prodigal son?" Pastor Voss asked.

The son who left his father's house and lived a life of sin, only to end up eating pig slop and returning home? Of course Davis knew that story. He was that story.

"It's powerful, don't you think? The father running out to the wayward-turned-repentant son, giving him the best clothes, preparing a giant feast.

All to celebrate his return. I always wonder, when I read that story, how different it would have been, if instead of accepting his father's gift, the son would have worn sackcloth and worked in his father's pigsty."

A squadron of goose bumps marched up Davis's arms.

"Loses some of its power that way, doesn't it?"

"You think that's what I'm doing?"

Pastor Voss squeezed his shoulder. "God's calling you to be His son, not His slave. He doesn't want you to wear shackles, Davis. Not when He's already cut you free."

Davis scratched his temple, trying not to feel like a yo-yo stringed to Marilyn's house. Back and forth, back and forth. Only this time, he was back to tell Ivy the good news about finding a venue and to see if it wasn't too late to accept Joan's offer. As soon as he did that, he needed to hightail it to the airport, pick up his mom, and get to Sara's party.

For the second time that day, an unfamiliar car was parked in Marilyn's driveway. This time, a yellow Mustang with rental plates. Who was here now? He looked up at the second-story porch, where Sara liked to sit, and saw nothing but an empty rocker and potted plants. He jangled his keys and walked up the drive. Before he reached the front door, it opened and a man stepped outside. The image of James, only less gray and slightly shorter. Bruce stepped into the sunlight and gave Davis a squinty smile.

"What are you doing here?" Davis asked.

"On my way to a modeling convention in Miami. Scheduled a short layover here so I could speak to my dear niece. Who, oddly, hasn't returned a single one of my phone calls. Have you seen her?"

"I'm looking for her too."

Bruce puffed his cheeks with air and let it escape through pursed lips. "Well, hey, I don't have much time here. Not enough to chase Ivy around Greenbrier, at least."

"Is there something I can do for you?"

"You tell me. Are you coming to New York City after the fashion show or what?"

New York City after the fashion show? "I'm not sure what—"

Bruce waved his hands. "No time for uncertainty, Davis. The shoot is only a week and a half away. Vera Wang wants you." He let his hands clap against his thighs and smiled. "To tell you the truth, I'm surprised Ivy hasn't convinced you yet. She can be awfully convincing, especially when her future is on the line. So what do you say, Davis? Shooting pictures for Vera Wang. An opportunity of a lifetime. For you and for Ivy."

33

Ivy paced outside the doors of Something New. Through the display window, Marilyn flitted from dress rack to dress rack, rearranging and straightening. The last thing Ivy wanted to tell her was that she had lost the venue. That, along with the all-too-fresh memory of throwing herself at Davis did not make a good combination.

Had she gone too far this time? Surely the venue snafu combined with her desperate attempt to entice him to New York this morning had shown Davis the real Ivy Clark was still alive and well. And now that he'd seen that, would he throw her away like James had done to Mom? Ivy twisted her hands together. In an attempt to rectify her wrongs, she'd gone to the theater and used the only weapon she knew to get the venue back—her looks. Only it didn't work. Duncan drooled all over the counter and even asked her out to dinner, but in the end, it came to nothing. The place was already booked and there was nothing he could do about it. She took a deep breath.

Just do it. Stop being a coward and go in there and tell Marilyn the truth.

Ivy swung open the door.

Marilyn had her Big Band music playing extra loud. She looked up from a cerulean satin bridesmaid's dress and smiled. "I was about to close up and come find you. Did you get a chance to straighten things out with the theater?"

Ivy couldn't look her in the face, not when Marilyn's eyes held such unwavering, unmerited confidence in them.

"Is Marilyn invisible to you?" Ivy closed her eyes, refusing to contemplate Sara's question. She had enough emotions swirling inside her without inviting more into the mix. "No, I didn't."

The door opened behind her. Ivy looked over her shoulder. Davis stood in the doorframe, his face dark, as if a black thundercloud had cast a giant shadow over it. Ivy wondered if he was more disgusted with her for how she acted earlier or more upset with her for losing the venue.

"You ready, Marilyn?"

Ivy turned all the way around. Was he really going to ignore her?

Marilyn hung the bridesmaid dress on the rack, looking at Ivy. "Did we find out what happened with Crestledown? Can we really not have the fashion show at the theater?"

"I found us a new venue," Davis said.

"What?" Marilyn and Ivy asked the question at the same time.

"Pastor Voss offered the church. It'll work just as well for the show, and he's not charging us anything. On the way to pick up my mom and Mike from the airport, I made some phone calls to get the word out about the change in location."

Ivy almost melted with relief. "Davis, that's great."

The shadow across his face grew darker.

Marilyn looked between them, a frown tugging at her lips. "Why don't you escort Ivy to the party, Davis? I've got my bike. Hoppin' John's is only a few blocks away." She grabbed her purse and a set of keys. "Ivy, would you mind locking up for me?"

Ivy looked at Davis, who still had yet to acknowledge her. "No, of course not."

Marilyn handed over the keys, kissed Davis on the cheek, and left the boutique.

The silence crackled with tension until Ivy couldn't stand it anymore. "Davis, I'm sorry."

"You really had me fooled."

His cold tone made her take a step back. "What do you mean?"

"For a while there, I actually believed you cared."

"About what?"

"About Sara. This show. Me."

"Of course I care." She cared too much, in fact. So much it scared her. She'd grown to care about him and Sara and this show more than she'd ever cared about anything, and all of it was feeling like pretty rocky terrain.

"Give it up, Ivy. Bruce stopped by the house today."

Warmth drained from her face. "Bruce?"

"All the work you did for the fashion show. Raising money for the art program. Pressuring me to photograph Twila? You never cared about me or Sara—or worse, Twila. All of it was so I'd say yes to a Vera Wang shoot."

No, Davis had it all wrong. "I admit that's what I wanted at first, but it hasn't been about that for a long time." Not since Sara wheedled her way into her heart. Not since Twila had too. And Davis. Especially Davis.

"Then what was this afternoon about? You came on to me and begged me to come to New York." His chest rose and fell. Heated breaths for heated words.

Could she pull the "I don't know" card?

"You tried to play me."

She stepped toward him. "No, that's not what it was about. I promise."

He held up his hand as if to stop her from coming any closer, then paced to the counter, the back of his neck red with anger. Ivy couldn't stand it. She hated his anger. She hated even more that his anger mattered so much. Hadn't she promised herself a long time ago that she would never let it matter? Hadn't she promised to never ever become like her mother?

"I should have listened to my grandfather."

And just like that, his words undid her.

"If you don't mind, I'd rather you not come to Sara's party," Davis said.

"I helped plan the party. Of course I'm going."

"Well, consider yourself officially uninvited. Unlike you, Sara's love is actually genuine." He dug out his wallet from the back of his jeans, snagged some bills, and tossed them toward her feet. They swept the air and rested at her toes. "Payment for your time and energy."

And with that, he turned and stalked out of the boutique.

Ivy stood like a statue, mouth slightly open, processing what had happened until her insides drooped like day-old party balloons. She felt sick to her stomach. Davis had found out about Vera Wang and New York City and disinvited her to Sara's birthday party. She kicked at the money and dug inside her purse for her cell phone.

Bruce answered halfway through the first ring. "What were you thinking?" she asked.

"Well, hello to you too."

"Are you still in Greenbrier?"

"No. I just landed in Miami. Modeling convention. I have a layover in South Carolina tomorrow on my way home. Listen, we need to talk."

"How could you spring Vera Wang and New York City on Davis like that?"

"Spring it on him? Ivy, the shoot's a week and a half away. You promised you'd be able to get Davis, and I promised Juliette you'd follow through. But I have to tell ya, he looked a little shell-shocked when I mentioned it this afternoon."

"He's not going to do it, Bruce. He wants nothing to do with New York City." Or me.

Bruce laughed. "Please tell me you're joking."

"I'm not joking. Listen, you've got to find another photographer. You know a million of them. Surely you can get somebody."

"Juliette wants Davis."

"Well, Davis is out. Find somebody else."

"You're giving me a headache, Ivy. And an ulcer. I can't believe you couldn't convince one guy to come to New York City."

His words were like a prick to an open wound. "Not helping, Bruce."

"Listen, I have to go. We'll talk about this tomorrow."

And that was it. No *Good-bye.* No *Take care.* Nothing but an irritated reprimand. What was she going to tell him tomorrow that she hadn't told him already?

Low-hanging lights drooped from the ceiling, casting a dim glow along the dingy bar top as a country tune about cheating wives droned from crackly speakers and a football game flickered over half-filled bottles of liquor. On her aimless stroll down the strip, she'd spotted the flashing sign for Piper's Bar and Grill, cold beer, and fried pickles. Only the bulbs didn't work for the *C,* so apparently they served old beer and fried pickles. Beer was beer was beer. She'd take it cold or old or halfway warm. She didn't care, so long as it had alcohol.

Ivy needed to think. Or stop thinking. Which was it? Think about her future. Stop thinking about Davis. There it was. If only she could do those two things, life might start making sense again. But Davis refused to leave her brain and her future refused to enter. What was wrong with her? She looked over her shoulder out the smudged windowpanes. Greenbrier, that's what. It was this town's fault. How could she think clearly here? She needed overcrowded streets and honking horns, not ocean waves and country music.

Ivy walked to the bar and sidled onto one of the wooden stools.

"Well, well, well, if it isn't Ivy Clark." The voice crawled up her skin. It belonged to Doyle Flanning. He sat several seats down, the only other patron at the bar, same red baseball cap and same smarmy grin. "The gal nobody will shut up about."

The gray-haired, heavyset man behind the bar finished drying off a beer glass. "You start causing trouble, Doyle, and I'm kicking you out of here."

Doyle let go of his tall mug of foam-topped amber and held up his hands. "I'm saying hello is all, Cal."

Cal gave Doyle a beady stare down before turning to Ivy. "What can I get you?"

Forget the beer. She needed something stronger. "You have Jose Cuervo Gold?"

"Sure do."

The metal legs of Doyle's stool scraped against the floor as he scooted back and moved to the seat beside Ivy. "Where's your boyfriend?"

"He's not my boyfriend."

"You sure? Because he looked pretty goo-goo eyed last time I saw you two together."

Ivy scooted her stool away. "Could you make it a double, Cal?"

"You think you're too good to talk to me, Ivy Clark? Because I can tell you right now, you're not." Doyle held up his fist, showcasing what she could only presume to be one of his state championship football rings.

She couldn't help herself—the eye roll came on its own volition.

His eyes narrowed. "I know women like you. I was married to a woman like you. Two of them, in fact. Women who think they're all that and a bag of chips, all because of a pretty face."

Cal set a shot glass in front of Ivy. "All right, Doyle, you're done. Get out."

"What'd I say?"

"You're disrespecting one of my customers. Which means if you want any more beer tonight, you're going to have to get it elsewhere."

"Aw, c'mon, Cal. The game's not even at halftime."

"You're cut off."

Doyle let out a string of curse words and stood. He threw a wad of bills on the bar and leaned next to Ivy's ear. "Until we meet again, Ms. Clark."

His breath was hot and stale on her neck.

"Out, Doyle!"

Laughing, Doyle stumbled outside. Ivy didn't relax until the door closed.

"You want to be careful around him. Doyle's a bit of a hothead." Cal opened the tequila bottle and poured it into her shot glass. It glugged until the golden liquid reached the top.

"Don't worry. I can handle men like Doyle." Ivy knocked the drink back, her throat catching fire.

Cal grinned. "So I take it you're the gal Sara Knight's been parading around town. The one organizing that fashion show my daughter Rachel's walking in."

Ivy tapped her empty shot glass on the bar. "That would be me."

"My wife Trudy told me you were engaged to Davis. Then my sister Barbara Jean says you're his cousin. You don't seem the type to marry your cousin."

Ivy twirled her hand. "You going to pour me that drink or talk all night?"

His grin widened. "A little spitfire, aren't you?" He poured her another round. "Isn't Sara's party tonight?"

"Sure is." Ivy emptied her glass and pursed her lips. Man, that burned.

"What are you doing here, then?"

"That's a great question." She folded her arms over the bar, the alcohol starting a fire in her stomach. Davis had disinvited her—but so what? He wasn't the party police. It wasn't even his party. She looked around the bar. She could sit here and sulk all night, worrying about Bruce's visit tomorrow, or she could go to Sara's party and celebrate with her friend.

Friend.

The word hummed in her throat. That's what Sara was—a friend. Ivy loved her. And despite what Davis might think, it had nothing to do with New York City. She fished a twenty from her purse, threw it on the bar, and left. She had a party to attend.

34

He had to give his sister credit. She feigned surprise well. Expressed appreciation and gratitude too. Only those weren't fake. Mom, Mike, Marilyn, and a whole host of party guests swept Sara into hugs, shook her hand, kissed her cheek, wished her happy birthday. His sister—twenty-three. Where had time gone?

He took a sip of his Coke and wrapped his hand around the strap of the Nikon hanging around his neck. Ever since he arrived at Hoppin' John's, he'd hidden in the back, away from Grandfather and Grandma Eleanor and Marilyn and Mom and anybody else who might ask about Ivy. What would he tell them? That he'd disinvited her? Marilyn would have his head and Grandfather would shake his hand. Davis didn't like the thought of either.

Blowing out a deep breath, he ran his hand through his hair and closed his eyes. The heated emotions of anger and betrayal had cooled into a sludge of regret and embarrassment. He'd overreacted. So Ivy wanted him to go to New York City. There was no reason for it to come as such a huge shock.

But it had.

It really had. All this time, he'd thought she cared for him as much as he cared for her. Bruce's news wounded his pride, and just as he'd lashed out at Sara in New York City two years ago, he'd done the exact same thing to Ivy in that boutique. To make matters worse, he'd thrown money at her.

Once Sara emerged from all the guests, he stood from his back-corner seat and wrapped her in a hug. "Happy birthday."

She hugged him back. "Where's Ivy?"

He stepped back and scratched the back of his neck, Sara's eager expression exacerbating his jerk-like feelings. "I'm not sure."

"Weren't you supposed to come together?"

"Um..." What could he say? He couldn't lie. But telling the truth would only make her angry, especially after their heated conversation at the house earlier today. Sara was already annoyed with him. Did he need to make it worse?

Thankfully, Mom saved him from answering. She glided over and gripped Sara's shoulders. "Were you surprised or what?" She winked and nodded at Davis's Nikon. "Picture time!"

Mom and Sara flashed identical smiles.

He took the picture with half his heart. Was it too late to find Ivy and re-invite her?

"I can't believe you're twenty-three, Sara." Mom's dewy-eyed gaze swept over Sara as if she were rewinding the past twenty-three years and reliving each day. "Your father would be so proud of the woman you've become."

The mention of Dad didn't help Davis's mood. Dad never would have treated a woman the way Davis treated Ivy tonight.

A throat cleared. Jordan Ludd stood awkwardly to the side, cheeks stained scarlet, holding a single white rose in his hand. "Hello, Sara."

"Hello, Jordan." Sara stepped away from Mom and reached for Jordan's hand.

"Happy birthday." Jordan twined his fingers with hers and handed her the rose. "It's white. Your favorite."

"Thank you." She blushed and buried her nose in the blossom. She resurfaced with the same question she asked before. "So where's Ivy, Davis?"

He looked at the door, willing her to walk through it. To tell him to shove aside because, regardless of what he'd said, regardless of the way he'd treated her at the boutique, she cared about Sara and she'd be attending her party. His attention fell on Sara and Jordan's interlaced fingers. They wouldn't be together if not for Ivy butting in when he told her not to. And Sara wouldn't be wearing the delighted expression she wore right now.

He tugged at his collar. "I'm going to go pick her up right now."

Ivy's heels clicked down the deserted strip. Shafts of white moonlight peeked through ink-blotched clouds, then disappeared as she turned down a darkened path—one that led through a small park. Jose Cuervo sloshed inside her belly and made her legs feel like overplucked bowstrings. She wasn't drunk. She knew what that felt like. But after two months of zero alcohol, she was plenty tipsy. She walked beneath a canopy of Spanish moss and listened to the crickets' serenade.

Davis was at the party right now, probably telling everybody about the changed location for the show. Well, she could help. When she got there, she would help. She'd also make him listen. She hadn't been manipulating him. Maybe at first, but not later. Not after he stood up for her to Marshall or protected her from a belligerent Doyle at the festival. Not after watching him take pictures of Twila or the hug he gave her afterward. Not after falling in love with him…

Her heart stuttered. So did her stride.

Is that what was happening? Was she in love with Davis Knight?

An image of her mother flashed through her mind—wasting away, slipping away, losing more and more of herself every single day James remained absent and left her phone calls unanswered. The only reason Mom made Ivy go on those summertime visits was so she could stay linked to James somehow. Ivy reached out trembling fingers and felt for the lone bench alongside the path. She gripped the backrest and eased onto the seat.

Davis Knight.

Her heart throbbed at the thought of him, which was reason enough to walk away. She imagined going to New York and never looking back. She forced herself to picture it. The thought of never seeing Davis again made the alcohol in her stomach turn sour.

She hugged her middle, digesting the truth. Ivy had gone and done what she promised herself she'd never do. She'd fallen in love. The image of

Mom's wasted form blurred out of focus, and in its place came a different one. Of Jordan when he looked at Sara. Sara when she listened to Jordan. The tenderness they shared for one another. Maybe love didn't have to be bad. Davis wasn't anything like James. Maybe loving a man like him wouldn't ruin her.

Ivy's chest flooded with hope. She kept her eyes closed and clamped her arms tighter around her middle, like the feeling might leak out of her if she didn't hold everything together. Could she let herself love Davis? She bent over her knees. What if Davis didn't love her back? What if he didn't want anything to do with her ever again? Ivy exhaled the worry.

One thing was clear. She wouldn't find any answers huddled into a ball on this bench. She needed to get up and find him. She needed to try. Gathering the hope close, she straightened from her scrunched position and noticed that the dark path was no longer deserted.

A big man stumbled toward her, beer bottle in hand. That man wasn't Davis, either. It was Doyle, and he was already much too close for comfort. Her heart spiked, shooting heated prickles all the way into her fingertips. She was alone. In the dark. In a deserted park. With a man who was clearly drunk and, according to Davis, had an ex-wife who felt threatened enough to get a restraining order against him.

Relax. He's not an ax murderer. Or a rapist.

He could be. She didn't know.

A long-ago warning tumbled through her mind, words from a friend she missed. *"One of these days, you are going to mess with the wrong man. Tread carefully, my friend. You don't want to get hurt."* All of a sudden, Annalise's lighthearted warning felt terribly prophetic.

Taking a deep breath, Ivy reached inside her purse and clenched her fist around Marilyn's keys—her only weapon. Pinpricks of perspiration wrapped beneath her arms and slicked her palms. Blood whooshed past her ears so loud and fast she could hardly think. She looked down at her shoes.

Run, you idiot.

Her muscles poised for flight, but it was too late to run. Doyle stood right in front of her, his meaty fingers wrapped around the neck of an almost empty bottle of beer. He sure hadn't wasted any time finding another place to get his hands on one.

"We just can't seem to stop running into each other." The tail end of each word slurred into the beginning of the next. He wobbled in place, like the ground rocked him back and forth.

Her attention zipped left, then right, as if searching for an escape. She looked ahead, past the canopy of live oaks, their gorgeousness morphing into a death sentence. Nobody from the street could see them. She took a few steps away.

Doyle's hand darted out like a snake and wrapped rough fingers around her elbow. Apparently, he wasn't so drunk that he'd lost his reflexes. "Hey now, where you going?"

A scream built in her lungs, but would anybody even hear her? Judging by the empty strip, it seemed everybody was crammed into Hoppin' John's, enjoying Sara's birthday party. She looked past the trees, into the darkness, and cursed the sea turtles. Doyle's fingers bit into her flesh. "You're hurting my arm."

He released her as quickly as he'd grabbed her but didn't step away. Instead, he narrowed his eyes. "I really don't like women like you."

Ivy took another step back. Closer to the street.

"Full of yourself. Too good."

Another step back.

He took a swig from the bottle. Beer dribbled down his chin. "Just like my first ex-wife. Two peas in a pod. I can tell."

Two more steps. Her heart squeezed. *Thump. Squeeze. Thump.* She was getting closer to the street. Farther from him. But he demolished the gap in two long strides. He grabbed her chin, mashing it between rough fingers. "You know what?"

Ivy's heart jumped to her throat. *Please, God…*

"I think it would serve you good if you didn't have that pretty face." He shoved her back, jarring her neck.

Ivy stumbled. Recovered. Turned to flee. Escape. Breathe. But he grabbed her elbow and wrenched her arm. Pain exploded in her shoulder as if he'd ripped her bone from its joint. She gasped. She couldn't lift it. She tried to pull a ragged breath into her lungs, but they wouldn't work. Nothing worked.

And before she could run away, Doyle brought the empty beer bottle back and crashed it against her cheek.

An explosion of pain.

Then nothing but blackness.

Davis jogged down Palmetto Boulevard, anxiety mounting the farther he got from Hoppin' John's. Why was he so unsettled? He didn't stop until he came to Something New and peeked into the display window. But he knew it was no good as soon as he spotted the darkened awning.

The lights were off. Ivy had already left. He tapped the middle of his forehead with his fist. He had told her he should have listened to his grandfather. He threw money at her feet and walked away. All her life, men treated her like nothing and she believed them. Tonight, he'd added himself to the mix. Of course she wanted to model for Vera Wang. She loved modeling just like Sara had loved painting. Why did he have to be such a jerk about it?

He pulled on the door. It gave a centimeter and clicked. Just to make sure she wasn't sitting in the dark, he rapped on the window. He tried her cell again but got shuffled to voice mail.

Come on, Ivy, where are you?

She might have walked back to Marilyn's or maybe to the beach or the bar. Trying to think, he looked both ways down the strip. Only one light was on and it filtered from the windows of Piper's Bar and Grill. Might as well try there. Davis jogged in that direction, peering at the beach as he did. Except for a distant flicker of firelight—probably a teenage beach party—he found nothing but darkness. One more block and he reached Cal's. He swung open the door to the twang of country music and cigarette smoke and spotted a couple, heads dipped together in a corner booth. Cal was wiping down the bar top.

"Hey, Cal."

"Well, hi there, Davis. Isn't your sister celebrating her birthday tonight?"

"She is." Davis stepped farther inside. "Hey, you haven't happened to see a girl around, have you? Tall and beautiful? Pretty hard to miss."

"Sure have. She had two rounds and headed out."

"Do you know where she was headed?"

"Can't say that I do. But I can say Doyle Flanning was giving her grief when she arrived."

Davis's uneasy feeling quadrupled. "Doyle was here?"

"Sure was. Had one too many, like usual. I kicked him out before he could get too nasty."

Oh, man. This was not good. Doyle had harassed Ivy, got himself kicked out of a bar, and now Ivy was out there somewhere, not answering her cell phone. Davis thanked Cal and slipped out of the bar, back into the night, his heart still thundering. He took a deep breath and wiped cold sweat from his palms, trying not to let panic have its way. Ivy and Doyle did not leave the bar together. She was probably fine. Davis would find her and apologize. Maybe he'd even agree to go to New York with her. It was only one photo shoot. After all she'd done for the fashion show, couldn't he give her that much?

Help me find her, Lord. I need to find her.

He twirled around, searching for a clue. Searching for direction. He spotted a familiar path up ahead. Palmetto Boulevard curved like a *C* around a small park. If a person wanted to take a short route from one end of the strip to the other, that person would cut through the park. He could do it now and head back to Hoppin' John's. Maybe that was his best bet. Maybe, despite his harsh words, she'd gone to Sara's party. It wouldn't be the first time she ignored his requests. He picked up his pace and jogged down the path leading through the park. He didn't stop until he heard something rustle.

His muscles coiled. "Hello?"

A low groan—up ahead.

He squinted through the darkness and saw the outline of a person on the ground. Davis hurried forward, his shoes crunching over glass. The person lay on the ground, long tangles of hair splayed across the pavement.

Oh God…

It was Ivy. Dread lodged in his throat as he bent over and touched her hair. Warm and wet. He brought his hands in front of his face, his fingers wet with blood. He put his hand on her shoulder. Another moan escaped her lips.

Oh God, oh God, oh God…

As gently as possible, he scooped Ivy into his arms and spun in a frantic circle. What could he do? How bad was she hurt? He couldn't see anything. He only knew there was a lot of blood.

Lord, tell me what to do!

Moonlight peeked through the clouds and filtered through the canopy of Spanish moss. He stepped out from under it and spotted the top of a familiar antebellum home not more than a block away.

He cradled Ivy to his chest and sprinted to Doc Armstrong's.

As soon as he got there, Davis pounded on the door. The deep bark of a dog sounded from the other side. Davis pounded again, air thick in his throat, Ivy limp in his arms. Had he hurt her by running? How much pain was she in?

The light flickered on and then flooded the porch. He blinked against the brightness. A chain rattled. A bolt clicked.

C'mon, Doc, hurry up!

The door opened and Doc Armstrong's face peered out, his thick glasses magnifying his eyes. "Hush up, Neil."

The barking stopped.

"Doc, I need help."

Doc flung open the door, his already large eyes widening at the sight of Ivy in his arms. Davis didn't look down. Couldn't look down. He was too afraid to see the damage.

35

Muffled voices wiggled their way into Ivy's consciousness. She stirred, kicking damp sheets off her legs as she tried wading out of the darkness. The voices rose, then quieted. She cracked open one eye. Muted sunlight pierced her pupil. She squeezed her eye shut. Her stomach rolled with nausea. Her throat felt as though somebody had swabbed it dry with cotton balls. Where was she? What was going on?

She tried to push herself up in bed, but her shoulder protested and her face caught fire. It itched and burned like somebody had rubbed it raw with a Brillo pad. When she tried opening both eyes, she found that one refused to cooperate. She managed a one-eyed blink, adjusting to the sunlit room. Somebody needed to shut the blinds.

And her face. What was wrong with her face?

A familiar voice floated inside the white room. "I'd like to see her."

Bruce? What was he doing here? And where was here?

"You can as soon as she's awake." The unfamiliar voice belonged to a woman.

Ivy's face itched and her eye wouldn't open. She reached up to scratch it, but her fingers touched gauze, and the frightening memory slowly took shape in her mind. Her heart went from a barely there gurgle to full-throttle panic attack.

Doyle and the beer bottle. Darkness. Fear. The smell of alcohol on his breath. Him pulling back his arm and smashing the bottle against her face.

She reached up and touched the gauze again. Pain blistered beneath the bandages and panic clawed up her throat. The room spun, then shrunk. Ivy gripped the sheets and cried out for help. What was wrong with her face?

Ivy's cry cut through Bruce's request. Davis wanted to bury his head in his hands. Cover his ears. Or maybe run inside her room and do something to soothe her pain. Her call reached out like a dull knife and gutted him.

Last night, the ambulance came to Doc's and brought Ivy to the hospital. Her injuries were too severe for Doc to treat in his home. Mom and Sara had come and gone, but Marilyn waited with him as late night turned into early morning. Davis paced in the waiting room, wanting to see her. Terrified to see her, battling much too familiar feelings of guilt, until Bruce waltzed inside the hospital not more than ten minutes ago. Davis had followed him to Ivy's room before he could barge inside. Now Ivy was awake. Davis dragged his hand down his face and stepped toward her door. Bruce stepped with him. Davis grabbed his arm and glared.

"Let me go check on her." The nurse, who looked weary of them both, disappeared inside the room.

"I'm her agent. She's my client and she's sustained injuries. It's my right to see her."

"It's your right to see her?" Who did he think he was—Ivy's owner? He'd certainly never been her caretaker. Bruce only cared about Ivy so long as she made him money. As far as Davis was concerned, he lost all his rights to Ivy a long time ago.

The nurse returned.

"How bad is it?" Bruce asked.

"The injury needed a number of stitches, and there's a lot of swelling. It won't look as bad once the swelling goes down."

"Will there be scarring?"

Davis hated Bruce for asking that question.

"The glass bottle caused some nasty damage. I don't see how there won't be. Now, if you'll let me change her bandages, you can go inside and say hello."

Bruce looked at the linoleum. He didn't have to say it. It was written all over his posture. Ivy's modeling career was over.

The nurse gave Ivy a large pill and a glass of water. She drank it down, wishing the medicine would erase the pain in her chest too. The nurse had poked and prodded her shoulder, tipped up her chin and peered at her face, then reapplied the bandages. Ivy had wanted a mirror, but fear kept the request nestled inside. The nurse smiled—the way Sara might have smiled—patted Ivy's hand, and left the room.

A minute later, Bruce stepped inside.

Ivy ducked her head. Even though her face was wrapped, she couldn't let Bruce see her. Not like this. If he saw the extent of her injuries… She closed her working eye and hurled the thought away. He wouldn't fire her. She was his niece. And her face would heal. That's what injuries did—they healed. A tear slipped from the corner of her eye and raced down the side of her nose. The Vera Wang photo shoot was less than two weeks away. The opportunity of a lifetime. Her last chance to hold on, and it had slipped between her fingers and disappeared.

"Rough night."

She didn't look up.

"Davis said the police caught this Doyle guy. He was already on parole for aggravated assault."

"Do you think that's really what I want to hear right now?"

Bruce didn't respond.

"Why don't you say what's on your mind, Bruce?"

"Ivy…"

Like a criminal facing the firing squad, she knew what was coming. Best to get it over with. And best to look him in the eye when he delivered the blow. It was the first time she'd ever seen him look uncomfortable.

"This isn't the time or the place," he said.

"Sure it is. This is the perfect time and place." Years and years of suppressed anger swirled together and blistered beneath her skin. She refused to look away from him. Refused to let him off the hook. "Quit being a coward and say it."

"What is it you want me to say?"

"What use am I now, right?"

He shook his head.

"It's written all over your face." Emptiness expanded, pushing her anger and everything else aside. She was empty. Empty, empty, empty. Only now, she had no beautiful shell to hide it. She fisted the sheets in her hands. "Well, thanks for the ride, Brucey. It was fun while it lasted."

The pity in his eyes made Ivy loathe him more. "We're not sure of anything right now. You could heal, do some commercial work. I can help you find a commercial agent."

Ivy shook her head. Empty words for empty promises.

He slipped his hands inside the pockets of his slacks. "What am I supposed to do?"

Hug me. Hold me. Treat me like your niece instead of your client. Tell me everything will be okay. That I'll heal and you'll see me in New York in a couple months and you'll find me a job.

Another tear raced down her cheek.

"Davis is outside. He wants to see you."

A wave of nausea rolled up her torso. "No." Davis couldn't see her like this. He would take one look and walk away revolted. She couldn't let him do that to her. She wouldn't survive it. "Send him away. He's the last person I want to see."

Davis stepped away from the door, Ivy's words tearing him straight through. Sara was an artist. She'd wanted to be a painter of watercolors. She needed her eyes. Ivy was a model. She'd wanted to model for Vera Wang. She needed her face. Somehow, he had played a role in destroying both.

He stared down at his hands—healthy and strong. They were hands that should have protected his sister. Hands that should have protected Ivy. But, instead, his hands tossed money at Ivy and left her alone. He'd disinvited her to Sara's party, and she'd ended up running from a man who'd injured her in a permanent way. All because he lost his temper. Just like he'd done with Sara. Somebody else had gotten hurt because of his poor choices. Somebody else had lost her dreams because of his swollen pride. Now Ivy never wanted to see him again. Davis felt sick to his stomach. He was the one who deserved blindness. He was the one who deserved to have his face pulverized.

Not Sara. The sister he loved. Not Ivy. The woman he loved.

Oh God…

He loved her. He did. But it was too late. Before Bruce could deliver Ivy's request, Davis turned around and walked away.

36

Davis left, but Marilyn stayed. She stayed while the doctors ran more scans and x-rays. She stayed when the police came with their questions. She stayed when Ivy asked her to leave.

A doctor asked, "Are you family?"

And Marilyn said, "Yes. I'm her mother."

She took care of filling out insurance and medical forms. She stood by Ivy's bedside while the nurse showed them how to dress and treat the wounds. She scheduled a follow-up appointment when Ivy would have her stitches removed. She called Sara, who came with Jordan to bring Ivy clean clothes. And when all that was finished, she checked Ivy out of the hospital and helped her to the car.

Marilyn gripped the steering wheel with white knuckles and a bereft heart as Ivy sat in the passenger seat—pale and pinched and tight-lipped, half her face hidden beneath gauze as she looked out her window. Every time Marilyn tried to find her voice and ask a question, the words got stuck. What was there to say? So they drove in silence until she pulled into the garage and turned off the car.

"Are you hungry? I can make you something to eat. Maybe some soup."

Ivy shook her head, unstrapped her seat belt.

Marilyn unstrapped hers as well and hurried out of the car, around to the passenger side, opened Ivy's door, and offered her arm.

But Ivy shrugged her away and got out on her own.

Marilyn hurried ahead and helped Ivy inside the house. Georgia greeted them with happy barks that did not match the mood. Marilyn nudged her away with her foot. "Do you need any pain medicine? Would you like to lie down on the couch?"

"I don't want your help!"

Georgia stopped yipping.

Ivy glared, broken and bruised and shut away. Impossible to reach. Each smile Ivy had extended to Marilyn over the last couple of weeks had become treasured blocks of hope, one stacked on top of the next until a tall tower of them rose in her heart. God was doing great things. She could feel it. He was restoring all that had been lost. But now the tower tumbled and crashed. Ivy looked like she would never smile again. "I just want you to leave me alone."

What else could Marilyn do but nod?

Clutching the small bag of medicine to her chest, Ivy walked up the stairs and disappeared. Marilyn sunk down onto the couch, her heart fissuring, every doubtful thought she'd ignored over the accumulating years seeping through the cracks. Rising to the surface.

What was the purpose of all this pain?

A long time ago, Marilyn had thought she understood. Nobody else did—certainly not James or her parents—but Marilyn knew God had a purpose. A story was unfolding. The moment she'd laid eyes on Ivy, it was as if God had said, *Woman, here is your daughter,* and all of a sudden, her barren womb made sense. God was going to take the ashes of infertility and betrayal and make something beautiful. But now all that remained was confusion. Why would God give her this burdensome love if all it would bring was more pain? What was the point in giving Ivy beauty if He was only going to snatch it away?

Marilyn felt like a tragic figure in a play, the last one to catch on that the ending would not be a happy one. The fool who had given her heart away and would never get it back.

But the whisper came…just as it had ten years ago when Ivy left for New York.

I am not finished.

She gathered the words in her hands and grasped them to her chest as if the tighter she clung, the truer they would be.

Ivy felt mean as she walked up the steps. She didn't want food or water. Despite her throbbing shoulder and pounding head, she didn't even want medicine. All she wanted was to rewind time, go back and have a giant redo. Not just to last night, but all of it. Her entire Greenbrier experience, before Davis found a way into her heart.

She had told Bruce she didn't want to see him. She had pushed Davis away as she had pushed every other man before him, but maybe, this time, this man wouldn't let her. She had sat in her bed while Bruce walked out of her hospital room, hoping Davis would barge through the door and cup her face in his hands and whisper words of love and assurance. She was not a bouquet of dead flowers. She was not a snow globe. Her entire body had ached with the hope of it. Until Bruce came back into her room alone.

"He already left," he'd said.

And whatever remained of Ivy's heart shriveled into nothing.

Through the rest of her hospital stay, Ivy managed to avoid her reflection. Now, as she stood on the landing in front of the door that led to the guest apartment, the task barreled toward her like an unavoidable freight train. She twisted the knob. The door creaked open with an unenthusiastic squeak. Ivy stepped over the threshold, flicked on the light, and tiptoed across the carpet, her stomach clenching tighter and tighter with each step closer to the mirror.

She stared down at her sandals. Some flecks of blood had dried over her French pedicure. She squeezed her unswollen eye shut, filled her cramped lungs with a long, deep breath of stale air, and began removing the gauze from her face. When the dressings lay at her feet, she brought her hand to her cheek. Bumpy ridges pressed into her fingertips. She placed her palm over her chest as if the pressure might still her heart. Then she opened her eye. Brought up her head. And looked at her reflection.

The air in her lungs swooshed away.

The stranger staring back at her was half monster—purple and swollen with lacerations spidering across her cheek, climbing over her jaw, and dribbling down her neck. Deep, red, raw wounds laced with black stitching.

Ivy gasped.

The monster in the mirror gasped too.

Her fingers fluttered to her chin.

The monster in the mirror did the same.

Revulsion grabbed hold of her stomach. The doctor had said the swelling would go down. The purple welts would fade. The stitches would come out. But the scars? Ivy knew all too well that scars stayed. A cry clawed up her throat as ravaged and raw as her wounds. It bubbled from her lips and snapped whatever composure she'd clung to. A tsunami of grief and anger crashed through her body. She ripped the bouquet of dead flowers off the mirror and tore them to shreds, rage and sorrow possessing the beast in the mirror.

Her father never wanted her. Bruce only loved her for her beauty and the money she could make him. And for all Davis's words, he didn't want her either. Nobody did. She scrambled on top of the dresser, gripped the heavy mirror, and wrenched it from the wall, pain exploding in her shoulder as she heaved the mirror from her body. Marilyn's box, with all her pictures, fell with it. The mirror crashed against the ground with a sickening crack. Shards of glass popped from the frame and tumbled on top of each other.

"You can't hide from Him, Ivy. He sees you. He sees all of you."

Ivy slid off the dresser and sank onto the glass-strewn floor. She wrapped her arms around her shins and buried her face in her knees. What did God see—an unwanted child? An unfortunate mistake? A woman who finally got what she deserved? "Oh, God, who do you see?"

Who am I?

She hugged herself tighter and rocked back and forth, trying to squeeze the hopeless question away. A sliver of glass bit into her thigh. A sharp breath hissed through her teeth. She jerked her head up from her knees and saw the mess she'd made. Pictures scattered across broken glass. Pictures of a stranger with her face. Marilyn's box tipped on its side. And a card resting at her knee.

I have called you by name, you are Mine.

A sob rent loose from somewhere deep inside her, followed by another and another. The words swept through her. She longed for them to be true. She ached for them to be true. But how could they be when nobody had ever loved her like that?

Except…

Her bedroom door flew open. "Ivy!"

And Marilyn came. Despite Ivy's rejections, despite pushing her away again and again and again, Marilyn didn't even hesitate. She moved through the shards of glass with bare feet and gathered a broken Ivy in her arms, holding her tighter than she'd ever been held.

Fragments of memory stirred and gathered in Ivy's mind, impossible to ignore. It was Marilyn who brought her flowers. Marilyn who saw her when James looked the other way. Marilyn who did everything she could to make Ivy feel wanted whenever she came for those summer visits. It was Marilyn who collected Ivy's pictures and Marilyn who gave her a home when her mother no longer could. It was Marilyn who tried to stop Ivy from going to New York, even though Ivy hated her for it. Marilyn who gave her a job when there were no more jobs to be had. And Marilyn with her Bible, forever on her knees, praying for her. Despite the humiliation Ivy's existence must have caused. Despite being betrayed by the same man. Marilyn fought for her when nobody else would fight. Marilyn loved her even when Ivy threw that love back in her face. Marilyn had taken an unwanted child and made her into a beloved daughter.

I have called you by name, you are Mine.

Everything collapsed. The walls Ivy had built. The fear that hounded her. The fleeting, temporary beauty she clung to with desperate fingers. It collapsed into rubble and left her contracting with pain. So much that she was left gasping for breath, curled into a ball against Marilyn's chest, hope ricocheting through her soul, breaking what wasn't already broken.

Maybe, if Marilyn could love her like that, maybe if Marilyn could forgive James for such unfathomable betrayal, then just maybe the God she worshiped so fervently could love and forgive Ivy too.

Oh, God, if it's true, You can have me. You can have every broken piece…

And while Marilyn helped Ivy birth the pain, somehow, some way, Ivy clasped Sara's truth to her chest and made it her own. Slowly, slowly, the pain receded. Not every single bit, but enough to know that she was His. He called her by name.

37

When daylight turned to dusk, Marilyn let Ivy go. Together, and with an understanding that required few words, they cleaned the rubble of glass and pictures and gauze from the carpet. And when that was done, Marilyn carefully combed pieces of glass from Ivy's hair. By the time Ivy had taken a shower and dressed into her pajamas, her stomach grumbled and her shoulder and face throbbed. Marilyn gave Ivy her medicine and redressed her wounds. They ate big bowls of potato soup at the small table in the kitchenette. Then Marilyn helped her to bed. Ivy curled under the blankets and slept like the dead.

She awoke in the morning to a glass of water, her pills, and a handwritten note.

Breakfast is on the counter. Coffee is all ready to brew. The dress rehearsal for the show is this morning, so I had to leave. Please call if you need anything.

Love, M.

Love, M. Funny how something that would have baffled, if not angered a few months ago could lift her spirits this morning. Ivy sat up slowly, gave herself a moment to acclimate to being vertical, then took her medicine and headed over to the white bag on the counter. She knew what was inside before she saw it; she could tell by the delicious smell. Ivy pressed Start on the coffee maker, and the bag crinkled as Ivy pulled out a giant cinnamon roll. Whenever Ivy came to Greenbrier as a kid, Marilyn would take her to the bakery on Sundays and let her pick whatever she wanted. Ivy had always chosen a cinnamon roll.

Smiling, she pulled the gooey bread apart and ate half, poured herself a hot cup of coffee, and ate the rest. A silver lining. No Vera Wang shoot meant no more careful diet. When she finished, she licked the glaze from her fingers, cleaned up the mess with her good arm and found herself sitting in front of the vanity in her bathroom, examining the angry lacerations with her unswollen eye.

Ivy inhaled a deep breath.

Her career was over. Her face would never be what it was, not even with plastic surgery. Yet somehow, despite the impossibility, Ivy knew she was going to be okay. Maybe not right away. Maybe not for a long time. But she'd get there.

The church buzzed with chaotic energy. Davis messed with the lighting while Marilyn directed models around the stage, and Big Bubba, their emcee, fiddled with the sound system. Jordan wheeled racks of dresses to the back rooms of the church. Sara greeted the hair stylists and makeup artists. And Pastor Voss directed Arabella's kitchen assistant to the lobby, where they'd arrange meals and appetizers for tomorrow's lunch. But despite all the motion and excitement, Davis couldn't drum up any enthusiasm. After tomorrow, he'd put his camera away for good. And, of course, Ivy was nowhere in sight. Several times yesterday he'd picked up his phone to call her, but something stopped him every time. This morning had been the same.

Mrs. Ludd tapped Davis on the shoulder. "Where did you want to set up the packages you're going to auction?"

Right. Auctioning wedding-related packages had been Ivy's idea, an excellent one too. They'd likely make more money for the art program with the silent auction than the ticket sales, and that was saying something, as they'd already sold a lot of tickets. More than he ever expected. "Somewhere in the lobby?"

"It's already full with the ticket booth and the food."

Static blasted through the sanctuary. Davis cringed. Several models shrieked. One tripped on her shoe and fell on the stage. Big Bubba must have hit the wrong button on one of the microphones. Marilyn waved her hands for attention and pointed to the opposite end of the platform. Good grief, they needed Ivy.

"Man, Bubba, I thought you knew how to work that stuff," Davis called.

The D.J. grimaced. "I know how to work new stuff. This equipment's prehistoric."

"It's all we have." So he'd better figure out how to use it without deafening their audience tomorrow. Davis scratched the back of his neck, wondering how he could create space when there was none left. Was there an extra room he was forgetting about? A place for Mrs. Ludd and all the others to showcase their auction items? "What about that small conference room off the lobby? Do you think that could be big enough?"

"I'll go check it out." Mrs. Ludd bustled away.

Davis made a beeline for Marilyn.

Two hours into the rehearsal and the models still looked lost. How hard could it be to walk across a stage in a wedding gown? Ivy showed them how to walk a week ago. They couldn't have forgotten everything already. Marilyn turned away from the ladies, a brightness in her eyes that definitely wasn't there in the waiting room of the hospital.

"How's Ivy?" he asked.

"Okay, I think." Marilyn looked him up and down. "Where did you go off to? One minute you were at the hospital and the next you were gone."

"I guess I figured you had it covered." He couldn't meet her eyes when he said it.

Marilyn tucked her clipboard under her arm. "Davis, are you okay?"

"I can't do pictures anymore."

She raised her eyebrows. "The fashion show is tomorrow."

"I know that. I mean once it's over. I know you and Joan had hoped I'd do some more work once this campaign was over, but I can't." He had asked God for guidance regarding Joan's offer, and God had answered loud and clear. He just wished God wouldn't have used the woman he loved to give it.

"Do you mind if I ask why not?"

"C'mon, Marilyn, you know why. First Sara, now Ivy. She would have been at Hoppin' John's if not for me uninviting her to the party. Instead, she was getting her face wrecked by Doyle." He shook away the memory of Ivy unconscious in his arms. It didn't matter that he'd washed her blood from his hands. Every time he looked at his palms, it was still there. "Why should I get to do what I love when Sara and Ivy can't do what they love?"

Mrs. Ludd bustled back inside and relayed some information to Marilyn. She flipped a page on her clipboard, wrote something down, then turned back to Davis. "Did you ever wonder why there's an eight-year age gap between you and Sara?"

"What?"

"You and Sara, did you ever wonder about the age gap?"

Davis furrowed his brow. What did that have to do with anything?

"After you were born, your mom stopped trying to have kids."

"Why?"

"Because I was her sister and I couldn't have kids." Marilyn took a deep breath. "When your mom got pregnant with you, I was over the moon. But I was also sad. James and I had been trying for almost two years at that point and I still had no baby in my arms. So Rose calls me one day—you were a couple months old at the time—and she says she's done. She wouldn't have any more kids if I couldn't." Marilyn called out to Jordan, who was moving a table into the sanctuary, and waved her hand for him to move it back out. "I think you got your martyr gene from her."

"Martyr gene?"

"Here was a woman who could have as many babies as she wanted, and she was going to stop because I couldn't? It was the stupidest thing I'd ever heard. And it only made my inability to have kids worse."

"Why?"

"Because I never asked her to stop having babies."

He shifted his weight. "Well, she must have changed her mind at some point."

"Thank the Lord, otherwise there'd be no Sara."

Davis looked over at the sound booth, where his sister spoke with Big Bubba, most likely going over the music selection. He couldn't fathom a world without her. "So what are you saying—I should take pictures?"

"That's between you and God. All I'm saying is you should think long and hard before sacrificing something nobody is asking you to sacrifice. Now, could you take these ladies to the back and show them how things are going to work backstage? I'd like Sara to start running the music so the girls can time their walks better."

Davis blinked several times. "Yeah. Sure."

Marilyn pivoted on her heel and headed for Sara.

"Um, okay, ladies." Davis climbed onto the stage. "Come with me."

He led them to the back room, where they would change and get their hair done and makeup fixed. He pointed to eight separate clothing racks, feeling mechanical in his movements. "Each of you has your own. Arabella, this is yours. See these Polaroids?" A few days ago, after the fitting, he'd taken pictures of each model in the outfits they would wear for the show. Now the pictures were tacked to the racks. Another one of Ivy's ideas. "They show exactly what you're wearing and in what order. You'll have somebody here tomorrow to help you get in and out of your clothes."

Arabella gave him a thumbs-up.

"Why don't the rest of you go through your rack and make sure everything is where it needs to be?"

The models dispersed.

Arabella motioned toward a deserted rack in the corner. "Who's going to model Ivy's dresses?"

The muscles across Davis's chest pulled tight. Marilyn had saved the best dresses for Ivy. The likelihood of finding a five-foot-ten-inch, rail-thin model this late in the game was close to nil. "Nobody. Unless you have any ideas."

"Put a veil over her face and have her walk."

Davis frowned. "I don't think she wants to see anybody right now."

"Yeah, you're probably right." Arabella patted his forearm. "It's really too bad what happened, but I'm sure she'll get back up again. You'll see."

It was the same thing people used to say about Sara after her accident. Davis never believed them. But despite his doubts, Sara had gotten back up.

Arabella stepped past him and began shuffling through her dresses.

With the models occupied, Davis made his way back onto the stage and spotted Sara laughing behind the sound booth with Jordan and Big Bubba. Marilyn's words buzzed around his thoughts like a pesky mosquito.

Was he really playing a martyr?

He gripped the familiar strap around his neck. After what happened to Sara, Davis had assumed God wanted him to put away his camera. It was, after all, what had gotten Davis wrapped up in the fashion industry to begin with. But what if his assumption was exactly that—an assumption? What if Davis had gone and created a yoke for himself he was never meant to wear?

Jordan wrapped his arm around Sara's waist and kissed her cheek.

All those people had been right. His sister had gotten back up.

Yet he'd languished on the ground for the last two years and, somewhere along the line, put his guilt on a pedestal. He turned it into an idol, focusing on his mistakes instead of God. Ivy pointed it out on the beach. Said he didn't live like he was forgiven.

And she'd been right. That's exactly how he'd been living.

He was done acting like his mistakes were too big for God. The past was the past. It was time to leave it behind once and for all.

Marilyn was anxious to get home. The rehearsal had been barely organized chaos. She had no idea how they'd pull it off tomorrow, but that didn't matter nearly as much as getting home to Ivy. She was partly excited and partly terrified, worried that whatever nebulous bond had formed between them yesterday might have floated away in the night.

I'm not finished. Not even close.

The whisper made tears well in Marilyn's eyes as she stepped inside and petted Georgia. Why was hope such a scary thing? She put her keys on the counter and turned toward the stairs when a rustle sounded from the living room off the kitchen. Ivy twisted around, her arm draped over the back of the couch, a Robert Frost poetry book in hand.

Marilyn stopped, unsure what to say. Too much seemed to be riding on these first words. In the end, it was Ivy who broke the ice. "Hi."

"Hello," Marilyn said back.

"Thanks for the cinnamon roll."

"You're welcome."

Ivy turned all the way around.

Marilyn stepped closer.

Georgia scampered to the couch and jumped up onto a cushion. "No Sara?" Ivy asked.

"She's spending the afternoon with Jordan."

"How was the rehearsal?"

Marilyn relaxed a little and smiled. "Disorganized." Honestly, they were all lost. Ivy had her thumb in every aspect of the show, and without her, nothing seemed to work right.

Tell her.

Marilyn frowned. If she told Ivy that, she might think Marilyn was trying to make her feel guilty for not being there. She might take it as pressure to do something she wasn't ready for. And then whatever spell that had been cast upon them would officially lose its magic. Marilyn couldn't risk it.

But the nudge came again, more forcefully this time. Marilyn fiddled with the silver chain of her necklace, came around the couch, and sat down.

Ivy brought the book into her lap. "I'm sure it wasn't that bad."

"I'm afraid we're all sort of clueless without you, Ivy."

The half of her face that wasn't swollen and bruised turned pink.

"Any way you'd consider coming tomorrow and helping us out?"

Ivy's attention darted to her lap.

Marilyn held her breath, waiting.

"I...I'm not sure I want anyone to see me."

The softly spoken response had Marilyn exhaling. She couldn't help but wonder if by *anyone,* Ivy was thinking most about Davis. "I don't want you to think there's any pressure. It's just that you've worked so hard on this. It might be fun to see the fruits of that labor."

"Yeah...it would."

They sat in comfortable silence for a while. Marilyn petting Georgia's head, Ivy fanning her thumb across the pages of her book.

"Marilyn?"

"Yes?"

Ivy looked up, tears welling in her eyes. "Thanks."

It was just one word, and a common one at that. Spoken a million times a day throughout the world. But coming from Ivy, that one word meant everything. This wasn't the end. After sixteen years, Marilyn was certain, this was just the beginning.

38

A model was late. Big Bubba couldn't get a handle on the church's sound system. And people stared and whispered.

"Poor girl."

"Got attacked by some guy."

"Bless her heart. The scarring will be bad."

The whispers followed her through the sanctuary and around the lobby as she directed a makeup artist, a hair stylist, and seven overexcited models. Ivy did her best to ignore the whispers and take hold of her new mantra.

I am His... I am His...

It wasn't easy.

Especially since everything seemed to be going wrong. Marilyn was busy with Arabella's staff and setting up the food, and Mrs. Ludd only brought six bouquets when they needed seven. One of the models showed up late with a limp and a swollen ankle. They were already down one, thanks to her. What kind of show would it be sans two models? It's not like the remaining six could all wear an extra dress. Not when each gown was tailored for a specific fit. Ivy worried the paying ticket holders wouldn't get their money's worth or, worse, the industry professionals would give Marilyn's dresses bad reviews.

Her nerves tangled into knots. She forced herself to take steady, even breaths. Marilyn believed in her. She could do this. She walked to the back of the sanctuary toward the sound booth. "You got it figured out yet, Bubba?"

The heavyset D.J. had a large headset around his ears. He removed them and looked down at the complicated panel, careful to keep his attention diverted from her face. Just like everybody else. "I think so."

"Good."

Ivy turned around, headed to the lobby, and found Jordan, sans his grease-stained blue jeans. Instead, he wore a pair of khaki shorts and a Hawaiian-style button-up. Unlike everybody else, he looked her in the eye. It was altogether welcomed. "Jordan, I'm so glad you're here. Has Sara arrived yet?"

Her stomach dipped. Sara was supposed to arrive with Davis as soon as she finished her Braille lesson. No sign of them yet. Ivy held on to a hope that Davis wouldn't come at all, which, of course, was a silly hope. Davis was a man of his word. He would never leave them high and dry. Still, imagining him actually seeing her face when the mere thought had sent him running a few days ago made her heart squeeze with dread.

"She should be here soon," Jordan said. "I'm glad you're okay, Ivy."

His sincerity soothed her. "Thanks."

"And I never got a chance to tell you before, but that was awfully nice of you, what you did for Twila. Organizing that photo shoot with her and Davis. It was all she talked about last week."

Twila! How in the world could she have forgotten about Twila? She would have had her bone marrow transplant already—the Hail Mary pass—and Ivy had no idea how it went. She put her hand on Jordan's arm. "Have you seen her? Is she doing okay?"

"She's pretty nauseous, but the doctors aren't worried. So far they seem really pleased with how she's responding."

Ivy cupped her hand over her mouth, unprepared for the lump that lodged in her throat. *Thank You, God. Thank You.*

A startling pop sounded from the sanctuary.

She jumped. So did Jordan.

Big Bubba poked his head out from the arched double doors. "One of the overhead lights just busted."

The door behind them opened, bringing in a gust of warm air.

Big Bubba smiled. "Well, hey there, Sara, Davis. 'Bout time you two showed up."

Without thinking, Ivy turned around and found herself facing the one man she wasn't ready to see. He stood not more than four feet away, staring straight at her. And what he saw made his face turn white.

Heat burned Ivy's cheeks. She ducked away from his scrutiny and turned around, heart hammering in her chest. She wasn't ready for this. Davis could fix the lighting. Marilyn could manage the models. Ivy shouldn't have come.

Davis couldn't feel his fingers or toes as Ivy turned and walked away. Seeing her was like someone had shot him with Novocaine. He tried to shove away the image of her broken body on the cement. The image of her in the dark, trying to escape Doyle. How terrified she must have been. How much pain she must have endured. He took a step to go after her, then reconsidered. If Ivy didn't want to see him, he needed to respect her wishes.

"Davis, we have a busted light. Think you might be able to take a look?" Big Bubba jerked his head for Davis to follow him.

Jordan reached out to take Sara's arm. She accepted the invitation by slipping hers around his waist. Bubba waited beneath the arched doorway.

Fix a light. He could do that. It would take his mind off Ivy. He followed Bubba onto the stage, into a hub of activity, and looked at the light in question. While he surveyed the damage, he scanned the room. He could only imagine how hard being here was for Ivy. Yet she'd come. Because she cared about Sara and Marilyn and this show.

He finished his examination. "If I can't fix it, it shouldn't be too big of a deal." Not with its location—off center and toward the back. If he needed to, he could go out to his car and grab some extra lighting from his Jeep. He'd brought every piece of equipment he owned, just in case. He stepped off the ladder and checked his pockets for his keys to the church's supply closet, but he'd given them to Sara to put in her purse.

He spotted his sister at the back, with Jordan, manning the sound booth as she filled the sanctuary with classy, upbeat music—her smile reminding him that hope wasn't lost. On the drive over Sara had told him that she had been accepted into the University of South Carolina Beaufort. Starting the spring semester, she'd be on her way to becoming an elementary school teacher.

"I know you want to give me that art program, Davis," Sara had said in the parking lot. "But I was thinking, what if we used the proceeds of the show to help Annie with Twila's medical bills instead?"

He'd been shocked. "But I thought you wanted to paint again."

"If you would have asked me a few months ago, I would have absolutely said yes. But anymore, I'm not sure. I think God is ready for me to close that chapter of my life for good." She squeezed his elbow. "And besides, wouldn't it be great to bless Annie with this?"

Davis couldn't help but smile at the thought.

"Do you think it would be possible?" she asked.

"I'm not sure. We'd have to run it past everyone first." Somehow, he didn't think anyone would object. The town's enthusiasm surrounding the fashion show was much less about the art program and much more about having some fun. Davis shook his head, amazed that God could use a tragedy like Sara's to accomplish His purposes not only in her life but in the life of a sick little girl. He'd taken his sister off one path and set her onto another. She would make a wonderful teacher.

God, will you do the same for Ivy?

He hoped so. And even though he knew it was unlikely to happen, he found himself wishing, as he walked over to Sara, that he could take part in the journey. He reached over the sound booth and touched his sister's elbow. "I need my keys."

Sara handed over her purse, her attitude decidedly different than it had been in the parking lot.

He pulled apart the straps. "Are you upset about something?"

"I'm upset about you. You're being a fool."

Jordan ducked his head and pretended to fiddle with the volume.

Davis raised an eyebrow. "Excuse me?"

"I thought you loved her."

"Loved who?"

"Ivy! Who else?"

He sputtered like a waterlogged engine.

"Because she's in love with you."

No. Sara had it all wrong. Ivy wasn't in love with him; Ivy wanted nothing to do with him. Sara couldn't see the way Ivy looked at him. She couldn't see the severity of Ivy's injury. She didn't understand what he'd done.

"Do you love her, Davis?"

He opened his mouth, only nothing came out.

She stuck her fist on her hip. "Well?"

Davis groaned. "So much it's killing me."

"Then be a man and go tell her."

In her quest to escape, Ivy had found a small room—something like an old-fashioned hat closet—and sat in the corner on a balance beam. Why the church had one, she had no idea. Ivy put her hands on either side of her legs and looked down at the ground.

Who was she kidding? She couldn't run a fashion show. Even on a good day, but especially not on this one, with her heart aching for Davis and her face unrecognizable. Her skin itched beneath the gauze, so badly it was next to unbearable. She carefully pulled away the bandages and resisted the urge to scratch.

Old familiar voices rose up in Ivy's mind—the ones that said she was nothing more than an empty, beautiful shell who wasn't even beautiful anymore. Only this time, Ivy was tired of listening to them. Could an empty shell have accomplished all that she had in the last few months? Everything she'd done to make the fashion show as big as it was going to be. Convincing Davis to take pictures of Twila. Getting Sara and Jordan back together. Helping Marilyn at the boutique. None of those things had anything to do with modeling or her looks. And here she was, sitting in a closet, dwelling on all the wrong things, listening to all the wrong voices.

Where would it get her? In a closet, that's where. What would it get her? Nothing.

This was her chance to show herself that she was more than a beautiful face. And even if she failed, life would still go on. Because this wasn't her identity. This didn't quantify her worth. It was a discovery that had set her free last night. So where was her freedom now? She stood from her makeshift seat and headed for the door, determined to be the person Marilyn believed her to be, when the door creaked open.

Davis stood on the other side.

Her knees went wobbly. Ivy took a step back and looked away. At the wall. Down at the carpet. Anywhere but at him. She didn't want to see the revulsion on his face. Not when she'd finally mustered up the gumption to get back out there and kick some charity show butt. But Davis stood in her path, blocking the door. She stared at a spot on the carpet, next to one of the balance beam's legs, wishing she'd never removed the gauze. "Excuse me, please."

He didn't move.

"I need to get by," she said, a little louder this time.

He stepped inside the room and closed the door.

She took another step away, her heart flip-flopping inside her chest, feeling suddenly claustrophobic.

He stepped closer.

She held out her hand for him to stop. Right there. Because as much as her heart ached for his nearness, she knew she'd only end up hurt. And her heart could only break into so many pieces. "I came to run a fashion show. Could you please let me by?"

He ignored her hand and took another step closer. "I was looking all over for you. Why are you in here?"

Keeping her eyes trained on the ground, she stepped back. Her calves hit the balance beam. "I needed to gather my thoughts. But I'm done now, and I'm ready to get back out there."

"I know you're angry with me. You have every right to be."

Her heart wedged inside her throat. He was close. Much too close. His nearness hurt worse than her wounded shoulder and face combined. "You have no idea how I feel."

"Tell me then."

She ran a trembling hand through her hair, wishing she could cover her face with it. Or maybe flip off the lights altogether. Why had she taken off her bandages? She kept her face turned down, away. "We don't have time for this right now."

"I'm sorry about Doyle. I wish more than anything I could take that night back. I wish you had never ended up alone with him."

She couldn't help herself. She looked up and threw his words back in his face. "You think I care about Doyle?"

She didn't miss the shock on his face as his eyes took in the full extent of her injuries.

"You think I want your apology? Or your sympathy?" Ivy swallowed, hating the lump building in her throat. She needed to get away from Davis and the things he made her feel. "Those are the last things I want."

"What do you want then, Ivy? I'm not a mind reader. I can't read yours."

"I wanted you to fight for me!" The words exploded inside the small room. "Just once, I wanted somebody to fight for me. To chase after me. To not let me push them away. But you know what? I don't need you to chase after me anymore. I don't need you to tell me I'm beautiful. I don't need any of that because—"

But she didn't get to explain, not about Marilyn's love or Sara's card or the words that had become Ivy's new motto. She didn't get to explain any of it. Because before she could get it out, Davis grabbed her arms, pulled her to his chest, and kissed her. And all she could think, all she could wrap her mind around was one thing. A kiss like this had nothing to do with sympathy.

He pulled away, his chest rising and falling with hers as he looked at her face. Her breath snagged in her chest. Her face. She tried to turn away, to look down, but he brought his knuckles beneath her chin and, with a barely there touch, skimmed the edge of her jaw with the pad of his thumb, studying her wounds, her bruises, her stitches…not with revulsion but a tenderness that melted through her like warm chocolate.

"Because why?" he asked.

She grasped at her thoughts, trying to piece them together, but she couldn't think past the thudding of her heart. "Why what?"

"You were about to tell me why you don't need me to chase after you anymore." His warm breath whispered against her uninjured cheek as he laid the gentlest of kisses against her earlobe. "Or tell you that you're beautiful."

Oh, right. "Because I know who I am now."

"And who is that?"

She was the word that made her mother cry. The word she looked up in the dictionary all those years ago. To buy back, to gain or regain possession of. "Redeemed."

Davis face brightened.

Ivy bit her lip. The very one he'd kissed moments ago. "You told me once that the next time you kissed a girl, it would be because you love her."

His eyes crinkled in the corner. And without saying a word, he tipped her chin, kissed the uninjured side of her jaw, her neck, the tip of her nose, the middle of her forehead. Kisses so gentle, so soft, so warm that her insides melted. "I may have faults, but lying isn't one of them."

"Well then." She leaned into his embrace and brought her lips to his ear. "I love you too."

Ivy picked up a white carton left in one of the pews and plunked it inside the large garbage bag Davis held out for her. He wouldn't stop smiling. All through the pictures. All through the entire show. The grin never left his face. And, heaven help her, she had turned into a goofy, gushy smiler too.

She swatted his arm. "You're making my stitches hurt."

"I can't help it. You're amazing."

Amazing.

She smiled again.

The show couldn't have gone better. As soon as she stopped paying attention to her face, so did everybody else. She even managed to find a replacement for the model who sprained her ankle. Arabella had tried to talk Ivy into walking, since they couldn't find anyone to fill Ivy's spot, but that wasn't her place today. Today, she wasn't a model. Today, she was Ivy Clark, a woman capable of pulling off a charity event.

She plunked a plastic fork into the garbage bag, still reeling over the outpouring of donations that came in after Sara's announcement. When she broached the idea of donating the proceeds toward the Twila Welch Fund, Marilyn asked the audience to consider the possibility and vote anonymously at the end of the event. Instead, they received a standing ovation. It seemed Ivy wasn't the only one who'd been taken captive by the young girl. "Any guesses on how much money we made?"

"No idea." The garbage bag crinkled in Davis's hand as he turned toward the back of the sanctuary, where Marilyn stood over a foldout table, organizing the money from the metal lockbox. "Have you finished counting yet?"

Marilyn slid several bills through her hands. "Not yet. But I tell you what. I've never seen this church so crowded in my life."

Pastor Voss popped up from a pew, his own garbage bag slung over his shoulder. "Hey!"

"No offense, Pastor."

Sara laughed.

Ivy bent over and picked up a torn ticket. Something New Fashion Show Extravaganza.

Davis finished his row and joined Ivy in hers. "How about as soon as we finish cleaning, we all head over to the hospital with some 'mater sandwiches and share the news with Annie and Twila?"

With a widening smile, Ivy folded up the ticket and slipped it inside her pocket. The show might be over, but the best part was yet to come.

EPILOGUE

Ivy never went back to New York. She stayed in Greenbrier and lived with Marilyn and Sara in the house that had once belonged to James. Sara attended college, and Ivy and Marilyn became a dynamic force in the bridal industry. Then Sara married Jordan, and Ivy married Davis, and they moved out of James's house and into their own homes and started their own families.

The barren woman became a grandmother of six.

Davis made a name for himself doing what his father taught him all those years ago in the mountains of Telluride—capturing God's creation behind a lens and sharing that beauty with a hurting world. With time, Ivy's injuries healed, but the scars remained—a maze of thin white lines along her cheek and jaw. Reminding her that, yes, she had been hurt. And, yes, something had been stolen. But she didn't remain that way.

God did not leave her broken.

Like the name of the boutique Marilyn had opened all those years ago when Ivy ran off to New York City, He gathered her broken pieces and made something new.

Readers Guide

1. Do you think *A Broken Kind of Beautiful* is a good title for this book? What do you think it means? If you were to give this novel a different title, what would it be?
2. Ivy Clark is not your typical Christian novel heroine. Did you like her? Why or why not? What are some of Ivy's redeemable qualities? Do you know any women like Ivy?
3. Our past plays a huge role in shaping who we become and what we believe. How did Ivy's past shape her beliefs and who she became? In what ways has your own past shaped who you are today and what you believe? Do you think it's possible to overcome our pasts? Why or why not?
4. All right, let's gush! This is a romance novel, after all. What was your favorite romantic moment between Davis and Ivy?
5. Although this is technically a romance novel, there was a romantic thread that went deeper than the burgeoning love between Ivy Clark and Davis Knight. What was it?
6. Beauty is an important theme in this novel. How does the world define beauty? In what ways do you struggle to measure up to the world's definition?
7. Marilyn Olsen is nothing at all like the archetypical wicked stepmother. Of all the characters in this novel, what made Marilyn best suited to be an example of Christlike love for Ivy? How would the novel have changed if Davis replaced Marilyn in this particular role? Who has exemplified Christ's love in your life?
8. Marilyn felt God calling her to love Ivy, the daughter of her cheating husband and his mistress. How would you have reacted if you were

Marilyn? Have you ever had a moment where you felt called to something that didn't make sense?

9. Davis struggles with fully accepting God's forgiveness. Because he can't let go of the guilt he feels over what happened to Sara, he punishes himself by refusing to do what he loves—photography. Could you relate to Davis's struggle? Why or why not? If you were Sara, would you want Davis to continue as a photographer?
10. "It doesn't matter if I forgive you. It doesn't even matter if you forgive you. What matters, Davis, is that God already has." Discuss Sara's comment. Do you agree or disagree? Why?
11. Sara came to see the blessing in her blindness. Has God ever used a tragedy in your life to bring about blessing? Share with the group.

Acknowledgments

You would think that writing books would get easier with practice. Alas, it does not.

My second novel was more challenging than my first, and this one was more challenging than the second. But as long as God keeps giving me stories to tell, then tell them I shall. But not without thanking some people first…

My husband, who deserves an award. Being married to a writer is no easy feat, and yet he does it so well. Cooking and cleaning and entertaining our son, all so his neurotic wife can meet her deadlines. Thank you, Ryan, for loving me…even when I'm pulling out my hair or locked away in my office. I don't deserve you.

My family, with mad props to my dad and my mom and my aunt Peggy for entertaining the B-man for hours on end, all so I can have some working time. You have no idea how much easier you make my life or how much richer you make Brogan's. I could not do this without you.

My church family and small group and women's Bible study, my crazy junior high girls, adoption comrades (with a special shout out to Corie G. and Carrie P.), and every single one of my writerly soul mates. Your support keeps me going.

My agent, Rachelle Gardner, for assuring me that, yes, I can do this.

My editors, Shannon Marchese, Lissa Halls Johnson, and Laura Wright, for refusing to let me settle for good enough.

The entire phenomenal team at WaterBrook Multnomah who truly go above and beyond. Each and every one of you cares deeply in the power of story to change lives, and it absolutely shines through in your work. I know I've said it before, but I will say it again (and again and again). It is an honor to work with you.

Every single reader, with an extraspecial squeeze to my fabulous launch team. If this book has any measure of success, it is because you picked it up and shared it. Thank you for reading. Thank you for sharing. Thank you for encouraging. My prayer forever and always is that the stories I tell would draw hearts closer to the only One who can redeem.

And "to him who is able to do immeasurably more than all we ask or imagine, according to his power that is at work within us, to him be the glory in the church and in Christ Jesus throughout all generations, for ever and ever! Amen."